BY R.A. SALVATORE

THE LEGEND OF DRIZZT

The Dark Elf Trilogy
Homeland
Exile
Sojourn

The Icewind Dale Trilogy
The Crystal Shard
Streams of Silver
The Halfling's Gem

The Legacy of the Drow Series
The Legacy
Starless Night
Siege of Darkness
Passage to Dawn

The Paths of Darkness Series
The Silent Blade
The Spine of the World
Sea of Swords

The Sellswords Trilogy
Servant of the Shard
Promise of the Witch-King
Road of the Patriarch

The Hunter's Blades Trilogy
The Thousand Orcs
The Lone Drow
The Two Swords

The Transitions Series
The Orc King
The Pirate King
The Ghost King

The Neverwinter Saga
Gauntlgrym
Neverwinter
Charon's Claw
The Last Threshold

The Sundering Series
The Companions

The Companions Codex
Night of the Hunter
Rise of the King
Vengeance of the Iron Dwarf

The Homecoming Trilogy
Archmage
Maestro
Hero

Generations
Timeless
Boundless
Relentless

The Way of the Drow
Starlight Enclave
Glacier's Edge
Lolth's Warrior

OTHER NOVELS

DUNGEONS & DRAGONS

THE
CRYSTAL
SHARD

DUNGEONS & DRAGONS

THE LEGEND OF DRIZZT

THE CRYSTAL SHARD

R.A. SALVATORE

RANDOM HOUSE WORLDS

New York

Published in the United States by Random House Worlds, an imprint of Random House, a division of Penguin Random House LLC, New York.

Originally published in 1988 as *The Icewind Dale Trilogy, Book 1: The Crystal Shard* by TSR, Inc. and in 2005 by Wizards of the Coast LLC.

ISBN 978-0-593-87309-0

Printed in the United States of America on acid-free paper

randomhousebooks.com

2 4 6 8 9 7 5 3 1

First Random House Worlds Edition

Book design by Alexis Flynn

To my wife, Diane, and to Bryan, Geno, and Caitlin
for their support and patience through this experience.
And to my parents, Geno and Irene,
for believing in me even when I didn't.

DUNGEONS & DRAGONS

THE
CRYSTAL
SHARD

BLOOD MELTS
THE ARCTIC SNOW!

Wulfgar was heavily engaged with the remaining giant, easily maneuvering Aegis-fang to deflect the monster's powerful blows, but he was able to catch glimpses of the battle to his side. The scene painted a grim reminder of the value of what Drizzt had taught him, for the drow was toying with the verbeeg, using its uncontrolled rage against it. Again and again, the monster reared for a killing blow, and each time Drizzt was quick to strike and dance away. Verbeeg blood flowed freely from a dozen wounds, and Wulfgar knew that Drizzt could finish the job at any time.

But he was amazed that the dark elf was enjoying the tormenting game he played.

PRELUDE

The demon sat back on the seat it had carved in the stem of the giant mushroom. Sludge slurped and rolled around the rock island, the eternal oozing and shifting that marked this layer of the Abyss.

Errtu drummed its clawed fingers, its horned, apelike head lolling about on its shoulders as it peered into the gloom. "Where are you, Telshazz?" the demon hissed, expecting news of the relic. Crenshinibon pervaded all of the demon's thoughts. With the shard in its grasp, Errtu could rise over an entire layer, maybe even several layers.

And Errtu had come so close to possessing it!

The demon knew the power of the artifact; Errtu had been serving seven lichs when they combined their evil magics and made the Crystal Shard. The lichs, undead spirits of powerful wizards that refused to rest when their mortal bodies had passed from the realms of the living, had gathered to create the most vile artifact ever made, an evil that fed and flourished off of that which the purveyors of good considered most precious—the light of the sun.

But they had gone beyond even their own considerable powers. The forging actually consumed the seven, Crenshinibon stealing the magical strength that preserved the lichs' undead state to fuel its own first flickers of life. The ensuing bursts of power had hurtled Errtu back to the Abyss, and the demon had presumed the shard destroyed.

But Crenshinibon would not be so easily destroyed. Now, centuries later, Errtu had stumbled upon the trail of the Crystal Shard again: a crystal tower, Cryshal-Tirith, with a pulsating heart the exact image of Crenshinibon.

Errtu knew the magic was close by; the demon could sense the powerful presence of the relic. If only it could have found the thing earlier . . . if only it could have grasped . . .

But then Al Dimeneira had arrived, an angelic being of tremendous power. Al Dimeneira banished Errtu back to the Abyss with a single word.

Errtu peered through the swirling smoke and gloom when it heard the sucking footsteps.

"Telshazz?" the demon bellowed.

"Yes, my master," the smaller demon answered, cowering as it approached the mushroom throne.

"Did he get it?" Errtu roared. "Does Al Dimeneira have the Crystal Shard?"

Telshazz quivered and whimpered, "Yes, my lord . . . uh, no, my lord!"

Errtu's evil red eyes narrowed.

"He could not destroy it," the little demon was quick to explain. "Crenshinibon burned his hands!"

"Hah!" Errtu snorted. "Beyond even the power of Al Dimeneira! Where is it, then? Did you bring it, or does it remain in the second crystal tower?"

Telshazz whimpered again. It didn't want to tell its cruel master the truth, but it would not dare to disobey. "No, master, not in the tower," the little demon whispered.

"No!" Errtu roared. "Where is it?"

"Al Dimeneira threw it."

"Threw it?"

"Across the planes, merciful master!" Telshazz cried. "With all of his strength!"

"Across the very planes of existence!" Errtu growled.

"I tried to stop him, but . . ."

The horned head shot forward. Telshazz's words gurgled indecipherably as Errtu's canine maw tore its throat out.

FAR REMOVED FROM THE GLOOM OF THE ABYSS, CRENSHINIBON came to rest upon the world. Far up in the northern mountains of Faerûn, the Crystal Shard, the ultimate perversion, settled into the snow of a bowl-shaped dell.

And waited.

PART ONE
TEN-TOWNS

If I could choose what life would be mine, it would be this life that I now have, at this time. I am at peace, and yet, the world around me swirls with turmoil, with the ever-present threat of barbarian raids and goblin wars, with tundra yetis and gigantic polar worms. The reality of existence here in Icewind Dale is harsh indeed, an environment unforgiving, where one mistake will cost you your life.

That is the joy of the place, the very edge of disaster, and not because of treachery, as I knew in my home of Menzoberranzan. I can accept the risks of Icewind Dale; I can revel in them and use them to keep my warrior instincts finely honed. I can use them to remind me every day of the glory and joy of life. There is no complacency here, in this place where safety cannot be taken for granted, where a turn of the wind can pile snow over your head, where a single misstep on a boat can put you into water that will steal your breath away and render muscles useless in mere seconds, or a simple lapse on the tundra can put you in the belly of a fierce yeti.

When you live with death so close, you come to appreciate life all the more.

And when you share that life with friends like those that I have come to know these last years, then you know paradise. Never could I have imagined in my years in Menzoberranzan, or in the wilds of the Underdark, or even when I first came to the surface world, that I would ever surround myself with such friends as these. They are of different races, all three, and all three different from my own, and yet, they are more alike what is in my heart than anyone I have ever known, save, perhaps, my father, Zaknafein, and the ranger, Montolio, who trained me in the ways of Mielikki.

I have met many folk up here in Ten-Towns, in the savage land of Icewind Dale, who accept me despite my dark elf heritage, and yet, these three, above all others, have become as family to me.

Why them? Why Bruenor, Regis, and Catti-brie above all others, three friends whom I treasure as much as Guenhwyvar, my companion for all these years?

Everyone knows Bruenor as blunt—that is the trademark of many dwarves, but in Bruenor, the trait runs pure. Or so he wants all to believe. I know better. I know the other side of Bruenor, the hidden side, that soft and warm place. Yes, he has a heart, though he tries hard to bury it! He is blunt, yes, particularly with criticism. He speaks of errors without apology and without judgment, simply telling the honest truth and leaving it up to the offender to correct, or not correct the situation. Bruenor never allows tact or empathy to get in the way of his telling the world how it can be better!

But that is only half of the tale concerning the dwarf; on the other side of the coin, he is far from blunt. Concerning compliments, Bruenor is not dishonest, just quiet.

Perhaps that is why I love him. I see in him Icewind Dale itself, cold and harsh and unforgiving, but ultimately honest. He keeps me at my best, all the time, and in doing that, he helps me to survive in this place. There is only one Icewind Dale, and only one Bruenor Battlehammer, and if ever I met a creature and a land created for each other . . .

Conversely, Regis stands (or more appropriately, reclines), as a reminder to me of the goals and rewards of a job well done — not that Regis is ever the one who does that job. Regis reminds me, and Bruenor, I would guess, that there is more to life than responsibility, that there are times for personal relaxation and enjoyment of the rewards brought about by good work and vigilance. He is too soft for the tundra, too round in the belly and too slow on his feet. His fighting skills are lacking and he could not track a herd of caribou on fresh snow. Yet he survives, even thrives up here with wit and attitude, with an understanding, better than Bruenor's surely, and even better than my own, of how to appease and please those around him, of how to anticipate, rather than just react to the moves of others. Regis knows more than just what people do, he knows why they do it, and that ability to understand motivation allowed him to see past the color of my skin and the reputation of my people. If Bruenor is honest in expressing his observations, then Regis is honest in following the course of his heart.

And finally there is Catti-brie, wonderful and so full of life. Catti-brie is the opposite side of the same coin to me, a different reasoning to reach the same conclusions. We are soulmates who see and judge different things in the world to arrive at the same place. Perhaps we thus validate each other. Perhaps in seeing Catti-brie arriving at the same place as myself, and knowing that she arrived there along a different road, tells me that I followed my heart truly. Is that it? Do I trust her more than I trust myself?

That question is neither indictment of my feelings, nor any self-incrimination. We share beliefs about the way of the world and the way the world should be. She is akin to my heart as is Mielikki, and if I found my goddess by looking honestly into my own heart, then so I have found my dearest friend and ally.

They are with me, all three, and Guenhwyvar, dear Guenhwyvar, as well. I am living in a land of stark beauty and stark reality, a place where you have to be wary and alert and at your very best at all times.

I call this paradise.

—Drizzt Do'Urden

1

THE STOOGE

When the wizards' caravan from the Hosttower of the Arcane saw the snowcapped peak of Kelvin's Cairn rising from the flat horizon, they were more than a little relieved. The hard journey from Luskan to the remote frontier settlement known as Ten-Towns had taken them more than three tendays.

The first tenday hadn't been too difficult. The troop held close to the Sword Coast, and though they were traveling along the northernmost reaches of the Realms, the summer breezes blowing in off the Trackless Sea were comfortable enough.

But when they rounded the westernmost spurs of the Spine of the World, the mountain range that many considered the northern boundary of civilization, and turned into Icewind Dale, the wizards quickly understood why they had been advised against making this journey. Icewind Dale, a thousand square miles of barren, broken tundra, had been described to them as one of the most unwelcoming lands in all the Realms, and within a single day of traveling on the northern side of the Spine of the World, Eldeluc, Dendybar the Mottled, and the other wizards from Luskan considered the reputation well-earned. Bordered by impassable mountains on the south, an expanding glacier on the east, and an unnavigable sea of countless icebergs on the north and west, Icewind Dale was attainable only through the pass between the Spine of the World and the coast, a trail rarely used by any but the most hardy of merchants.

For the rest of their lives, two memories would ring clear in the wizards' minds whenever they thought about this trip, two facts of life on Icewind Dale that travelers here never forgot. The first was the endless moaning of the wind, as though the land itself was continuously groaning in torment. And the second was the emptiness of the dale, mile after mile of gray and brown horizon lines.

The caravan's destination marked the only varying features in all the dale—ten small towns positioned around the three lakes of the region, under the shadow of the only mountain, Kelvin's Cairn. Like everyone else who came to this harsh land the wizards sought Ten-Towns' scrimshaw, the fine ivory carvings made from the headbones of the knucklehead trout which swam in the waters of the lakes.

Some of the wizards, though, had even more devious gains in mind.

THE MAN MARVELED AT HOW EASILY THE SLENDER DAGGER slipped through the folds in the older man's robe and then cut deeper into the wrinkled flesh.

Morkai the Red turned on his apprentice, his eyes locked into a widened, amazed set at the betrayal by the man he had raised as his own son for a quarter of a century.

Akar Kessell let go of the dagger and backed away from his master, horrified that the mortally wounded man was still standing. He ran out of distance for his retreat, stumbling into the rear wall of the small cabin the wizards of Luskan had been given as temporary quarters by the host city of Easthaven. Kessell trembled visibly, pondering the grisly consequences he would face in light of the growing possibility that the magical expertise of the old mage had found a way to defeat even death itself.

What terrible fate would his mighty mentor impose upon him for his betrayal? What magical torments could a true and powerful wizard such as Morkai conjure that would outdo the most agonizing of the tortures common throughout the land?

The old man held his gaze firmly on Akar Kessell, even as the last light began to fade from his dying eyes. He didn't ask why, he didn't even outwardly question Kessell about the possible motives. The gain of power was involved somewhere, he knew—that was always the case in such betrayals. What confused him was the instrument, not the motive. Kessell? How could Kessell, the bumbling apprentice whose stuttering lips could barely call out the simplest of cantrips, possibly hope to profit from the death of the only man who had ever shown him more than basic, polite consideration?

Morkai the Red fell dead. It was one of the few questions he had never found the answer to.

Kessell remained against the wall, needing its tangible support, and continued to shake for long minutes. Gradually, the confidence that had put him in this dangerous position began to grow again within him. He was the boss now—Eldeluc, Dendybar the Mottled, and the other wizards who had made the trip had said so. With his master gone, he, Akar Kessell, would be rightfully awarded his own meditation chamber and alchemy lab in the Hosttower of the Arcane in Luskan.

Eldeluc, Dendybar the Mottled, and the others had said so.

"IT IS DONE, THEN?" THE BURLY MAN ASKED WHEN KESSELL entered the dark alley designated as the meeting place.

Kessell nodded eagerly. "The red-robed wizard of Luskan shan't cast again!" he proclaimed too loudly for the likes of his fellow conspirators.

"Speak quietly, fool," Dendybar the Mottled, a frail-looking man tucked defensively within the alleyway's shadows, demanded in the same monotonous voice that he always used. Dendybar rarely spoke at all and never displayed any semblance of passion when he did. Ever was he hidden beneath the low-pulled cowl of his robe. There was something cold-blooded about Dendybar that unnerved most people who met him. Though the wizard was physically the smallest and least imposing man on the merchant caravan that had made the four-hundred mile journey to the frontier settlement of Ten-Towns, Kessell feared him more than any of the others.

"Morkai the Red, my former master, is dead," Kessell reiterated softly.

"Akar Kessell, this day forward known as Kessell the Red, is now appointed to the Wizard's Guild of Luskar!"

"Easy, friend," said Eldeluc, putting a comforting hand on Kessell's nervously twitching shoulder. "There will be time for a proper coronation when we return to the city." He smiled and winked at Dendybar from behind Kessell's head.

Kessell's mind was whirling, lost in a daydream search through all of the ramifications of his pending appointment. Never again would he be taunted by the other apprentices, boys much younger than he who climbed through the ranks in the guild step by tedious step. They would show him some respect now, for he would leap beyond even those who had passed him by in the earliest days of his apprenticeship, into the honorable position of wizard.

As his thoughts probed every detail of the coming days, though, Kessell's radiant face suddenly grayed over. He turned sharply on the man at his side, his features tensed as though he had discovered a terrible error. Eldeluc and several of the others in the alley became uneasy. They all fully understood the consequences if the archmage of the Hosttower of the Arcane ever learned of their murderous deed.

"The robe?" Kessell asked. "Should I have brought the red robe?"

Eldeluc couldn't contain his relieved chuckle, but Kessell merely took it as a comforting gesture from his newfound friend.

I should have known that something so trivial would throw him into such a fit, Eldeluc told himself, but to Kessell he merely said,

"Have no fear about it. There are plenty of robes in the Hosttower. It would seem a bit suspicious, would it not, if you showed up at the archmage's doorstep claiming the vacated seat of Morkai the Red and holding the very garment that the murdered wizard was wearing when he was slain?"

Kessell thought about it for a moment, then agreed.

"Perhaps," Eldeluc continued, "you should not wear the red robe."

Kessell's eyes squinted in panic. His old self-doubts, which had haunted him for all of his days since his childhood, began to bubble up within him. What was Eldeluc saying? Were they going to change their minds and not award him the seat he had rightfully earned?

Eldeluc had used the ambiguity of his statement as a tease, but he didn't want to push Kessell into a dangerous state of doubt. With a second wink at Dendybar, who was inwardly thoroughly enjoying this game, he answered the poor wretch's unspoken question. "I only meant that perhaps a different color would better suit you. Blue would complement your eyes."

Kessell cackled in relief. "Perhaps," he agreed, his fingers nervously twiddling.

Dendybar suddenly grew tired of the farce. He motioned for his burly companion to be rid of the annoying little wretch.

Eldeluc obediently led Kessell back down the alleyway. "Go on, now, back to the stables," he instructed. "Tell the master there that the wizards shall be leaving for Luskan this very night."

"But what of the body?" Kessell asked.

Eldeluc smiled evilly. "Leave it. That cabin is reserved for visiting merchants and dignitaries from the south. It will most probably remain vacant until next spring. Another murder in this part of the world will cause little excitement, I assure you, and even if the good people of Easthaven were to decipher what had truly happened, they are wise enough to tend to their own business and leave the affairs of wizards to wizards!"

The group from Luskan moved out into the waning sunlight on

the street. "Now be off!" Eldeluc commanded. "Look for us as the sun sets." He watched as Kessell, like some elated little boy, scurried away.

"How fortunate to find so convenient a tool," Dendybar noted. "The wizard's stupid apprentice saved us much trouble. I doubt that we would have found a way to get at that crafty old one. Though the gods alone know why, ever did Morkai have a soft spot for his wretched little apprentice!"

"Soft enough for a dagger's point!" laughed a second voice.

"And so convenient a setting," remarked yet another. "Unexplained bodies are considered no more than an inconvenience to the cleaning wenches in this uncivilized outpost."

The burly Eldeluc laughed aloud. The gruesome task was at last completed; they could, finally, leave this barren stretch of frozen desert and return home.

KESSELL'S STEP WAS SPRIGHTLY AS HE MADE HIS WAY ACROSS the village of Easthaven to the barn where the wizards' horses had been stabled. He felt as though becoming a wizard would change every aspect of his daily life, as if some mystical strength had somehow been infused into his previously incompetent talents.

He tingled in anticipation of the power that would be his. An alleycat crossed before him, casting him a wary glance as it pranced by.

Slit-eyed, Kessell looked around to see if anyone was watching. "Why not?" he muttered. Pointing a deadly finger at the cat, he uttered the command words to call forth a burst of energy. The nervous feline bolted away at the spectacle, but no magical bolts struck it, or even near it.

Kessell looked down at his singed fingertip and wondered what he had done wrong.

But he wasn't overly dismayed. His own blackened nail was the strongest effect he had ever gotten from that particular spell.

2

ON THE BANKS OF
MAER DUALDON

Regis the halfling, the only one of his kind for hundreds of miles in any direction, locked his fingers behind his head and leaned back against the mossy blanket of the tree trunk. Regis was short, even by the standards of his diminutive race, with the fluff of his curly brown locks barely cresting the three-foot mark, but his belly was amply thickened by his love of a good meal, or several, as the opportunities presented themselves.

The crooked stick that served as his fishing pole rose up above him, clenched between two of his furry toes, and hung out over the quiet lake, mirrored perfectly in the glassy surface of Maer Dualdon. Gentle ripples rolled down the image as the red-painted wooden bobber began to dance slightly. The line had floated in toward shore and hung limply in the water, so Regis couldn't feel the fish nibbling at the bait. In seconds, the hook was cleaned with no catch to show for it, but the halfling didn't know, and it would be hours before he'd even bother to check. Not that he'd have cared, anyway.

This trip was for leisure, not work. With winter coming on, Regis figured that this might well be his last excursion of the year to the lake; he didn't go in for winter fishing, like some of the fanatically greedy humans of Ten-Towns. Besides, the halfling already had enough ivory stocked up from other people's catches to keep him busy for all seven months of snow. He was truly a credit to his less-than-ambitious race, carving out a bit of civilization in a land where none existed, hundreds of miles from the most remote settlement that could rightly be called a city. Other halflings never came this far north, even during the summer months, preferring the comfort of the southern climes. Regis, too, would have gladly packed up his belongings and returned to the south, except for a little problem he had with a certain guildmaster of a prominent thieves' guild.

A four-inch block of the "white gold" lay beside the reclining halfling, along with several delicate carving instruments. The beginnings of a horse's muzzle marred the squareness of the block. Regis had meant to work on the piece while he was fishing.

Regis meant to do a lot of things.

"Too fine a day," he had rationalized, an excuse that never seemed to grow stale for him. This time, though, unlike so many others, it truly bore credibility. It seemed as though the weather demons that bent this harsh land to their iron will had taken a holiday, or perhaps they were just gathering their strength for a brutal winter. The result was an autumn day fitting for the civilized lands to the south. A rare day indeed for the land that had come to be called Icewind Dale, a name well-earned by the eastern breezes that always seemed to blow in, bringing with them the chilled air of Reghed Glacier. Even on the few days that the wind shifted there was little relief, for Ten-Towns was bordered on the north and west by miles of empty tundra and then more ice, the Sea of Moving Ice. Only southern breezes promised any relief, and any wind that tried to reach this desolate area from that direction was usually blocked by the high peaks of the Spine of the World.

Regis managed to keep his eyes open for a while, peering up through the fuzzy limbs of the fir trees at the puffy white clouds as they sailed across the sky on the mild breezes. The sun rained down golden warmth, and the halfling was tempted now and then to take off his waistcoat. Whenever a cloud blocked out the warming rays, though, Regis was reminded that it was Eleint on the tundra. In a month there would be snow. In two, the roads west and south to Luskan, the nearest city to Ten-Towns, would be impassable to any but the sturdy or the stupid.

Regis looked across the long bay that rolled in around the side of his little fishing hole. The rest of Ten-Towns was taking advantage of the weather, too; the fishing boats were out in force, scrambling and weaving around each other to find their special "hitting spots." No matter how many times he witnessed it, the greed of humans always amazed Regis. Back in the southern land of Calimshan, the halfling had been climbing a fast ladder to Associate Guildmaster in one of the most prominent thieves' guilds in the port city of Calimport. But as he saw it, human greed had cut short his career. His guildmaster, the Pasha Pook, possessed a wonderful collection of rubies—a dozen, at least—whose facets were so ingeniously cut that they seemed to cast an almost hypnotic spell on anyone who viewed them. Regis had marveled at the scintillating stones whenever Pook put them out on display, and after all, he'd only taken one. To this day, the halfling couldn't figure out why the Pasha, who had no less than eleven others, was still so angry with him.

"Alas for the greed of humans," Regis would say whenever the Pasha's men showed up in another town that the halfling had made his home, forcing him to extend his exile to an even more remote land. But he hadn't needed that phrase for a year and a half now, not since he had arrived in Ten-Towns. Pook's arms were long, but this frontier settlement, in the middle of the most inhospitable and untamed land imaginable, was a longer way still, and Regis was quite content in the security of his new sanctuary. There was wealth here, and for those nimble and talented enough to be a scrimshander, someone who could transform the ivorylike bone of a knucklehead trout into an artistic carving, a comfortable living could be made with a minimum amount of work.

And with Ten-Towns' scrimshaw fast becoming the rave of the

south, the halfling meant to shake off his customary lethargy and turn his newfound trade into a booming business.

Someday.

DRIZZT DO'URDEN TROTTED ALONG SILENTLY, HIS SOFT, LOW-cut boots barely stirring the dust. He kept the cowl of his brown cloak pulled low over the flowing waves of his stark white hair and moved with such effortless grace that an onlooker might have thought him to be no more than an illusion, an optical trick of the brown sea of tundra.

The dark elf pulled his cloak tighter about him. He felt as vulnerable in the sunlight as a human would in the dark of night. More than half a century of living many miles below ground had not been erased by several years on the sunlit surface. To this day, sunlight drained and dizzied him.

But Drizzt had traveled right through the night and was compelled to continue. Already he was overdue for his meeting with Bruenor in the dwarf's valley, and he had seen the signs.

The reindeer had begun their autumn migration southwest to the sea, yet no human track followed the herd. The caves north of Ten-Towns, always a stopover for the nomadic barbarians on their way back to the tundra, had not even been stocked to re-provision the tribes on their long trek. Drizzt understood the implications. In normal barbarian life, the survival of the tribes depended on their following the reindeer herd. The apparent abandonment of their traditional ways was more than a little disturbing.

And Drizzt had heard the battle drums.

Their subtle rumblings rolled over the empty plain like distant thunder, in patterns usually recognizable only to the other barbarian tribes. But Drizzt knew what they foretold. He was an observer who understood the value of knowledge of friend or foe, and he had often used his stealth prowess to observe the daily routines and traditions of the proud natives of Icewind Dale, the barbarians.

Drizzt picked up his pace, pushing himself to the limits of his endurance. In five short years, he had come to care for the cluster of villages known as Ten-Towns and for the people who lived there. Like so many of the other outcasts who had finally settled there, the drow had found no welcome anywhere else in the Realms. Even here he was only tolerated by most, but in the unspoken kinship of fellow rogues, few people bothered him. He'd been luckier than most; he'd found a few friends who could look beyond his heritage and see his true character.

Anxiously, the dark elf squinted at Kelvin's Cairn, the solitary mountain that marked the entrance to the rocky dwarven valley between Maer Dualdon and Lac Dinneshere, but his violet-colored almond eyes, marvelous orbs that could rival an owl's in the night, could not penetrate the blur of daylight enough to gauge the distance.

Again he ducked his head under the cowl, preferring a blind run to the dizziness of prolonged exposure to the sun, and sank back into the dark dreams of Menzoberranzan, the lightless underworld city of his ancestors. The drow elves had actually once walked on the surface world, dancing beneath the sun and the stars with their fair-skinned cousins. Yet the dark elves were malicious, passionless killers beyond the tolerance of even their normally unjudging kin. And in the inevitable war of the elven nations, the drow were driven into the bowels of the ground. Here they found a world of dark secrets and dark magics and were content to remain. Over the centuries, they had flourished and grown strong once more, attuning themselves to the ways of mysterious magics. They became more powerful than even their surface-dwelling cousins, whose dealings with the arcane arts under the life-giving warmth of the sun were hobby, not necessity.

As a race, though, the drow had lost all desire to see the sun and the stars. Both their bodies and minds had adapted to the depths, and luckily for all who dwelt under the open sky, the evil dark elves were content to remain where they were, only occasionally resurfacing to raid and pillage. As far as Drizzt knew, he was the only one of his kind living on the surface. He had learned some tolerance of the light, but he still suffered the hereditary weaknesses it imparted upon his kind.

Yet even considering his disadvantage under daytime conditions, Drizzt was outraged by his own carelessness when the two bearlike tundra yetis, their camouflaging coats of shaggy fur still colored in summer brown, suddenly rose up before him.

A RED FLAG ROSE FROM THE DECK OF ONE OF THE FISHING BOATS, signaling a catch. Regis watched as it moved higher and higher. "A four-footer, or better," the halfling mumbled approvingly when the flag topped out just below the mast's crosspiece. "There'll be singing in one house tonight!"

A second ship raced up beside the one that had signaled the catch, banging into the anchored vessel in its rush. The two crews immediately drew weapons and faced off, though each remained on its respective ship. With nothing between him and the boats but empty water, Regis clearly heard the shouts of the captains.

"Ere, ye stole me catch!" the captain of the second ship roared.

"You're water-weary!" the captain of the first ship retorted. "Never it was! It's our fish fairly hooked and fairly hauled! Now be gone with your stinking tub before we take you out of the water!"

Predictably, the crew of the second ship was over the rail and swinging before the captain of the first ship had finished speaking.

Regis turned his eyes back to the clouds; the dispute on the boats did not hold any interest for him, though the noises of the battle were certainly disturbing. Such squabbles were common on the lakes, always over the fish, especially if someone landed a big one. Generally they weren't too serious, more bluster and parrying than actual fighting, and only rarely did someone get badly wounded or killed. There were exceptions, though. In one skirmish involving no less than seventeen boats, three full crews and half of a fourth were cut down and left floating in the bloodied water. On that same day, that particular lake, the southernmost of the three, had its name changed from Dellon-lune to Redwaters.

"Ah little fishes, what trouble you bring," Regis muttered softly, pondering the irony of the havoc the silvery fish wreaked on the lives of the greedy people of Ten-Towns. These ten communities owed their very existence to the knucklehead trout, with their oversized, fist-shaped heads and bones the consistency of fine ivory. The three lakes were the only spots in the world where the valuable fish were known to swim, and though the region was barren and wild, overrun with humanoids and barbarians and sporting frequent storms that could flatten the sturdiest of buildings, the lure of quick wealth brought in people from the farthest reaches of the Realms.

As many inevitably left as came in, though. Icewind Dale was a bleak, colorless wasteland of merciless weather and countless dangers. Death was a common visitor to the villagers, stalking any who could not face the harsh realities of Icewind Dale.

Still, the towns had grown considerably in the century that had passed since the knuckleheads were first discovered. Initially, the nine villages on the lakes were no more than the shanties where individual frontiersmen had staked out a claim on a particularly good fishing hole. The tenth village, Bryn Shander, though now a walled, bustling settlement of several thousand people, had been merely an empty hill sporting a solitary cabin where the fishermen would meet once a year, exchanging stories and goods with the traders from Luskan.

Back in the early days of Ten-Towns a boat, even a one-man rowboat, out on the lakes, whose waters year-round were cold enough to kill in minutes anyone unfortunate enough to fall overboard, was a rare sight, but now every town on the lakes had a fleet of sailing vessels flying its flag. Targos alone, largest of the fishing towns, could put over a hundred vessels onto Maer Dualdon, some of them two-masted schooners with crews of ten or more.

A death cry sounded from the embattled ships, and the clang of steel on steel rang out loudly. Regis wondered, and not for the first time, if the people of Ten-Towns would be better off without the troublesome fish.

The halfling had to admit that Ten-Towns had been a haven for him, though. His practiced, nimble fingers adapted easily to the instruments of the scrimshander, and he had even been elected as the council spokesman of one of the villages. Granted, Lonelywood was the smallest and northernmost of the ten towns, a place where the rogues of rogues hid out, but Regis still considered his appointment an honor. It was convenient as well. As the only true scrimshander in Lonelywood, Regis was the sole person in the town with reason or desire to travel regularly to Bryn Shander, the principal settlement and market hub of Ten-Towns. This had proved to be quite a boon to the halfling. He became the primary courier to bring the catches of Lonelywood's fishermen to market, for a commission equaling a tenth-piece of the goods. This alone kept him deep enough in ivory to make an easy living.

Once a month during the summer season and once every three in the winter, weather permitting, Regis had to attend council meetings and fulfill his duties as spokesman. These meetings took place in Bryn Shander, and though they normally broke down into nothing more than petty arguments over fishing territories between villages, they usually lasted only a few hours. Regis considered his attendance a small price to pay for keeping his monopoly on trips to the southern marketplace.

The fighting on the boats soon ended, only one man dead, and Regis drifted back into quiet enjoyment of the sailing clouds. The halfling looked back over his shoulder at the dozens of low wooden cabins dotting the thick rows of trees that comprised Lonelywood. Despite the reputation of its inhabitants, Regis found this town to be the best in the region. The trees provided a measure of protection from the howling wind and good corner posts for the houses. Only its distance from Bryn Shander had kept the town in the wood from being a more prominent member of Ten-Towns.

Abruptly, Regis pulled the ruby pendant out from under his waistcoat and stared at the wondrous gem he had appropriated from his former master a thousand miles and more to the south, in Calimport.

"Ah, Pook," he mused, "if only you could see me now."

THE ELF WENT FOR THE TWO SCIMITARS SHEATHED ON HIS HIPS, but the yetis closed quickly. Instinctively, Drizzt spun to his left, sacrificing his opposite flank to accept the rush of the closest monster. His right arm became helplessly pinned to his side as the yeti wrapped its great arms around him, but he managed to keep his left arm free enough to draw his second weapon. Ignoring the pain of the yeti's squeeze, Drizzt set the hilt of the scimitar firmly against his hip and allowed the momentum of the second charging monster to impale it on the curving blade.

In its frenzied death throes, the second yeti pulled away, taking the scimitar with it.

The remaining monster bore Drizzt to the ground under its weight. The drow worked his free hand frantically to keep the deadly teeth from gaining a hold on his throat, but he knew that it was only a matter of time before his stronger foe finished him.

Suddenly Drizzt heard a sharp crack. The yeti shuddered violently. Its head contorted weirdly, and a gout of blood and brains poured over its face from above its forehead.

"Yer late, elf!" came the rough edge of a familiar voice. Bruenor Battlehammer walked up the back of his dead foe, disregarding the fact that the heavy monster lay on top of his elven friend. In spite of the added discomfort, the dwarf's long, pointed, often-broken nose and gray-streaked though still-fiery red beard came as a welcome sight to Drizzt. "Knew I'd find ye in trouble if I came out an' looked for ye!"

Smiling in relief, and also at the mannerisms of the ever-amazing dwarf, Drizzt managed to wriggle out from under the

monster while Bruenor worked to free his axe from the thick
skull.

"Head's as hard as frozen oak," grumbled the dwarf. He planted
his feet behind the yeti's ears and pulled the axe free with a mighty
jerk. "Where's that kitten o' yers, anyway?"

Drizzt fumbled around in his pack for a moment and produced
a small onyx statue of a panther. "I'd hardly label Guenhwyvar a
kitten," he said with fond reverence. He turned the figurine over in
his hands, feeling the intricate details of the work to ensure that it
had not been damaged in the fall under the yeti.

"Bah, a cat's a cat!" insisted the dwarf. "An' why isn't it here
when ye needed it?"

"Even a magical animal needs its rest," Drizzt explained.

"Bah," Bruenor spouted again. "It's sure to be a sorry day when
a drow—and a ranger, what's more—gets taken off 'is guard on an
open plain by two scab tundra yetis!" Bruenor licked his stained
axe blade, then spat in disgust.

"Foul beasts!" he grumbled. "Can't even eat the damn things!"
He pounded the axe into the ground to clean the blade and
stomped off toward Kelvin's Cairn.

Drizzt put Guenhwyvar back into the pack and went to retrieve
his scimitar from the other monster.

"Come on, elf," scolded the dwarf. "We've five miles an' more of
road to go!"

Drizzt shook his head and wiped the bloodstained blade on the
felled monster's fur. "Roll on, Bruenor Battlehammer," he whispered under his smile. "And know to your pleasure that every
monster along our trail will mark well your passing and keep its
head safely hidden!"

3

THE MEAD HALL

Many miles north of Ten-Towns, across the trackless tundra to the northernmost edge of land in all the Realms, the frosts of winter had already hardened the ground in a white-tipped glaze. There were no mountains or trees to block the cold bite of the relentless eastern wind, carrying the frosty air from Reghed Glacier. The great bergs of the Sea of Moving Ice drifted slowly past, the wind howling off of their high-riding tips in a grim reminder of the coming season. And yet, the nomadic tribes who summered there with the reindeer had not journeyed with the herd's migration southwest along the coast to the more hospitable sea on the south side of the peninsula.

The unwavering flatness of the horizon was broken in one small corner by a solitary encampment, the largest gathering of barbarians this far north in more than a century. To accommodate the leaders of the respective tribes, several deerskin tents had been laid out in a circular pattern, each encompassed in its own ring of campfires. In the center of this circle, a huge deerskin hall had been constructed, designed to hold every warrior of the tribes. The tribesmen called it Hengorot, "The Mead Hall," and to the northern barbarians this was a place of reverence, where food and drink were shared in toasts to Tempus, the god of battle.

The fires outside the hall burned low this night, for King Heaf staag and the Tribe of the Elk, the last to arrive, were expected in the camp before moonset. All the barbarians already in the encampment had assembled in Hengorot and begun the pre-council festivities. Great flagons of mead dotted every table, and good-natured contests of strength sprang up with growing frequency. Though the tribes often warred with each other, in Hengorot all differences were put aside.

King Beorg, a robust man with tousled blond locks, a beard fading to white, and lines of experience etched deeply into his tanned face, stood solemnly at the head table. Representing his people, he stood tall and straight, his wide shoulders proudly squared. The barbarians of Icewind Dale stood a full head and more above the average inhabitant of Ten-Towns, sprouting as though to take advantage of the wide and roomy expanses of empty tundra.

They were indeed much akin to their land. Like the ground they roamed over, their often-bearded faces were browned from the sun and cracked by the constant wind, giving them a leathery, toughened appearance, a foreboding, expressionless mask that did not welcome outsiders. They despised the people of Ten-Towns, whom they considered weak wealth-chasers possessed of no spiritual value whatsoever.

Yet one of those wealth-chasers stood among them now in their most revered hall of meeting. At Beorg's side was deBernezan, the dark-haired southerner, the only man in the room who was not born and bred of the barbarian tribes. The mousey deBernezan kept his shoulders defensively hunched as he glanced nervously about the hall. He was well aware that the barbarians were not overly fond of outsiders and that any one of them, even the youngest attendant, could break him in half with a casual flick of his huge hands.

"Hold steady!" Beorg instructed the southerner. "Tonight you hoist mead flagons with the Tribe of the Wolf. If they sense your fear . . ." He left the rest unspoken, but deBernezan knew well how the barbarians dealt with weakness. The small man took a steadying deep breath and straightened his shoulders.

Yet Beorg, too, was nervous. King Heafstaag was his primary rival on the tundra, commanding a force as dedicated, disciplined, and numerous as his own. Unlike the customary barbarian raids, Beorg's plan called for the total conquest of Ten-Towns, enslaving the surviving fishermen and living well off of the wealth they harvested from the lakes. Beorg saw an opportunity for his people to abandon their precarious nomadic existence and find a measure of luxury they had never known. Everything now hinged on the assent of Heafstaag, a brutal king interested only in personal glory and triumphant plunder. Even if the victory over Ten-Towns was achieved, Beorg knew that he would eventually have to deal with his rival, who would not easily abandon the fervent bloodlust that had put him in power. That was a bridge the King of the Tribe of the Wolf would have to cross later; the primary issue now was the initial conquest, and if Heafstaag refused to go along, the lesser tribes would split in their alliances among the two. War might be joined as early as the next morning. This would prove devastating to all their people, for even the barbarians who survived the initial battles would be in for a brutal struggle against winter. The reindeer had long since departed for the southern pastures, and the caves along the route had not been stocked in preparation. Heafstaag was a cunning leader; he knew that at this late date the tribes were committed to following the initial plan, but Beorg wondered what terms his rival would impose.

Beorg took comfort in the fact that no major conflicts had broken out among the assembled tribes, and this night, when they all met in the common hall, the atmosphere was brotherly and jovial, with every beard in Hengorot lathered in foam. Beorg's gamble had been that the tribes could be united by a common enemy and the promise of continued prosperity. All had gone well . . . so far.

But the brute, Heafstaag, remained the key to it all.

THE HEAVY BOOTS OF HEAFSTAAG'S COLUMN SHOOK THE GROUND beneath their determined march. The huge, one-eyed king himself led the procession, his great, swinging strides indicative of the nomads of the tundra. Intrigued by Beorg's proposal and wary of winter's early onset, the rugged king had chosen to march straight through the cold nights, stopping only for short periods of food and rest. Though primarily known for his ferocious proficiency in battle, Heafstaag was a leader who carefully weighed his every move. The impressive march would add to the initial respect given his people by the warriors of the other tribes, and Heafstaag was quick to pounce on any advantage he could get.

Not that he expected any trouble at Hengorot. He held Beorg in high respect. Twice before he had met the King of the Tribe of the Wolf on the field of honor with no victory to show for it. If Beorg's plan was as promising as it initially seemed, Heafstaag would go along, insisting only on an equal share in the leadership with the blond king. He didn't care for the notion that the tribesmen, once they had conquered the towns, could end their nomadic lifestyle and be contented with a new life trading knucklehead trout, but he was willing to allow Beorg his fantasies if they delivered to him the thrill of battle and easy victory. Let the plunder be taken and warmth secured for the long winter before he changed the original agreement and redistributed the booty.

When the lights of the campfires came into view, the column quickened its pace. "Sing, my proud warriors!" Heafstaag commanded. "Sing hearty and strong! Let those gathered tremble at the approach of the Tribe of the Elk."

Beorg had an ear cocked for the sound of Heafstaag's arrival. Knowing well the tactics of his rival, he was not surprised in the least when the first notes of the Song of Tempus rolled in from the night. The blond king reacted at once, leaping onto a table and calling silence to the gathering. "Harken, men of the north!" he cried. "Behold the challenge of the song!"

Hengorot immediately burst into commotion as the men dashed from their seats and scrambled to join the assembling groups of their respective tribes. Every voice was lifted in the common refrain to the god of battle, singing of deeds of valor and of glorious deaths on the field of honor. This verse was taught to every barbarian boy from the time he could speak his first words, for the Song of Tempus was actually considered a measure of a tribe's strength. The only variance in the words from tribe to tribe was the refrain that identified the singers. Here the warriors sang at crescendo pitch, for the challenge of the song was to determine whose call to the god of battle was most clearly heard by Tempus.

Heafstaag led his men right up to the entrance of Hengorot. Inside the hall the calls of the Tribe of the Wolf were obviously drowning out the others, but Heafstaag's warriors matched the strength of Beorg's men.

One by one, the lesser tribes fell silent under the dominance of the Wolf and the Elk. The challenge dragged on between the two remaining tribes for many more minutes, neither willing to relinquish superiority in the eyes of their deity. Inside the mead hall, men of the beaten tribes nervously put their hands to their weapons. More than one war had erupted on the plains because the challenge of the song could determine no clear winner.

Finally, the flap of the tent opened admitting Heafstaag's standard bearer, a youth, tall and proud, with observing eyes that carefully weighed everything about him and belied his age. He put a whalebone horn to his lips and blew a clear note. Simultaneously, according to tradition, both tribes stopped their singing.

The standard bearer walked across the room toward the host

king, his eyes never blinking or turning away from Beorg's imposing visage, though Beorg could see that the youth marked the expressions that were upon him. Heafstaag had chosen his herald
well, Beorg thought.

"Good King Beorg," the standard bearer began when all commotion had ceased, "and other assembled kings. The Tribe of the
Elk asks leave to enter Hengorot and share mead with you, that we
might join together in toast to Tempus."

Beorg studied the herald a bit longer, testing to see if he could
shake the youth's composure with an unexpected delay.

But the herald did not blink or turn aside his penetrating stare,
and the set of his jaw remained firm and confident.

"Granted," answered Beorg, impressed. "And well met." Then
he mumbled under his breath, "A pity that Heafstaag is not possessed of your patience."

"I announce Heafstaag, King of the Tribe of the Elk," the herald cried out in a clear voice, "son of Hrothulf the Strong, son of
Angaar the Brave; thrice killer of the great bear; twice conqueror
of Termalaine to the south; who slew Raag Doning, King of the
Tribe of the Bear, in single combat in a single stroke . . ." (this
drawing uneasy shuffles from the Tribe of the Bear, and especially
their king, Haalfdane, son of Raag Doning). The herald went on
for many minutes, listing every deed, every honor, every title, ac-
cumulated by Heafstaag during his long and illustrious career.

As the challenge of the song was competition between the
tribes, the listing of titles and feats was a personal competition
between men, especially kings, whose valor and strength reflected
directly upon their warriors. Beorg had dreaded this moment, for
his rival's list exceeded even his own. He knew that one of the
reasons Heafstaag had arrived last was so that his list could be
presented to all in attendance, men who had heard Beorg's own
herald in private audience upon their arrival days before. It was the
advantage of a host king to have his list read to every tribe in attendance, while the heralds of visiting kings would only speak to

the tribes present upon their immediate arrival. By coming in last, and at a time when all the other tribes would be assembled together, Heafstaag had erased that advantage.

At length, the standard bearer finished and returned across the hall to hold open the tent flap for his king. Heafstaag strode confidently across Hengorot to face Beorg.

If men were impressed with Heafstaag's list of valor, they were certainly not disappointed by his appearance. The red-bearded king was nearly seven feet tall, with a barrel-shaped girth that dwarfed even Beorg's. And Heafstaag wore his battle scars proudly. One of his eyes had been torn out by the antlers of a reindeer, and his left hand was hopelessly crumpled from a fight with a polar bear. The King of the Tribe of the Elk had seen more battles than any man on the tundra, and by all appearances he was ready and anxious to fight in many more.

The two kings eyed each other sternly, neither blinking or diverting his glance for even a moment.

"The Wolf or the Elk?" Heafstaag asked at length, the proper question after an undecided challenge of the song.

Beorg was careful to give the appropriate response. "Well met and well fought," he said. "Let the keen ears of Tempus alone decide, though the god himself will be hard-pressed to make such a choice!"

With the formalities properly carried out, the tension eased from Heafstaag's face. He smiled broadly at his rival. "Well met, Beorg, King of the Tribe of the Wolf. It does me well to face you and not see my own blood staining the tip of your deadly spear!"

Heafstaag's friendly words caught Beorg by surprise. He couldn't have hoped for a better start to the war council. He returned the compliment with equal fervor. "Nor to duck the sure cut of your cruel axe!"

The smile abruptly left Heafstaag's face when he took notice of the dark-haired man at Beorg's side. "What right, by valor or by blood, does this weakling southerner have in the mead hall of

Tempus?" the red-bearded king demanded. "His place is with his own, or with the women at best!"

"Hold to faith, Heafstaag," Beorg explained. "This is deBernezan, a man of great import to our victory. Valuable is the information he has brought to me, for he has dwelt in Ten-Towns for two winters and more."

"Then what role does he play?" Heafstaag pressed.

"He has informed," Beorg reiterated.

"That is past," said Heafstaag. "What value is he to us now? Certainly he cannot fight beside warriors such as ours."

Beorg cast a glance at deBernezan, biting back his own contempt for the dog who had betrayed his people in a pitiful attempt to fill his own pockets. "Plead your case, southerner. And may Tempus find a place in his field for your bones!"

DeBernezan tried futilely to match the iron gaze of Heafstaag. He cleared his throat and spoke as loudly and confidently as he could. "When the towns are conquered and their wealth secured, you shall need one who knows the southern marketplace. I am that man."

"At what price?" growled Heafstaag.

"A comfortable living," answered deBernezan. "A respected position, nothing more."

"Bah!" snorted Heafstaag. "He would betray his own, he would betray us!" The giant king tore the axe from his belt and lurched at deBernezan. Beorg grimaced, knowing that this critical moment could defeat the entire plan.

With his mangled hand Heafstaag grabbed deBernezan's oily black hair and pulled the smaller man's head to the side, exposing the flesh of his neck. He swung his axe mightily at the target, his gaze locked onto the southerner's face. But even against the unbending rules of tradition, Beorg had rehearsed deBernezan well for this moment. The little man had been warned in no uncertain terms that if he struggled at all he would die in any case. But if he accepted the stroke and Heafstaag was merely testing him, his life would probably be spared. Mustering all of his willpower, deBernezan steeled his gaze on Heafstaag and did not flinch at the approach of death.

At the very last moment, Heafstaag diverted the axe, its blade whistling within a hair's breadth of the southerner's throat. Heafstaag released the man from his grasp, but he continued to hold him in the intense lock of his single eye.

"An honest man accepts all judgments of his chosen kings," deBernezan declared, trying to keep his voice as steady as possible.

A cheer erupted from every mouth in Hengorot, and when it died away, Heafstaag turned to face Beorg. "Who shall lead?" the giant asked bluntly.

"Who won the challenge of the song?" Beorg answered.

"Well settled, good king." Heafstaag saluted his rival. "Together, then, you and I, and let no man dispute our rule!"

Beorg nodded. "Death to any who dare!"

DeBernezan sighed in deep relief and shifted his legs defensively. If Heafstaag, or even Beorg, ever noticed the puddle between his feet, his life would certainly be forfeit. He shifted his legs again nervously and glanced around, horrified when he met the gaze of the young standard bearer. DeBernezan's face blanched white in anticipation of his coming humiliation and death. The standard bearer unexpectedly turned away and smiled in amusement but in an unprecedented merciful act for his rough people, he said nothing.

Heafstaag threw his arms above his head and raised his gaze and axe to the ceiling. Beorg grabbed his axe from his belt and quickly mimicked the movement. "Tempus!" they shouted in unison. Then, eyeing each other once more, they gashed their shield arms with their axes, wetting the blades with their own blood. In a synchronous movement, they spun and heaved the weapons across the hall, each axe finding its mark in the same keg of mead. Immediately, the closest men grabbed flagons and scrambled to catch the first drops of spilling mead that had been blessed with the blood of their kings.

"I have drawn a plan for your approval," Beorg told Heafstaag.

"Later, noble friend," the one-eyed king replied. "Let tonight be a time of song and drink to celebrate our coming victory." He clapped Beorg on the shoulder and winked with his one eye. "Be glad of my arrival, for you were sorely unprepared for such a gathering," he said with a hearty laugh. Beorg eyed him curiously, but Heafstaag gave him a second grotesque wink to quench his suspicions.

Abruptly, the lusty giant snapped his fingers at one of his field lieutenants, nudging his rival with his elbow as if to let him in on the joke.

"Fetch the wenches!" he commanded.

4

THE CRYSTAL SHARD

There was only blackness.

Mercifully, he couldn't remember what had happened, where he was. Only blackness, comforting blackness.

Then a chilling burn began to grow on his cheeks, robbing him of the tranquility of unconsciousness. Gradually, he was compelled to open his eyes, but even when he squinted, the blinding glare was too intense.

He was facedown in the snow. Mountains towered all about him, their jagged peaks and deep snowcaps reminding him of his location. They had dropped him in the Spine of the World. They had left him to die.

Akar Kessell's head throbbed when he finally managed to lift it. The sun was shining brightly, but the brutal cold and swirling winds dispelled any warmth the bright rays could impart. Ever was it winter in these high places, and Kessell wore only flimsy robes to protect him from the cold's killing bite.

They had left him to die.

He stumbled to his feet, knee-deep in white powder, and looked around. Far below, down a deep gorge and moving northward, back toward the tundra and the trails that would take them around the foreboding range of impassable mountains, Kessell saw the black specks that marked the wizards' caravan beginning its long journey back to Luskan. They had deceived him. He understood now that he had been no more than a pawn in their devious designs to rid themselves of Morkai the Red.

Eldeluc, Dendybar the Mottled, and the others.

They'd never had any intentions of granting him the title of wizard.

"How could I have been so stupid?" Kessell groaned. Images of Morkai, the only man who had ever granted him any measure of respect, flashed across his mind in a guilt-driven haze. He remembered all the joys that the wizard had allowed him to experience. Morkai had once turned him into a bird so that he could feel the freedom of flight; and once a fish, to let him experience the blurry world of the undersea.

And he had repaid that wonderful man with a dagger.

Far down the trails, the departing wizards heard Kessell's anguished scream echoing off the mountain walls.

Eldeluc smiled, satisfied that their plan had been executed perfectly, and spurred his horse on.

KESSELL TRUDGED THROUGH THE SNOW. HE DIDN'T KNOW WHY he was walking—he had nowhere to go. Kessell had no escape. Eldeluc had dropped him into a bowl-shaped, snow-filled depression, and with his fingers numbed beyond feeling, he had no chance of climbing out.

He tried again to conjure a wizard's fire. He held his outstretched palm skyward and through chattering teeth uttered the words of power.

Nothing.

Not even a wisp of smoke.

So he started moving again. His legs ached; he almost believed that several of his toes had already fallen away from his left foot. But he didn't dare remove his boot to verify his morbid suspicion.

He began to circumnavigate the bowl again, following the same trail he had left behind on his first pass. Abruptly, he found himself veering toward the middle. He didn't know why, and in his delirium, he didn't pause to try and figure it out. All the world had become a white blur. A frozen white blur. Kessell felt himself falling. He felt the icy bite of the snow on his face again. He felt the tingling that signaled the end of the life of his lower extremities.

Then he felt . . . warmth.

Imperceptible at first, but growing steadily stronger. Something was beckoning to him. It was beneath him, buried under the snow, yet even through the frozen barrier, Kessell felt the life-giving glow of its warmth.

He dug. Visually guiding hands that could not feel their work, he dug for his life. And then he came upon something solid and felt the heat intensify. Scrambling to push the remaining snow away from it, he managed at last to pull it free. He couldn't understand what he was seeing. He blamed it on delirium. In his frozen hands, Akar Kessell held what appeared to be a square-sided icicle. Yet its warmth flowed through him, and he felt the tingles again, this time signaling the rebirth of his extremities.

Kessell had no idea what was happening, and he didn't care in the least. For now, he had found hope for life, and that was enough. He hugged the Crystal Shard to his chest and moved back toward the rocky wall of the dell, searching out the most sheltered area he could find.

Under a small overhang, huddled in a small area where the heat of the crystal had pushed the snow away, Akar Kessell survived his first night in the Spine of the World. His bedfellow was the Crystal Shard, Crenshinibon, an ancient, sentient relic that had waited throughout ages uncounted for one such as he to appear in the bowl. Awakened again, it was even now pondering the methods it would use to control the weak-willed Kessell. It was a relic enchanted in the earliest days of the world, a perversion that had been lost for centuries, to the dismay of those evil lords who sought its strength.

Crenshinibon was an enigma, a force of the darkest evil that drew its strength from the light of day. It was an instrument of destruction, a tool for scrying, a shelter and home for those who would wield it. But foremost among the powers of Crenshinibon was the strength it imparted to its possessor.

Akar Kessell slept comfortably, unaware of what had befallen him. He knew only—and cared only—that his life was not yet at an end. He would learn the implications soon enough. He would come to understand that he would never again play the role of stooge to pretentious dogs like Eldeluc, Dendybar the Mottled, and the others.

He would become the Akar Kessell of his own fantasies, and all would bow before him.

"Respect," he mumbled from within the depths of his dream, a dream that Crenshinibon was imposing upon him.

Akar Kessell, the Tyrant of Icewind Dale.

KESSELL AWAKENED TO A DAWN THAT HE THOUGHT HE WOULD never see. The Crystal Shard had preserved him through the night, yet it had done much more than simply prevent him from freezing. Kessell felt strangely changed that morning. The night before, he had been concerned only with the quantity of his life, wondering how long he could merely survive. But now he pondered the quality of his life. Survival was no longer a question; he felt strength flowing within him.

A white deer bounded along the rim of the bowl.

"Venison," Kessell whispered aloud. He pointed a finger in the direction of his prey and spoke the command words of a spell, tingling with excitement as he felt the power surge through his blood. A searing white bolt shot out from his hand felling the hart where it stood.

"Venison," he declared, mentally lifting the animal through the air toward him without a second thought to the act, though tele-

kinesis was a spell that hadn't even been in the considerable reper-
toire of Morkai the Red, Kessell's sole teacher. Though the shard
would not have let him, Kessell the greedy did not stop to ponder
the sudden appearance of abilities he'd felt long overdue him.

Now he had food and warmth from the shard. Yet a wizard
should have a castle, he reasoned. A place where he might practice
his darkest secrets undisturbed. He looked to the shard for an answer to his dilemma and found a duplicate crystal lying next to the
first. Instinctively, so he presumed (though, in reality, it was another
subconscious suggestion from Crenshinibon that guided him), Kessell understood his role in fulfilling his own request. He knew the
original Shard at once from the warmth and strength that it exuded,
but this second one intrigued him as well, holding an impressive
aura of power of its own. He took up the copy of the shard and
carried it to the center of the bowl, setting it down on the deep snow.

"Ibssum dal abdur," he mumbled without knowing why, or even
what it meant.

Kessell backed away as he felt the force within the image of the
relic begin to expand. It caught the rays of the sun and drew them
within its depths. The area surrounding the bowl fell into shadow
as it stole the very light of day. It began to pulse with an inner,
rhythmic light.

And then it began to grow.

It widened at the base, nearly filling the bowl, and for a while
Kessell feared that he would be crushed against the rocky walls.
And in accordance with the crystal's widening, its tip rose up into
the morning sky, keeping the dimensions aligned with its power
source. Then it was complete, still an exact image of Crenshinibon,
but now of mammoth proportions.

A crystalline tower. Somehow—the same way Kessell knew
anything about the Crystal Shard—he knew its name.

Cryshal-Tirith.

KESSELL WOULD HAVE BEEN CONTENTED, FOR THE TIME BEING, at least, to remain in Cryshal-Tirith and feast off of the unfortunate animals that wandered by. He had come from a meager background of unambitious peasants, and though he outwardly boasted of aspirations beyond his station, he was intimidated by the implications of power. He didn't understand how or why those who had gained prominence had risen above the common rabble, and even lied to himself, passing off the accomplishments of others, and conversely, the lack of his own, as a random choice of fate.

Now that he had power within his grasp he had no notion of what to do with it.

But Crenshinibon had waited too long to see its return to life wasted as a hunting lodge for a puny human. Kessell's wishy-washiness was actually a favorable attribute from the relic's perspective. Over a period of time, it could persuade Kessell to follow almost any course of action with its nighttime messages.

And Crenshinibon had the time. The relic was anxious to again taste the thrill of conquest, but a few years did not seem long to an artifact that had been created at the dawn of the world. It would mold the bumbling Kessell into a proper representative of its power, nurture the weak man into an iron-fisted glove to deliver its message of destruction. It had done likewise a hundred times in the initial struggles of the world, creating and nurturing some of the most formidable and cruel opponents of law across any of the planes.

It could do so again.

That very night, Kessell, sleeping in the comfortably adorned second level of Cryshal-Tirith, had dreams of conquest. Not violent campaigns waged against a city such as Luskan, or even on the scale of battle against a frontier settlement, like the villages of Ten-Towns, but a less ambitious and more realistic start to his kingdom. He dreamed that he had forced a tribe of goblins into servitude, using them to assume the roles as his personal staff, catering to his every need. When he awakened the next morning, he remembered the dream and found that he liked the idea.

Later that morning, Kessell explored the third level of the tower, a room like all the others, made of smooth yet stone-strong crystal, this particular one filled with various scrying devices. Suddenly, an urge came over him to make a certain gesture and speak an arcane word of command that he assumed he must have heard in the presence of Morkai. He complied with the feeling and watched in amazement as the dimension within the depths of one of the mirrors in the room suddenly swirled in a gray fog. When the fog cleared, an image came into focus.

Kessell recognized the area depicted as a valley he had passed a short distance down the trail when Eldeluc, Dendybar the Mottled, and the others had left him to die.

The image of the region was bustling with a tribe of goblins at work constructing a campsite. These were nomads, probably, for war bands rarely brought females and young ones along on their raids. Hundreds of caves dotted the sides of these mountains, but they weren't numerous enough to hold the tribes of orcs, goblins, ogres, and even more powerful monsters. Competition for lairs was fierce, and the lesser goblin tribes were usually forced above ground, enslaved, or slaughtered.

"How convenient," Kessell mused, wondering if the subject of his dream had been a coincidence or a prophecy. On another sudden impulse, he sent his will through the mirror toward the goblins. The effect startled him.

As one, the goblins turned, apparently confused, in the direction of the unseen force. The warriors apprehensively drew their clubs and stone-headed axes, and the females and children huddled in the back of the group.

One larger goblin, the leader presumably, holding its club defensively before it, took a few cautious steps ahead of its soldiers.

Kessell scratched his chin, pondering the extent of his newfound power.

"Come to me," he called to the goblin chieftain. "You cannot resist!"

THE TRIBE ARRIVED AT THE BOWL A SHORT TIME LATER, REMAIN-
ing a safe distance away while they tried to figure out exactly what
the tower was and where it had come from. Kessell let them mar-
vel over the splendor of his new home, then called again to the
chieftain, compelling the goblin to approach Cryshal-Tirith.

Against its own will, the large goblin strode from the ranks of
the tribe. Fighting every step, it walked right up to the base of the
tower. It couldn't see any door, for the entrance to Cryshal-Tirith
was invisible to all except denizens of foreign planes and those
that Crenshinibon, or its wielder, allowed to enter.

Kessell guided the terrified goblin into the first level of the
structure. Once inside, the chieftain remained absolutely motionless, its eyes darting around nervously for some indication of the
overpowering force that had summoned it to this structure of dazzling crystal.

The wizard (a title rightfully imparted to the possessor of Crenshinibon, even if Kessell had never been able to earn it by his own
deeds) let the miserable creature wait for a while, heightening its
fear. Then he appeared at the top of the stairwell through a secret
mirror door. He looked down upon the wretched creature and
cackled with glee.

The goblin trembled visibly when it saw Kessell. It felt the wizard's will imposing upon it once again, compelling the creature to
its knees.

"Who am I?" Kessell asked as the goblin groveled and whimpered.

The chieftain's reply was torn from within by a power that it
could not resist.

"Master."

5
SOMEDAY

Bruenor walked up the rocky slope with measured steps, his boots finding the same footholds he always used when he ascended to the high point of the southern end of the dwarven valley. To the people of Ten-Towns, who often saw the dwarf standing meditatively on the perch, this high column of stones in the rocky ridge that lined the valley had come to be known as Bruenor's Climb. Just below the dwarf, to the west, were the lights of Termalaine, and beyond them the dark waters of Maer Dualdon, spotted occasionally by the running lights of a fishing boat whose resolute crew stubbornly refused to come ashore until they had landed a knucklehead.

The dwarf was well above the tundra floor and the lowest of the countless stars that sparkled the night. The celestial dome seemed polished by the chill breeze that had blown since sunset, and Bruenor felt as though he had escaped the bonds of earth.

In this place he found his dreams, and ever they took him back to his ancient home. Mithral Hall, home of his fathers and theirs before them, where rivers of the shining metal ran rich and deep and the hammers of dwarven smiths rang out in praise to Moradin and Dumathoin. Bruenor was merely an unbearded boy when his people had delved too deep into the bowels of the world and had been driven out by the dark things in dark holes. He was now the eldest surviving member of his small clan and the only one among them who had witnessed the treasures of Mithral Hall.

They had made their home in the rocky valley between the two northernmost of the three lakes long before any humans, other than the barbarians, had come to Icewind Dale. They were a poor remnant of what had been a thriving dwarven society, a band of refugees beaten and broken by the loss of their homeland and heritage. They continued to dwindle in numbers, their elders dying as much of sadness as old age. Though the mining under the fields of the region was good, the dwarves seemed destined to fade away into oblivion.

When Ten-Towns had sprung up, though, the luck of the dwarves rose considerably. Their valley was just north of Bryn Shander, as close to the principal city as any of the fishing villages, and the humans, often warring with each other and fighting off invaders, were happy to trade for the marvelous armor and weapons that the dwarves forged.

But even with the betterment of their lives, Bruenor, particularly, longed to recover the ancient glory of his ancestors. He viewed the arrival of Ten-Towns as a temporary stay from a problem that would not be resolved until Mithral Hall had been recovered and restored.

"A cold night for so high a perch, good friend," came a call from behind.

The dwarf turned around to face Drizzt Do'Urden, though he realized that the drow would be invisible against the black backdrop of Kelvin's Cairn. From this vantage point, the mountain was the only silhouette that broke the featureless line of the northern horizon. The cairn had been so named because it resembled a mound of purposely piled boulders; barbarian legend claimed that it truly served as a grave. Certainly the valley where the dwarves now made their home did not resemble any natural landmark. In every direction the tundra rolled on, flat and earthen. But the valley had only sparse patches of dirt sprinkled in among broken boulders and walls of solid stone. It, and the mountain on its northern border, were the only features in all of Icewind Dale with any mentionable quantities of rock, as if they had been misplaced by some god in the earliest days of creation.

Drizzt noted the glazed look of his friend's eyes. "You seek the sights that only your memory can see," he said, well aware of the dwarf's obsession with his ancient homeland.

"A sight I'll see again!" Bruenor insisted. "We'll get there, elf."

"We do not even know the way."

"Roads can be found," said Bruenor. "But not until ye look for them."

"Someday, my friend," Drizzt humored. In the few years that he and Bruenor had been friends, the dwarf had constantly badgered Drizzt about accompanying him on his adventure to find Mithral Hall. Drizzt thought the idea foolish, for no one that he had ever spoken with had even a clue as to the location of the ancient dwarven home, and Bruenor could only remember disjointed images of the silvery halls. Still, the drow was sensitive to his friend's deepest desire, and he always answered Bruenor's pleas with the promise of "someday."

"We have more urgent business at the moment," Drizzt reminded Bruenor. Earlier that day, in a meeting in the dwarven halls, the drow had detailed his findings to the dwarves.

"Yer sure they'll be comin' then?" Bruenor asked now.

"Their charge will shake the stones of Kelvin's Cairn," Drizzt replied as he left the darkness of the mountain's silhouette and joined his friend. "And if Ten-Towns does not stand united against them, the people are doomed."

Bruenor settled into a crouch and turned his eyes to the south, toward the distant lights of Bryn Shander. "They'll not, the stubborn fools," he muttered.

"They might, if your people went to them."

"No," growled the dwarf. "We'll fight beside them if they choose to stand together, an' pity then to the barbarians! Go to them, if ye wish, an' good luck to ye, but nothing o' the dwarves. Let us see what grit an' guts the fisherfolk can muster."

Drizzt smiled at the irony of Bruenor's refusal. Both of them knew well that the drow was not trusted, not even openly welcomed, in any of the towns other than Lonelywood, where their friend Regis was spokesman. Bruenor marked the drow's look, and it pained him as it pained Drizzt, though the elf stoically pretended otherwise.

"They owe ye more than they'll ever know," Bruenor stated flatly, turning a sympathetic eye on his friend.

"They owe me nothing!"

Bruenor shook his head. "Why do ye care?" he growled. "Ever yer watchin' over the folk that show ye no good will. What do ye owe to them?"

Drizzt shrugged, hard-pressed to find an answer. Bruenor was right. When the drow had first come to this land the only one who had shown him any friendship at all was Regis. He often escorted and protected the halfling through the dangerous first legs of the journey from Lonelywood, around the open tundra north of Maer Dualdon and down toward Bryn Shander, when Regis went to the principal city for business or council meetings. They had actually met on one such trek: Regis tried to flee from Drizzt because he'd heard terrible rumors about him. Luckily for both of them, Regis was a halfling who was usually able to keep an open mind about people and make his own judgments concerning their character. It wasn't long before the two were fast friends.

But to this day, Regis and the dwarves were the only ones in the area who considered the drow a friend. "I do not know why I care," Drizzt answered honestly. His eyes turned back to his ancient homeland where loyalty was merely a device to gain an advantage over a common foe. "Perhaps I care because I strive to be different from my people," he said, as much to himself as to Bruenor. "Perhaps I care because I am different from my people. I may be more akin to the races of the surface . . . that is my hope at least. I care because I have to care about something. You are not so different, Bruenor Battlehammer. We care lest our own lives be empty."

Bruenor cocked a curious eye.

"You can deny your feelings for the people of Ten-Towns to me, but not to yourself."

"Bah!" Bruenor snorted. "Sure that I care for them! My folk need the trade!"

"Stubborn," Drizzt mumbled, smiling knowingly. "And Cattibrie?" he pressed. "What of the human girl who was orphaned in the raid those years ago on Termalaine? The waif that you took in and raised as your own child?" Bruenor was glad that the cover of night offered some protection from his revealing blush. "She lives with you still, though even you would have to admit that she is able to go back to her own kind. Might it be, perhaps, that you care for her, gruff dwarf?"

"Aw, shut yer mouth," Bruenor grumbled. "She's a servin' wench and makes my life a bit easier, but don't ye go gettin' sappy about her!"

"Stubborn," Drizzt reiterated more loudly this time. He had one more card to play in this discussion. "What of myself, then? Dwarves are not overly fond of the light elves, let alone the drow. How do you justify the friendship you have shown me? I have nothing to offer you in return but my own friendship. Why do you care?"

"Ye bring me news when—" Bruenor stopped short, aware that Drizzt had cornered him.

But the drow didn't press the issue any further.

So the friends watched in silence as the lights of Bryn Shander went down, one by one. Despite his outward callousness, Bruenor realized how true some of the drow's accusations had rung; he had come to care for the people who had settled on the banks of the three lakes.

"What do ye mean to do then?" the dwarf asked at length.

"I mean to warn them," Drizzt replied. "You underestimate your neighbors, Bruenor. They're made of tougher stuff than you believe."

"Agreed," said the dwarf, "but my questions are of their character. Every day we see fightin' on the lakes, an' always over the damned fish. The people cling to their own towns an' goblins take the others, for all they care! Now they've to show me an' mine that they've the will to fight together!"

Drizzt had to admit the truth of Bruenor's observations. The fishermen had grown more competitive over the last couple of years as the knucklehead trout took to the deeper waters of the lakes and became harder to catch. Cooperation among the towns was at a low point as each town tried to gain an economic advantage over the rival towns on its lake.

"There is a council in Bryn Shander in two days," Drizzt continued. "I believe that we still have some time before the barbarians come. Though I fear for any delays, I do not believe that we would be able to bring the spokesmen together any sooner. It will take me that long to properly instruct Regis on the course of action that he must take with his peers, for he must carry the tidings of the coming invasion."

"Rumblebelly?" snorted Bruenor, using the name he had tagged on Regis for the halfling's insatiable appetite. "He sits on the council for no better reason than t'keep his stomach well-stocked! They'll hear 'im less than they'd hear yerself, elf."

"You underestimate the halfling, more so even than you underestimate the people of Ten-Towns," answered Drizzt. "Remember always that he carries the stone."

"Bah! A fine-cut gem, but no more!" Bruenor insisted. "I've seen it meself, an' it holds no spell on me."

"The magic is too subtle for the eyes of a dwarf, and perhaps not strong enough to penetrate your thick skull," laughed Drizzt. "But it is there—I see it clearly and know the legend of such a stone.

Regis may be able to influence the council more than you would believe—and certainly more than I could. Let us hope so, for you know as well as I that some of the spokesmen might be reluctant to pursue any plan of unity, whether in their arrogant independence, or in their belief that a barbarian raid upon some of their less protected rivals might actually help their own selfish ambitions. Bryn Shander remains the key, but the principal city will only be spurred to action if the major fishing towns, Targos in particular, join in."

"Ye know that Easthaven'll help," said Bruenor. "They're ever ones for bringing all o' the towns together."

"And Lonelywood, too, with Regis speaking for them. But Kemp of Targos surely believes that his walled city is powerful enough to stand alone, whereas its rival, Termalaine, would be hard-pressed to hold back the horde."

"He's not likely to join anythin' that includes Termalaine. An' yer in for more trouble then, drow, for without Kemp ye'll never get Konig and Dineval to shut up!"

"But that is where Regis comes in," Drizzt explained. "The ruby he possesses can do wondrous things, I assure you!"

"Again ye speak of the power o' the stone," Bruenor. "But Rumblebelly claims that his master o' old had twelve o' the things," he reasoned. "Mighty magics don't come in dozens!"

"Regis said that his master had twelve similar stones," Drizzt corrected. "In truth, the halfling had no way of knowing if all twelve, or any of the others, were magical."

"Then why would the man have given the only one o' power to Rumblebelly?"

Drizzt left the question unanswered, but his silence soon led Bruenor to the same inescapable conclusion. Regis had a way of collecting things that didn't belong to him, and though the halfling had explained the stone as a gift. . . .

6

BRYN SHANDER

Bryn Shander was unlike any of the other communities of Ten-Towns. Its proud pennant flew high from the top of a hill in the middle of the dry tundra between the three lakes, just south of the southern tip of the dwarven valley. No ships flew the flags of this city, and it had no docks on any of the lakes, yet there was little argument that it was not only the geographical hub of the region but the center of activity as well.

This was where the major merchant caravans from Luskan put in, where the dwarves came to trade, and where the vast majority of craftsmen, scrimshanders, and scrimshaw evaluators were housed. Proximity to Bryn Shander was second only to the quantity of fish hooked in determining the success and size of the fishing towns. Thus, Termalaine and Targos on the southeastern banks of Maer Dualdon, and Caer-Konig and Caer-Dineval on the western shores of Lac Dinneshere, four towns less than a day's journey from the principal city, were the dominant towns on the lakes.

High walls surrounded Bryn Shander, as much protection from the biting wind as from invading goblins or barbarians. Inside, the buildings were similar to those of the other towns: low, wooden structures, except that in Bryn Shander they were more tightly packed together and often subdivided to house several families. Congested as it was, though, there was a measure of comfort and security in the city, the largest taste of civilization a person could find for four hundred long and desolate miles.

Regis always enjoyed the sounds and smells that greeted him when he walked through the iron-bound wooden gates on the northern wall of the principal city. Though on a smaller scale than the great cities of the south, the bustle and shouts of Bryn Shander's open markets and plentiful street vendors reminded him of his days back in Calimport. And as in Calimport, the people of Bryn Shander's streets were a cross section of every heritage that the Realms had to offer. Tall, dark-skinned desert folk mingled among fair-skinned travelers from the Moonshaes. The loud boasts of swarthy southerners and robust mountain men trading fanciful tales of love and battle in one of the many taverns echoed on nearly every street corner.

And Regis took it all in, for though the location was changed, the noise remained the same. If he closed his eyes as he skipped along down one of the narrow streets he could almost recapture the zest for life that he had known those years before in Calimport.

This time, though, the halfling's business was so grave that it dampened even his ever-lifted spirits. He had been horrified at the drow's grim news and was nervous about being the messenger who would deliver it to the council.

Away from the noisy market section of the city, Regis passed the palatial home of Cassius, the spokesman of Bryn Shander. This was the largest and most luxurious building in all of Ten-Towns, with a columned front and bas-relief artwork adorning all its walls. It had originally been built for the meetings of the ten spokesmen, but as interest in the councils had died away, Cassius, skilled in diplomacy and not above using strong-arm tactics, had appropriated the palace as his official residence and moved the council hall to a vacant warehouse tucked away in a remote corner of the city. Several of the other spokesmen had complained about the change, but though the fishing towns could often exert some influence on the principal city in matters of public concern, they had little recourse in an issue as trivial to the general populace as this. Cassius understood his city's position well and knew how to keep most of the other communities under his thumb. The militia of Bryn Shander could defeat the combined forces of any five of the other nine towns combined, and Cassius's officers held a monopoly on connections to the necessary marketplaces in the south. The other spokesmen might grumble about the change in the meeting place, but their dependence on the principal city would prevent them from taking any actions against Cassius.

Regis was the last to enter the small hall. He looked around at the nine men who had gathered at the table and realized how out of place he truly was. He had been elected spokesman because nobody else in Lonelywood cared enough to want to sit on the council, but his peers had attained their positions through valorous and heroic deeds. They were the leaders of their communities, the men who had organized the structure and defenses of the towns. Each of these spokesmen had seen a score of battles and more, for goblin and barbarian raiders descended upon Ten-Towns more often than sunny days. It was a simple rule of life in Icewind Dale that if you couldn't fight, you couldn't survive, and the spokesmen of the council were some of the most proficient fighters in all of Ten-Towns.

Regis had never been intimidated by the spokesmen before because normally he had nothing to say at council. Lonelywood, a secluded town hidden away in a small, thick wood of fir trees, asked for nothing from anyone. And with an insignificant fishing fleet, the other three towns it shared Maer Dualdon with imposed no demands upon it. Regis never offered an opinion unless pressed and had been careful always to cast his vote on an issue in the way of the general consensus. And if the council was split on an issue,

Regis simply followed the lead of Cassius. In Ten-Towns, one couldn't go wrong by following Bryn Shander.

This day, though, Regis found that he was intimidated by the council. The grim news that he bore would make him vulnerable to their bullying tactics and often-angry reprisals. He focused his attention on the two most powerful spokesmen, Cassius of Bryn Shander and Kemp of Targos, as they sat at the head of the rectangular table and chatted. Kemp looked the part of rugged frontiersman: not too tall but barrel-chested, with gnarled and knotted arms, and a stern demeanor that frightened friend and foe alike.

Cassius, though, hardly seemed a warrior. He was small of frame, with neatly trimmed gray hair and a face that never showed a hint of stubble. His big, bright blue eyes forever seemed locked into an inner contentment. But anyone who had ever seen the spokesman from Bryn Shander raise a sword in battle or maneuver his charge on the field had no doubts concerning his fighting prowess or his bravery. Regis truly liked the man, yet he was careful not to fall into a situation that left him vulnerable. Cassius had earned a reputation for getting what he wanted at another's expense.

"Come to order," Cassius commanded, rapping his gavel on the table. The host spokesman always opened the meeting with the Formalities of Order, readings of titles and official proposals that had originally been intended to give the council an aura of importance, impressing especially the ruffians that sometimes showed up to speak for the more remote communities. But now, with the degeneration of the council as a whole, the Formalities of Order served only to delay the end of the meeting, to the regret of all ten spokesmen. Consequently, the Formalities were pared down more and more each time the group gathered, and there had even been talk of eliminating them altogether.

When the list had finally been completed, Cassius turned to the important issues. "The first item on the agenda," he said, hardly glancing at the notes that were laid out before him, "concerns the territorial dispute between the sister cities, Caer-Konig and Caer-Dineval, on Lac Dinneshere. I see that Dorim Lugar of Caer-Konig has brought the documents that he promised at the last meeting, so I turn the floor over to him. Spokesman Lugar."

Dorim Lugar, a gaunt, dark-complected man whose eyes never seemed to stop darting about nervously, nearly leaped out of his chair when he was introduced.

"I have in my hand," he yelled, his upraised fist closed about an old parchment, "the original agreement between Caer-Konig and Caer-Dineval, signed by the leaders of each town"—he shot an accusing finger in the direction of the spokesman from Caer-Dineval—"including your own signature, Jensin Brent!"

"An agreement signed during a time of friendship and in the spirit of good will," retorted Jensin Brent, a younger, golden-haired man with an innocent face that often gave him an advantage over people who judged him naive. "Unroll the parchment, Spokesman Lugar, and let the council view it. They shall see that it makes no provisions whatsoever for Easthaven." He looked around at the other spokesmen. "Easthaven could hardly be called even a hamlet when the agreement to divide the lake in half was signed," he explained, and not for the first time. "They had not a single boat to put in the water."

"Fellow spokesmen!" Dorim Lugar yelled, jolting some of them from the lethargy that had already begun to creep in. This same debate had dominated the last four councils with no ground gained by either side. The issue held little importance or interest for any but the two spokesmen and the spokesman from Easthaven.

"Surely Caer-Konig cannot be blamed for the rise of Easthaven," pleaded Dorim Lugar. "Who could have foreseen the Eastway?" he asked, referring to the straight and smooth road that Easthaven had constructed to Bryn Shander. It was an ingenious move and proved a boon to the small town on the southeastern corner of Lac Dinneshere. Combining the appeal of a remote community with easy access to Bryn Shander had made Easthaven the fastest growing community in all of Ten-Towns, with a fishing fleet that had swelled to nearly rival the boats of Caer-Dineval.

"Who indeed?" retorted Jensin Brent, now a bit of fluster showing through his calm facade. "It is obvious that Easthaven's growth has put Caer-Dineval in stiff competition for the southern waters of the lake, while Caer-Konig sails freely in the northern half. Yet Caer-Konig has flatly refused to renegotiate the original terms to compensate for the imbalance! We cannot prosper under such conditions!"

Regis knew that he had to act before the argument between Brent and Lugar got out of control. Two previous meetings had been adjourned because of their volatile debates, and Regis couldn't let this council disintegrate before he had told them of the impending barbarian attack.

He hesitated, having to admit to himself once again that he had no options and could not back away from this urgent mission; his haven would be destroyed if he said nothing. Although Drizzt had reassured him of the power he possessed, he retained his doubts about the true magic of the stone. Yet due to his own insecurity, a trait common among little folk, Regis found himself blindly trusting in Drizzt's judgment. The drow was possibly the most knowledgeable person he had ever known, with a list of experiences far beyond the tales that Regis could tell. Now was the time for action, and the halfling was determined to give the drow's plan a try.

He closed his fingers around the little wooden gavel that was set out on the table before him. It felt unfamiliar to his touch, and he realized then that this was the first time that he had ever used the instrument. He tapped it lightly on the wooden table, but the others were intent on the shouting match that had erupted between Lugar and Brent. Regis reminded himself of the urgency of the drow's news once again and boldly pounded the gavel down.

The other spokesmen turned immediately to the halfling, blank expressions stamped upon their faces. Regis rarely spoke at the meetings, and then only when cornered with a direct question.

Cassius of Bryn Shander brought his heavy gavel down. "The council recognizes Spokesman . . . uh . . . the spokesman from Lonelywood," he said, and from his uneven tone Regis could guess that he had struggled to address the halfling's request for the floor seriously.

"Fellow spokesmen," Regis began tentatively, his voice cracking into a squeak. "With all due respect to the seriousness of the debate between the spokesmen from Caer-Dineval and Caer-Konig, I believe that we have a more urgent problem to discuss." Jensin Brent and Dorim Lugar were livid at being interrupted, but the others eyed the halfling curiously. Good start, Regis thought, I've got their full attention.

He cleared his throat, trying to steady his voice and sound a bit more impressive. "I have learned beyond doubt that the barbarian tribes are gathering for a united attack on Ten-Towns!" Though he tried to make the announcement dramatic, Regis found himself facing nine apathetic and confused men.

"Unless we form an alliance," Regis continued in the same urgent tones, "the horde will overrun our communities one by one, slaughtering any who dare to oppose them!"

"Certainly, Spokesman Regis of Lonelywood," said Cassius in a voice he meant to be calming but was, in effect, condescending, "we have weathered barbarian raids before. There is no need for—"

"Not like this one!" Regis cried. "All the tribes have come together. The raids before matched one tribe against one city, and usually we fared well. But how would Termalaine or Caer-Konig—or even Bryn Shander—stand against the combined tribes of Icewind Dale?" Some of the spokesmen settled back into their chairs to contemplate the halfling's words; the rest began talking among themselves, some in distress, some in angry disbelief. Finally Cassius pounded his gavel again, calling the hall to silence.

Then, with familiar bravado, Kemp of Targos slowly rose from his seat. "May I speak, friend Cassius?" he asked with unnecessary politeness. "Perhaps I may be able to put this grave pronouncement in the proper light."

Regis and Drizzt had made some assumptions about alliances when they had planned the halfling's actions at this council. They knew that Easthaven, founded and thriving on the principle of brotherhood among the communities of Ten-Towns, would openly embrace the concept of a common defense against the barbarian horde. Likewise Termalaine and Lonelywood, the two most accessible and raided towns of the ten, would gladly accept any offers of help.

Yet even Spokesman Agorwal of Termalaine, who had so much to gain from a defensive alliance, would hedge and hold his silence if Kemp of Targos refused to accept the plan. Targos was the largest and mightiest of the nine fishing villages, with a fleet more than twice the size of the second largest.

"Fellow members of the council," Kemp began, leaning forward over the table to loom larger in the eyes of his peers. "Let us learn more of the halfling's tale before we begin to worry. We have fought off barbarian invaders and worse enough times to be confident that the defenses of even the smallest of our towns are adequate."

Regis felt his tension growing as Kemp rolled into his speech, building on points designed to destroy the halfling's credibility. Drizzt had decided early on in their planning that Kemp of Targos was the key, but Regis knew the spokesman better than the drow and knew that Kemp would not be easily manipulated. Kemp illustrated the tactics of the powerful town of Targos in his own mannerisms. He was large and bullying, often taking to sudden fits of violent rage that intimidated even Cassius. Regis had tried to steer Drizzt away from this part of their plan, but the drow was adamant.

"If Targos agrees to accept the alliance with Lonelywood," Drizzt had reasoned, "Termalaine will gladly join and Bremen, being the only other village on the lake, will have no choice but to go along. Bryn Shander will certainly not oppose a unified alliance of the four towns on the largest and most prosperous lake, and Easthaven will make six in the pact, a clear majority."

The rest would then have no choice but to join in the effort. Drizzt had believed that Caer-Dineval and Caer-Konig, fearing that Easthaven would receive special consideration in future councils, would put on a blusterous show of loyalty, hoping themselves to gain favor in the eyes of Cassius. Good Mead and Dougan's Hole, the two towns on Redwaters, though relatively safe from an invasion from the north, would not dare to stand apart from the other eight communities.

But all of this was merely hopeful speculation, as Regis clearly realized when he saw Kemp glaring at him from across the table. Drizzt had conceded the point that the greatest obstacle in forming the alliance would be Targos. In its arrogance, the powerful town might believe that it could withstand any barbarian raid. And if it did manage to survive, the destruction of some of its competitors might actually prove profitable.

"You say only that you have learned of an invasion," Kemp began. "Where could you have gathered this valuable and, no doubt, hard-to-find information?"

Regis felt sweat beading on his temples. He knew where Kemp's question would lead, but there was no way that he could avoid the truth. "From a friend who often travels the tundra," he answered honestly.

"The drow?" Kemp asked.

With his neck bent up and Kemp towering over him, Regis found himself quickly placed on the defensive. The halfling's father had once warned him that he would always be at a disadvantage when dealing with humans because they physically had to look down when speaking to him, as they would to their own children. At times like this, the words of his father rang painfully true to Regis. He wiped a bead of moisture from his upper lip.

"I cannot speak for the rest of you," Kemp continued, adding a chuckle to place the halfling's grave warning in an absurd light, "but I have too much serious work to do to go into hiding on the words of a drow elf!" Again the burly spokesman laughed, and this time he was not alone.

Agorwal of Termalaine offered some unexpected assistance to the halfling's failing cause. "Perhaps we should let the spokesman from Lonelywood continue. If his words are true—"

"His words are the echoes of a drow's lies!" Kemp snarled. "Pay them no heed. We have fought off the barbarians before, and—"

But then Kemp, too, was cut short as Regis suddenly sprang up on the council table. This was the most precarious part of Drizzt's plan. The drow had shown faith in it, describing it matter-of-factly, as though it would pose no problems. But Regis felt impending disaster hovering all about him. He clasped his hands behind his back and tried to appear in control so that Cassius wouldn't take any immediate actions against his unusual tactics.

During Agorwal's diversion, Regis had slipped the ruby pendant out from under his waistcoat. It sparkled on his chest as he walked up and down, treating the table as though it were his personal stage.

"What do you know of the drow to jest of him so?" he demanded of the others, pointedly Kemp. "Can any of you name a single person that he has harmed? No! You chastise him for the crimes of his race, yet have none of you ever considered that Drizzt Do'Urden walks among us because he has rejected the ways of his people?" The silence in the hall convinced Regis that he had either been impressive or absurd. In any case, he was not so arrogant or foolish to think his little speech sufficient to accomplish the task.

He walked over to face Kemp. This time he was the one looking down, but the spokesman from Targos seemed on the verge of exploding into laughter.

Regis had to act quickly. He bent down slightly and raised his hand to his chin, by appearance to scratch an itch though in truth to set the ruby pendant spinning, tapping it with his arm as it passed. He then held the silence of the moment patiently and counted as Drizzt had instructed. Ten seconds passed and Kemp had not blinked. Drizzt had said that this would be enough, but Regis, surprised and apprehensive at the ease with which he had accomplished the task, let another ten go by before he dared begin testing the drow's beliefs.

"Surely you can see the wisdom of preparing for an attack," Regis suggested calmly. Then in a whisper that only Kemp could hear he added, "These people look to you for guidance, great Kemp. A military alliance would only enhance your stature and influence."

The effect was dazzling.

"Perhaps there is more to the halfling's words than we first believed," Kemp said mechanically, his glazed eyes never leaving the ruby.

Stunned, Regis straightened up and quickly slipped the stone back under his waistcoat. Kemp shook his head as though clearing a confusing dream from his thoughts, and he rubbed his dried eyes. The spokesman from Targos couldn't seem to recall the last few moments, but the halfling's suggestion was planted deeply into his mind. Kemp found, to his own amazement, that his attitudes had changed.

"We should hear well the words of Regis," he declared loudly. "For we shall be none the worse from forming such an alliance, yet the consequences of doing nothing may prove to be grave, indeed!"

Quick to seize an advantage, Jensin Brent leaped up from his chair. "Spokesman Kemp speaks wisely," he said. "Number the people of Caer-Dineval, ever proponents of the united efforts of Ten-Towns, among the army that shall repel the horde!"

The rest of the spokesmen lined up behind Kemp as Drizzt had expected, with Dorim Lugar making an even bigger show of loyalty than Brent's.

Regis had much to be proud of when he left the council hall later that day, and his hopes for the survival of Ten-Towns had returned. Yet the halfling found his thoughts consumed by the implications of the power he had discovered in his ruby. He worked to figure the most fail-safe way in which he could turn this new-found power of inducing cooperation into profit and comfort.

"So nice of the Pasha Pook to give me this one!" he told himself as he walked through the front gate of Bryn Shander and headed for the appointed spot where he would meet with Drizzt and Bruenor.

7

THE COMING STORM

They started at dawn, charging across the tundra like an angry whirlwind. Animals and monsters alike, even the ferocious yetis, fled before them in terror. The frozen ground cracked beneath the stamp of their heavy boots, and the murmur of the endless tundra wind was buried under the strength of their song, the song to the god of battle.

They marched long into the night and were off again before the first rays of dawn, more than two thousand barbarian warriors hungry for blood and victory.

DRIZZT DO'URDEN SAT NEARLY HALFWAY UP ON THE NORTHERN face of Kelvin's Cairn, his cloak pulled tight against the bitter wind that howled through the boulders of the mountain. The drow had spent every night up here since the council in Bryn Shander, his violet eyes scanning the blackness of the plain for the first signs of the coming storm. At Drizzt's request, Bruenor had arranged for Regis to sit beside him. With the wind nipping at him like an invisible animal, the halfling squeezed in between two boulders as further protection from the unwelcoming elements.

Given a choice, Regis would have been tucked away into the warmth of his own soft bed in Lonelywood, listening to the quiet moan of the swaying tree branches beyond his warm walls. But he understood that as a spokesman everyone expected him to help carry out the course of action he had suggested at the council. It quickly became obvious to the other spokesmen and to Bruenor, who had joined in the subsequent strategy meetings as the representative of the dwarves, that the halfling wouldn't be much help in organizing the forces or drawing any battle plans, so when Drizzt told Bruenor that he would need a courier to sit watch with him, the dwarf was quick to volunteer Regis.

Now the halfling was thoroughly miserable. His feet and fingers were numbed from the cold, and his back ached from sitting against the hard stone. This was the third night out, and Regis grumbled and complained constantly, punctuating his discomfort with an occasional sneeze. Through it all, Drizzt sat unmoving and oblivious to the conditions, his stoic dedication to duty overriding any personal distress.

"How many more nights do we have to wait?" Regis whined. "One morning, I'm sure—maybe even tomorrow—they'll find us up here, dead and frozen to this cursed mountain!"

"Fear not, little friend," Drizzt answered with a smile. "The wind speaks of winter. The barbarians will come all too soon, determined to beat the first snows." Even as he spoke, the drow caught the tiniest flicker of light in the corner of his eye. He rose from his crouch suddenly, startling the halfling, and turned toward the direction of the flicker, his muscles tensed with reflexive wariness, his eyes straining to spot a confirming sign.

"What's—" Regis began, but Drizzt silenced him with an outstretched palm. A second dot of fire flashed on the edge of the horizon.

"You have gotten your wish," Drizzt said with certainty.

"Are they out there?" Regis whispered. His vision wasn't nearly as keen as the drow's in the night.

Drizzt stood silently in concentration for a few moments, mentally trying to measure the distance of the campfires and calculate the time it would take the barbarians to complete their journey.

"Go to Bruenor and Cassius, little friend," he said at length. "Tell them that the horde will reach Bremen's Run when the sun peaks tomorrow."

"Come with me," said Regis. "Surely they'll not put you out when you bear such urgent news."

"I have a more important task at hand," Drizzt answered. "Now be off! Tell Bruenor—and Bruenor alone—that I shall meet him on Bremen's Run at the first light of dawn." And with that, the drow padded off into the darkness. He had a long journey before him.

"Where are you going?" Regis called after him.

"To find the horizon's horizon!" came a cry from the black night.

And then there was only the murmur of the wind.

THE BARBARIANS HAD FINISHED SETTING UP THEIR ENCAMPment shortly before Drizzt reached its outer perimeter. This close to Ten-Towns, the invaders were on their guard; the first thing Drizzt noticed was that they had set many men on watch. But alert as they were, their campfires burned low and this was the night, the time of the drow. The normally effective watchmen were outmatched by an elf from a world that knew no light, one who could conjure a magical darkness that even the keenest eyes could not penetrate and carry it beside him like a tangible cloak. Invisible as a shadow in the darkness, with footfalls as silent as a stalking cat's, Drizzt passed by the guards and entered the inner rings of the camp.

Just an hour earlier, the barbarians had been singing and talking of the battle they would fight the next day. Yet even the adrenaline and bloodlust that pumped through their veins could not dispel the exhaustion from their hard march. Most of the men slept soundly, their heavy, rhythmic breathing comforting Drizzt as he picked his way among them in search of their leaders, who would no doubt be finalizing the battle plans.

Several tents were grouped together within the encampment. Only one, though, had guards posted outside its entrance. The flap was closed, but Drizzt could see the glow of candles within, and he could hear gruff voices, often raised in anger. The drow slipped around to the back. Luckily, no warriors had been permitted to make their beds close to the tent, so Drizzt was fairly secluded. As a precaution, he pulled the panther figurine out of his pack. Then, taking out a slender dagger, he poked a tiny hole in the deerskin tent and peeked in.

There were eight men inside, the seven barbarian chiefs and a smaller dark-haired man that Drizzt knew could not have been from northern stock. The chiefs sat on the ground in a semicircle around the standing southerner, asking him questions about the terrain and forces they would encounter the next day.

"We should destroy the town in the wood first," insisted the largest man in the room, possibly the largest man Drizzt had ever seen, who bore the symbol of the Elk. "Then we can follow your plan to the town called Bryn Shander."

The smaller man appeared absolutely flustered and outraged, though Drizzt could see that fear of the huge barbarian king would temper his response. "Great King Heafstaag," he answered tentatively, "if the fishing fleets sight trouble and land before we get to Bryn Shander, we shall find an army that outnumbers our own waiting for us within the solid walls of that city."

"They are only weakly southerners!" growled Heafstaag, thrusting out his barrel chest in pride.

"Mighty king, I assure you that my plan will satisfy your hunger for southern blood," said the dark-haired man.

"Then speak, deBernezan of Ten-Towns. Prove your worth to my people!"

Drizzt could see that the last statement rattled the one called deBernezan, for the undertones of the barbarian king's demand clearly showed his contempt for the southerner. Knowing how barbarians generally felt about outsiders, the drow realized that the slightest error during any part of this campaign would probably cost the little man his life.

DeBernezan reached down into the side of his boot and produced a scroll. He unrolled it and held it out for the barbarian kings to see. It was a poor map, roughly drawn, its lines further blurred by the slight tremble of the southern man's hand, but Drizzt could clearly make out many of the distinctive features that marked Ten-Towns on the otherwise featureless plain.

"To the west of Kelvin's Cairn," deBernezan explained, running his finger along the western bank of the largest lake on the map, "there is a clear stretch of high ground called Bremen's Run that goes south between the mountain and Maer Dualdon. From our location, this is the most direct route to Bryn Shander and the path that I believe we should take."

"The town on the banks of the lake," Heafstaag reasoned, "should then be the first that we crush!"

"That is Termalaine," replied deBernezan. "All of its men are fishermen and will be out on the lake as we pass. You would not find good sport there!"

"We will not leave an enemy alive behind us!" Heafstaag roared, and several other kings cried out their agreement.

"No, of course not," said deBernezan. "But it will not take many men to defeat Termalaine when the boats are out. Let King Haalfdane and the Tribe of the Bear sack the town while the rest of the force, led by yourself and King Beorg, presses on to Bryn Shander. The fires of the burning town should bring the entire fleet, even the ships from the other towns of Maer Dualdon, into Termalaine where King Haalfdane can destroy them on the docks. It is important that we keep them away from the stronghold of Targos. The people of Bryn Shander will receive no aid from the other lakes in time to support them and will have to stand alone against your charge. The Tribe of the Elk will flank around the base of the hill below the city and cut off any possible escape or any last-minute reinforcements."

Drizzt watched closely as deBernezan described this second division of the barbarian forces on his map. Already the drow's calculating mind was formulating initial defense plans. Bryn Shander's hill wasn't very high but its base was thick, and the barbarians who were to swing around the back of the hill would be a long way from the main force.

A long way from reinforcements.

"The city will fall before sunset!" deBernezan declared triumphantly. "And your men will feast on the finest booty in all of Ten-Towns!" A sudden cheer went up on cue from the seated kings at the southerner's declaration of victory.

Drizzt put his back to the tent and considered what he had heard. This dark-haired man named deBernezan knew the towns well and understood their strengths and weaknesses. If Bryn Shander fell, no organized resistance could be formed to drive off the invaders. Indeed, once they held the fortified city, the barbarians would be able to strike at their leisure at any of the other towns.

"Again you have shown me your worth," Drizzt heard Heafstaag tell the southerner, and the ensuing of conversations told the drow that the plans had been accepted as final. Drizzt then focused his keen senses on the encampment around him, seeking the best path for his escape. He noticed suddenly that two guards were walking his way and talking. Though they were too far away for their human eyes to see him as anything but a shadow on the side of the tent, he knew that any movement on his part would surely alert them.

Acting immediately, Drizzt dropped the black figurine to the ground. "Guenhwyvar," he called softly. "Come to me, my shadow."

SOMEWHERE IN A CORNER OF THE VAST ASTRAL PLANE, THE EN-
tity of the panther moved in sudden, subtle steps as it stalked the
entity of the deer. The beasts of this natural world had played out
this scenario countless times, following the harmonious order that
guided the lives of their descendents. The panther crouched low
for the final spring, sensing the sweetness of the upcoming kill.
This strike was the harmony of natural order, the purpose of the
panther's existence, and the meat its reward.

It stopped at once, though, when it heard the call of its true
name, compelled above any other directives to heed the call of its
master.

The great cat's spirit rushed down the long, darkened corridor
that marked the void between the planes, seeking the solitary
speck of light that was its life on the Material Plane. And then it
was beside the dark elf, its soulmate and master, crouching in the
shadows by the hanging skins of a human dwelling.

It understood the urgency of its master's call and quickly opened
its mind to the drow's instructions.

The two barbarian guards approached cautiously, trying to make
out the dark forms that stood beside their kings' tent. Suddenly
Guenhwyvar sprang toward them and soared in a mighty leap past
their drawn swords. The guards swung the weapons futilely and
charged off after the cat, screaming an alert to the rest of the camp.

In the excitement of the diversion, Drizzt moved calmly and
stealthily away in a different direction. He heard the shouts of
alarm as Guenhwyvar darted through the campsites of the sleeping warriors and couldn't help but smile when the cat crossed
through one particular group. Upon sighting this feline, who
moved with so much grace and speed that it appeared as no more
than a cat's spirit, the Tribe of the Tiger, instead of giving chase,
fell to their knees and raised their hands and voices in thanks to
Tempus.

Drizzt had little trouble escaping the perimeter of the camp, as
all of the sentries were rushing off in the direction of the commo-

tion. When the drow gained the blackness of the open tundra, he turned south toward Kelvin's Cairn and sped off across the lonely plain in full flight, all the while concentrating on finalizing a deadly counter-plan of defense. The stars told him that there were less than three hours left before dawn, and he knew that he mustn't be late for his meeting with Bruenor if the ambush were to be properly set.

The noise of the surprised barbarians soon died away, except for the prayers of the Tribe of the Tiger, which would continue until dawn. A few minutes later, Guenhwyvar was trotting easily by Drizzt's side.

"A hundred times you have saved my life, trusted friend," Drizzt said as he patted the great cat's muscled neck. "A hundred times and more!"

"THEY'VE BEEN ARGUIN' AND SCUFFLIN' FOR TWO DAYS NOW," Bruenor remarked disgustedly. "A blessing it is that the greater enemy has finally arrived!"

"Better to name the coming of barbarians in a different way," Drizzt replied, though a smile had found its way onto his normally stoic features. He knew that his plan was solid and that the battle this day would belong to the people of Ten-Towns. "Go now and lay the trap—you've not much time."

"We began loadin' the womenfolk and children onto the boats as soon as Rumblebelly told us yer news," Bruenor explained. "We'll chase the vermin from our borders before the day is through!" The dwarf spread his feet wide in his customary battle stance and banged his axe onto his shield to emphasize his point. "Ye've a good eye for battle, elf. Yer plan'll turn the surprise on the barbarians and it still splits the glory evenly among them that needs glory."

"Even Kemp of Targos should be pleased," Drizzt agreed.

Bruenor clapped his friend on the arm and turned to leave.

"Ye'll fight beside me, then?" he asked over his shoulder, though he already knew the answer.

"As it should be," Drizzt assured him.

"An' the cat?"

"Guenhwyvar has already played its part in this battle," replied the drow. "I'll be sending my friend home soon."

Bruenor was pleased with the answer; he didn't trust the drow's strange beast. "It ain't natural," he said to himself as he trekked down Bremen's Run toward the gathered hosts of Ten-Towns.

Bruenor was too far away for Drizzt to make out his final words, but the drow knew the dwarf well enough to gather the general meaning of his grumblings. He understood the uneasiness that Bruenor, and many others, felt around the mystical cat. Magic was a prominent part of the underworld of his people, a necessary fact of their everyday existence, but it was much rarer and less understood among the common folk of the surface. Dwarves in particular were usually uncomfortable with it, except for the crafted magical weapons and armor they often made themselves.

The drow, though, had no anxiety around Guenhwyvar from the very first day he had met the cat. The figurine had belonged to Masoj Hun'ett, a drow of high standing in a prominent family of the great city of Menzoberranzan, a gift from a demon lord in exchange for some assistance that Masoj had given him in a matter concerning some troublesome gnomes. Drizzt and the cat had crossed paths many times over the years in the dark city, often in planned meetings. They shared an empathy with each other that transcended the relationship that the cat felt with its then-master.

Guenhwyvar had even rescued Drizzt from certain death, uncalled for, as if the cat had been watching protectively over the drow who was not yet its master. Drizzt had struck out alone from Menzoberranzan on a journey to a neighboring city when he fell prey to a cave fisher, a crablike denizen of the dark caverns that customarily found a niche high above the floor of a tunnel and dropped an invisible, sticky line of webbing. Like an angler, this cave fisher had waited, and like a fish, Drizzt had fallen into its trap. The sticky line entangled him completely, rendering him helpless as he was dragged up the side of the corridor's stone wall.

He saw no hope for surviving this encounter and vividly understood that a terrible death certainly awaited him.

But then Guenhwyvar had arrived, leaping among the broken clefts and ridges along the wall at the same level as the monster. Without any regard to its own safety and following no orders, the cat charged right in on the fisher, knocking it from its perch. The monster, seeking only its own safety, tried to scramble away, but Guenhwyvar pounced upon it vindictively, as if to punish it for attacking Drizzt.

Both the drow and the cat knew from that day on that they were destined to run together. Yet the cat had no power to disobey the will of its master, and Drizzt had no right to claim the figurine from Masoj, especially since the house of Hun'ett was much more powerful than Drizzt's own family in the structured hierarchy of the underworld.

And so the drow and the cat continued their casual relationship as distant comrades.

Soon after, though, came an incident that Drizzt could not ignore. Guenhwyvar was often taken on raids with Masoj, whether against enemy drow houses or other denizens of the underworld. The cat normally carried out its orders efficiently, thrilled to aid its master in battle. On one particular raid, though, against a clan of svirfnebli, the deep mining, unassuming gnomes that often had the misfortune of running up against the drow in their common habitat, Masoj went too far in his maliciousness.

After the initial assault on the clan, the surviving gnomes scattered down the many corridors of their mazework mines. The raid had been successful; the treasures that had been sought were taken, and the clan had been dispatched, obviously never to bother the drow again. But Masoj wanted more blood.

He used Guenhwyvar, the proud, majestic hunter, as his instrument of murder. He sent the cat after the fleeing gnomes one by one until they were all destroyed.

Drizzt and several other drow witnessed the spectacle. The others, in their characteristic vileness, thought it great sport, but Drizzt found himself absolutely disgusted. Furthermore, he recognized the humiliation painfully etched on the proud cat's features. Guenhwyvar was a hunter, not an assassin, and to use it in such a role was criminally degrading, to say nothing of the horrors that Masoj was inflicting upon the innocent gnomes.

This was actually the final outrage in a long line of outrages which Drizzt could no longer bear. He had always known that he was unlike his kin in many ways, though he had many times feared that he would prove to be more akin to them than he believed. Yet he was rarely passionless, considering the death of another more important than the mere sport it represented to the vast majority of drow. He couldn't label it, for he had never come across a word in the drow language that spoke of such a trait, but to the surface-dwellers that later came to know Drizzt, it was called conscience.

One day the very next tenday, Drizzt managed to catch Masoj alone outside the cluttered grounds of Menzoberranzan. He knew that there could be no turning back once the fatal blow had been struck, but he didn't even hesitate, slipping his scimitar through the ribs of his unsuspecting victim. That was the only time in his life that he had ever killed one of his own race, an act that thoroughly revolted him despite his feelings toward his people.

Then he took the figurine and fled, meaning only to find another of the countless dark holes in the vast underworld to make his home, but eventually winding up on the surface. And then, unaccepted and persecuted for his heritage in city after city in the populated south, he had made his way to the wilderness frontier of Ten-Towns, a melting pot of outcasts, the last outpost of humanity, where he was at least tolerated.

He didn't care much about the shunning he usually received

even here. He had found friendship with the halfling, and the dwarves, and Bruenor's adopted daughter, Catti-brie.

And he had Guenhwyvar by his side.

He patted the great cat's muscled neck once again and left Bremen's Run to find a dark hole where he could rest before the battle.

8

BLOODY FIELDS

The horde entered the mouth of Bremen's Run just before mid-day. They longed to announce their glorious charge with a song of war, but they understood that a certain degree of stealth was vital to the ultimate success of deBernezan's battle plan.

DeBernezan was comforted by the familiar sight of sails dotting the waters of Maer Dualdon as he jogged beside King Haalfdane. The surprise would be complete, he believed, and then with ironic amusement he noted that some of the ships already flew the red flags of the catch. "More wealth for the victors," he hissed under his breath. The barbarians had still not begun their song when the Tribe of the Bear split away from the main group and headed toward Termalaine, though the cloud of dust that followed their run would have told a wary observer that something out of the ordinary was happening. They rolled on toward Bryn Shander and cried out their first cheer when the pennant of the principal city came into sight.

The combined forces of the four towns of Maer Dualdon lay hidden in Termalaine. Their goal was to strike fast and hard at the small tribe that attacked the city, overrunning them as quickly as possible, then charge to the aid of Bryn Shander, trapping the rest of the horde between the two armies. Kemp of Targos was in command of this operation, but he had conceded the first blow to Agorwal, spokesman of the home city.

Torches set the first buildings of the city ablaze as Haalfdane's wild army rushed in. Termalaine was second only to Targos among the nine fishing villages in population, but it was a sprawling, uncluttered town, with houses spread out over a large area and wide avenues running between them. Its people had retained their privacy and a measure of breathing room, giving the town an air of solitude that belied its numbers. Still, deBernezan sensed that the streets seemed unusually deserted. He mentioned his concern to the barbarian king at his side, though Haalfdane assured him that the rats had gone into hiding at the approach of the Bear.

"Pull them out of their holes and burn their houses!" the barbarian king roared. "Let the fishermen on the lake hear the cries of their women and see the smoke of their burning town!"

But then an arrow thudded into Haalfdane's chest, burying itself deep within his flesh and biting through, tearing into his heart. The shocked barbarian looked down in horror at the vibrating shaft, though he couldn't even utter a final cry before the blackness of death closed in around him.

With his ashwood bow, Agorwal of Termalaine had silenced the King of the Tribe of the Bear. And on signal from Agorwal's strike, the four armies of Maer Dualdon sprang to life.

They leaped from the rooftops of every building, from the alleys and doorways of every street. Against the ferocious assault of the multitude, the confused and stunned barbarians realized immediately that their battle would soon be at an end. Many were cut down before they could even ready their weapons.

Some of the battle-hardened invaders managed to form into small groups, but the people of Ten-Towns, fighting for their homes and the lives of their loved ones and armed with crafted weapons and shields forged by dwarven smiths, pressed in immediately. Fearlessly, the defenders bore the remaining invaders down under the weight of their greater numbers.

In an alley on the edge of Termalaine, Regis dived behind the concealment of a small cart as two fleeing barbarians passed by. The halfling fought with a personal dilemma: He didn't want to be labeled a coward, but he had no intention of jumping into the battle of big folk. When the danger had passed, he walked back around the cart and tried to figure out his next move.

Suddenly a dark-haired man, a member of Ten-Towns' militia, Regis supposed, entered the alley and spotted the halfling. Regis knew that his little game of hiding was over; the time had come for him to make his stand. "Two of the scum just passed this way," he called boldly to the dark-haired southerner. "Come, if we're quick we can catch them yet!"

DeBernezan had different plans, though. In a desperate attempt to save his own life, he had decided to slip down one alley and emerge from another as a member of the Ten-Towns force. He had no intention of leaving any witnesses to his treachery. Steadily he walked toward Regis, his slender sword at the ready.

Regis sensed that the mannerisms of the closing man weren't quite right. "Who are you?" he asked, though he somehow expected no reply. He thought that he knew nearly everyone in the city, though he didn't believe that he had ever seen this man before. Already, he had the uncomfortable suspicion that this was the traitor Drizzt had described to Bruenor. "How come I didn't see you come in with the others earli—"

DeBernezan thrust his sword at the halfling's eye. Regis, dexterous and ever-alert, managed to lurch out of the way, though the blade scratched the side of his head and the momentum of his dodge sent him spinning to the ground. With an unemotional, disturbingly cold-blooded calm, the dark-haired man closed in again.

Regis scrambled to his feet and backed away, step for step with his assailant. But then he bumped up against the side of the small cart. DeBernezan advanced methodically. The halfling had nowhere left to run.

Desperate, Regis pulled the ruby pendant from under his waist-coat. "Please don't kill me," he pleaded, holding the sparkling stone out by its chain and letting it dance seductively. "If you let me live, I'll give you this and show you where you can find many more!" Regis was encouraged by deBernezan's slight hesitation at the sight of the stone. "Surely, it's a beautiful cut and worth a dragon's hoard of gold!"

DeBernezan kept his sword out in front of him, but Regis counted as the seconds passed and the dark-haired man did not blink. The halfling's left hand began to steady, while his right, concealed behind his back, clasped firmly onto the handle of the small but heavy mace crafted for him personally by Bruenor.

"Come, look closer," Regis suggested softly. DeBernezan, firmly under the spell of the sparkling stone, stooped low to better examine its fascinating dance of light.

"This isn't really fair," Regis lamented aloud, confident that deBernezan was oblivious to anything he might say at that moment. He cracked the spiked ball of the mace onto the back of the bending man's head.

Regis eyed the result of his dirty work and shrugged absently. He had only done what was necessary.

The sounds of the battle in the street rang closer to his alley sanctuary and dispelled his contemplation. Again the halfling acted on instinct. He crawled under the body of his felled enemy, then twisted around underneath to make it look as if he had gone down under the weight of the larger man.

When he inspected the damage of deBernezan's initial thrust, he was glad that he hadn't lost his ear. He hoped that his wound was serious enough to give credence to this image of a death struggle.

THE MAIN HOST OF THE BARBARIAN FORCE REACHED THE LONG, low hill that led up to Bryn Shander unaware of what had befallen their comrades in Termalaine. Here they split again, with Heafstaag leading the Tribe of the Elk around the eastern side of the hill and Beorg taking the rest of the horde straight toward the walled city. Now they took up their song of battle, hoping to further unnerve the shocked and terrified people of Ten-Towns.

But behind the wall of Bryn Shander was a very different scene than the barbarians imagined. The army of the city, along with the forces of Caer-Konig and Caer-Dineval, sat ready with bows and spears and buckets of hot oil.

In a dark twist of irony, the Tribe of the Elk, out of sight of the front wall of the city, took up a cheer when the first screams of death rang out on the hill, thinking the victims to be the unprepared people of Ten-Towns. A few seconds later, as Heafstaag led his men around the easternmost bend in the hill, they too met with disaster. The armies of Good Mead and Dougan's Hole were firmly dug in and waiting, and the barbarians were hard-pressed before they even knew what had hit them.

After the first few moments of confusion, though, Heafstaag managed to regain control of the situation. These warriors had been through many battles together, seasoned fighting men who knew no fear. Even with the losses of the initial attack, they were not outnumbered by the force before them, and Heafstaag was confident that he could overrun the fishermen quickly and still get his men into position.

But then, shouting as they came, the army of Easthaven charged down the Eastway and pressed the barbarians on their left flank. And Heafstaag, still unshaken, had just ordered his men to make the proper adjustments to protect against the new foe when ninety battle-hardened and heavily armored dwarves tore into them from behind. The grim-faced dwarven host attacked in a wedge formation with Bruenor as its deadly tip. They cut into the Tribe of the Elk, felling barbarians like a low-swinging scythe through tall grass.

The barbarians fought bravely, and many fishermen died on the eastern slopes of Bryn Shander. But the Tribe of the Elk was out-numbered and outflanked, and barbarian blood ran freer than the blood of their foes. Heafstaag worked wildly to rally his men, but all semblance of formation and order disintegrated around him. To his worst horror and disgrace, the giant king realized that every one of his warriors would die on this field if they didn't find a way to escape the ring of enemies and flee back to the safety of the tundra.

Heafstaag himself, who had never before retreated in battle, led the desperate break. He and as many warriors as he could gather together rushed around the dwarven host, seeking a route between them and the army of Easthaven. Most of the tribesmen were cut down by the blades of Bruenor's people, but some managed to break free of the ring and bolt away toward Kelvin's Cairn.

Heafstaag got through the gauntlet, killing two dwarves as he passed, but suddenly the giant king was engulfed in an impenetra-ble globe of absolute blackness. He dived headlong through it and emerged back into the light only to find himself face-to-face with a dark elf.

BRUENOR HAD SEVEN NOTCHES TO PUT ON HIS AXE HANDLE AND he bore down on number eight, a tall, gangly barbarian youth, too young even to show any stubble on his tanned face, but bearing the standard of the Tribe of the Elk with the composure of an experi-enced warrior. Bruenor curiously considered the engaging stare and calm visage as he closed in on the youth. It surprised him that he did not find the savage fire of barbarian bloodlust contorting the youth's features, but rather an observant, understanding depth. The dwarf found himself truly lamenting having to kill one so young and unusual, and his pity caused him to hesitate slightly as the two joined battle.

Ferocious as his heritage dictated, though, the youth showed no fear, and Bruenor's hesitation had given him the first swing. With deadly accuracy, he slammed his standard pole down onto his foe, snapping it in half. The amazingly powerful blow dented Bruenor's helm and jolted the dwarf into a short bounce. Tough as the mountain stone he mined, Bruenor put his hands on his hips and glared up at the barbarian, who nearly dropped his weapon, so shocked was he that the dwarf still stood.

"Silly boy," Bruenor growled as he cut the youth's legs out from under him. "Ain't ye never been told not to hit a dwarf on the head?" The youth desperately tried to regain his footing, but Bruenor slammed an iron shield into his face.

"Eight!" roared the dwarf as he stormed away in search of number nine. But he looked back for a moment over his shoulder to consider the fallen youth, shaking his head at the waste of one so tall and straight, with intelligent eyes to match his physical prowess, a combination uncommon among the wild and ferocious natives of Icewind Dale.

HEAFSTAAG'S RAGE DOUBLED WHEN HE RECOGNIZED HIS NEWest opponent as a drow elf. "Sorcerous dog!" he bellowed, raising his huge axe high into the sky.

Even as he spoke, Drizzt flicked a finger and purple flames limned the tall barbarian from head to toe. Heafstaag roared in horror at the magical fire, though the flames did not burn his skin. Drizzt bore in, his two scimitars whirling and jabbing, thrusting high and low too quickly for the barbarian king to deflect both.

Blood trickled from many small wounds, but Heafstaag seemed able to shake off the punctures of the slender scimitars as no more than a discomfort. The great axe arced down, and though Drizzt was able to deflect its path, the effort numbed his arm. Again the barbarian swung his axe. This time Drizzt was able to spin out of its killing sweep, and the completion of the drow's rotation left the overbalanced Heafstaag stumbling and open to a counter. Drizzt didn't hesitate, driving one of his blades deep into the barbarian king's side.

Heafstaag howled in agony and launched a backhand swing in retaliation. Drizzt thought his last thrust to be fatal, and his surprise was total when the flat head of Heafstaag's axe smashed into his ribs and launched him through the air. The barbarian charged quickly after, meaning to finish this dangerous opponent before he could regain his footing.

But Drizzt was as nimble as a cat. He landed in a roll and came up to meet Heafstaag's charge with one of his scimitars firmly set. His axe helplessly poised above his head, the surprised barbarian couldn't stop his momentum before he impaled his belly on the wicked point. Still, he glared at the drow and began to swing his axe. Already convinced of the superhuman strength of the barbarian, Drizzt had kept up his guard this time. He knifed his second blade just under the first, opening the lower part of Heafstaag's abdomen from hip to hip.

Heafstaag's axe fell harmlessly to the ground as he grabbed at the wound, desperately trying to keep his belly from spilling out. His huge head lolled from side to side, the world spun about him, and he felt himself endlessly falling.

Several other tribesmen, in full flight and with dwarves hot on their heels, came by at that moment and caught their king before he hit the ground. So great was their dedication to Heafstaag that two of them lifted him and carried him away while the others turned to face the coming tide of dwarves, knowing that they would certainly be cut down, but hoping only to give their comrades enough time to bear their king to safety.

Drizzt rolled away from the barbarians and leaped to his feet, meaning to give chase to the two who bore Heafstaag. He had a sickening feeling that the terrible king would survive even the last grievous wounds, and he was determined to finish the job. But when he rose, he, too, found the world spinning. The side of his cloak was stained with his own blood, and he suddenly found it difficult to catch his breath. The blazing midday sun burned into his night eyes, and he was lathered in sweat.

Drizzt collapsed into darkness.

THE THREE ARMIES WAITING BEHIND BRYN SHANDER'S WALL had quickly dispatched the first line of invaders and then driven the remaining barbarian host halfway back down the hill. Undaunted and thinking that time would play in their favor, the ferocious horde had regrouped around Beorg and begun a steady, cautious march back toward the city.

When the barbarians heard the charge coming up the eastern slope, they assumed that Heafstaag had finished his battle on the side of the hill, had learned of the resistance at the front gate, and was returning to help them smash into the city. Then Beorg spotted tribesmen fleeing to the north toward Icewind Pass, the stretch of ground opposite Bremen's Run that passed between Lac Dinneshere and the western side of Kelvin's Cairn. The king of the Tribe of the Wolf knew that his people were in trouble. Offering no explanation beyond the promised thrust of the tip of his spear to any who questioned his orders, Beorg started to turn his men around to head away from the city, hoping to regroup with Haalfdane and the Tribe of the Bear and salvage as many of his people as he could.

Before he had even completed the reversal of the march, he found Kemp and the four armies of Maer Dualdon behind him, their deep ranks barely thinned by the slaughter in Termalaine. Over the wall came the armies of Bryn Shander, Caer-Konig, and Caer-Dineval, and around the hill came Bruenor, leading the dwarven clan and the last three armies of Ten-Towns.

Beorg ordered his men into a tight circle. "Tempus is watching," he yelled at them. "Make him proud of his people!"

Nearly eight hundred barbarians remained, and they fought with the confidence of the blessing of their god. They held their formation for almost an hour, singing and dying, before the lines broke down and chaos erupted.

Less than fifty escaped with their lives.

AFTER THE FINAL BLOWS HAD AT LAST BEEN SWUNG, THE EX-hausted warriors of Ten-Towns set about the grim task of sorting out their losses. More than five hundred of their companions had been killed and two hundred more would eventually die of their wounds, yet the toll wasn't heavy considering the two thousand barbarians who lay dead in the streets of Termalaine and on the slopes of Bryn Shander.

Many heroes had been made that day, and Bruenor, though anxious to get back to the eastern battlefields to search for missing companions, paused for a long moment as the last of them was carried in glory up the hill to Bryn Shander.

"Rumblebelly?" exclaimed the dwarf.

"The name is Regis," the halfling retorted from his high perch, proudly folding his arms across his chest.

"Respect, good dwarf," said one of the men carrying Regis. "In single combat Spokesman Regis of Lonelywood slew the traitor that brought the horde upon us, though he was wickedly injured in the battle!"

Bruenor snorted in amusement as the procession passed. "There's more to that tale than what's been told, I'll wager!" he chuckled to his equally amused companions. "Or I'm a bearded gnome!"

KEMP OF TARGOS AND ONE OF HIS LIEUTENANTS WERE THE FIRST to come upon the fallen form of Drizzt Do'Urden. Kemp prodded the dark elf with the toe of his bloodstained boot, drawing a semi-conscious groan in response.

"He lives," Kemp said to his lieutenant with an amused smile.

"A pity." He kicked the injured drow again, this time with more enthusiasm. The other man laughed in approval and lifted his own foot to join in the fun.

Suddenly, a mailed fist slammed into Kemp's kidney with enough force to carry the spokesman over Drizzt and send him bouncing down the long decline of the hill. His lieutenant whirled around, conveniently ducking low to receive Bruenor's second swing square in the face.

"One for yerself, too!" the enraged dwarf growled as he felt the man's nose shatter under his blow.

Cassius of Bryn Shander, viewing the incident from higher up on the hill, screamed in anger and rushed down the slope toward Bruenor. "You should be taught some diplomacy!" he scolded.

"Stand where y' are, son of a swamp pig!" was Bruenor's threatening response. "Ye owe the drow yer stinkin' lives and homes," he roared to all around who could hear him, "and ye treat him as vermin!"

"Ware your words, dwarf!" retorted Cassius, tentatively grabbing at his sword hilt. The dwarves formed a line around their leader, and Cassius's men gathered around him.

Then a third voice sounded clearly. "Ware your own, Cassius," warned Agorwal of Termalaine. "I would have done the same thing to Kemp if I was possessed of the courage of the dwarf!" He pointed to the north. "The sky is clear," he yelled. "Yet were it not for the drow, it would be filled with the smoke of burning Termalaine!" The spokesman from Termalaine and his companions moved over to join Bruenor's line. Two of the men gently lifted Drizzt from the ground.

"Fear not for your friend, valiant dwarf," said Agorwal. "He will be well tended in my city. Never again shall I, or my fellow men of Termalaine, prejudge him by the color of his skin and the reputation of his kin!"

Cassius was outraged. "Remove your soldiers from the grounds of Bryn Shander!" he screamed at Agorwal, but it was an empty threat, for the men of Termalaine were already departing.

Satisfied that the drow was in safe hands, Bruenor and his clan moved on to search the rest of the battleground.

"I'll not forget this!" Kemp yelled at him from far down the hill.

Bruenor spat at the spokesman from Targos and continued on unshaken.

And so it went that the alliance of the people of Ten-Towns lasted only as long as their common enemy.

EPILOGUE

All along the hill, the fishermen of Ten-Towns moved among their fallen enemies, looting the barbarians of what small wealth they possessed and putting the sword to the unfortunate ones who were not quite dead.

Yet amid the carnage of the bloody scene, a finger of mercy was to be found. A man from Good Mead rolled the limp form of an unconscious young barbarian over onto its back, preparing to finish the job with his dagger. Bruenor came upon them then and, recognizing the youth as the standard bearer who had dented his helmet, stayed the fisherman's thrust. "Don't kill 'im. He's nothing but a boy, and he can't have known truly what he an' his people did."

"Bah!" huffed the fisherman. "What mercy would these dogs have shown to our children, I ask you? He's half in the grave anyway."

"Still I ask ye to let him be!" Bruenor growled, his axe bouncing impatiently against his shoulder. "In fact, I insist!"

The fisherman returned the dwarf's scowl, but he had witnessed Bruenor's proficiency in battle and thought the better of pushing him too far. With a disgusted sigh, he headed off around the hill to find less-protected victims.

The boy stirred on the grass and moaned.

"So ye've a bit of life left in ye yet," said Bruenor. He knelt beside the lad's head and lifted it by the hair to meet his eyes. "Hear me well, boy. I saved yer life here—why, I'm not quite knowin'—but don't ye think ye've been pardoned by the people of Ten-Towns. I want ye to see the misery yer people have brung. Maybe killing is in yer blood, and if it is, then let the fisherman's blade end ye here and now! But I'm feelin' there's more to ye, and ye'll have the time to show me right.

"Ye're to serve me and me people in our mines for five years and a day to prove yourself worthy of life and freedom."

Bruenor saw that the youth had slumped back into unconsciousness. "Never mind," he muttered. "Ye'll hear me well before all's done, be sure o' that!" He moved to drop the head back to the grass, but laid it down gently instead.

Onlookers to the spectacle of the gruff dwarf showing kindness to the barbarian youth were indeed startled, but none could guess the implications of what they had witnessed. Bruenor himself, for all of his assumptions of this barbarian's character, could not have foreseen that this boy, Wulfgar, would grow into the man who would reshape this harsh region of the tundra.

FAR TO THE SOUTH, IN A WIDE PASS AMONG THE TOWERING peaks of the Spine of the World, Akar Kessell languished in the soft life that Crenshinibon had provided for him. His goblin slaves had captured yet another female from a merchant caravan for him to play with, but now something else had caught his eye. Smoke, rising into the empty sky from the direction of Ten-Towns.

"Barbarians," Kessell guessed. He had heard rumors that the tribes were gathering when he and the wizards from Luskan had been visiting Easthaven. But it didn't matter to him, and why should it? He had all that he needed right here in Cryshal-Tirith and had no desire to travel anywhere else.

No desires that were wrought of his own will.

Crenshinibon was a relic that was truly alive in its magic. And part of its life was the desire to conquer and command. The Crystal Shard was not content with an existence in a desolate mountain range, where the only servants were lowly goblins. It wanted more. It wanted power.

Kessell's own subconscious recollections of Ten-Towns when he had spotted the column of smoke had stirred the relic's hunger, so it now used the same empathetic power of suggestion on Kessell.

A sudden image grasped at the wizard's deepest needs. He saw himself seated on a throne in Bryn Shander, immeasurably wealthy and respected by all in his court. He imagined the response from the Hosttower of the Arcane in Luskan when the mages there, especially Eldeluc and Dendybar, learned of Akar Kessell, lord of Ten-Towns and ruler of all Icewind Dale! Would they offer him a robe in their puny order then?

Despite Kessell's true enjoyment of the leisurely existence he had found, the thought appealed to him. He let his mind continue through the fantasy, exploring the paths that he might take to accomplish such an ambitious goal.

He ruled out trying to dominate the fisherfolk as he had dominated this goblin tribe, for even the least intelligent of the goblins had held out against his imposing will for quite a long time. And when any of these had gotten away from the immediate area of the tower, they regained their ability to determine their own actions and had fled into the mountains. No, simple domination would not work against the humans.

Kessell pondered using the power that he felt pulsing within the structure of Cryshal-Tirith, destructive forces beyond anything he had ever heard of, even in the Hosttower. This would help, but it wouldn't be enough. Even the strength of Crenshinibon was limited, requiring lengths of time under the sun to gather new power to replace expended energy. Furthermore, in Ten-Towns there were too many people too widely scattered to be corralled by a single sphere of influence, and Kessell didn't want to destroy them all. Goblins were convenient; but the wizard longed to have humans bowing before him, real men like the ones who had persecuted him for all of his life.

For all of his life before he had gained the shard.

His ponderings eventually led him inevitably down the same line of reasoning. He would need an army.

He considered the goblins he presently commanded. Fanatically devoted to his every wish, they would gladly die for him (in fact, several had). Yet even they weren't nearly numerous enough to engulf the wide region of the three lakes with any semblance of strength.

And then an evil thought, again covertly insinuated into his will by the Crystal Shard, came upon the wizard. "How many holes and caves," Kessell cried aloud, "are there in this vast and rugged mountain range? And how many goblins, ogres, even trolls and giants, do they harbor?" The beginnings of a devious vision took shape in his mind. He saw himself at the head of a huge goblin and giant army, sweeping across the plains, unstoppable and irresistible.

How he would make men tremble!

He lay back on a soft pillow and called for the new harem girl. He had another game in mind, one that had also come to him in a strange dream; it called for her to beg and whimper, and finally, to die. The wizard decided, though, that he would certainly consider the possibilities of lordship over Ten-Towns that had opened wide before him. But there was no need to hurry; he had time. The goblins could always find him another plaything.

Crenshinibon, too, seemed to be at peace. It had placed the seed within Kessell's mind, a seed that it knew would germinate into a plan of conquest. But like Kessell, the relic had no need for haste.

The Crystal Shard had waited ten thousand years to return to life and see this opportunity of power flicker again. It could wait a few more.

PART TWO
WULFGAR

Tradition.

The very sound of the word invokes a sense of gravity and solemnity. Tradition. Suuz'chok in the drow language, and there, too, as in every language that I have heard, the word rolls off of one's tongue with tremendous weight and power.

Tradition. It is the root of who we are, the link to our heritage, the reminder that we as a people, if not individually, will span the ages. To many people and many societies, tradition is the source of structure and of law, the abiding fact of identity that denies the contrary claims of the outlaw, or the misbehavior of the rogue. It is that echoing sound deep in our hearts and our minds and our souls that reminds us of who we are by reinforcing who we were. To many it is even more than the law; it is the religion, guiding faith as it guides morality and society. To many, tradition is a god itself, the ancient rituals and holy texts, scribbled on unreadable parchments yellowed with age or chiseled into eternal rocks.

To many, tradition is all.

Personally, I view it as a double-edged sword, and one that can cut even more deeply in the way of error.

I saw the workings of tradition in Menzoberranzan, the ritualistic sacrifice of the third male child (which was almost my own fate), the workings of the three drow schools. Tradition justified my sister's advances toward me in the graduation of Melee-Magthere, and denied me any claims against that wretched ceremony. Tradition holds the Matrons in power, limiting the ascent of any males. Even the vicious wars of Menzoberranzan, house against house, are rooted in tradition, are justified because that is the way it has always been.

Such failings are not exclusive to the drow. Often I sit on the northern face of Kelvin's Cairn looking out over the empty tundra and the twinkling lights of the campfires in the vast barbarian encampments. There, too, is a people wholly consumed by tradition, a people clinging to ancient codes and ways that once allowed them to survive as a society in an inhospitable land but that now hinder them as much as, or more than, help them. The barbarians of Icewind Dale follow the caribou herd from one end of the dale to the other. In days long past that was the only way they could have survived up here, but how much easier might their existence be now if they only traded with the folk of Ten-Towns, offering pelts and good meat in exchange for stronger materials brought up from the south so they might construct more permanent homes for themselves?

In days long past, before any real civilization crept this far to the north, the barbarians refused to speak with, or even to accept, anyone else within Icewind Dale, the various tribes often joining for the sole purpose of driving out any intruders. In those past times, any newcomers would inevitably become rivals for the meager food and other scarce supplies, and so such xenophobia was necessary for basic survival.

The folk of Ten-Towns, with their advanced fishing techniques, and their rich trade with Luskan, are not rivals of the barbarians—most have never even eaten venison, I would *guess. And yet, tradition demands of the barbarians that they do not make friends with those folk, and indeed, often war upon them.*

Tradition.

What gravity indeed does that word impart! What power it wields! As it roots us and grounds us and gives us hope for who we are because of who we were, so it also wreaks destruction and denies change.

I would never pretend to understand another people well enough to demand that they change their traditions, yet how foolish it seems to me to hold fast and unyieldingly to those mores and ways without regard for any changes that have taken place in the world about us.

For that world is a changing place, moved by advancements in technology and magic, by the rise and fall of populations, even by the blending of races, as in the half-elf communities. The world is not static, and if the roots of our perceptions, traditions, hold static, then we are doomed, I say, into destructive dogma.

Then we fall upon the darker blade of that double-edged sword.

—Drizzt Do'Urden

9
NO MORE A BOY

Regis stretched out lazily against his favorite tree and enjoyed a drawn-out yawn, his cherubic dimples beaming in the bright ray of sunlight that somehow found its way to him through the thickly packed branches. His fishing pole stood poised beside him, though its hook had long since been cleaned of any bait. Regis rarely caught any fish, but he prided himself on never wasting more than one worm.

He had come out here every day since his return to Lonelywood. He wintered in Bryn Shander now, enjoying the company of his good friend, Cassius. The city on the hill didn't compare to Calimport, but the palace of its spokesman was the closest thing to luxury in all of Icewind Dale. Regis thought himself quite clever for persuading Cassius to invite him to spend the harsh winters there.

A cool breeze wafted in off Maer Dualdon, drawing a contented sigh from the halfling. Though Kythorn had already passed its midpoint, this was the first hot day of the short season. And Regis was determined to make the most of it. For the first time in over a year he had been out before noon, and he planned to stay in this spot, stripped of his clothes, letting the sun sink its warmth into every inch of his body until the last red glow of sunset.

An angry shout out on the lake caught his attention. He lifted his head and half-opened one heavy eyelid. The first thing he noticed, to his complete satisfaction, was that his belly had grown considerably over the winter, and from this angle, lying flat on his back, he could see only the tips of his toes.

Halfway across the water, four boats, two from Termalaine and two from Targos, jockeyed for position, running past each other with sudden tacks and turns, their sailors cursing and spitting at the boats that flew the flag of the other city. For the last four and a half years, since the Battle of Bryn Shander, the two cities had virtually been at war. Though their battles were more often fought with words and fists than weapons, more than one ship had been rammed or driven into rocks or up to beach in shallow waters.

Regis shrugged helplessly and dropped his head back to his folded waistcoat. Nothing had changed much around Ten-Towns in the last few years. Regis and some of the other spokesmen had entertained high hopes of a united community, despite the heated argument after the battle between Kemp of Targos and Agorwal of Termalaine over the drow.

Even on the banks of the lake across the way, the period of goodwill was short-lived among the long-standing rivals. The truce between Caer-Dineval and Caer-Konig had lasted only until the first time one of Caer-Dineval's boats landed a valuable and rare five-footer, on the stretch of Lac Dinneshere that Caer-Konig had relinquished to her as compensation for the waters she had lost to Easthaven's expanding fleet.

Furthermore, Good Mead and Dougan's Hole, the normally unassuming and fiercely independent towns on the southernmost lake, Redwaters, had boldly demanded compensation from Bryn Shander and Termalaine. They had suffered staggering casualties in the battle on Bryn Shander's slopes, though they had never even considered the affair their business. They reasoned that the two towns which had gained the most from the united effort should be made to pay. The northern cities, of course, balked at the demand.

And so the lesson of the benefits of unification had gone unheeded. The ten communities remained as divided as ever before.

In truth, the town which had benefited the most from the battle was Lonelywood. The population of Ten-Towns as a whole had remained fairly constant. Many fortune hunters or hiding scoundrels continued to filter into the region, but an equal number were killed or grew disenchanted with the brutal conditions and returned to the more hospitable south.

Lonelywood, though, had grown considerably. Maer Dualdon, with its consistent yield of knucklehead, remained the most profitable of the lakes, and with the fighting between Termalaine and Targos, and Bremen precariously perched on the banks of the unpredictable and often flooding Shaengarne River, Lonelywood appeared the most appealing of the four towns. The people of the small community had even launched a campaign to draw newcomers, citing Lonelywood as the "Home of the Halfling Hero," and as the only place with shade trees within a hundred miles.

Regis had given up his position as spokesman shortly after the battle, a choice mutually arrived at by himself and the townsfolk. With Lonelywood growing into greater prominence and shaking off its reputation as a melting pot of rogues, the town needed a more aggressive person to sit on the council. And Regis simply didn't want to be bothered with the responsibility anymore.

Of course, Regis had found a way to turn his fame into profit. Every new settler in the town had to pay out a share of his first catches in return for the right to fly Lonelywood's flag, and Regis had persuaded the new spokesman and the other leaders of the town that since his name had been used to help bring in the new settlers, he should be cut in for a portion of these fees.

The halfling wore a broad smile whenever he considered his good fortune. He spent his days in peace, coming and going at his leisure, mostly just lying against the moss of his favorite tree, putting a line in the water once and letting the day pass him by.

His life had taken a comfortable turn, though the only work he ever did now was carving scrimshaw. His crafted pieces carried ten times their old value, the price partially inflated by the halfling's small degree of fame, but more so because he had persuaded some connoisseurs who were visiting Bryn Shander that his unique style and cut gave his scrimshaw a special artistic and aesthetic worth.

Regis patted the ruby pendant that rested on his bare chest. It seemed that he could "persuade" almost anyone of almost anything these days.

THE HAMMER CLANGED DOWN ON THE GLOWING METAL. SPARKS leaped off the anvil platform in a fiery arc, then died into the dimness of the stone chamber. The heavy hammer swung again and again, guided effortlessly by a huge, muscled arm.

The smith wore only a pair of pants and a leather apron tied about his waist in the small, hot chamber. Black lines of soot had settled in the muscular grooves across his broad shoulders and chest, and he glistened with sweat in the orange glow of the forge. His movements were marked by such rhythmic, tireless ease that they seemed almost preternatural, as though he were the god who had forged the world in the days before mortal man.

An approving grin spread across his face when he felt the rigidity of the iron finally give a bit under the force of his blows. Never before had he felt such strength in the metal; it tested him to the limits of his own resilience, and he felt a shiver as alluring as the thrill of battle when he had at last proven himself the stronger.

"Bruenor will be pleased."

Wulfgar stopped for a moment and considered the implications of his thoughts, smiling in spite of himself as he remembered his first days in the mines of the dwarves. What a stubborn, angry youth he had been then, cheated out of his right to die on the field of honor by a grumbling dwarf who justified unasked-for compassion by labeling it "good business."

This was his fifth and final spring indentured to the dwarves in tunnels that kept his seven-foot frame continually hunched. He longed for the freedom of the open tundra, where he could stretch his arms up high to the warmth of the sun or to the intangible pull of the moon. Or lie flat on his back with his legs unbent, the ceaseless wind tickling him with its chill bite and the crystalline stars filling his mind with mystical visions of unknown horizons.

And yet, for all of their inconveniences, Wulfgar had to admit that he would miss the hot drafts and constant clatter of the dwarven halls. He had clung to the brutal code of his people, which defined capture as disgrace, during the first year of his servitude, reciting the Song of Tempus as a litany of strength against the insinuation of weakness in the company of the soft, civilized southerners.

Yet Bruenor was as solid as the metal he pounded. The dwarf openly professed no love for battle, but he swung his notched axe with deadly accuracy and shrugged off blows that would fell an ogre.

The dwarf had been an enigma to Wulfgar in the early days of their relationship. The young barbarian was compelled to grant Bruenor a degree of respect, for Bruenor had bested him on the field of honor. Even then, with the battle lines firmly defining the two as enemies, Wulfgar had recognized a genuine and deeply rooted affection in the eyes of the dwarf that had confused him. He and his people had come to pillage Ten-Towns, yet Bruenor's underlying attitude seemed more the concern of a stern father than the callous perspective of a slave's master. Wulfgar always remembered his rank in the mines, however, for Bruenor was often gruff and insulting, working Wulfgar at menial, sometimes degrading, tasks.

Wulfgar's anger had dissipated over the long months. He came to accept his penance with stoicism, heeding Bruenor's commands without question or complaint. Gradually, conditions had improved.

Bruenor had taught him to work the forge, and later, to craft the metal into fine weapons and tools. And finally, on a day that Wulfgar would never forget, he had been given his own forge and anvil where he could work in solitude and without supervision—though Bruenor often stuck his head in to grumble over an inexact strike or to spout a few pointers. More than the degree of freedom, though, the small workshop had restored Wulfgar's pride. Since the first time he lifted the smithy hammer he called his own, the methodical stoicism of a servant had been replaced by the eagerness and meticulous devotion of a true craftsman. The barbarian found himself fretting over the smallest burr, sometimes reworking an entire piece to correct a slight imperfection. Wulfgar was pleased about this change in his perspective, viewing it as an attribute that might serve him well in the future, though he didn't as yet understand how.

Bruenor called it "character."

The work paid dividends physically as well. Chopping stone and pounding metal had corded the barbarian's muscles, redefining the gangly frame of his youth into a hardened girth of unrivaled strength. And he possessed great stamina, for the tempo of the tireless dwarves had strengthened his heart and stretched his lungs to new limits.

Wulfgar bit his lip in shame as he vividly remembered his first conscious thought after the Battle of Bryn Shander. He had vowed to pay Bruenor back in blood as soon as he had fulfilled the terms of his indenture. He understood now, to his own amazement, that he had become a better man under the tutelage of Bruenor Battlehammer, and the mere thought of raising a weapon against the dwarf sickened him.

He turned his sudden emotion into motion, slamming his hammer against the iron, flattening its incredibly hard head more and more into the semblance of a blade. This piece would make a fine sword.

Bruenor would be pleased.

10

THE GATHERING GLOOM

Torga the orc faced Grock the goblin with open contempt. Their respective tribes had been warring for many years, as long as any living member of either group could remember. They shared a valley in the Spine of the World and competed for ground and food with the brutality indicative of their warlike races.

And now they stood on common ground with no weapons drawn, compelled to this spot by a force even greater than their hatred for each other. In any other place, at any other time, the tribes could never have been this close without joining in fierce battle. But now, they had to be content with idle threats and dangerous glares, for they had been commanded to put aside their differences.

Torga and Grock turned and walked, side by side, to the structure that held the man who would be their master.

They entered Cryshal-Tirith and stood before Akar Kessell.

TWO MORE TRIBES HAD JOINED HIS SWELLING RANKS. ALL ABOUT the plateau that harbored his tower were the standards of various bands of goblins: the Goblins of Twisting Spears, Slasher Orcs, the Orcs of the Severed Tongue, and many others, all come to serve the master. Kessell had even pulled in a large clan of ogres, a handful of trolls, and two score rogue verbeeg, the least of the giants but giants nonetheless.

But his crowning achievement was a group of frost giants that had simply wandered in, desiring only to please the wielder of Crenshinibon.

Kessell had been quite content with his life in Cryshal-Tirith, with all of his whims obediently served by the first tribe of goblins that he had encountered. The goblins had even been able to raid a trading caravan and supply the wizard with a few human women for his pleasures. Kessell's life had been soft and easy, just the way that he liked it.

But Crenshinibon was not contented. The relic's hunger for power was insatiable. It would settle for small gains for a short time, and then demand that its wielder move on to greater conquests. It wouldn't openly oppose Kessell, for in their constant war of wills Kessell ultimately held the power of decision. The small crystal shard bridled a reserve of incredible power, but without a wielder, it was akin to a sheathed sword with no hand to draw it. Thus Crenshinibon exerted its will through manipulation, insinuating illusions of conquest into the wizard's dreams, allowing Kessell to view the possibilities of power. It dangled a carrot before the nose of the once-bumbling apprentice that he could not refuse—respect.

Kessell, ever a spit bucket for the pretentious wizards in Luskan—and everyone else, it seemed—was easy prey for such ambitions. He, who had been down in the dirt beside the boots of the important people, ached for the chance to reverse the roles.

And now he had the opportunity to turn his fantasies into reality, Crenshinibon often assured him. With the relic close to his heart, he could become the conqueror; he could make people, even the wizards in the Hosttower, tremble at the mere mention of his name.

He had to remain patient. He had spent several years learning the subtleties of controlling one, and then a second, goblin tribe. Yet the task of bringing together dozens of tribes and bending their natural enmity into a common cause of servitude to him was far more challenging. He had to bring them in, one at a time at first, and ensure that he had enslaved them to his will wholeheartedly before he dared summon another group.

But it was working, and now he had brought in two rival tribes simultaneously with positive results. Torga and Grock had entered Cryshal-Tirith each searching for a way to kill the other without bringing on the wrath of the wizard. When they left, though, after a short discussion with Kessell, they were chatting like old friends about the glory of their coming battles in the army of Akar Kessell.

Kessell lounged back on his pillows and considered his good fortune. His army was indeed taking shape. He had frost giants for his field commanders, ogres as his field guard, verbeeg as a deadly strike force, and trolls, wretched, fear-inspiring trolls, as his personal bodyguard. And by his count thus far, ten thousand fanatically loyal goblin kin troops to carry out his swath of destruction.

"Akar Kessell!" he shouted to the harem girl that manicured his long fingernails as he sat in contemplation, though the girl's mind had long ago been destroyed by Crenshinibon. "All glory to the Tyrant of Icewind Dale!"

FAR TO THE SOUTH OF THE FROZEN STEPPES, IN THE CIVILIZED lands where men had more time for leisure activities and contemplation and every action wasn't determined by sheer necessity, wizards and would-be wizards were less rare. The true mages, lifelong students of the arcane arts, practiced their trade with due respect for the magic, ever wary of the potential consequences of their spellcastings.

Unless consumed by the lust for power, which was a very dangerous thing, the true mages tempered their experiments with caution and rarely caused disasters.

The would-be mages, however, men who somehow had come into a degree of magical prowess, whether they had found a scroll or a master's spellbook or some relic, were often the perpetrators of colossal calamities.

Such was the case that night in a land a thousand miles from Akar Kessell and Crenshinibon. A wizard's apprentice, a young man who had shown great promise to his master, came into possession of a diagram of a powerful magic circle, and then sought and found a spell of summoning. The apprentice, lured by the promise of power, managed to extract the true name of a demon from his master's private notes.

Sorcery, the art of summoning entities from other planes into servitude, was this young man's particular love. His master had allowed him to bring midges and manes through a magical portal—closely supervised—hoping to demonstrate the potential dangers of the practice and reinforce the lessons of caution. Actually, the demonstrations had only served to heighten the young man's appetite for the art. He had begged his master to allow him to try for a true demon, but the wizard knew that he wasn't nearly ready for such a test.

The apprentice disagreed.

He had completed inscribing the circle that same day. So confident was he in his work that he didn't spend an extra day (some wizards would spend a tenday) checking the runes and symbols or bother to test the circle on a lesser entity, such as a mane.

And now he sat within it, his eyes focused on the fire of the brazier that would serve as the gate to the Abyss. With a self-assured, overly proud smile, the would-be sorcerer called the demon.

Errtu, a major demon of catastrophic proportions, faintly heard its name being uttered on the faraway plane. Normally, the great beast would have ignored such a weak call; certainly the summoner hadn't demonstrated any ability of sufficient strength to compel the demon to comply.

Yet Errtu was glad of the fateful call. A few years before, the demon had felt a surge of power on the Material Plane that it believed would culminate a quest it had undertaken a millennium ago. The demon had suffered through the last few years impatiently, eager for a wizard to open a path for it so that it could come to the Material Plane and investigate.

The young apprentice felt himself being drawn into the hypnotic dance of the brazier's fire. The blaze had unified into a single flame, like the burn of a candle only many times larger, and it swayed tantalizingly, back and forth, back and forth.

The mesmerized apprentice wasn't even aware of the growing intensity of the fire. The flame leaped higher and higher, its flickering sped up, and its color moved through the spectrum toward the ultimate heat of whiteness.

Back and forth. Back and forth.

Faster, now, wagging wildly and building its strength to support the mighty entity that waited on the other side.

Back and forth. Back and forth.

The apprentice was sweating. He knew that the power of the spell was growing beyond his bounds, that the magic had taken over and was living a life of its own. That he was powerless to stop it.

Back and forth. Back and forth.

Now he saw the dark shadow within the flame, the great clawed hands, and the leathery, batlike wings. And the size of the beast! A giant even by the standards of its kind.

"Errtu!" the young man called, the words forced from him by the demands of the spell. The name hadn't been completely identified in his master's notes, but he saw clearly that it belonged to a mighty demon, a monster ranking just below the demon lords in the hierarchy of the Abyss.

Back and forth. Back and forth.

Now the grotesque, monkeylike head, with the maw and muzzle of a dog and the oversized incisors of a boar, was visible, the huge, blood-red eyes squinting from within the brazier's flame. The acidic drool sizzled as it fell to the fire.

Back and forth. Back and forth.

The fire surged into a final climax of power, and Errtu stepped through. The demon didn't pause at all to consider the terrified young human that had foolishly called its name. It began a slow stalk around the magic circle in search of clues to the extent of this wizard's power.

The apprentice finally managed to steady himself. He had summoned a major demon! That fact helped him to reestablish his confidence in his abilities as a sorcerer. "Stand before me!" he commanded, aware that a firm hand was necessary to control a creature from the chaotic lower planes.

Errtu, undisturbed, continued its stalk.

The apprentice grew angry. "You will obey me!" he screamed. "I brought you here, and I hold the key to your torment! You shall obey my command and then I shall release you, mercifully, back to your own filthy world! Now, stand before me!"

The apprentice was defiant. The apprentice was proud.

But Errtu had found an error in the tracing of a rune, a fatal imperfection in a magic circle that could not afford to be almost perfect.

The apprentice was dead.

ERRTU FELT THE FAMILIAR SENSATION OF POWER MORE DIS-tinctly on the Material Plane and had little trouble discerning the direction of the emanations. It soared on its great wings over the cities of the humans, spreading a panic wherever it was noticed, but not delaying its journey to savor the erupting chaos below.

Arrow-straight and with all speed Errtu soared, over lakes and mountains, across great expanses of empty land. Toward the northernmost range in the Realms, the Spine of the World, and the ancient relic that it had spent centuries searching for.

KESSELL WAS AWARE OF THE APPROACHING DEMON LONG BEfore his assembled troops began scattering in terror from under the swooping shadow of darkness. Crenshinibon had imparted the information to the wizard, the living relic anticipating the movements of the powerful creature from the lower planes that had been pursuing it for ages uncounted.

Kessell wasn't worried, though. Inside his tower of strength he was confident that he could handle even a nemesis as mighty as Errtu. And he had a distinct advantage over the demon. He was the rightful wielder of the relic. It was attuned to him, and like so many other magical artifacts from the dawn of the world, Crenshinibon could not be wrested from its possessor by sheer force. Errtu desired to wield the relic and, therefore, would not dare to oppose Kessell and invoke Crenshinibon's wrath.

Acid drool slipped freely from the demon's mouth when it saw the tower image of the relic. "How many years?" it bellowed victoriously. Errtu saw the tower's door clearly, for the demon was a creature not of the Material Plane, and approached at once. None of Kessell's goblins, or even giants, stood to hinder the demon's entrance.

Flanked by his trolls, the wizard was waiting for Errtu in Cryshal-Tirith's main chamber, the tower's first level. The wizard understood that the trolls would be of little use against a fire-wielding demon, but he wanted them present to enhance the demon's first impression of him. He knew that he held the power to send Errtu away easily enough, but another thought, again implanted through a suggestion of the Crystal Shard, had come to him.

The demon could be very useful.

Errtu pulled up short when it passed through the narrow entryway and came upon the wizard's entourage. Because of the remote
location of the tower, the demon had expected to find an orc, or
perhaps a giant, holding the shard. It had hoped to intimidate and
trick the slow-witted wielder into surrendering the relic, but the
sight of a robed human, probably even a mage, threw a snag into
its plans.

"Greetings, mighty demon," Kessell said politely, bowing low.
"Welcome to my humble home."

Errtu growled in rage and started forward, forgetting the draw-
backs of destroying the possessor in its all-consuming hatred and
envy for the smug human.

Crenshinibon reminded the demon.

A sudden flare of light pulsed from the tower walls, engulfing
Errtu in the painful brightness of a dozen desert suns. The demon
halted and covered its sensitive eyes. The light dissipated, soon
enough, but Errtu held its ground and did not approach the wizard again.

Kessell smirked. The relic had supported him. Brimming with
confidence, he addressed the demon again, this time a stern edge
in his voice. "You have come to take this," he said, reaching within
the folds of his robe to produce the shard. Errtu's eyes narrowed
and locked onto the object it had pursued for so long.

"You cannot have it," Kessell said flatly, and he replaced it under
his robe. "It is mine, rightfully found, and you have no claim over
it that it would honor!" Kessell's foolish pride, the fatal flaw in his
personality that had always pushed him down a road of certain
tragedy, wanted him to continue his taunting of the demon in its
helpless situation.

"Enough," warned a sensation within him, the silent voice he
had come to suspect was the sentient will of the shard.

"This is none of your affair," Kessell shot back aloud. Errtu
looked around the room, wondering who the wizard was address-
ing. Certainly the trolls had paid him no heed. As a precaution, the

demon invoked various detection spells, fearing an unseen assailant.

"You taunt a dangerous foe," the shard persisted. "I have protected you from the demon, yet you persist in alienating a creature that would prove a valuable ally!"

As was usually the case when Crenshinibon communicated with the wizard, Kessell began to see the possibilities. He decided upon a course of compromise, an agreement mutually beneficial to both himself and the demon.

Errtu considered its predicament. It couldn't slay the impertinent human, though the demon would have truly savored such an act. Yet leaving without the relic, putting off the quest that had been its primary motivation for centuries, was not an acceptable option.

"I have a proposal to offer, a bargain that might interest you," Kessell said temptingly, avoiding the death-promising glare that the demon was throwing him. "Stay by my side and serve as commander of my forces! With you leading them and the power of Crenshinibon and Akar Kessell behind them, they shall sweep through the northland!"

"Serve you?" Errtu laughed. "You have no hold over me, human."

"You view the situation incorrectly," retorted Kessell. "Think of it not as servitude but as an opportunity to join in a campaign that promises destruction and conquest! You have my utmost respect, mighty demon. I would not presume to call myself your master."

Crenshinibon, with its subconscious intrusions, had coached Kessell well. Errtu's less threatening stance showed that it was intrigued by the wizard's proposition.

"And consider the gains that you shall someday make," Kessell continued. "Humans do not live a very long time by your ageless estimations. Who, then, shall take the Crystal Shard when Akar Kessell is no more?"

Errtu smiled wickedly and bowed before the wizard. "How could I refuse such a generous offer?" the demon rasped in its horrible, unearthly voice. "Show me, wizard, what glorious conquests lie in our path."

Kessell nearly danced with joy. His army was, in effect, complete.

He had his general.

11

AEGIS-FANG

Sweat beaded on Bruenor's hand as he put the key into the dusty lock of the heavy wooden door. This was the beginning of the process that would put all of his skill and experience to the ultimate trial. Like all master dwarven smiths, he had been waiting for this moment with excitement and apprehension since the beginning of his long training.

He had to push hard to swing the door in on the small chamber. Its wood creaked and groaned in protest, having warped and settled since it was last opened many years before. This was a comfort to Bruenor, though, for he dreaded the thought of anyone looking in on his most prized possessions. He glanced around at the dark corridors of this little-used section of the dwarven complex, making sure once more that he hadn't been followed, then he entered the room, putting his torch in before him to burn away the hanging fringes of many cobwebs.

The only piece of furniture in the room was a wooden, iron-bound box, banded by two heavy chains joined by a huge padlock. Spiderwebs crisscrossed and flowed from every angle of the chest, and a thick layer of dust covered its top. Another good sign, Bruenor noted. He looked out into the hall again, then shut the wooden door as quietly as he could.

He knelt before the chest and placed his torch on the floor beside him. Several webs, licked by its flame, puffed into orange for just an instant, then died away. Bruenor took a small block of wood from his belt pouch and removed a silver key that hung on a chain about his neck. He held the wood block firmly in front of him and, keeping the fingers of his other hand below the level of the padlock as much as possible, gently slid the key into the lock.

Now came the delicate part. Bruenor turned the key slowly, listening. When he heard the tumbler in the lock click, he braced himself and quickly pulled his hand from the key, allowing the mass of the padlock to drop away from its ring, releasing a spring-loaded lever that had been pressed between it and the chest. The small dart knocked into the block of wood, and Bruenor breathed a sigh of relief. Though he had set the trap nearly a century before, he knew that the poison of the Tundra Widowmaker snake had kept its deadly sting.

Sheer excitement overwhelmed Bruenor's reverence of this moment, and he hurriedly threw the chains back over the chest and blew the dust from its lid. He grasped the lid and started to lift it but suddenly slowed again, recovering his solemn calm and reminding himself of the importance of every action.

Anyone who had come upon this chest and managed to get by the deadly trap would have been pleased with the treasures he found inside. A silver goblet, a bag of gold, and a jeweled though poorly balanced dagger were mixed in among other more personal and less valuable items: a dented helm, old boots, and other similar pieces that would hold little appeal for a thief.

Yet these items were merely a foil. Bruenor pulled them out and dropped them on the dirty floor without a second thought.

The bottom of the heavy chest sat just above the level of the floor, giving no indication that anything more was to be found here. But Bruenor had cunningly cut the floor lower under the chest, fitting the box into the hole so perfectly that even a scrutinizing thief would swear that it sat on the floor. The dwarf poked out a small knothole in the box's bottom and hooked a stubby finger through the opening. This wood, too, had settled over the years, and Bruenor had to tug mightily to finally pull it free. It came out with a sudden snap, sending Bruenor tumbling backward. He was back at the chest in an instant, peering cautiously over its edge at his greatest treasures.

A block of the purest mithral, a small leather bag, a golden coffer, and a silver scroll tube capped on one end by a diamond were spaced exactly as Bruenor had lain them so long ago.

Bruenor's hands trembled, and he had to stop and wipe the perspiration from them several times as he removed the precious items from the chest, placing those that would fit in his pack and laying the mithral block on a blanket he had unrolled. Then he quickly replaced the false bottom, taking care to fit the knothole back into the wood perfectly, and put his phony treasure back in place. He chained and locked the box, leaving everything exactly as he had found it, except that he saw no reason to chance accidents by rearming the needle trap.

BRUENOR HAD CONSTRUCTED HIS OUTDOOR FORGE IN A HIDDEN nook tucked away at the base of Kelvin's Cairn. This was a seldom-traveled portion of the dwarven valley, the northern end, with Bremen's Run widening out into the open tundra around the western side of the mountain, and Icewind Pass doing likewise on the east. To his surprise, Bruenor found that the stone here was hard and pure, deeply imbued with the strength of the earth, and would serve his small temple well.

As always, Bruenor approached this sacred place with measured, reverent steps. Carrying now the treasures of his heritage, his mind drifted back over the centuries to Mithral Hall, ancient home of his people, and to the speech his father had given him on the day he received his first smithy hammer.

"If yer talent for the craft is keen," his father had said, "and ye're lucky enough to live long and feel the strength of the earth, ye'll find a special day. A special blessin'—some would say a curse—has been placed upon our people, for once, and only once, the very best of our smiths may craft a weapon of their choosing that outdoes any work they'd ever done. Be wary of that day, son, for ye'll put a great deal of yerself into that weapon. Ye'll never match its perfection in yer life again and knowing this, ye'll lose a lot of the craftsman's desire that drives the swing of yer hammer. Ye may find an empty life after yer day, but if yer good as yer line says ye'll be, ye'll have crafted a weapon of legend that will live on long after yer bones are dust."

Bruenor's father, cut down in the coming of the darkness to Mithral Hall, hadn't lived long enough to find his special day, though if he had, several of the items that Bruenor now carried would have been used by him. But the dwarf saw no disrespect in his taking the treasures as his own, for he knew that he would craft a weapon to make the spirit of his father proud.

Bruenor's day had come.

THE IMAGE OF A TWO-HEADED HAMMER HIDDEN WITHIN THE block of mithral had come to Bruenor in a dream earlier that tenday. The dwarf had understood the sign at once and knew that he would have to move quickly to get everything ready for the night of power that was fast approaching. Already the moon was big and bright in the sky. It would reach its fullness on the night of the solstice, the gray time between the seasons when the air tingled with magic. The full moon would only enhance the enchantment of that night, and Bruenor believed that he would capture a mighty spell indeed when he uttered the dweomer of power.

The dwarf had much work before him if he was to be prepared. His labor had begun with the construction of the small forge. That had been the easy part and he went about it mechanically, trying to hold his thoughts to the task at hand and away from the disrupting anticipation of crafting the weapon.

Now the time he had waited for was upon him. He pulled the heavy block of mithral from his pack, feeling its pureness and strength. He had held similar blocks before and grew apprehensive for a moment. He stared into the silvery metal.

For a long moment, it remained a squared block. Then its sides appeared to round as the image of the marvelous warhammer came clear to the dwarf. Bruenor's heart raced, and he breathed in short gasps.

His vision had been real.

He fired up the forge and began his work at once, laboring through the night until the light of dawn dispelled the charm that was upon him. He returned to his home that day only to collect the adamantite rod he had set aside for the weapon, returning to the forge to sleep and later to pace nervously while he waited for darkness to fall.

As soon as daylight faded, Bruenor eagerly went back to work. The metal molded easily under his skilled manipulations, and he knew that before the dawn could interrupt him, the head of the hammer would be formed. Though he still had hours of work ahead of him, Bruenor felt a surge of pride at that moment. He knew that he would meet his demanding schedule. He would attach the adamantite handle the next night, and all would be ready for the enchantment under the full moon on the night of the summer solstice.

THE OWL SWOOPED SILENTLY DOWN ON THE SMALL RABBIT, guided toward its prey by senses as acute as any living creature's. This would be a routine kill, with the unfortunate beast never even aware of the coming predator. Yet the owl was strangely agitated, and its hunter's concentration wavered at the last moment. Seldom did the great bird miss, but this time it flew back to its home on the side of Kelvin's Cairn without a meal.

Far out on the tundra, a lone wolf sat as still as a statue, anxious but patient as the silver disk of the huge summer moon broke the flat rim of the horizon. It waited until the alluring orb came full in the sky, then it took up the ancient howling cry of its breed. It was answered, again and again, by distant wolves and other denizens of the night, all calling out to the power of the heavens.

The night of the summer solstice, when magic tingled in the air, exciting all but the rational beings who had rejected such base instinctual urges, had begun.

In his emotional state, Bruenor felt the magic distinctly. But absorbed in the culmination of his life's labors, he had attained a level of calm concentration. His hands did not tremble as he opened the golden lid of the small coffer.

The mighty warhammer lay clamped to the anvil before the dwarf. It represented Bruenor's finest work, powerful and beautifully crafted even now, but waiting for the delicate runes and intonations that would make it a weapon of special power.

Bruenor reverently removed the small silver mallet and chisel from the coffer and approached the warhammer. Without hesitation, for he knew that he had little time for such intricate work, he set the chisel on the mithral and solidly tapped it with the mallet. The untainted metals sang out a clear, pure note that sent shivers through the appreciative dwarf's spine. He knew in his heart that all of the conditions were perfect, and he shivered again when he thought of the result of this night's labors.

He did not see the dark eyes peering intently at him from a ridge a short distance away.

Bruenor needed no model for the first carvings; they were symbols etched into his heart and soul. Solemnly, he inscribed the hammer and anvil of Moradin the Soulforger on the side of one of the warhammer's heads, and the crossed axes of Clangeddin, the dwarven god of battle, across from the first on the side of the other head. Then he took the silver scroll tube and gently removed its diamond cap. He sighed in relief when he saw that the parchment inside had survived the decades. Wiping the oily sweat from his hands, he removed the scroll and slowly unrolled it, laying it on the flat of the anvil. At first, the page seemed blank, but gradually the rays of the full moon coaxed its symbols, the secret runes of power, to appear.

These were Bruenor's heritage, and though he had never seen them before, their arcane lines and curves seemed comfortably familiar to him. His hand steady with confidence, the dwarf placed the silver chisel between the symbols he had inscribed of the two gods and began etching the secret runes onto the warhammer. He felt their magic transferring from the parchment through him to the weapon and watched in amazement as each one disappeared from the scroll after he had inscribed it onto the mithral. Time had no meaning to him now as he fell deeply into the trance of his work, but when he had completed the runes, he noticed that the moon had passed its peak and was on the wane.

The first real test of the dwarf's expertise came when he overlaid the rune carvings with the gem inside the mountain symbol of Dumathoin, the Keeper of Secrets. The lines of the god's symbol aligned perfectly with those of the runes, obscuring the secret tracings of power.

Bruenor knew then that his work was nearly complete. He removed the heavy warhammer from its clamp and took out the small leather bag. He had to take several deep breaths to steady himself, for this was the final and most decisive test of his skill. He loosened the cord at the top of the bag and marveled at the gentle shimmering of the diamond dust in the soft light of the moon.

From behind the ridge, Drizzt Do'Urden tensed in anticipation, but he was careful not to disturb his friend's complete concentration.

Bruenor steadied himself again, then suddenly snapped the bag into the air, releasing its contents high into the night. He tossed the bag aside, grasped the warhammer in both hands, and raised it above his head. The dwarf felt his very strength being sucked from him as he uttered the words of power, but he would not truly know how well he had performed until his work was complete. The level

of perfection of his carvings determined the success of his intonations, for as he had etched the runes onto the weapon, their
strength had flowed into his heart. This power then drew the magical dust to the weapon and its power, in turn, could be measured
by the amount of shimmering diamond dust it captured.

A fit of blackness fell over the dwarf. His head spun, and he did
not understand what kept him from toppling. But the consuming
power of the words had gone beyond him. Though he wasn't even
conscious of them, the words continued to flow from his lips in an
undeniable stream, sapping more and more of his strength. Then,
mercifully, he was falling, though the void of unconsciousness took
him long before his head hit the ground.

Drizzt turned away and slumped back against the rocky ridge;
he, too, was exhausted from the spectacle. He didn't know if his
friend would survive this night's ordeal, yet he was thrilled for
Bruenor. For he had witnessed the dwarf's most triumphant moment, even if Bruenor had not, as the hammer's mithral head
flared with the life of magic and pulled in the shower of diamond.

And not a single speck of the glittering dust had escaped Bruenor's beckon.

12

THE GIFT

Wulfgar sat high up on the northern face of Bruenor's Climb, his eyes trained on the expanse of the rocky valley below, intently seeking any movement that might indicate the dwarf's return. The barbarian came to this spot often to be alone with his thoughts and the mourn of the wind. Directly before him, across the dwarven vale, were Kelvin's Cairn and the northern section of Lac Dinneshere. Between them lay the flat stretch of ground known as Icewind Pass that led to the northeast and the open plain.

And for the barbarian, the pass that led to his homeland.

Bruenor had explained that he would be gone for a few days, and at first Wulfgar was happy for the relief from the dwarf's constant grumbling and criticism. But he found his relief short-lived.

"Worried for him, are you?" came a voice behind him. He didn't have to turn to know that it was Catti-brie.

He left the question unanswered, figuring that she had asked it rhetorically anyway and would not believe him if he denied it.

"He'll be back," Catti-brie said with a shrug in her voice. "Bruenor's as hard as mountain stone, and there is nothing on the tundra that can stop him."

Now the young barbarian did turn to consider the girl. Long ago, when a comfortable level of trust had been reached between Bruenor and Wulfgar, the dwarf had introduced the young barbarian to his "daughter," a human girl the barbarian's own age.

She was an outwardly calm girl, but packed with an inner fire and spirit that Wulfgar had been unaccustomed to in a woman. Barbarian girls were raised to keep their thoughts and opinions, unimportant by the standards of men, to themselves. Like her mentor, Catti-brie said exactly what was on her mind and left little doubt as to how she felt about a situation. The verbal sparring between her and Wulfgar was nearly constant and often heated, but still, Wulfgar was glad to have a companion his own age, someone who didn't look down at him from a pedestal of experience.

Catti-brie had helped him through the difficult first year of his indenture, treating him with respect (although she rarely agreed with him) when he had none for himself. Wulfgar even had the feeling that she had something indirectly to do with Bruenor's decision to take Wulfgar under his tutorship.

She was his own age, but in many ways Catti-brie seemed much older, with a solid inner sense of reality that kept her temperament on an even level. In other ways, however, such as the skipping spring in her step, Catti-brie would forever be a child. This unusual balance of spirit and calm, of serenity and unbridled joy, intrigued Wulfgar and kept him off balance whenever he spoke with the girl.

Of course, there were other emotions that put Wulfgar at a disadvantage when he was with Catti-brie. Undeniably, she was beautiful, with thick waves of rich, auburn hair rolling down over her shoulders and the darkest blue, penetrating eyes that would make any suitor blush under their knowing scrutiny. Still, there was something beyond any physical attraction that interested Wulfgar. Catti-brie was beyond his experience, a young woman who did not fit the role as it had been defined to him on the tundra. He wasn't sure if he liked this independence or not. But he found himself unable to deny the attraction that he felt for her.

"You come up here often, do you not?" Catti-brie asked. "What is it you look for?"

Wulfgar shrugged, not fully knowing the answer himself.

"Your home?"

"That, and other things that a woman would not understand."

Catti-brie smiled away the unintentional insult. "'Tell me, then," she pressed, hints of sarcasm edging her tone. "Maybe my ignorance will bring a new perspective to these problems." She hopped down the rock to circle the barbarian and take a seat on the ledge beside him.

Wulfgar marveled at her graceful movements. Like the polarity of her curious emotional blend, Catti-brie also proved an enigma physically. She was tall and slender, delicate by all appearances, but growing into womanhood in the caverns of the dwarves, she was accustomed to hard and heavy work.

"Of adventures and an unfulfilled vow," Wulfgar said mysteriously, perhaps to impress the young girl, but more so to reinforce his own opinion about what a woman should and should not care about.

"A vow you mean to fulfill," Catti-brie reasoned, "as soon as you're given the chance."

Wulfgar nodded solemnly. "It is my heritage, a burden passed on to me when my father was killed. The day will come . . ." He let his voice trail away, and he looked back longingly to the emptiness of the open tundra beyond Kelvin's Cairn.

Catti-brie shook her head, the auburn locks bouncing across her shoulders. She saw beyond Wulfgar's mysterious facade enough to understand that he meant to undertake a very dangerous, probably suicidal, mission in the name of honor. "What drives you, I cannot tell. Luck to you on your adventure, but if you're taking it for no better reason than you have named, you're wasting your life."

"What could a woman know of honor?" Wulfgar shot back angrily.

But Catti-brie was not intimidated and did not back down. "What indeed?" she echoed. "Do you think that you hold it all in your oversized hands for no better reason than what you hold in your pants?"

Wulfgar blushed a deep red and turned away, unable to come to terms with such nerve in a woman.

"Besides," Catti-brie continued, "you can say what you want about why you have come up here this day. I know that you're worried about Bruenor, and I'll hear no denying."

"You know only what you desire to know!"

"You are a lot like him," Catti-brie said abruptly, shifting the subject and disregarding Wulfgar's comments. "More akin to the dwarf than you'd ever admit." She laughed. "Both stubborn, both proud, and neither about to admit an honest feeling for the other. Have it your own way, then, Wulfgar of Icewind Dale. To me you can lie, but to yourself . . . there's a different tale!" She hopped from her perch and skipped down the rocks toward the dwarven caverns.

Wulfgar watched her go, admiring the sway of her slender hips and the graceful dance of her step, despite the anger that he felt. He didn't stop to think of why he was so mad at Catti-brie.

He knew that if he did, he would find, as usual, that he was angry because her observations hit the mark.

DRIZZT DO'URDEN KEPT A STOIC VIGIL OVER HIS UNCONSCIOUS friend for two long days. Worried as he was about Bruenor and curious about the wondrous warhammer, the drow remained a respectful distance from the secret forge.

Finally, as morning dawned on the third day, Bruenor stirred and stretched. Drizzt silently padded away, moving down the path he knew the dwarf would take. Finding an appropriate clearing, he hastily set up a small campsite.

The sunlight came to Bruenor as only a blur at first, and it took him several minutes to reorient himself to his surroundings. Then his returning vision focused on the shining glory of the warhammer.

Quickly, he glanced around him, looking for signs of the fallen dust. He found none, and his anticipation heightened. He was trembling once again as he lifted the magnificent weapon, turning it over in his hands, feeling its perfect balance and incredible strength. Bruenor's breath flew away when he saw the symbols of the three gods on the mithral, diamond dust magically fused into their deeply etched lines. Entranced by the apparent perfection of his work, Bruenor understood the emptiness his father had spoken of. He knew that he would never duplicate this level of his craft, and he wondered if, knowing this, he would ever be able to lift his smithy hammer again.

Trying to sort through his mixed emotions, the dwarf put the silver mallet and chisel back into their golden coffer and replaced the scroll in its tube, though the parchment was blank and the magical runes would never reappear. He realized that he hadn't eaten in several days, and his strength hadn't fully recovered from the drain of the magic. He collected as many things as he could carry, hoisted the huge warhammer over his shoulder, and trudged off toward his home.

The sweet scent of roasting coney greeted him as he came upon Drizzt Do'Urden's camp.

"So, yer back from yer travels," he called in greeting to his friend.

Drizzt locked his eyes onto the dwarf's, not wanting to give away his overwhelming curiosity for the warhammer. "At your request, good dwarf," he said, bowing low. "Surely you had enough people looking for me to expect that I'd return."

Bruenor conceded the point, though for the present he only offered absently, "I needed ye," as an explanation. A more pressing need had come over him at the sight of the cooking meat.

Drizzt smiled knowingly. He had already eaten and had caught and cooked this coney especially for Bruenor. "Join me?" he asked.

Before he had even finished the offer, Bruenor was eagerly reaching for the rabbit. He stopped suddenly, though, and turned a suspicious eye upon the drow.

"How long have ye been in?" the dwarf asked nervously.

"Just arrived this morning," Drizzt lied, respecting the privacy of the dwarf's special ceremony. Bruenor smirked at the answer and tore into the coney as Drizzt set another on the spit.

The drow waited until Bruenor was engrossed with his meal, then quickly snatched up the warhammer. By the time Bruenor could react, Drizzt had already lifted the weapon.

"Too big for a dwarf," Drizzt remarked casually. "And too heavy for my slender arms." He looked at Bruenor, who stood with his forearms crossed and his foot stamping impatiently. "Who then?"

"Ye've a talent for puttin' yer nose where it don't belong, elf," the dwarf answered gruffly.

Drizzt laughed in response. "The boy, Wulfgar?" he asked in mock disbelief. He knew well that the dwarf harbored strong feelings for the young barbarian, though he also realized that Bruenor would never openly admit it. "A fine weapon to be giving a barbarian. Did you craft it yourself?"

Despite his chiding, Drizzt was truly awe-stricken by Bruenor's workmanship. Though the hammer was far too heavy for him to wield, he could clearly feel its incredible balance.

"Just an old hammer, that's all," Bruenor mumbled. "The boy lost 'is club; I couldn't well turn 'im loose in this wild place without a weapon!"

"And its name?"

"Aegis-fang," Bruenor replied without thinking, the name flowing from him before he even had time to consider it. He didn't remember the incident, but the dwarf had determined the name of the weapon when he had enchanted it as part of the magical intonations of the ceremony.

"I understand," Drizzt said, handing the hammer back to Bruenor. "An old hammer, but good enough for the boy. Mithral, adamantite, and diamond will simply have to do."

"Aw, shut yer mouth," snapped Bruenor, his face flushed red with embarrassment. Drizzt bowed low in apology.

"Why did you request my presence, friend?" the drow asked, changing the subject.

Bruenor cleared his throat. "The boy," he grumbled softly. Drizzt saw the uncomfortable lump well in Bruenor's throat and buried his next taunt before he spoke it.

"He comes free afore winter," continued Bruenor, "an' he's not rightly trained. Stronger than any man I've ever seen and moves with the grace of a fleeing deer, but he's green to the ways o' battle."

"You want me to train him?" Drizzt asked incredulously.

"Well, I can't do it!" Bruenor snapped suddenly. "He's seven foot and wouldn't be takin' well to the low cuts of a dwarf!"

The drow eyed his frustrated companion curiously. Like everyone else who was close to Bruenor, he knew that a bond had grown between the dwarf and the young barbarian, but he hadn't guessed just how deep it ran.

"I didn't take 'im under me eye for five years just to let him get cut down by a stinkin' tundra yeti!" Bruenor blurted, impatient with the drow's hesitance, and nervous that his friend had guessed more than he should. "Will ye do it, then?"

Drizzt smiled again, but there was no teasing in it this time. He remembered his own battle with tundra yetis nearly five years before. Bruenor had saved his life that day, and it hadn't been the first and wouldn't be the last time that he had fallen into the dwarf's debt. "The gods know that I owe you more than that, my friend. Of course I'll train him."

Bruenor grunted and grabbed the next coney.

THE RING OF WULFGAR'S POUNDING ECHOED THROUGH THE dwarven halls. Angered by the revelations he had been forced to see in his discussion with Catti-brie, he had returned to his work with fervor.

"Stop yer hammerin', boy," came a gruff voice behind him.

Wulfgar spun on his heel. He had been so engrossed in his work that he hadn't heard Bruenor enter. An involuntary smile of relief widened across his face. But he caught the show of weakness quickly and repainted a stern mask.

Bruenor regarded the young barbarian's great height and girth and the scraggly beginnings of a blond beard upon the golden skin of his face. "I can't rightly be callin' ye 'boy' anymore," the dwarf conceded.

"You have the right to call me whatever you wish," retorted Wulfgar. "I am your slave."

"Ye've a spirit as wild as the tundra," Bruenor said, smiling. "Ye've ne'er been, nor will ye ever be, a slave to any dwarf or man!"

Wulfgar was caught off guard by the dwarf's uncharacteristic compliment. He tried to reply but could find no words.

"Never have I seen ye as a slave, boy," Bruenor continued. "Ye served me to pay for the crimes of yer people, and I taught ye much in return. Now put yer hammer away." He paused for a moment to consider Wulfgar's fine workmanship.

"Yer a good smith, with a good feel for the stone, but ye don't belong in a dwarf's cave. It's time ye felt the sun on yer face again."

"Freedom?" Wulfgar whispered.

"Get the notion outta yer head!" Bruenor snapped. He pointed a stubby finger at the barbarian and growled threateningly. "Yer mine 'til the last days of fall, don't ye forget that!"

Wulfgar had to bite his lip to stem a laugh. As always, the dwarf's awkward combination of compassion and borderline rage had confused him and kept him off balance. It no longer came as a shock, though. Four years at Bruenor's side had taught him to expect—and disregard—the sudden outbursts of gruffness.

"Finish up whatever ye got here to do," Bruenor instructed. "I take ye out to meet yer teacher tomorrow morning, and by yer vow, ye'll heed to him as ye would to me!"

Wulfgar grimaced at the thought of servitude to yet another, but he had accepted his indenture to Bruenor unconditionally for a period of five years and a day, and he would not dishonor himself by going back on his oath. He nodded his consent.

"I won't be seein' much more o' ye," Bruenor continued, "so I'll have yer oath now that ye'll never again raise a weapon against the people o' Ten-Towns."

Wulfgar set himself firmly. "That you may not have," he replied boldly. "When I have fulfilled the terms you set before me, I shall leave here a man of free will!"

"Fair enough," Bruenor conceded, Wulfgar's stubborn pride actually enhancing the dwarf's respect for him. He paused for a moment to look over the proud young warrior and found himself pleased at his own part in Wulfgar's growth.

"Ye broke that stinkin' pole o' yers on me head," Bruenor began tentatively. He cleared his throat. This final order of business made the tough dwarf uncomfortable. He wasn't quite sure of how he could get through it without appearing sentimental and foolish. "Winter'll be fast upon ye after yer term to me is ended. I can't rightly send ye out into the wild without a weapon." He reached back into the hallway quickly and grabbed the warhammer.

"Aegis-fang," he said gruffly as he tossed it to Wulfgar. "I'll place no bonds on yer will, but I'll have yer oath, for me own good conscience, that ye'll never raise this weapon against the people o' Ten-Towns!"

As soon as his hands closed around the adamantite handle, Wulfgar sensed the worth of the magical warhammer. The diamond-filled runes caught the glow of the forge and sent a myriad of reflections dancing about the room. The barbarians of Wulfgar's tribe had always prided themselves on the fine weapons they kept, even measuring the worth of a man by the quality of his spear or sword, but Wulfgar had never seen anything to match the exquisite detail and sheer strength of Aegis-fang. It balanced so well in his huge hands and its height and weight fit him so perfectly that he felt as if he had been born to wield this weapon. He told himself at once that he would pray for many nights to the gods of fate for delivering this prize unto him. Certainly they deserved his thanks.

As did Bruenor.

"You have my word," Wulfgar stammered, so overcome by the magnificent gift that he could hardly speak. He steadied himself so that he could say more, but by the time he was able to pull his gaze from the magnificent hammer, Bruenor was gone.

The dwarf stomped through the long corridors toward his private chambers, mumbling curses at his weakness, and hoping that none of his kin came upon him. With a cautious look around, he wiped the moisture from his gray eyes.

13

AS THE WIELDER BIDS

"Gather together your people and go, Biggrin," the wizard told the enormous frost giant that stood before him in Cryshal-Tirith's throne room. "Remember that you represent the army of Akar Kessell. You are the first group to go into the area, and secrecy is the key to our victory! Do not fail me! I shall be watching over your every move."

"We'll not fail ye, master," the giant responded. "The lair'll be set and readied for your coming!"

"I have faith in you," Kessell assured the huge commander. "Now be off."

The frost giant lifted the blanketed mirror that Kessell had given it, gave one final bow to its master, and walked out of the room.

"You should not have sent them," hissed Errtu, who had been standing invisibly beside the throne during the conversation. "The verbeeg and their frost giant leader will be easy to mark in a community of humans and dwarves."

"Biggrin is a wise leader," Kessell shot back, angered at the demon's impertinence. "The giant is cunning enough to keep troops out of sight!"

"Yet the humans would have been better suited for this mission, as Crenshinibon has shown you."

"I am the leader!" screamed Kessell. He pulled the Crystal Shard out from under his robes and waved it menacingly at Errtu, leaning forward in an attempt to emphasize the threat. "Crenshinibon advises, but I decide! Do not forget your place, mighty demon. I am the wielder of the shard, and I shall not tolerate your questioning my every move."

Errtu's blood-red eyes narrowed dangerously, and Kessell straightened back in his throne, suddenly reconsidering the wisdom of threatening the demon. But Errtu calmed quickly, accepting the minor inconveniences of Kessell's foolish outbursts for the long-term gains it stood to make.

"Crenshinibon has existed since the dawn of the world," the demon rasped, making one final point. "It has orchestrated a thousand campaigns much grander than the one you are about to undertake. Perhaps you would be wise to give more credence to its advice."

Kessell twitched nervously. The shard had indeed counseled him to use the humans he would soon command in the first excursion into the region. He had been able to create a dozen excuses to validate his choice of sending the giants, but in truth, he had sent Biggrin's people more to illustrate his undeniable command to himself, to the shard, and to the impertinent demon, than for any possible military gains.

"I shall follow Crenshinibon's advice when I deem it appropriate," he told Errtu. He pulled a second crystal, an exact duplicate of Crenshinibon and the crystal he had used to raise this tower, out from one of the many pockets of his robe. "Take this to the appropriate spot and perform the ceremony of raising," he instructed. "I shall join you through a mirror door when all is ready."

"You wish to raise a second Cryshal-Tirith while the first still stands?" Errtu balked. "The drain on the relic shall be enormous!"

"Silence!" Kessell ordered, trembling visibly, "Go and perform the ceremony! Let the shard remain my concern!"

Errtu took the replica of the relic and bowed low. Without a further word, the demon stalked out of the room. It understood that Kessell was foolishly demonstrating his control over the shard at the expense of proper restraint and wise military tactics. The wizard did not have the capacity or the experience to orchestrate this campaign, yet the shard continued to back him.

Errtu had made a secret offer to it to dispose of Kessell and take over as wielder. But Crenshinibon had refused the demon. It preferred the demonstrations that Kessell demanded of it to appease his own insecurities over the constant struggle of control it would face against the powerful demon.

THOUGH HE WALKED AMONG GIANTS AND TROLLS, THE PROUD barbarian king's stature was not diminished. He strode defiantly through the iron door of the black tower and pushed through the wretched troll guards with a threatening growl. He hated this place of sorcery and had decided to ignore the calling when the singular spinet of the tower appeared on the horizon like an icy finger risen from the flat ground. Yet in the end he could not resist the summons of the master of Cryshal-Tirith.

Heafstaag hated the wizard. By all measures of a tribesman Akar Kessell was weak, using tricks and demonic callings to do the work of muscle. And Heafstaag hated him even more because he could not refute the power that the wizard commanded.

The barbarian king threw aside the dangling, beaded strands that sectioned off Akar Kessell's private audience hall on the tower's second level. The wizard reclined on a huge, satin pillow in the middle of the room, his long, painted fingernails tapping impatiently on the floor. Several nude slave girls, their minds bent and broken under the shard's domination, waited on every whim of the shard's wielder.

It angered Heafstaag to see women enslaved to such a puny, pitiful shell of a man. He considered, and not for the first time, a sudden charge, burying his great axe deep into the wizard's skull. But the room was filled with strategically located screens and pillars, and the barbarian knew, even if he refused to believe that the wizard's will could deny his rage, that Kessell's pet demon wouldn't be far from its master.

"So good that you could join me, noble Heafstaag," said Kessell in a calm, disarming way. Errtu and Crenshinibon were close at hand. He felt quite secure, even in the presence of the rugged barbarian king. He fondled one of the slaves absently, showing off his absolute rule. "Really, you should have come sooner. Already many of my forces are assembled; the first group of scouts has already departed."

He leaned forward toward the barbarian to emphasize his point. "If I can find no room for your people in my plans," he said with an evil snicker, "then I shall have no need for your people at all."

Heafstaag didn't flinch or change his expression in the least.

"Come now, mighty king," the wizard crooned, "sit and share in the riches of my table."

Heafstaag clung to his pride and remained unmoving.

"Very well!" snapped Kessell. He clenched his fist and uttered a command word. "To whom do you owe your fealty?" he demanded.

Heafstaag's body went rigid. "To Akar Kessell!" he responded, to his own repulsion.

"And tell me again who it is that commands the tribes of the tundra."

"They follow me," Heafstaag replied, "and I follow Akar Kessell. Akar Kessell commands the tribes of the tundra!"

The wizard released his fist, and the barbarian king slumped back.

"I take little joy in doing that to you," said Kessell, rubbing a burr in one of his painted nails. "Do not make me do it again." He pulled a scroll out from behind the satin pillow and tossed it to the floor. "Sit before me," he instructed Heafstaag. "Tell me again of your defeat."

Heafstaag took his place on the floor in front of his master and unrolled the parchment.

It was a map of Ten-Towns.

14

LAVENDER EYES

Bruenor had regained his dour visage by the time he called on Wulfgar the following morning. Still, it touched the dwarf deeply, though he was able to hide the fact, to see Aegis-fang casually slung over the young barbarian's shoulder as if it had always been there—and always belonged there.

Wulfgar, too, was wearing a sullen mask. He passed it off as anger at being put into the service of another, but if he had examined his emotions more closely, he would have recognized that he was truly saddened about separating from the dwarf.

Catti-brie was waiting for them at the junction of the final passage that led to the open air.

"Sure that you're a sour pair this fine morning!" she said as they approached. "But not to mind, the sun will put a smile on your faces."

"You seemed pleased at this parting," Wulfgar answered, a bit perturbed though the sparkle in his eyes at the sight of the girl belied his anger. "You know, of course, that I am to leave the dwarven town this day?"

Catti-brie waved her hand nonchalantly. "You will be back soon enough." She smiled. "And be happy for your going! Consider the lessons you will soon learn needed if you're ever to reach your goals."

Bruenor turned toward the barbarian. Wulfgar had never spoken with him about what lay ahead after the term of indenture, and the dwarf, though he meant to prepare Wulfgar as well as he could, hadn't honestly come to terms with Wulfgar's resolve to leave.

Wulfgar scowled at the girl, showing her beyond doubt that their discussion of the unfulfilled vow was a private matter. Of her own discretion, Catti-brie hadn't intended to discuss the issue any further anyway. She simply enjoyed teasing some emotion out of Wulfgar. Catti-brie recognized the fire that burned in the proud young man. She saw it whenever he looked upon Bruenor, his mentor whether he would admit it or not. And she marked it whenever Wulfgar looked at her.

"I am Wulfgar, son of Beornegar," he boasted proudly, throwing back his broad shoulders and straightening his firm jaw. "I have grown among the Tribe of the Elk, the finest warriors in all of Icewind Dale! I know nothing of this tutor, but he will be hard-pressed indeed to teach me anything of the ways of battle!"

Catti-brie exchanged a knowing smile with Bruenor as the dwarf and Wulfgar passed her. "Farewell, Wulfgar, son of Beornegar," she called after them. "When next we meet, I'll mark well your lessons of humility!"

Wulfgar looked back and scowled again, but Catti-brie's wide smile diminished not at all.

The two left the darkness of the mines shortly after dawn, traveling down through the rocky valley to the appointed spot where they were to meet the drow. It was a cloudless, warm summer day, the blue of the sky paled by the morning haze. Wulfgar stretched high into the air, reaching to the limits of his long muscles. His people were meant to live in the wide expanses of the open tundra, and he was relieved to be out of the stifling closeness of the dwarven-made caverns.

Drizzt Do'Urden was at the spot waiting for them when they arrived. The drow leaned against the shadowed side of a boulder, seeking relief from the glare of the sun. The hood of his cloak was pulled low in front of his face as further protection. Drizzt considered it the curse of his heritage that no matter how many years he remained among the surface dwellers his body would never fully adapt to the sunlight.

He held himself motionless, though he was fully aware of the approach of Bruenor and Wulfgar. Let them make the first moves, he thought, wanting to judge how the boy would react to the new situation.

Curious about the mysterious figure who was to be his new teacher and master, Wulfgar boldly walked over and stood directly in front of the drow. Drizzt watched him approach from under the shadows of his cowl, amazed at the graceful interplay of the huge man's corded muscles. The drow had originally planned to humor Bruenor in his outrageous request for a short while, then make some excuse and be on his way. But as he noted the smooth flow and spring of the barbarian's long strides, an ease unusual in someone his size, Drizzt found himself growing interested in the challenge of developing the young man's seemingly limitless potential.

Drizzt realized that the most painful part of meeting this man, as it was with everyone he met, would be Wulfgar's initial reaction to him. Anxious to get it over with, he pulled back his hood and squarely faced the barbarian.

Wulfgar's eyes widened in horror and disgust. "A dark elf!" he cried incredulously. "Sorcerous dog!" He turned on Bruenor as though he had been betrayed. "Surely you cannot ask this of me! I have no need nor desire to learn the magical deceits of his decrepit race!"

"He'll teach ye to fight—no more," Bruenor said. The dwarf had expected this. He wasn't worried in the least, fully aware, as was Catti-brie, that Drizzt would teach the overly proud young man some needed humility.

Wulfgar snorted defiantly. "What can I learn of fighting from a weakling elf? My people are bred as true warriors!" He eyed Drizzt with open contempt. "Not trickster dogs like his kind!"

Drizzt calmly looked to Bruenor for permission to begin the day's lesson. The dwarf smirked at the barbarian's ignorance and nodded his consent.

In an eyeblink, the two scimitars leaped from their sheaths and challenged the barbarian. Instinctively, Wulfgar raised his warhammer to strike.

But Drizzt was the quicker. The flat sides of his weapons slapped in rapid succession against Wulfgar's cheeks, drawing thin streaks of blood. Even as the barbarian moved to counter, Drizzt spun one of the deadly blades in a declining arc, its razor edge diving at the back of Wulfgar's knee. Wulfgar managed to slip his leg out of the way, but the action, as Drizzt had anticipated, put him off balance. The drow casually slipped the scimitars back into their leather scabbards as his foot slammed into the barbarian's stomach, sending him sprawling into the dust, the magical hammer flying from his hands.

"Now that ye understand each other," declared Bruenor, trying to hide his amusement for the sake of Wulfgar's fragile ego, "I'll be leavin' ye!" He looked questioningly at Drizzt to make sure that the drow was comfortable with the situation.

"Give me a few tendays," Drizzt answered with a wink, returning the dwarf's smile.

Bruenor turned back to Wulfgar, who had retrieved Aegis-fang and was resting on one knee, eyeing the elf with blank amazement. "Heed his words, boy," the dwarf instructed one last time. "Or he'll cut ye into pieces small enough for a vulture's gullet."

FOR THE FIRST TIME IN NEARLY FIVE YEARS, WULFGAR looked out beyond the borders of Ten-Towns to the open stretch of Icewind Dale that spread wide before him. He and the drow had spent the remainder of their first day together hiking down the length of the valley and around the eastern spurs of Kelvin's Cairn. Here, just above the base of the northern side of the mountain, was the shallow cave where Drizzt made his home.

Sparsely furnished with a few skins and some cooking pots, the cave had no luxuries to speak of. But it served the unpretentious drow ranger well, allowing him the privacy and seclusion that he preferred above the taunts and threats of the humans. To Wulfgar, whose people rarely stayed in any place longer than a single night, the cave itself seemed a luxury.

As dusk began to settle over the tundra, Drizzt, in the comfortable shadows deeper in the cave, stirred from his short nap. Wulfgar was pleased that the drow had trusted him enough to sleep easily, so obviously vulnerable, on their first day together. This, coupled with the beating Drizzt had given him earlier, had caused Wulfgar to question his initial outrage at the sight of a dark elf.

"Do we begin our sessions this night, then?" Drizzt asked.

"You are the master," Wulfgar said bitterly. "I am only the slave!"

"No more a slave than I," replied Drizzt. Wulfgar turned to him curiously.

"We are both indebted to the dwarf," Drizzt explained. "I owe him my life many times over and thus have agreed to teach you my skill in battle. You follow an oath that you made to him in exchange for your life. Thus you are obliged to learn what I have to teach. I am no man's master, nor would I ever want to be."

Wulfgar turned back to the tundra. He didn't fully trust Drizzt yet, though he couldn't figure out what ulterior motives the drow could possibly be pursuing with the friendly facade.

"We fulfill our debts to Bruenor together," said Drizzt. He empathized with the emotions Wulfgar was feeling as the young man gazed out over the plains of his homeland for the first time in years. "Enjoy this night, barbarian. Go about as you please and remember again the feel of the wind on your face. We shall begin at the fall of tomorrow's night." He left then to allow Wulfgar the privacy he desired.

Wulfgar could not deny that he appreciated the respect the drow had shown him.

DURING THE DAYTIME, DRIZZT RESTED IN THE COOL SHADOWS OF the cave while Wulfgar acclimated himself to the new area and hunted for their supper.

By night, they fought.

Drizzt pressed the young barbarian relentlessly, slapping him with the flat of a scimitar every time he opened a gap in his defenses. The exchanges often escalated dangerously, for Wulfgar was a proud warrior and grew enraged and frustrated at the drow's superiority. This only put the barbarian at a further disadvantage, for in his rage all semblance of discipline flew from him. Drizzt was ever quick to point this out with a series of slaps and twists that ultimately left Wulfgar sprawled on the ground.

To his credit, though, Drizzt never taunted the barbarian or tried to humiliate him. The drow went about his task methodically, understanding that the first order of business was to sharpen the barbarian's reflexes and teach him some concern for defense.

Drizzt was truly impressed with Wulfgar's raw ability. The incredible potential of the young warrior staggered him. At first he feared that Wulfgar's stubborn pride and bitterness would render him untrainable, but the barbarian had risen to the challenge. Recognizing the benefits he could reap from one as adept with weapons as Drizzt, Wulfgar listened attentively. His pride, instead of limiting him into believing that he was already a mighty warrior and needed no further instruction, pushed him to grab at every advantage he could find that would help him to achieve his ambitious goals. By the end of the first tenday, during those times he could control his volatile temper, he was already able to deflect many of Drizzt's cunning attacks.

Drizzt said little during that first tenday, though he would occasionally compliment the barbarian about a good parry or counter, or more generally on the improvement Wulfgar was showing in such a short time. Wulfgar found himself eagerly anticipating the drow's remarks whenever he executed an especially difficult maneuver, and dreading the inevitable slap whenever he foolishly left himself vulnerable.

The young barbarian's respect for Drizzt continued to grow. Something about the drow, living without complaint in stoic solitude, touched Wulfgar's sense of honor. He couldn't yet guess why Drizzt had chosen such an existence, but he was certain from what he had already seen of the drow that it had something to do with principles.

By the middle of the second tenday, Wulfgar was in complete control of Aegis-fang, twisting its handle and head deftly to block the two whirring scimitars, and responding with cautiously measured thrusts of his own. Drizzt could see the subtle change taking place as the barbarian stopped reacting after the fact to the scimitars' deft cuts and thrusts and began recognizing his own vulnerable areas and anticipating the next attack.

When he became convinced that Wulfgar's defenses were sufficiently strengthened, Drizzt began the lessons of attack. The drow knew that his style of offense would not be the most effective mode for Wulfgar. The barbarian could use his unrivaled strength more effectively than deceptive feints and twists. Wulfgar's people were naturally aggressive fighters, and striking came more easily to them than parrying. The mighty barbarian could fell a giant with a single, well-placed blow.

All that he had left to learn was patience.

EARLY ONE DARK, MOONLESS NIGHT, AS HE PREPARED HIMSELF for the evening's lesson, Wulfgar noticed the flare of a campfire far out on the plain. He watched, mesmerized, as several others sprang suddenly into sight, wondering if it might even be the fires of his own tribe.

Drizzt silently approached, unnoticed by the engrossed barbarian. The drow's keen eyes had noted the stirrings of the distant camp long before the firelight had grown strong enough for Wulfgar to see. "Your people have survived," he said to comfort the young man.

Wulfgar started at the sudden appearance of his teacher. "You know of them?" he asked.

Drizzt moved beside him and stared out over the tundra. "Their losses were great at the Battle of Bryn Shander," he said. "And the winter that followed bit hard at the many women and children who had no men to hunt for them. They fled west to find the reindeer, banding together with other tribes for strength. The peoples still hold to the names of the original tribes, but in truth there are only two remaining: the Tribe of the Elk and the Tribe of the Bear.

"You were of the Tribe of the Elk, I believe," Drizzt continued, drawing a nod from Wulfgar. "Your people have done well. They dominate the plain now, and though more years will have to pass before the people of the tundra regain the strength they held before the battle, the younger warriors are already coming into manhood."

Relief flooded through Wulfgar. He had feared that the Battle of Bryn Shander had decimated his people to a point from which they could never recover. The tundra was doubly harsh in the frozen winter, and Wulfgar often considered the possibility that the sudden loss of so many warriors—some of the tribes had lost every one of their menfolk—would doom the remaining people to slow death.

"You know much about my people," Wulfgar remarked.

"I have spent many days watching them," Drizzt explained, wondering what line of thought the barbarian was drawing, "learning their ways and tricks for prospering in such an unwelcoming land."

Wulfgar chuckled softly and shook his head, further impressed by the sincere reverence the drow showed whenever he spoke of the natives of Icewind Dale. He had known the drow less than two tendays, but already he understood the character of Drizzt Do'Urden well enough to know that his next observation about the drow was true to the mark.

"I'll wager you even felled deer silently in the darkness, to be found in the morning light by people too hungry to question their good fortune."

Drizzt neither answered the remark nor changed the set of his gaze, but Wulfgar was confident in his guess.

"Do you know of Heafstaag?" the barbarian asked after a few moments of silence. "He was king of my tribe, a man of many scars and great renown."

Drizzt remembered the one-eyed barbarian well. The mere mention of his name sent a dull ache into the drow's shoulder, where he had been wounded by the huge man's heavy axe. "He lives," Drizzt replied, somewhat shielding his contempt. "Heafstaag speaks for the whole of the north now. None of true enough blood remain to oppose him in combat or speak out against him to hold him in check."

"He is a mighty king," Wulfgar said, oblivious to the venom in the drow's voice.

"He is a savage fighter," Drizzt corrected. His lavender eyes bore into Wulfgar, catching the barbarian completely by surprise with their sudden flash of anger. Wulfgar saw the incredible character in those violet pools, an inner strength within the drow whose pure quality would make the most noble of kings envious.

"You have grown into a man in the shadow of a dwarf of indisputable character," Drizzt scolded. "Have you gained nothing for the experience?"

Wulfgar was dumbfounded and couldn't find the words to reply.

Drizzt decided that the time had come for him to lay bare the barbarian's principles and judge the wisdom and worth of teaching the young man. "A king is a man strong of character and conviction who leads by example and truly cares for the sufferings of his people," he lectured. "Not a brute who rules simply because he is the strongest. I should think you would have learned to understand the distinction."

Drizzt noted the embarrassment on Wulfgar's face and knew that the years in the dwarven caves had shaken the very ground that the barbarian had grown on. He hoped that Bruenor's belief in Wulfgar's sense of conscience and principle proved true, for he, too, like Bruenor years before, had come to recognize the promise of the intelligent young man and found that he cared about Wulfgar's future. He turned suddenly and started away, leaving the barbarian to find the answers to his own questions.

"The lesson?" Wulfgar called after him, still confused and surprised.

"You have had your lesson for this night," Drizzt replied without turning or slowing. "Perhaps it was the most important that I will ever teach." The drow faded into the blackness of the night, though the distinct image of lavender eyes remained clearly imprinted in Wulfgar's thoughts.

The barbarian turned back to the distant campfire.

And wondered.

15

ON THE WINGS OF DOOM

They came in under the cover of a violent squall line that swept down upon Ten-Towns from the open east. Ironically, they followed the same trail along the side of Kelvin's Cairn that Drizzt and Wulfgar had traveled just two tendays earlier. This band of verbeeg, though, headed south toward the settlements, rather than north to the open tundra. Though tall and thin—the smallest of the giants—they were still a formidable force.

A frost giant led the advance scouts of Akar Kessell's vast army. Unheard beneath the howling blasts of wind, they moved with all speed to a secret lair that had been discovered by orc scouts in a rocky spur on the southern side of the mountain. There was barely a score of the monsters, but each carried a huge bundle of weapons and supplies.

The leader pressed on toward its destination. Its name was Biggrin, a cunning and immensely strong giant whose upper lip had been torn away by the ripping maw of a huge wolf, leaving the grotesque caricature of a smile forever stamped upon its face. This disfigurement only added to the giant's stature, instilling the respect of fear in its normally unruly troops. Akar Kessell had hand-picked Biggrin as the leader of his forward scouts, though the wizard had been counseled to send a less conspicuous party, some of Heafstaag's people, for the delicate mission. But Kessell held Biggrin in high regard and was impressed with the enormous amount of supplies the small band of verbeeg could carry.

The troop settled into their new quarters before midnight and immediately went about fashioning sleeping areas, storage rooms, and a small kitchen. Then they waited, silently poised to strike the first lethal blows in Akar Kessell's glorious assault on Ten-Towns.

An orc runner came every couple of days to check on the band and deliver the latest instructions from the wizard, informing Biggrin of the progress of the next supply troop that was scheduled to arrive. Everything was proceeding according to Kessell's plan, but Biggrin noted with concern that many of his warriors grew more eager and anxious every time a new runner appeared, hoping that the time to march to war was finally upon them.

Always the instructions were the same, though: Stay hidden and wait.

In less than two tendays in the tense atmosphere of the stuffy cave, the camaraderie between the giants had disintegrated. Verbeeg were creatures of action, not contemplation, and boredom led them inescapably to frustration.

Arguments became the norm, often leading to vicious fights. Biggrin was never far away, and the imposing frost giant usually managed to break up the scuffles before any of the troops were seriously wounded. The giant knew beyond any doubt that it could not keep control of the battle-hungry band for much longer.

The fifth runner slipped into the cave on a particularly hot and uncomfortable night. As soon as the unfortunate orc entered the common room, it was surrounded by a score of grumbling verbeeg.

"What's the news, then?" one of them demanded impatiently.

Thinking that the backing of Akar Kessell was sufficient protection, the orc eyed the giant in open defiance. "Fetch your master, soldier," it ordered.

Suddenly a huge hand grabbed the orc by the scruff of the neck and shook the creature roughly. "Yous was asked a question, scum," said a second giant. "What's the news?"

The orc, now visibly unnerved, shot back an angry threat at its giant assailant. "The wizard will peel the skin from your hide while you watch!"

"I heared enough," growled the first giant, reaching down to clamp a huge hand around the orc's neck. It lifted the creature clear off the ground, using only one of its massive arms. The orc slapped and twisted pitifully, not bothering the verbeeg in the least.

"Aw, squeeze its filthy neck," came one call.

"Put its eyes out an' drop it in a dark hole!" said another.

Biggrin entered the room, quickly pushing through the ranks to discover the source of the commotion. The giant wasn't surprised to find the verbeeg tormenting an orc. In truth, the giant leader was amused by the spectacle, but it understood the danger of angering the volatile Akar Kessell. It had seen more than one unruly goblin put to a slow death for disobeying, or simply to appease the wizard's distorted taste for pleasure. "Put the miserable thing down," Biggrin ordered calmly.

Several groans and angry grumbles sprang up around the frost giant.

"Bash its 'ead in!" cried one.

"Bites its nose!" yelled another.

By now, the orc's face had grown puffy from lack of air, and it hardly struggled at all. The verbeeg holding it returned Biggrin's threatening stare for a few moments longer, then tossed its helpless victim at the frost giant's booted feet.

"Keep it then," the verbeeg snarled at Biggrin. "But if it wags its tongue at me agin, I'll eats it fer sure!"

"I've 'ad too much o' this hole," complained a giant, from the back of the ranks. "An' a whole dale o' filthy dwarfs fer the takin'!" The grumbling renewed with heightened intensity.

Biggrin looked around and studied the seething rage that had crept into all of the troops, threatening to bring down the whole lair in one sudden fit of irrepressible violence.

"Tomorrow night we starts goin' out t'see what's about us," Biggrin offered in response. It was a dangerous move, the frost giant knew, but the alternative was certain disaster. "Only three at a time, an' no one's to know!"

The orc had regained a measure of composure and heard Biggrin's proposal. It started to protest, but the giant leader silenced it immediately.

"Shut yer mouth, orc dog," Biggrin commanded, looking to the verbeeg that had threatened the runner and smiling wryly, "or I'll lets me friend eat!"

The giants howled their glee and exchanged shoulder claps with their companions, comrades again. Biggrin had given them back the promise of action, though the giant leader's doubts about its decision were far from dispelled by the lusty enthusiasm of the soldiers. Shouts of the various dwarven recipes the verbeegs had concocted—"Dwarf o' the Apple" and "Bearded, Basted, an' Baked" to name two—rang out to overwhelming hoots of approval.

Biggrin dreaded what might happen if any of the verbeeg came upon some of the short folk.

BIGGRIN LET THE VERBEEG OUT OF THE LAIR IN GROUPS OF THREE, and only during the nighttime hours. The giant leader thought it unlikely that any dwarves would travel this far north up the valley, but knew that it was taking a huge gamble. A sigh of relief escaped from the giant's mouth whenever a patrol returned without incident.

Simply being allowed out of the cramped cave improved the verbeeg's morale tenfold. The tension inside the lair virtually disappeared as the troops regained their enthusiasm for the coming war. Up on the side of Kelvin's Cairn they often saw the lights of Caer-Konig and Caer-Dineval, Termalaine across the way to the west, and even Bryn Shander far to the south. Viewing the cities allowed them to fantasize about their upcoming victories, and the thoughts were enough to sustain them in their long wait.

Another tenday slipped by. Everything seemed to be going along well. Witnessing the improvement the small measure of freedom had brought to his troops, Biggrin gradually began to relax about the risky decision.

But then two dwarves, having been informed by Bruenor that there was some fine stone under the shadow of Kelvin's Cairn, made the trip to the north end of the valley to investigate its mining potential. They arrived on the southern slopes of the rocky mountain late one afternoon, and by dusk had made camp on a flat rock beside a swift stream.

This was their valley, and it had known no trouble in several years. They took few precautions.

So it happened that the first patrol of verbeeg to leave the lair that night soon spotted the flames of a campfire and heard the distinctive dialect of the hated dwarves.

ON THE OTHER SIDE OF THE MOUNTAIN, DRIZZT DO'URDEN opened his eyes from his daytime slumber. Emerging from the cave into the growing gloom, he found Wulfgar in the customary spot, poised meditatively on a high stone, staring out over the plain.

"You long for your home?" the drow asked rhetorically.

Wulfgar shrugged his huge shoulders and answered absently, "Perhaps." The barbarian had come to ask many disturbing questions of himself about his people and their way of life since he had learned respect for Drizzt. The drow was an enigma to him, a confusing combination of fighting brilliance and absolute control. Drizzt seemed able to weigh every move he ever made in the scales of high adventure and indisputable morals.

Wulfgar turned a questioning gaze on the drow. "Why are you here?" he asked suddenly.

Now it was Drizzt who stared reflectively into the openness before them. The first stars of the evening had appeared, their reflections sparkling distinctively in the dark pools of the elf's eyes. But Drizzt was not seeing them; his mind was viewing long-past images of the lightless cities of the drow in their immense cavern complexes far beneath the ground.

"I remember," Drizzt recalled vividly, as terrible memories are often vivid, "the first time I ever viewed this surface world. I was a much younger elf then, a member of a large raiding party. We slipped out from a secret cave and descended upon a small elven village." The drow flinched at the images as they flashed again in his mind. "My companions slaughtered every member of the wood elf clan. Every female. Every child."

Wulfgar listened with growing horror. The raid that Drizzt was describing might well have been one perpetrated by the ferocious Tribe of the Elk.

"My people kill," Drizzt went on grimly. "They kill without mercy." He locked his stare onto Wulfgar to make sure that the barbarian heard him well.

"They kill without passion."

He paused for a moment to let the barbarian absorb the full weight of his words. The simple yet definitive description of the cold killers had confused Wulfgar. He had been raised and nurtured among passionate warriors, fighters whose entire purpose in life was the pursuit of battle glory—fighting in praise of Tempus. The young barbarian simply could not understand such emotionless cruelty. A subtle difference, though, Wulfgar had to admit. Drow or barbarian, the results of the raids were much the same.

"The demon goddess they serve leaves no room for the other races," Drizzt explained. "Particularly the other races of elves."

"But you will never come to be accepted in this world," said Wulfgar. "Surely you must know that the humans will ever shun you."

Drizzt nodded. "Most," he agreed. "I have few that I can call friends, yet I am content. You see, barbarian, I have my own respect, without guilt, without shame." He rose from his crouch and started away into the darkness. "Come," he instructed. "Let us fight well this night, for I am satisfied with the improvement of your skills, and this part of your lessons nears its end."

Wulfgar sat a moment longer in contemplation. The drow lived a hard and materially empty existence, yet he was richer than any man Wulfgar had ever known. Drizzt had clung to his principles against overwhelming circumstances, leaving the familiar world of his own people by choice to remain in a world where he would never be accepted or appreciated.

He looked at the departing elf, now a mere shadow in the gloom. "Perhaps we two are not so different," he mumbled under his breath.

"SPIES!" WHISPERED ONE OF THE VERBEEG.

"Stupid fer spyin' with a fire," said another.

"Lets go squash 'em!" said the first, starting toward the orange light.

"The boss said no!" the third reminded the others. "We's to watch, but no squashin'!"

They started down the rocky path toward the small camp of the dwarves with as much stealth as they could muster, which made them about as quiet as a rolling boulder.

The two dwarves were well aware that someone or something was approaching. They drew their weapons as a precaution, but figured that Wulfgar and Drizzt, or perhaps some fishermen from Caer-Konig, had seen their light and were coming to share dinner with them.

When the camp came into sight just below, the verbeeg could see the dwarves standing firm, weapons in hand.

"They's seen us!" said one giant, ducking into the darkness.

"Aw, shut up," ordered the second.

The third giant, knowing as well as the second that the dwarves could not as yet know who they were, grasped the second's shoulder and winked evilly "If they's seen us," it reasoned, "we's got no choice but to squash 'em!"

The second giant chuckled softly, poised its heavy club on its shoulder, and started for the camp.

The dwarves were completely stunned when the verbeeg came bounding around some boulders just a few yards from their camp and closed in on them. But a cornered dwarf is pound for pound as tough as anything in the world, and these were of the clan from Mithral Hall who had been waging battles on the merciless tundra for all of their lives. This fight would not be as easy as the verbeeg had expected.

The first dwarf ducked a lumbering swing from the lead verbeeg and countered by slamming his hammer onto the monster's toes. The giant instinctively lifted its injured foot and hopped on one leg, and the seasoned dwarf fighter promptly cut it down by bashing it in the knee.

The other dwarf had reacted quickly, launching his hammer with pinpoint accuracy. It caught another giant in the eye and spun the creature crashing into some rocks.

But the third verbeeg, the smartest of the three, had picked up a stone before it had charged and returned the dwarf's throw with tremendous force.

The stone deflected off the unfortunate dwarf's temple, snapping his neck violently to the side. His head lolled about uncontrollably on his shoulders as he fell dead to the ground.

The first dwarf would have soon finished off the giant he had felled, but the last of the monsters was upon him at once. The two combatants parried and countered, with the dwarf actually gaining a bit of an advantage. An advantage that lasted only until the giant who had been struck in the eye by the thrown hammer recovered enough to jump in.

The two verbeeg rained blow after heavy blow at the dwarf. He managed to dodge and deflect them for a short while, but then one landed squarely on his shoulder and dropped him to his back. He found his breath in a short time, for he was as tough as the stone he had landed on, but a heavy boot stomped on him and held him prone.

"Squish 'im!" begged the injured giant the dwarf had cut down. "Then we takes 'im to the cook!"

"We does not!" growled the giant above the dwarf. It ground its huge boot into the earth, slowly pressing the life from the unfortunate victim.

"Biggrin'll take us to the cook if 'e finds us out!" The other two grew genuinely afraid when they were reminded of the wrath of their brutal leader. They looked helplessly to their more cunning companion for a solution.

"We puts 'em an' their filthy things in a dark hole and says nothin' more o' this!"

MANY MILES TO THE EAST, IN HIS SOLITARY TOWER, AKAR KESsell waited patiently. In the autumn, the last—and largest—of the trading caravans would roll back into Ten-Towns from Luskan, laden with riches and supplies for the long winter. His vast armies would be assembled and on the move by then, marching gloriously to destroy the pitiful fishermen. The mere thought of the fruits of his easy victory sent shivers of delight through the wizard.

He had no way of knowing that the first blows of the war had already been struck.

16

SHALLOW GRAVES

When Wulfgar awakened just before midday, rested from his long night's work, he was surprised to see Drizzt already up and about, busily preparing a pack for a long hike.

"Today we start a different type of lesson," Drizzt explained to the barbarian. "We'll set out right after you've had something to eat."

"To where?"

"First, the dwarven mines," replied Drizzt. "Bruenor will want to see you so he might measure your progress for himself." He smiled at the big man. "He shan't be disappointed!"

Wulfgar smiled, confident that his newfound prowess with the hammer would impress even the grumpy dwarf. "And then?"

"To Termalaine, on the banks of Maer Dualdon. I have a friend there. One of my few," he added quickly with a wink, drawing a smile from Wulfgar. "A man named Agorwal. I want you to meet some of the people of Ten-Towns so that you might better judge them."

"What have I to judge?" Wulfgar asked angrily. The drow's dark and knowing eyes bore into him. Wulfgar clearly understood what Drizzt had in mind. The dark elf was trying to personalize the people the barbarians had declared enemies, to show Wulfgar the everyday existence of the men, women, and children who might have been victims of his own heavy pole if the fight on the slopes had turned out differently. Fearless in any battle, Wulfgar was truly frightened of facing those people. Already the young barbarian had begun to question the virtues of his warlike people; the innocent faces he would encounter in the town his people had casually marked for burning could well complete the destruction of the foundations of his entire world.

The two companions set out a short time later, retracing their steps around the eastern trails of Kelvin's Cairn. A dusty wind was blowing in steadily from the east, assaulting them with fine grains of stinging sand as they crossed the exposed face of the mountain. Though the glaring sun was especially draining on Drizzt, he kept a strong pace and did not stop for rest.

In the late afternoon, when they finally rounded a southern spur, they were exhausted but in good spirits.

"In the shelter of the mines, I had forgotten how cruel the tundra wind could be!" laughed Wulfgar.

"We'll have some protection below the rim of the valley," said Drizzt. He patted the empty waterskin at his side. "Come, I know where we might refill these before we continue."

He led Wulfgar westward, below the southern slopes of the mountain. The drow knew of an icy stream a short distance away, its waters fed from the snowmelt atop Kelvin's Cairn.

The brook sang merrily as it danced across the stones. Nearby birds cackled and cawed at the approach of the companions, and a lynx slipped silently away. Everything appeared as it should, but from the moment they arrived on the large, flat rock that was commonly used by travelers as a campsite, Drizzt sensed that something was terribly wrong. Moving in tentatively, he searched for some tangible sign that would confirm his growing suspicions.

Wulfgar, though, dived belly-down onto the stone and dunked his sweat- and dust-streaked face eagerly into the cold water.

When he pulled it back out, the luster had returned to his eyes, as if the icy water had given him back his vitality.

But then the barbarian noticed crimson stains on the rock and followed their gory trail to the hairy piece of skin that had gotten caught on the sharp tip of a stone just above the rushing stream.

Both skilled trackers, the ranger and barbarian had little difficulty in ascertaining that a battle had recently been fought on this spot. They recognized the coarse hair on the patch of skin as a piece of beard, which of course led them to think of the dwarves. They found three sets of giant-size footprints nearby. Following a tangent line of tracks that stretched southward a short distance to a sandy patch of ground, they soon found the shallow graves.

"Not Bruenor," Drizzt said grimly, examining the two corpses. "Younger dwarves—Bundo, son of Fellhammer, and Dourgas, son of Argo Grimblade, I believe."

"We should make all haste to the mines," Wulfgar suggested.

"Soon," replied the drow. "We still have much to learn about what happened here, and tonight may be our only chance. Were these giants simply passing rogues, or are they lairing in the area? And are there more of the foul beasts?"

"Bruenor should be told," Wulfgar argued.

"And so he will," said Drizzt. "But if these three are still nearby, as I believe they are since they took the time to bury their kill, they might well return for some more sport when night falls." He directed Wulfgar's gaze to the west, where the sky had already begun to take on the pink shades of twilight. "Are you ready for a fight, barbarian?"

With a determined grunt, Wulfgar brought Aegis-fang down from his shoulder and slapped the adamantite handle across his free hand. "We shall see who finds sport this night."

They moved behind the secrecy of a rocky bluff south of the flat stone and waited as the sun passed below the horizon and the dark shadows deepened into evening.

It wasn't very long a wait, for the same verbeeg that had killed the dwarves the night before were again the first out of the lair, anxious to seek fresh victims. Soon the patrol came crashing over the mountain slopes and onto the flat rock beside the stream.

Wulfgar immediately moved to charge, but Drizzt stayed him before he gave their position away. The drow had every intention of killing these giants, but he wanted to see if he could learn anything about why they were here first.

"Drats an' dingers," grumbled one of the giants. "Not a dwarf to be found!"

"Rotten luck, it is," groaned another. "An' our last night out, too." The creature's companions looked at it curiously.

"The other group's comin' in tomorrow," the verbeeg explained. "Our numbers'll double, an' stinkin' ogres an' orcs to boot, an' the boss ain't to let us out 'til everthin's calmed again."

"A score more in that stinkin' hole," complained one of the others. "Rightly t'send us flippin'!"

"Let's be movin', then," said the third. "No huntin' 'ere an' no night fer wastin'."

The two adventurers behind the bluff tensed reflexively when the giants spoke of leaving.

"If we can get to that rock," Wulfgar reasoned, unknowingly pointing to the same boulder that the giants had used for their ambush the night before, "we'll have them before they even realize we're here!" He turned anxiously to Drizzt but backed off immediately when he saw the drow. The lavender eyes burned with a luster that Wulfgar had never witnessed before.

"There are only three of them," said Drizzt, his voice holding a fragile edge of calm that threatened to explode at any moment. "We need no surprise."

Wulfgar didn't quite know how to take this unexpected change in the dark elf. "You taught me to seek every advantage," he said cautiously.

"In battle, yes," answered Drizzt. "This is vengeance. Let the giants see us, let them feel the terror of impending doom!" The scimitars suddenly appeared in his slender hands as he walked out around the bluff, his steady stride unnervingly holding the unswerving promise of death.

One of the giants yelled out in surprise, and they all froze in their tracks when they saw the drow step out before them. Apprehensive and confused, they formed a defensive line across the flat rock. The verbeeg had heard legends of the drow, even some where the dark elves had joined forces with giants, but the sudden appearance of Drizzt caught them totally by surprise.

Drizzt enjoyed their nervous twitchings, and he held back to savor the moment.

"What are ye fer, then?" one of the giants asked cautiously.

"A friend of dwarves," Drizzt replied with a wicked laugh. Wulfgar leaped out beside him as the largest of the giants charged without hesitation. But Drizzt stopped him cold. The drow pointed one of his scimitars at the advancing giant and stated with deathly calm, "You are dead." At once, the verbeeg was limned by purplish flames. It yelled in terror and retreated a step, but Drizzt stalked it methodically.

An overwhelming impulse came over Wulfgar to throw the warhammer, as though Aegis-fang was exerting a will of its own. The weapon whistled through the night air and exploded into the giant standing in the middle, hurling its broken body into the swollen stream.

Wulfgar was truly awe-stricken with the power and deadliness of the throw, but he worried about how effectively he could fight off the third giant with a small dagger, the only weapon he had left. The giant recognized the advantage as well and charged wildly. Wulfgar went for the dagger.

But instead he found Aegis-fang magically returned to his grasp. He had no idea of this special power Bruenor had imbued upon the weapon, and he had no time now to pause and ponder.

Terrified, but having nowhere to run, the largest giant attacked Drizzt with abandon, giving the elf even more of an advantage.

The monster lifted its heavy club high, the movement exaggerated by rage, and Drizzt quickly poked his pointed blades through the leather tunic and into the exposed belly. With only a slight hesitation, the giant continued its mighty swing, but the agile drow still had ample time to dodge the blow. And as the swing threw the lumbering giant off balance, Drizzt jabbed two more tiny holes into its shoulder and neck.

"Are you watching, boy?" the drow called gaily to Wulfgar. "It fights like one of your kind."

Wulfgar was heavily engaged with the remaining giant, easily maneuvering Aegis-fang to deflect the monster's powerful blows, but he was able to catch glimpses of the battle to his side. The scene painted a grim reminder of the value of what Drizzt had taught him, for the drow was toying with the verbeeg, using its uncontrolled rage against it. Again and again, the monster reared for a killing blow, and each time Drizzt was quick to strike and dance away. Verbeeg blood flowed freely from a dozen wounds, and Wulfgar knew that Drizzt could finish the job at any time. But he was amazed that the dark elf was enjoying the tormenting game he played.

Wulfgar hadn't yet struck a solid blow on his opponent, biding his time, as Drizzt had taught him, until the enraged verbeeg wore itself out. Already the barbarian could see that the giant's blows were coming with less frequency and vigor. Finally, lathered in sweat and breathing heavily, the verbeeg slipped up and dropped its guard. Aegis-fang pounded home once, and then again, and the giant toppled in a lump.

The verbeeg fighting Drizzt was down on one knee now, the drow having deftly sliced out one of its hamstrings. When Drizzt saw the second giant fall before Wulfgar, he decided to end the game. The giant took one more futile swing, and Drizzt waded in behind the flow of the weapon, jabbing with one scimitar and this time following the cruel point with his full weight. The blade slipped through the giant's neck and upward into its brain.

LATER, ONE QUESTION PRESSED UPON DRIZZT AS HE AND WULF-gar, resting on one knee, considered the results of their handiwork. "The hammer?" he asked simply.

Wulfgar looked down at Aegis-fang and shrugged. "I do not know," he answered honestly. "It returned to my hand by its own magic!"

Drizzt smiled to himself. He knew. How wondrous the crafting of Bruenor, he thought. And how deeply the dwarf must care for the boy to have given him such a gift!

"A score of verbeeg coming," groaned Wulfgar.

"And another twenty already here," added Drizzt. "Go straight away to Bruenor," he instructed. "These three just came from the lair; I shouldn't have much trouble backtracking and finding out where the rest of them are!"

Wulfgar nodded his assent, though he looked upon Drizzt with concern. The uncharacteristic smolder he had seen in the drow's eyes before they attacked the verbeeg had unnerved the barbarian. He wasn't quite sure just how daring the dark elf might be. "What do you mean to do when you find the lair?"

Drizzt said nothing but smiled wryly, adding to the barbarian's apprehension. Finally he eased his friend's worries. "Meet me back at this spot in the morning. I assure you that I shan't begin the fun without you!"

"I shall return before the first light of dawn," Wulfgar replied grimly. He spun on his heel and disappeared into the darkness, making his way as fast as he could under starlight.

Drizzt, too, started away, tracing the trail of the three giants westward across the face of Kelvin's Cairn. Eventually, he heard the baritone voices of giants, and shortly thereafter he saw the hastily constructed wooden doors that marked their lair, cunningly concealed behind some brush halfway up a rocky foothill.

Drizzt waited patiently and soon saw a second patrol of three giants emerge from the lair. And later on, when they returned, a third group came out. The drow was trying to discern if any alarms had gone up due to the absence of the first patrol. But verbeeg were almost always unruly and undependable, and Drizzt was reassured from the small snatches of conversation he was able to hear that the giants assumed their missing companions had either gotten lost or simply deserted. When the drow slipped away a few hours later to set his next plans, he was confident that he still had the element of surprise working for him.

WULFGAR RAN ALL THROUGH THE NIGHT. HE DELIVERED HIS message to Bruenor and started back to the north without waiting for the clan to be roused. His great strides took him to the flat rock more than an hour before the first light, even before Drizzt had returned from the lair. He went back behind the bluff to wait, his concern for the drow growing with every passing second.

Finally, able to stand the suspense no longer, he sought out the trail of the verbeeg and started tracking it toward the lair, determined to discover what was happening. He hadn't gone twenty feet when a hand cuffed him on the back of the head. Reflexively he spun to meet his attacker, but his astonishment turned to joy when he saw Drizzt standing before him.

Drizzt had returned to the rock shortly after Wulfgar but had remained hidden, watching the barbarian to see if the impulsive young warrior would trust in their pact or decide to take matters into his own hands. "Never doubt an appointed rendezvous until its hour has passed," the drow scolded sternly, touched as he was by the barbarian's concern for his well-being.

Any response that might have been coming from Wulfgar was cut short, for suddenly the two companions heard a gruff shout from a familiar voice. "Get me a pig-squealin' giant to kill!" Bruenor called from the flat stone by the stream behind them. Enraged dwarves can roll along at an incredible speed. In less than an hour,

Bruenor's clan had assembled and started after the barbarian, nearly matching his frantic pace.

"Well met," Drizzt called as he moved to join the dwarf. He found Bruenor eyeing the three dead verbeeg with grim satisfaction. Fifty iron-visaged, battle-ready dwarves, more than half the clan, stood around their leader.

"Elf," Bruenor greeted with his customary consideration. "A lair, is it?"

Drizzt nodded. "A mile to the west, but let that be not your first concern. The giants there are not going anywhere, but they are expecting guests this very day."

"The boy told me," said Bruenor. "A score of reinforcements!" He swung his axe casually. "Somehow I get the feelin' they're not goin' t' make the lair! Any notion o' where they're to be comin' in?"

"North and east is the only way," Drizzt reasoned. "Somewhere down Icewind Pass, around the north of Lac Dinneshere. Your people will greet them, then?"

"Of course," replied Bruenor. "They'll be passin' Daledrop for certain!" A twinkle edged his eye. "What do ye mean to do?" he asked Drizzt. "An what o' the boy?"

"The boy remains with me," Drizzt insisted. "He needs rest. We'll watch over the lair."

The eager gleam in Drizzt's eye gave Bruenor the impression that the drow had more in mind than watching. "Crazy elf," he said under his breath. "Probably'll take on the whole lot of 'em by himself!" He looked around curiously again at the dead giants. "And win!" Then Bruenor studied the two adventurers, trying to match their weapons with the types of wounds on the verbeeg.

"The boy felled two," Drizzt replied to the dwarf's unspoken question.

A hint of a rare smile found its way onto Bruenor's face. "Two to yer one, eh? Yer slippin', elf."

"Nonsense," Drizzt retorted. "I recognized that he needed the practice!"

Bruenor shook his head, surprised by the extent of the pride he felt toward Wulfgar, though of course he wasn't about to tell the boy and swell his head. "Yer slippin'!" he called again as he moved up to the head of the clan. The dwarves took up a rhythmic chanting, an ancient tune that had once echoed off the silvery halls of their lost homeland.

Bruenor looked back at his two adventurous friends and honestly wondered what would be left of the giant lair by the time he and his fellow dwarves returned.

17

VENGEANCE

Tirelessly, the heavily laden dwarves marched on. They had come prepared for war, some carrying heavy packs and others shouldering the great weight of large wooden beams.

The drow's guess about which direction the reinforcements would be coming from seemed the only possible way, and Bruenor knew exactly where to meet them. There was only one pass that afforded easy access down into the rocky valley: Daledrop, up on the level of the tundra yet below the southern slopes of the mountain.

Though they had marched without rest throughout half of the night and most of the morning, the dwarves set right to work. They had no idea what time the giants would be coming in, though it probably wouldn't happen under the light of day; they wanted to make certain that everything was ready. Bruenor was determined to take out this war party quickly and with minimal losses to his people. Scouts were posted on the high spots of the mountainside, and others were sent out onto the plain. Under Bruenor's direction, the remainder of the clan prepared the area for an ambush. One group set to digging a trip-trench and another began reassembling the wooden beams into two ballistae. Heavy crossbowmen sought out the best vantage points among the boulders on the nearby mountainside from which to launch their assault.

In a short time, all was ready. But the dwarves still did not stop to rest. They continued canvassing every inch of the area, searching for any possible advantage they could gain over the verbeeg.

Late in the day, the sun already dipping its lowest edges below the horizon, one of the lookouts on the mountain announced that he had sighted a dust cloud growing in the distant east. Soon after, a scout came in from the plain to report that a troop of twenty verbeeg, a few ogres, and at least a dozen orcs was making speed toward Daledrop. Bruenor signaled the crossbowmen into their concealed positions. The ballista crews inspected the camouflage on the great bows and added perfecting touches. Then the strongest fighters of the clan, with Bruenor himself among them, dug themselves into small holes along the worn path of Daledrop, carefully cutting the tufts of thick grass so that they could roll it back over them.

They would strike the first blows.

DRIZZT AND WULFGAR HAD TAKEN UP A POSITION AMONG THE boulders of Kelvin's Cairn above the giants' lair. They had slept in shifts throughout the day. The drow's only concern for Bruenor and his clan was that some of the giants would leave the lair to meet the incoming reinforcements and spoil the dwarves' advantage of surprise.

After several uneventful hours, Drizzt's worries proved true. The drow was resting in the shadow of a ledge while Wulfgar kept watch over the lair. The barbarian could hardly see the wooden doors concealed behind the brush, but he clearly heard the creak of a hinge when one of them opened. He waited for a few moments before moving to rouse the drow to make sure that some of the giants were actually coming out of the hole.

Then he heard giants talking within the blackness of the open door, and suddenly, a half dozen verbeeg emerged into the sunlight. He turned to Drizzt but found the ever-alert drow already standing behind him, his large eyes squinting as he watched the giants in the bright light.

"I do not know what they are about," Wulfgar told Drizzt.

"They're seeking their missing companions," Drizzt replied. He'd heard, more clearly with his keen ears than his friend, distinct pieces of the conversation that had taken place before the giants emerged. These verbeeg had been instructed to exercise all possible caution, but they were to find the long-overdue patrol, or at least determine where the missing giants had gone off to. They were expected to return that same night, with or without the others.

"We must warn Bruenor," said Wulfgar.

"This group will have found their dead companions and alerted the lair long before we could return," replied Drizzt. "Besides, I believe that Bruenor has enough giants to deal with already."

"What, then?" asked Wulfgar. "Surely the lair will be tenfold more difficult to defeat if they expect trouble." The barbarian noticed that the simmering flame had returned to the drow's eye.

"The lair will be none the wiser if these giants never return," Drizzt said matter-of-factly, as though the task of stopping six hunting verbeeg was a minor obstacle. Wulfgar listened in disbelief, though he had already guessed what Drizzt had in mind.

The drow noted Wulfgar's apprehension and smiled broadly. "Come, boy," he instructed, using the condescending title to stir up the barbarian's pride. "You have trained hard for many tendays in preparation for a moment such as this." He sprang lightly across a small chasm on the stone ledge and turned back on Wulfgar, his eyes sparkling wildly as they caught the afternoon sun.

"Come," the drow repeated, beckoning with one hand. "There are only six of them!"

Wulfgar shook his head resignedly and sighed. During the tendays of training, he had come to know Drizzt as a controlled and deadly swordsman who weighed every feint and strike with calm precision. But in the last two days, Wulfgar had seen an overly daring—even reckless—side of the drow. Drizzt's unwavering confidence was the only thing that convinced Wulfgar that the elf wasn't suicidal, and the only thing that compelled Wulfgar to follow him against his own better judgment. He wondered if there was any limit to how far he would trust the drow.

He knew then and there that Drizzt would someday lead him into a situation from which there was no escape.

THE GIANT PATROL TRAVELED SOUTHWARD FOR A SHORT WHILE, Drizzt and Wulfgar secretly in tow. The verbeeg found no immediate trace of the missing giants and feared that they were getting too close to the dwarven mines, so they turned sharply back to the northeast, in the general direction of the flat rock where the skirmish had taken place.

"We must move on them soon," Drizzt told his companion. "Let us close in on our prey."

Wulfgar nodded. A short time later, they approached a broken area of jagged stones, where the narrow path twisted and turned suddenly. The ground was sloping upward slightly, and the companions recognized that the path they traveled would move out to the rim of a small chasm. The daylight had faded enough to provide some cover. Drizzt and Wulfgar exchanged knowing glances; the time had come for action.

Drizzt, by far the more battle-seasoned of the two, quickly discerned the mode of attack that offered the best chance of success. He motioned silently for Wulfgar to pause. "We have to strike and move away," he whispered, "and then strike again."

"Not an easy task against a wary foe," Wulfgar said.

"I have something that may aid us." The drow pulled his pack from his back and took out the small figurine and called his shadow. When the wondrous feline abruptly appeared, the barbarian gasped in horror and leaped away.

"What demon have you conjured?" he cried as loudly as he

dared, his knuckles whitening under the pressure of his clutch on Aegis-fang.

"Guenhwyvar is no demon," Drizzt reassured his large companion. "She is a friend and a valuable ally." The cat growled, as if it understood, and Wulfgar took another step away.

"No natural beast," the barbarian retorted. "I shall not fight beside a demon conjured with sorcery!" The barbarians of Icewind Dale feared neither man nor beast, but the black arts were absolutely foreign to them, and their ignorance left them vulnerable.

"If the verbeeg learn the truth of the missing patrol, Bruenor and his kin will be in danger," Drizzt said darkly. "The cat will help us to stop this group. Will you allow your own fears to hinder the rescue of the dwarves?"

Wulfgar straightened and recaptured a measure of his composure. Drizzt's play on his pride and on the very real threat to the dwarves was pressuring him to temporarily put aside his revulsion for the black arts. "Send the beast away, we need no assistance."

"With the cat, we're certain to get them all. I will not risk the life of the dwarf because of your discomfort." Drizzt knew that it would take many hours for Wulfgar to accept Guenhwyvar as an ally, if it ever happened at all, but for now, all that he needed was Wulfgar's cooperation in the attack.

The giants had been marching for several hours. Drizzt watched patiently as their formation began to loosen, with one or two of the monsters occasionally lagging behind the others. Things were falling into place exactly as the drow had hoped.

The path took one last twist between two gigantic boulders, then widened considerably and sloped more steeply up the final expanse to the chasm rim. It turned sharply then, and continued along the ledge, a solid rock wall on one side, and a rocky drop on the other. Drizzt motioned to Wulfgar to stand ready, then sent the great cat into action.

THE WAR PARTY, A SCORE OF VERBEEG WITH THREE OGRES AND a dozen orcs beside them, moved at an easy pace, reaching Daledrop well after the night had fallen. There were more monsters than the dwarves had originally expected, but they weren't overly concerned by the orcs and knew how to deal with ogres. The giants were the key to this battle.

The long wait did nothing to temper the raw edge of the dwarves' nerves. None of the clan had slept in nearly a day, and they remained tense and eager to avenge their kin.

The first of the verbeeg tramped onto the sloping field without incident, but when the last of the invading party reached the limits of the ambush zone, the dwarves of Mithral Hall attacked. Bruenor's group struck first, springing from their holes, often right beside a giant or orc and hacking at the nearest target. They aimed their blows to cripple, using the basic tenet of dwarven giant-fighting philosophy: The sharp edge of an axe cuts the tendon and muscles on the back of a knee, the flat head of a hammer crushes the kneecap in the front.

Bruenor felled a giant with one swing, then turned to flee, but he found himself facing the readied sword of an orc. Having no time to trade blows, Bruenor tossed his weapon into the air, shouting, "Catch!" The orc's eyes stupidly followed the axe's diversionary flight. Bruenor decked the creature by slamming his helmeted forehead on its chin, caught his axe as it fell, and scampered off into the night, pausing only for a second to kick the orc as he passed.

The monsters had been taken absolutely by surprise, and many of them already lay screaming on the ground. Then the ballistae opened up. Spear-size missiles blasted into the front ranks, knocking giants aside and into each other. The crossbowmen sprang from their concealment and launched a deadly barrage, then dropped their bows and charged down the mountainside. Bruenor's group, now in their fighting V formation, rushed back into the fray.

The monsters never had the chance to regroup, and by the time they were even able to raise their weapons in response, their ranks had been decimated.

The Battle of Daledrop was over in three minutes.

Not a dwarf was even seriously injured, and of the invading monsters, only the orc that Bruenor had knocked out remained alive.

GUENHWYVAR UNDERSTOOD ITS MASTER'S WISHES AND LEAPED silently among the broken stones to the side of the trail, circling up ahead of the verbeeg and settling onto the rock wall above the path. It crouched low, no more than another of the deepening shadows. The first of the giants passed under, but the cat waited obediently, still as death, for the appropriate time. Drizzt and Wulfgar crept in closer, stealthily moving within clear sight of the back of the patrol's line.

The last of the giants, an extraordinarily fat verbeeg, paused for a moment to catch its breath.

Guenhwyvar struck quickly.

The lithe panther sprang from the wall and raked its long claws into the giant's face, then continued its bound over the monster, using the huge shoulder as a springboard, and returned to another spot on the wall. The giant howled in agony, clutching its torn face.

Aegis-fang took the creature in the back of the head, dropping it into the small gorge.

The giant in back of the remaining group heard the cry of pain and immediately charged back down the path, rounding the last bend just in time to see its unfortunate companion tumble down the rocky drop. The great cat didn't hesitate, dropping down upon its second victim, its sharp claws catching a firm hold on the giant's chest. Blood spurted wildly as the two-inch fangs sank deeply into the fleshy neck. Taking no chances, Guenhwyvar raked with all four of its mighty paws to deflect any counter, but the stunned giant was barely able to raise its arms in response before the deepest blackness closed over it.

With the rest of the patrol now coming fast, Guenhwyvar sprang away, leaving the gasping giant to drown in its own blood. Drizzt and Wulfgar took up positions behind the boulders on either side of the trail, the drow drawing his scimitars and the barbarian clutching the hammer that had returned to his hands.

The cat did not falter. It had played this scenario with its master many times before and understood well the advantage of surprise. It hesitated for a moment until the rest of the giants spotted it, then sprinted down the trail, darting between the rocks that hid its master and Wulfgar.

"Blimey!" cried one of the verbeeg, unconcerned with its dying companion. "A great huge cat, it is! An' black as me cook's kettles!"

"Be after it!" hollered another. "A new coat 'e'll make fer the one whats catches 'im!" They hopped over the fallen giant, never giving it a second thought, and charged down the trail after the panther.

Drizzt was the closest to the charging giants. He let the first two pass, concentrating on the remaining two. They crossed by the boulder side by side, and he jumped onto the path before them, jabbing the scimitar in his left hand deep into one giant's chest and blinding the other with a right-handed slash across the eyes. Using the scimitar that was planted into the first giant as a pivot, the drow wheeled behind his reeling foe and drove the other blade into the monster's back. He managed to free both blades with a subtle twist, dancing away as the mortally wounded giant toppled to the ground.

Wulfgar, too, let the lead giant go by. The second had pulled up nearly even with the barbarian when Drizzt attacked the back two. The giant stopped short and whirled, intending to help the others, but from his place behind the boulder, Wulfgar swung Aegis-fang in a sweeping arc and landed the heavy hammer squarely onto the verbeeg's chest. The monster dropped on its back, the air literally blasted from its lungs. Wulfgar reversed his swing quickly and launched Aegis-fang in the opposite direction. The lead giant spun about just in time to catch it in the face.

Without hesitation, Wulfgar pounced on the closest giant he had felled, wrapping his powerful arms around the monster's massive neck. The giant recovered quickly and put the barbarian in a bear hug, and though it was still sitting, it had little trouble lifting its smaller foe completely off the ground. But the years swinging a hammer and chopping stone in the dwarven mines had imbued the barbarian with the strength of iron. He tightened his grasp on the giant and slowly rotated his knotted arms. With a loud snap, the verbeeg's head lolled to the side.

The giant that Drizzt had blinded flailed about wildly with its huge club. The drow kept in constant motion, dancing around to each flank as the opportunity allowed, driving home thrust after thrust into the helpless monster. Drizzt aimed for any vital area he could safely reach, hoping to efficiently finish off his opponent.

Aegis-fang now securely back in his bands, Wulfgar walked over to the verbeeg he had struck in the face to make sure that it was dead. He kept an eye cautiously focused down the trail for any sign of the returning Guenhwyvar. Having seen the powerful cat at work, he had no desire to engage it personally.

When the last giant lay dead, Drizzt moved down the path to join his friend. "You have not yet come to understand your own prowess in battle!" he laughed, slapping the big man on the back. "Six giants are not beyond our ability!"

"Now do we go to find Bruenor?" Wulfgar asked, though he saw the fire still flickering dangerously in the drow's lavender eyes. He realized that they weren't leaving yet.

"No need," Drizzt replied. "I am confident that the dwarves have their situation well in hand.

"But we do have a problem," he continued. "We were able to kill the first group of giants and still retain the element of surprise. Very soon, though, with six more missing, the lair will become alert to any hint of danger."

"The dwarves should return in the morning," said Wulfgar. "We can attack the lair before midday."

"Too late," Drizzt said, pretending disappointment. "I fear that you and I may have to strike at them tonight, without delay."

Wulfgar wasn't surprised; he didn't even argue. He feared that he and the drow were taking on too much, that the drow's plan was too outrageous, but he was starting to accept one indisputable fact: He would follow Drizzt into any adventure, no matter how improbable their chances of surviving.

And he was beginning to admit to himself that he enjoyed gambling alongside the dark elf.

18

BIGGRIN'S HOUSE

Drizzt and Wulfgar were pleasantly surprised when they found the back entrance to the verbeeg lair. It sat high up on the steep incline on the western side of the rocky outcropping. Piles of garbage and bones lay strewn about the ground at the bottom of the rocks, and a thin but steady stream of smoke wafted out of the open cave, scented with the flavors of roasting mutton.

The two companions crouched in the brush below the entrance for a short while, noting the degree of activity. The moon had come up, bright and clear, and the night had lightened considerably. "I wonder if we'll be in time for dinner," remarked the drow, still smirking wryly. Wulfgar shook his head and laughed at the dark elf's uncanny composure.

Although the two often heard sounds from the shadows just beyond the opening, pots clanging and occasional voices, no giant showed itself outside the cave until shortly before moonset. A fat verbeeg, presumably the lair's cook from its dress, shuffled out onto the doorstep and dumped a load of garbage from a large iron pot down the slope.

"He's mine," said Drizzt, suddenly serious. "Can you provide a distraction?"

"The cat will do," Wulfgar answered, though he wasn't keen on being alone with Guenhwyvar.

Drizzt crept up the rocky slope, trying to stay in the dark shadows as he went. He knew that he would remain vulnerable in the moonlight until he got above the entrance, but the climb proved rougher than he had expected and the going was slow. When he was almost to the opening, he heard the giant chef stirring by the entrance, apparently lifting a second pot of garbage for dumping.

But the drow had nowhere to go. A call from within the cave diverted the cook's attention. Realizing how little time he had to get to safety, Drizzt sprinted the last few feet to the door level and peered around the corner into the torchlit kitchen.

The room was roughly square with a large stone oven on the wall across from the cave entrance. Next to the oven was a wooden door slightly ajar, and behind this Drizzt heard several giant voices. The cook was nowhere in sight, but a pot of garbage sat on the floor just inside the entrance.

"He'll be back soon," the drow muttered to himself as he picked his handholds and crept noiselessly up the wall and above the cave entrance. At the base of the slope, a nervous Wulfgar sat absolutely motionless as Guenhwyvar stalked back and forth before him.

A few minutes later the giant chef came out with the pot. As the verbeeg dumped the garbage, Guenhwyvar moved into view. One great leap took the cat to the base of the slope. Tilting its head up at the cook, the black panther growled.

"Ah, git outta here, ye mangy puss," snapped the giant, apparently unimpressed and unsurprised by the sudden appearance of the panther, "afore I squash yer head an' drop ye into a stewin' pot!"

The verbeeg's threat was an idle one. Even as it stood shaking an oversized fist, its attention fully on the cat, the dark shape that was Drizzt Do'Urden sprang from the wall onto its back. His scimitars already in hand, the drow wasted no time in cutting an ear-to-ear smile into the giant's throat. Without uttering a cry the verbeeg tumbled down the rocks to settle in with the rest of the garbage. Abruptly Drizzt dropped to the cave step and spun around, praying that no other giants had entered the kitchen.

He was safe for the moment. The room was empty. As Guenhwyvar and then Wulfgar crested the ledge, he signaled to them silently to follow him in. The kitchen was small (for giants) and sparsely stocked. There was one table on the right wall which held several pans. Next to it was a large chopping block with a garish cleaver, rusty and jagged and apparently unwashed for tendays, buried into it. Over to Drizzt's left were shelves holding spices and herbs and other supplies. The drow went to investigate these as Wulfgar moved to peer into the adjoining—and occupied—room.

Also square, this second area was a bit larger than the kitchen. A long table divided the room in half, and beyond it, directly across from where he stood, Wulfgar saw a second door. Three giants sat at the side of the table closest to Wulfgar, a fourth stood between them and the door, and two more sat on the opposite side. The group feasted on mutton and slurped thick stew, all the while cursing and taunting each other—a typical dinner gathering of verbeeg. Wulfgar noted with more than a passing interest that the monsters tore the meat from the bones with their bare hands. There weren't any weapons in the room.

Drizzt, holding a bag he had found on the shelves, drew one of his scimitars again and moved with Guenhwyvar to join Wulfgar. "Six," Wulfgar whispered, pointing to the room. The big barbarian hoisted Aegis-fang and nodded eagerly. Drizzt peeked through the door and quickly formulated an attack plan.

He pointed to Wulfgar, then to the door. "Right," he whispered. Then he indicated himself. "Behind you, left."

Wulfgar understood him perfectly, but wondered why he hadn't included Guenhwyvar. The barbarian pointed to the cat.

Drizzt merely shrugged and smiled, and Wulfgar understood. Even the skeptical barbarian was confident that Guenhwyvar would figure out where it best fit in.

Wulfgar shook the nervous tingles out of his muscles and clenched Aegis-fang tightly. With a quick wink to his companion, he burst through the door and pounced at the nearest target. The giant, the only one of the group standing at the time, managed to turn and face his attacker, but that was all. Aegis-fang swung in a low sweep and rose with deadly accuracy, smashing into its belly. Driving upward, it crushed the giant's lower chest. With his incredible strength, Wulfgar actually lifted the huge monster several feet off the ground. It fell, broken and breathless, beside the barbarian, but he paid it no more heed; he was already planning his second strike.

Drizzt, Guenhwyvar close on his heels, rushed past his friend toward the two stunned giants seated farthest to the left at the table. He jerked open the bag he held and twirled as he reached his targets, blinding them in a puff of flour. The drow never slowed as he passed, gouging his scimitar into the throat of one of the powdered verbeeg and then rolling backward over the top of the wooden table. Guenhwyvar sprang on the other giant, its powerful jaws tearing out the monster's groin.

The two verbeeg on the far side of the table were the first of their group to truly react. One leaped to stand ready to meet Drizzt's whirling charge, while the second, unwittingly singling itself out as Wulfgar's next target, bolted for the back door.

Wulfgar marked the escaping giant quickly and launched Aegis-fang without hesitation. If Drizzt, at that time in midroll across the table, had realized just how close his form had come to intercepting the twirling warhammer, he might have had a few choice words for his friend. But the hammer found its mark, bashing into the verbeeg's shoulder and knocking the monster into the wall with enough force to break its neck.

The giant Drizzt had gored lay squirming on the floor, clutching its throat in a futile attempt to quell the flow of its lifeblood. And Guenhwyvar was having little trouble dispatching the other. Only two verbeeg remained to fight.

Drizzt finished his roll and landed on his feet on the far side of the table, nimbly dodging the grasp of the waiting verbeeg. He darted around, putting himself between his opponent and the door. The giant, its huge hands outstretched, spun around and charged. But the drow's second scimitar was out with the first, interweaving in a mesmerizing dance of death. As each blade flashed out, it sent another of the giant's gnarled fingers spinning to the floor. Soon the verbeeg had nothing more than two bloodied stumps where its hands had once been. Enraged beyond sanity, it swung its clublike arms wildly. Drizzt's scimitar quickly slipped under the side of its skull, ending the creature's madness.

Meanwhile, the last giant had rushed the unarmed barbarian. It wrapped its huge arms around Wulfgar and lifted him into the air, trying to squeeze the life out of him. Wulfgar tightened his muscles in a desperate attempt to prevent his larger foe from snapping the bones in his back.

The barbarian had trouble finding his breath. Enraged, he slammed his fist into the giant's chin and raised his hand for a second blow.

But then, following the dweomer that Bruenor had cast upon it, the magical warhammer was back in his grasp. With a howl of glee, Wulfgar drove home the butt end of Aegis-fang and put out the giant's eye. The giant loosened its grip, reeling backward in agony. The world had become such a blur of pain to the monster that it didn't even see Aegis-fang arcing over Wulfgar's head and speeding toward its skull. It felt a hot explosion as the heavy hammer split open its head, bouncing the lifeless body into the table and knocking stew and mutton all over the floor.

"Don't spill the food!" cried Drizzt in mock anger as he rushed to retrieve a particularly juicy-looking chop.

Suddenly they heard heavy-booted footsteps and shouts coming down the corridor behind the second door. "Back outside!" yelled Wulfgar as he turned toward the kitchen.

"Hold!" shouted Drizzt. "The fun is just beginning!" He pointed to a dim, torchlit tunnel that ran off the left wall of the room. "Down there! Quickly!"

Wulfgar knew that they were pushing their luck, but once again he found himself listening to the elf.

And once again the barbarian was smiling.

Wulfgar passed the heavy wooden supports at the beginning of the tunnel and raced off into the dimness. He had gone about thirty feet, Guenhwyvar loping uncomfortably close at his side, when he realized that Drizzt wasn't following. He turned around just in time to see the drow stroll casually out of the room and past the wooden beams. Drizzt had sheathed his scimitars. Instead, he held a long dagger, its wicked tip planted firmly into a piece of mutton.

"The giants?" asked Wulfgar from the darkness.

Drizzt stepped to the side, behind one of the massive wooden beams. "Right behind me," he explained calmly as he tore another bite off of his meal. Wulfgar's jaw dropped open when a pack of frothing verbeeg charged into the tunnel, never noticing the concealed drow.

"Prayne de crabug ahm keike rinedere be-yogt iglo kes gron!" Wulfgar shouted as he spun on his heel and sprinted off down the corridor, hoping that it didn't lead to a dead end.

Drizzt pulled the mutton off the end of his blade and accidentally dropped it to the ground, cursing silently at the waste of good food. Licking the dagger clean, he waited patiently. As the last verbeeg rambled past, he darted from his concealment, whipped the dagger into the back of the trailing giant's knee, and scooted around the other side of the beam. The wounded giant howled in pain, but by the time it or its companions had turned back around, the drow was nowhere to be seen.

Wulfgar rounded a bend and slipped against the wall, easily guessing what had stopped the pursuit. The pack had turned back when they found that there was another intruder nearer the exit.

A giant leaped through the supports and stood with its legs

wide apart and its club ready, its eyes going from door to door as it tried to figure out which route the unseen assailant had taken. Behind it and off to the side, Drizzt pulled a small knife out of each of his boots and wondered how the giants could be stupid enough to fall for the same trick twice in a span of ten seconds. Not about to argue with good fortune, the elf scrambled out behind his next victim and before its companions still in the tunnel could shout a call of warning, drove one of the knives deep into the giant's thigh, severing the hamstring. The giant lurched over to the side and Drizzt, hopping by, marveled at how wonderful a target the thick veins in a verbeeg's neck make when the monster's jaw is clenched in pain.

But the drow had no time to pause and ponder the fortunes of battle. The rest of the pack—five angry giants—had already thrown aside their wounded companion in the tunnel and were only a few strides behind. He put the second knife deep into the verbeeg's neck and headed for the door leading deeper into the lair. He would have made it, except that the first giant coming back into the room happened to be carrying a stone. As a rule, verbeeg are quite adept at rock throwing, and this one was better than most. The drow's unhelmeted head was its target, and its throw was true.

Wulfgar's throw was on target, too. Aegis-fang shattered the backbone of the trailing giant as it passed its wounded companion in the tunnel. The injured verbeeg, working to get Drizzt's dagger out of its knee, stared in disbelief at its suddenly dead companion and at the berserk death charge of the ferocious barbarian.

Out of the corner of his eye, Drizzt saw the stone coming. He managed to duck enough to avoid getting his head caved in, but the heavy missile caught him in the shoulder and sent him flying to the floor. The world spun around him as though he was its axis. He fought to reorient himself, for in the back of his mind he understood that the giant was coming to finish him off. But everything seemed a blur. Then something lying close to his face managed to hold his attention. He fixed his eyes on it, straining to find a focus and force everything else to stop spinning.

A verbeeg finger

The drow was back. Quickly, he reached for his weapon.

He knew that he was too late when he saw the giant, club raised for a death blow, towering above him.

The wounded giant stepped into the middle of the tunnel to meet the barbarian's charge. The monster's leg had gone numb, and it could not plant its feet firmly. Wulfgar, Aegis-fang comfortably back in his hands, swatted it aside and continued into the room. Two of the giants were waiting for him.

Guenhwyvar wove between a giant's legs as it turned and launched itself as high and far as its sleek muscles could take it. Just as the verbeeg standing over Drizzt started to swing its club at the prone elf, Drizzt saw a shade of black cross in front of its face. A jagged tear lined the giant's cheek. Drizzt understood what had happened when he heard Guenhwyvar's padded paws set down on the table and propel the cat farther across the room. Though a second giant now joined the first and both had their clubs poised to strike, Drizzt had gained all the time that he needed. In a lightning movement, he slid one of the scimitars from its sheath and thrust it into the first giant's groin. The monster doubled over in agony, a shield for Drizzt, and caught the blow from its comrade on the back of its head. The drow mumbled "Thank you" as he rolled over the corpse, landing on his feet and again thrusting upward, this time lifting his body to follow the blade.

Hesitation had cost another giant its life. For as the stunned verbeeg stared dumbfoundedly at its friend's brains splattered all over its club, the drow's curved blade sliced under its rib cage, tearing through lungs and finding its mark in the monster's heart.

Time moved slowly for the mortally wounded giant. The club it had dropped seemed to take minutes to reach the floor. With the barely perceptible motion of a falling tree, the verbeeg slid back from the scimitar. It knew that it was falling, but the floor never came up to meet it. Never came up . . .

Wulfgar hoped that he had hit the wounded giant in the tunnel hard enough to keep it out of the fray for a while—he would be in a tight spot indeed if it came up behind him then. He had all that he could handle parrying and counterthrusting with the two giants he now faced. He needn't have worried about his backside, though, for the wounded verbeeg slumped against the wall in the tunnel, oblivious to its surroundings. And in the opposite direction, Drizzt had just finished off the other two giants. Wulfgar laughed aloud when he saw his friend wiping the blood from his blade and walking back across the room. One of the verbeeg noticed the dark elf, too, and it jumped out of its fight with the barbarian to engage this new foe.

"Ay, ye little runt, ye think ye can face me even up an' live to talk about it?" bellowed the giant.

Feigning desperation, Drizzt glanced all about him. As usual, he found an easy way to win this fight. Using a stalking belly-crawl, Guenhwyvar had slithered behind the giant bodies, trying to get into a favorable position. Drizzt took a small step backward, goading the giant into the great cat's path.

The giant's club crashed into Wulfgar's ribs and pushed him up against the wooden beam. The barbarian was made of tougher stuff than wood, though, and he took the blow stoically, returning it two-fold with Aegis-fang. Again the verbeeg struck, and again Wulfgar countered. The barbarian had been fighting with hardly a break for over ten minutes, but adrenaline coursed through his veins, and he barely felt winded. He began to appreciate the endless hours toiling for Bruenor in the mines, and the miles and miles of running Drizzt had led him through during their sessions as his blows started to fall with increasing frequency on his tiring opponent.

The giant advanced on Drizzt. "Arg, hold yer ground, ye miserable rat!" it growled. "An' none o' yer sneaky tricks! We wants to see how ye does in a fair fight."

Just as the two came together, Guenhwyvar darted the remaining few feet and sank its fangs deep into the back of the verbeeg's ankle. Reflexively, the giant shot a glance at the rear attacker, but it recovered quickly and shot its eyes back to the elf . . .

. . . just in time to see the scimitar entering its chest.

Drizzt answered the monster's puzzled expression with a question. "Where in the nine hells did you ever find the notion that I would fight fair?"

The verbeeg lurched away. The blade hadn't found its heart, but it knew that the wound would soon prove fatal if untended. Blood poured freely down the monster's leather tunic, and it labored visibly as it tried to breathe.

Drizzt alternated his attacks with Guenhwyvar, striking and ducking away from the lumbering counter while his partner rushed in on the monster's other side. They knew, and the giant did, too, that this fight would soon be over.

The giant fighting Wulfgar could no longer sustain a defensive posture with its heavy club. Wulfgar was beginning to tire as well, so he started to sing an old tundra war song, the Song of Tempus, its rousing notes inspiring him into one final barrage. He waited for the verbeeg's club to inch inevitably downward and then launched Aegis-fang once, twice, and then a third time. Wulfgar nearly collapsed in exhaustion after the third swing, but the giant lay crumpled on the floor. The barbarian leaned wearily on his weapon and watched his two friends nip and scratch their verbeeg to pieces.

"Well done!" Wulfgar laughed when the last giant fell. Drizzt walked over to the barbarian, his left arm hanging limply at his side. His jacket and shirt were torn where the stone had struck, and the exposed skin of his shoulder was swollen and bruised.

Wulfgar eyed the wound with genuine concern, but Drizzt answered his unspoken question by raising the arm above him, though he grimaced in pain with the effort. "It'll be quick to mend," he assured Wulfgar. "Just a nasty bump, and I find that a small cost to weigh against the bodies of thirteen verbeeg!"

A low groan issued from the tunnel.

"Twelve as yet," Wulfgar corrected. "Apparently one is not quite done kicking." With a deep breath, Wulfgar lifted Aegis-fang and turned to finish the task.

"A moment, first," insisted Drizzt, a thought pressing on his mind. "When the giants charged you in the tunnel, you yelled something in your home tongue, I believe. What was it you said?" Wulfgar laughed heartily. "An old Elk tribe battle cry," he explained. "Strength to my friends, and death to my foes!"

Drizzt eyed the barbarian suspiciously and wondered just how deep ran Wulfgar's ability to fabricate a lie on demand.

THE INJURED VERBEEG WAS STILL PROPPED AGAINST THE TUNNEL wall when the two companions and Guenhwyvar came upon it. The drow's dagger remained deeply buried in the giant's knee, its blade caught fast between two bones. The giant eyed the men with hate-filled yet strangely calm eyes as they approached.

"Ye'll pay fer all o' this," it spat at Drizzt. "Biggrin'll play with ye afore killin' ye, be sure o' that!"

"So it has a tongue," Drizzt said to Wulfgar. And then to the giant, "Biggrin?"

"Laird o' the cave," answered the giant. "Biggrin'll be wantin' to meet ye."

"And we'll be wanting to meet Biggrin!" stormed Wulfgar. "We have a debt to repay—a little matter concerning two dwarves!" As soon as Wulfgar mentioned the dwarves, the giant spat again. Drizzt's scimitar flashed and poised an inch from the monster's throat.

"Kill me then an' have done," laughed the giant, genuinely uncaring. The monster's ease unnerved Drizzt. "I serve the master!" proclaimed the giant. "Glory is to die for Akar Kessell!"

Wulfgar and Drizzt looked at each other uneasily. They had never seen or heard of this kind of fanatical dedication in a verbeeg, and the sight disturbed them. The primary fault of the verbeeg which had always kept them from gaining dominance over the smaller races was their unwillingness to devote themselves wholeheartedly to any cause and their inability to follow one leader.

"Who is Akar Kessell?" demanded Wulfgar.

The giant laughed evilly. "If friends o' the towns ye be, ye'll know soon enough!"

"I thought you said that Biggrin was laird of this cave," said Drizzt.

"The cave," answered the giant. "And once a tribe. But Biggrin follows the master now!"

"We've got trouble," Drizzt mumbled to Wulfgar. "Have you ever heard of a verbeeg chieftain giving up its dominance to another without a fight?"

"I fear for the dwarves," said Wulfgar.

Drizzt turned back to the giant and decided to change the subject so that he could extract some information more immediate to their situation. "What is at the end of this tunnel?"

"Nothin'," said the verbeeg, too quickly. "Er, just a place for us t' sleep, is all."

Loyal, but stupid, noted Drizzt. He turned to Wulfgar again. "We have to take out Biggrin and any others in the cave who might be able to get back to warn this Akar Kessell."

"What about this one?" asked Wulfgar. But the giant answered the question for Drizzt. Delusions of glory pushed it to seek death in the wizard's service. It tightened its muscles, ignoring the pain in its knee, and lunged at the companions.

Aegis-fang smashed the verbeeg's collarbone and neck at the same time Drizzt's scimitar was slipping through its ribs and Guenhwyvar was locking onto its gut.

But the giant's death mask was a smile.

THE CORRIDOR BEHIND THE BACK DOOR OF THE DINING ROOM was unlit, and the companions had to pull a torch from its sconce in the other corridor to take with them. As they wound their way down the long tunnel, moving deeper and deeper into the hill, they passed many small chambers, most empty, but some holding crated stores of various sorts: foodstuffs, skins, and extra clubs and spears. Drizzt surmised that Akar Kessell planned to use this cave as a home base for his army.

The blackness was absolute for some distance and Wulfgar, lacking the darkvision of his elven companion, grew nervous as the torch began to burn low. But then they came into a wide chamber, by far the largest they had seen, and beyond its reaches, the tunnel spilled out into the open night.

"We have come to the front door," said Wulfgar. "And it's ajar. Do you believe that Biggrin has left?"

"Sssh," hushed Drizzt. The drow thought that he had heard something in the darkness on the far right. He motioned for Wulfgar to stay in the middle of the room with the torch as he crept away into the shadows.

Drizzt stopped short when he heard gruff giant voices ahead, though he couldn't figure out why he couldn't see their bulky silhouettes. When he came upon a large hearth, he understood. The voices were echoing through the chimney.

"Biggrin?" asked Wulfgar when he came up.

"Must be," reasoned Drizzt. "Think you can fit through the chimney?"

The barbarian nodded. He hoisted Drizzt up first—the drow's left arm still wasn't of much use to him—and followed, leaving Guenhwyvar to keep watch.

The chimney snaked up a few yards, then came to an intersection. One way led down to a room from which the voices were coming, and the other thinned as it rose to the surface. The conversation was loud and heated now, and Drizzt moved down to investigate. Wulfgar held the drow's feet to help him inch down the final descent, as the slope became nearly vertical. Hanging upside down, Drizzt peeked under the rim of the hearth in another room.

He saw three giants: one by a door at the far end of the room, looking as though it wanted to leave, and a second with its back to the hearth, being scolded by the third, an immensely wide and tall frost giant. Drizzt knew by the twisted, lipless smile that he looked upon Biggrin.

"To tell Biggrin!" pleaded the smaller giant.

"Ye ran from a fight," scowled Biggrin. "Ye left yer friends t' die!"

"No . . ." protested the giant, but Biggrin had heard enough. With one swipe of its huge axe, it lopped the smaller giant's head off.

THE MEN FOUND GUENHWYVAR DILIGENTLY ON WATCH WHEN they came out of the chimney. The big cat turned and growled in recognition when it saw its companions, and Wulfgar, not understanding the throaty purr to be a friendly sound, took a cautious step away.

"There has to be a side tunnel off the main corridor farther down," Drizzt reasoned, having no time to be amused by his friend's nervousness.

"Let's get this over with, then," said Wulfgar.

They found the passage as the drow had predicted and soon came to a door they figured would lead to the room with the remaining giants. They clapped each other on the shoulder for luck and Drizzt patted Guenhwyvar, though Wulfgar declined the drow's invitation to do likewise. Then they burst in.

The room was empty. A door previously invisible to Drizzt from his vantage point at the hearth stood ajar.

BIGGRIN SENT ITS LONE REMAINING SOLDIER OUT THE SECRET side door with a message for Akar Kessell. The big giant had been disgraced, and it knew that the wizard wouldn't readily accept the loss of so many valuable troops. Biggrin's only chance was to take care of the two intruding warriors and hope that their heads would appease its unmerciful boss. The giant pressed its ear to the door and waited for its victims to enter the adjoining room.

WULFGAR AND DRIZZT PASSED THROUGH THE SECOND DOOR AND came into a lavish chamber, its floor adorned with plush furs and large, puffy pillows. Two other doors led out of the room. One was slightly open, a darkened corridor beyond, and the other was closed.

Suddenly Wulfgar stopped Drizzt with an outstretched hand and motioned for the drow to be quiet. The intangible quality of a true warrior, the sixth sense that allows him to sense unseen danger, had come into play. Slowly the barbarian turned to the closed door and lifted Aegis-fang above his head. He paused for a moment and cocked his head, straining to hear a confirming sound. None came, but Wulfgar trusted his instincts. He roared to Tempus and launched the hammer. It split the door asunder with a thunderous snap and dropped the planks—and Biggrin—to the floor.

Drizzt noticed the swing of the open secret door across the room beyond the giant chieftain and realized that the last of the giants must have slipped away. Quickly the drow set Guenhwyvar into motion. The panther understood, too, for it bolted away, clearing the writhing form of Biggrin with one great bound, and charged out of the cave to give chase to the escaping verbeeg.

Blood streamed down the side of the big giant's head, but the thick bone of its skull had rejected the hammer. Drizzt and Wulfgar looked on in disbelief as the huge frost giant shook its jowls and rose to meet them.

"It can't do that," protested Wulfgar.

"This giant's a stubborn one." Drizzt shrugged.

The barbarian waited for Aegis-fang to return to his grasp, then moved with the drow to face Biggrin.

The giant stayed in the doorway to prevent either of its foes from flanking it as Wulfgar and Drizzt confidently moved in. The three exchanged ominous stares and a few easy swings as they felt each other out.

"You must be Biggrin," Drizzt said, bowing.

"That I am," proclaimed the giant. "Biggrin! The last foe yer eyes'll see!"

"Confident as well as stubborn," Wulfgar remarked.

"Little human," the giant retorted, "I've squashed a hunnerd o' yer puny kin!"

"More reason for us to kill you," Drizzt stated calmly.

With sudden speed and ferocity that surprised its two opponents, Biggrin took a wide sweep with its huge axe. Wulfgar stepped back out of its deadly range, and Drizzt managed to duck under the blow, but the drow shuddered when he saw the axe blade take a fair-sized chunk out of the stone wall.

Wulfgar jumped right back at the monster as the axe passed him, pounding on Biggrin's broad chest with Aegis-fang. The giant flinched but took the blow.

"Ye'll have t' hit me harder 'an that, puny man!" it bellowed as it launched a mighty backswing with the flat head of the axe.

Again Drizzt slipped below the swing. Wulfgar, however, battle-weary as he was, did not move quickly enough to back out of range. The barbarian managed to get Aegis-fang up in front of him, but the sheer force of Biggrin's heavy weapon smashed him into the wall. He crumpled to the floor.

Drizzt knew that they were in trouble. His left arm remained useless, his reflexes were slowing with exhaustion, and this giant was simply too powerful for him to parry any blows. He managed to slip in one short thrust with his scimitar as the giant recovered for its next swing, and then he fled toward the main corridor.

"Run, ye dark dog!" roared the giant. "I'll after ye, an' I'll have ye!" Biggrin charged after Drizzt, smelling the kill.

The drow sheathed his scimitar as he reached the main passage and looked for a spot to ambush the monster. Nothing presented itself, so he went halfway to the exit and waited.

"Where can ye hide?" Biggrin taunted as its huge bulk entered the corridor. Poised in the shadows, the drow threw his two knives. Both hit home, but Biggrin hardly slowed.

Drizzt moved outside the cave. He knew that if Biggrin didn't follow him, he would have to go back in; he certainly couldn't leave Wulfgar to die. The first rays of dawn had found their way onto the mountain, and Drizzt worried that the growing light would spoil any chance he had for ambush. Scrambling up one of the small trees that concealed the exit, he pulled out his dagger.

Biggrin charged out into the sunlight and looked around for signs of the fleeing drow. "Yer about, ye miserable dog! Ye've no place to run!"

Suddenly Drizzt was on top of the monster, gouging its face and neck in a barrage of stabs and slices. The giant howled in rage and jerked its massive body backward violently, sending Drizzt, who could not gain a firm hold with his weakened arm, flying back into the tunnel. The drow landed heavily on his injured shoulder and nearly swooned in agony. He squirmed and twisted for a moment, trying to regain his feet, but he bumped into a heavy boot. He knew that Biggrin couldn't have gotten to him so quickly. He turned slowly onto his back, wondering where this new giant had come from.

But the drow's outlook changed dramatically when he saw that Wulfgar stood over him, Aegis-fang firmly in his hand and a grim look stamped upon his face. Wulfgar never took his eyes off of the giant as it entered the tunnel.

"He's mine," the barbarian said grimly.

Biggrin looked hideous indeed. The side of its head where the hammer had struck was caked with dark, dried blood, while the other, and several spots on its face and neck, ran bright with blood from new wounds. The two knives Drizzt had thrown were still sticking in the giant's chest like morbid medals of honor.

"Can you take it again?" Wulfgar challenged as he sent Aegis-fang on a second flight toward the giant.

In answer, Biggrin stuck out his chest defiantly to block the blow. "I can take whatere' ye have t'give!" it boasted.

Aegis-fang slammed home, and Biggrin staggered back a step. The hammer had cracked a rib or two, but the giant could handle that.

More deadly, though, and unknown to Biggrin, Aegis-fang had driven one of Drizzt's knives through the lining of its heart.

"I can run, now," Drizzt whispered to Wulfgar when he saw the giant advancing again.

"I stay," the barbarian insisted without the slightest tremor of fear in his voice.

Drizzt pulled his scimitar. "Well spoken, brave friend. Let us fell this foul beast—there's food to be eaten!"

"Ye'll find that more a task than ye talk!" Biggrin retorted. It felt a sudden stinging in its chest, but it grunted away the pain. "I've felt the best that ye can hit, an' still I come at ye! Ye can no' hope t' win!"

Both Drizzt and Wulfgar feared that there was more truth to the giant's boasts than either of them would admit. They were on their last legs, wounded and winded, yet determined to stay and finish the task.

But the complete confidence of the great giant as it steadily approached was more than a little unnerving.

Biggrin realized that something was terribly wrong when it got within a few steps of the two companions. Wulfgar and Drizzt knew, too, for the giant's stride suddenly slowed visibly.

The giant looked at them in outrage as though it had been deceived. "Dogs!" it gasped, a gout of blood bursting from its mouth. "What trick . . ."

Biggrin fell dead without another word.

"SHOULD WE GO AFTER THE CAT?" WULFGAR ASKED WHEN THEY got back to the secret door.

Drizzt was wrapping a torch out of some rags he had found. "Faith in the shadow," he answered. "Guenhwyvar will not let the verbeeg escape. Besides, I have a good meal waiting for me back in the cave."

"You go," Wulfgar told him. "I shall stay here and watch for the cat's return."

Drizzt clasped the big man's shoulder as he started to leave. They had been through a lot in the short time they had been together, and Drizzt suspected that the excitement was just beginning. The drow sang a feasting song as he started to the main passage, but only as a dodge to Wulfgar, for the dinner table wouldn't be his first stop. The giant they had spoken with earlier had been evasive when asked about what lay down the one tunnel they had yet to explore. And with everything else they had found, Drizzt believed that could only mean one thing—treasure.

THE GREAT PANTHER LOPED ALONG OVER THE BROKEN STONES, easily gaining on the heavy-footed giant. Soon Guenhwyvar could hear the verbeeg's labored breathing as the creature struggled with every leap and climb. The giant was making for Daledrop and the open tundra beyond. But so frenzied was its flight that it didn't move off the face of Kelvin's Cairn to the easier ground of the valley. It sought a straighter route, believing it to be the quicker path to safety.

Guenhwyvar knew the areas of the mountain as well as its master, knew where every creature on the mountain laired. The cat had already discerned where it wanted the giant to go. Like a shepherd's dog, it closed the remaining distance and scratched at the giant's flanks, veering it into the direction of a deep mountain pool. The terrified verbeeg, certain that the deadly warhammer or darting scimitar weren't far behind, didn't dare stop and engage the panther. It surged blindly along the path Guenhwyvar had chosen.

A short time later, Guenhwyvar broke away from the giant and raced ahead. When the cat reached the edge of the cold water, it tilted its head and concentrated its keen senses, hoping to spy something that could help it complete the task. Then Guenhwyvar noticed a tiny shimmer of movement under the sparkles of the first light on the water. Its sharp eyes sorted out the long shape lying deathly still. Satisfied that the trap was set, Guenhwyvar moved back behind a nearby ledge to wait.

The giant lumbered up to the pool, breathing heavily. It leaned against a boulder for a moment, despite its terror. Things seemed safe enough for the moment. As soon as it had caught its breath, the giant looked around quickly for signs of pursuit, then started forward again.

There was only one path across the pool, a fallen log that spanned the center, and all the alternative routes around the pool, though the water wasn't very wide, weaved around sheer drops and jutting rock faces and promised to be slow going.

The verbeeg tested the log. It seemed sturdy, so the monster cautiously started across. The cat waited for the giant to get close to the center of the pool, then charged from its hiding place and launched itself into the air at the verbeeg. The cat landed heavily into the surprised giant, planting its paws in the monster's chest and rebounding back toward the safety of the shore. Guenhwyvar splashed into the icy pool but scrambled quickly out of the perilous water. The giant, though, swung its arms wildly for a moment, trying to hold its precarious balance, then toppled in with a splash. The water rushed up to suck it down. Desperately, the giant lunged for a nearby floating log, the shape that Guenhwyvar had recognized earlier.

But as the verbeeg's hands came down, the form it had thought to be a log exploded into movement as the fifty-foot water constrictor threw itself around its prey with dizzying speed. The unrelenting coils quickly pinned the giant's arms to its side and began their merciless squeeze.

Guenhwyvar shook the freezing water from its glistening black coat and looked back to the pool. As yet another length of the monstrous snake locked under the verbeeg's chin and pulled the helpless monster under the surface, the panther was satisfied that the mission was complete. With a long, loud roar proclaiming victory, Guenhwyvar bounded off toward the lair.

19

GRIM TIDINGS

Drizzt padded through the tunnels and past the bodies of the dead giants, slowing only to grab another hunk of mutton from the large table. He crossed through the support beams and started down the dim hallway, tempering his eagerness with common sense. If the giants had hidden their treasure down here, the chamber holding it might be behind a concealed door, or there might even be some beast, though not likely another giant, since it would have joined in the fighting.

The tunnel was quite long, running straight northward, and Drizzt figured that he was now moving underneath the mass of Kelvin's Cairn. He had passed the last torch, but he was glad for the darkness. He had lived the majority of his life traveling tunnels in the lightless subterranean world of his people, and his large eyes guided him in absolute darkness more accurately than in areas of light.

The hallway ended abruptly at a barred, iron-bound door, its metal holding bar locked into place by a large chain and padlock. Drizzt felt a pang of guilt for leaving Wulfgar behind. The drow had two weaknesses: foremost was the thrill of battle, but a close second was the tingle of uncovering the booty of his vanquished foes. It wasn't the gold or gems that lured Drizzt; he didn't care for wealth and rarely even kept any of the treasures he had won. It was simply the thrill of viewing them for the first time, the excitement of sifting through them and, perhaps, discovering some incredible artifact that had been lost to knowledge in ages past, or maybe the spellbook of an ancient and powerful mage.

His guilt flew away as he pulled a small lockpick from his belt-pouch. He had never been formally trained in the thieving arts, but he was as agile and coordinated as any master burglar. With his sensitive fingers and acute hearing, he wasn't particularly challenged by the clumsy lock; in a matter of seconds, it fell open. Drizzt listened carefully for any sounds behind the door. Hearing none, he gently lifted the large bar and set it aside. Listening one last time, he drew one of his scimitars, held his breath in anticipation, and pushed in the door.

His breath came back out with a disappointed sigh. The room beyond glowed with the waning light of two torches. It was small and empty, except for a large, metal-rimmed mirror standing in its center. Drizzt dodged out of the mirror's path, well aware of some of the strange magical properties these items had been known to exhibit, and moved in to examine it more closely.

It was about half the height of a man but propped up to eye level by an intricately worked iron stand. That it was lined in silver and in such an out-of-the-way chamber led Drizzt to believe that there was something more here than an ordinary mirror. Yet his scrutinizing inspection revealed no arcane runes or markings of any kind that hinted at its properties.

Able to discover nothing unusual about the piece, Drizzt carelessly stepped in front of the glass. Suddenly a pinkish mist began to swirl within the mirror, giving the appearance of a three-dimensional space trapped within the flatness of the glass. Drizzt jumped to the side, more curious than afraid, and watched the growing spectacle.

The mist thickened and puffed as though fed by some hidden fire. Then its center mushroomed out and opened into a clear image of a man's face, a gaunt, hollowed visage painted in the tradition of some of the southern cities.

"Why do you bother me?" the face asked at the empty room before the mirror. Drizzt took another step to the side, farther away from the apparition's line of sight. He considered confronting the mysterious mage, but figured that his friends had too much at stake for him to take such a reckless chance.

"Stand before me, Biggrin!" commanded the image. It waited for several seconds, sneering impatiently and growing increasingly tense. "When I discover which of you idiots inadvertently summoned me, I shall turn you into a coney and put you in a pit of wolves!" the image screamed wildly. The mirror flashed suddenly and returned to normal.

Drizzt scratched his chin and wondered if there was anything more he could do or discover here. He decided that the risks were simply too great at this time.

WHEN DRIZZT RETURNED THROUGH THE LAIR, HE FOUND WULFgar sitting with Guenhwyvar in the main passage just a few yards from the closed and barred front doors. The barbarian stroked the cat's muscled shoulders and neck.

"I see that Guenhwyvar has won your friendship," Drizzt said as he approached.

Wulfgar smiled. "A fine ally," he said, giving the animal a playful shake. "And a true warrior!" He started to rise but was thrown violently back to the floor.

An explosion rocked the lair as a ballista bolt slammed into the heavy doors, splintering their wooden bar and blasting them in. One of the doors broke cleanly in half and the other's top hinge tore away, leaving the door hanging awkwardly by its twisted bottom hinge.

Drizzt drew his scimitar and stood protectively over Wulfgar as the barbarian tried to regain his balance.

Abruptly, a bearded fighter leaped onto the hanging door, a circular shield, its standard a mug of foaming ale, slung over one arm and a notched and bloodstained battle-axe poised in the other. "Come out and play, giants!" Bruenor called, banging his shield with his axe—as if his clan hadn't already made enough noise to rouse the lair!

"Rest easy, wild dwarf," Drizzt laughed. "The verbeeg are all dead."

Bruenor spotted his friends and hopped down into the tunnel, soon followed by the rest of the rowdy clan. "All dead!" the dwarf cried. "Damn ye, elf, I knew ye'd keep all the play to yerself!"

"What about the reinforcements?" Wulfgar asked.

Bruenor chuckled wickedly. "Some faith, will ye, boy? They're lumped in a common hole, though buryin's too good for 'em, I say! Only one's alive, a miserable orc who'll breathe only as long as 'e wags 'is stinkin' tongue!"

After the episode with the mirror, Drizzt was more than a little interested in interrogating the orc. "Have you questioned him?" he asked Bruenor.

"Ah, he's mum for now," the dwarf replied. "But I've a few things should make 'im squeal!"

Drizzt knew better. Orcs were not loyal creatures, but under the enchantment of a mage, torturing techniques weren't usually much good. They needed something to counteract the magic, and Drizzt had a notion of what might work. "Go for Regis," he instructed Bruenor. "The halfling can make the orc tell us everything we want to know."

"Torturin'd be more fun," lamented Bruenor, but he, too, understood the wisdom of the drow's suggestion. He was more than a bit curious—and worried—about so many giants working together. And now with orcs beside them . . .

DRIZZT AND WULFGAR SAT IN THE FAR CORNER OF THE SMALL chamber, as far from Bruenor and the other two dwarves as they could get. One of Bruenor's troops had returned from Lonely-wood with Regis that same night, and though they were all exhausted from marching and fighting, they were too anxious about the impending information to sleep. Regis and the captive orc had moved into the adjoining room for a private conversation as soon as the halfling had gotten the prisoner firmly under his control with his ruby pendant.

Bruenor busied himself preparing a new recipe—giantbrain stew—boiling the wretched, foul-smelling ingredients right in a hollowed-out verbeeg skull. "Use yer heads!" he had argued in response to Drizzt and Wulfgar's expressions of horror and disgust. "A barnyard goose tastes better 'an a wild one cause it don't use its muscles. The same oughta hold true for a giant's brains!"

Drizzt and Wulfgar hadn't seen things quite the same way. They didn't want to leave the area and miss anything that Regis might have to say, though, so they huddled in the farthest corner of the room, carrying on a private conversation.

Bruenor strained to hear them, for they were talking of something that he had more than a passing interest in.

"Half for the last one in the kitchen," Wulfgar insisted, "and half for the cat."

"And you only get half for the one at the chasm," Drizzt retorted.

"Agreed," said Wulfgar. "And we split the one in the hall and Biggrin down the middle?"

Drizzt nodded. "Then with all halves and shared kills added up, it's ten and one-half for me and ten and one-half for you."

"And four for the cat," added Wulfgar.

"Four for the cat," Drizzt echoed. "Well fought, friend. You've held your own up to now, but I've a feeling that we have a lot more fighting before us, and my greater experience will win out in the end!"

"You grow old, good elf," Wulfgar teased, leaning back against the wall, the whiteness of a confident grin showing through his blond beard. "We shall see. We shall see."

Bruenor, too, was smiling, both at the good-natured competition between his friends and at his continued pride in the young barbarian. Wulfgar was doing well to keep pace with a skilled veteran like Drizzt Do'Urden.

Regis emerged from the room, and the gray pall upon his usually jovial face deadened the lighthearted atmosphere. "We are in trouble," the halfling said grimly.

"Where's the orc?" Bruenor demanded as he pulled his axe from his belt, misunderstanding the halfling's meaning.

"In there. He's all right," Regis replied. The orc had been happy to tell its newfound friend everything about Akar Kessell's plans to invade Ten-Towns and the size of the gathering forces. Regis visibly trembled as he told his friends the news.

"All of the orc and goblin tribes and verbeeg clans of this region of the Spine of the World are banding together under a sorcerer named Akar Kessell," the halfling began. Drizzt and Wulfgar looked at each other, recognizing Kessell's name. The barbarian had thought Akar Kessell to be a huge frost giant when the verbeeg had spoken of him, but Drizzt had suspected differently, especially after the incident at the mirror.

"They plan to attack Ten-Towns," Regis continued. "And even the barbarians, led by some mighty, one-eyed leader, have joined their ranks!"

Wulfgar's face reddened in anger and embarrassment. His people fighting beside orcs! He knew the leader that Regis spoke of, for Wulfgar was of the Tribe of the Elk and had even once carried the tribe's standard as Heafstaag's herald. Drizzt painfully recalled the one-eyed king, too. He put a comforting hand on Wulfgar's shoulder.

"Go to Bryn Shander," the drow told Bruenor and Regis. "The people must prepare!"

Regis winced at the futility. If the orc's estimation of the assembling army had been correct, all of Ten-Towns joined together could not withstand the assault. The halfling dropped his head and mouthed silently, not wanting to alarm his friends any more than was necessary, "We have to leave!"

THOUGH BRUENOR AND REGIS WERE ABLE TO CONVINCE CASsius of the urgency and importance of their news, it took several days to round up the other spokesmen for council. It was the height of knucklehead season, late summer, and the last push was on to land a big catch for the final trading caravan to Luskan. The spokesmen of the nine fishing villages understood their responsibilities to their community, but they were reluctant to leave the lakes even for a single day.

And so, with the exceptions of Cassius of Bryn Shander; Muldoon, the new spokesman from Lonelywood, who looked up to Regis as the hero of his town; Glensather of Easthaven, the community ever-willing to join in for the good of Ten-Towns; and Agorwal of Termalaine who held fierce loyalty to Bruenor, the mood of the council was not very receptive.

Kemp, still bearing a grudge against Bruenor for the incident over Drizzt after the Battle of Bryn Shander, was especially disruptive. Before Cassius even had the opportunity to present the Formalities of Order, the gruff spokesman from Targos leaped up from his seat and slammed his fists down on the table. "Damn the formal readings and be on with it!" Kemp growled. "By what right do you order us in from the lakes, Cassius? Even as we sit around this table, the merchants in Luskan are preparing for their journey!"

"We have news of an invasion, Spokesman Kemp," Cassius answered calmly, understanding the fisherman's anger. "I would not have summoned you, any of you, at this time of the season if it were not urgent."

"Then the rumors are true," Kemp sneered. "An invasion, you say? Bah! I see beyond this sham of a council!"

He turned on Agorwal. The fighting between Targos and Termalaine had escalated in the past few tendays, despite Cassius's efforts to diffuse it and bring the principals of the warring towns to the bargaining table. Agorwal had agreed to a meeting, but Kemp was steadfastly against it. And so, with suspicions running high, the timing of this urgent council could not have been worse.

"This is a pitiful attempt indeed!" Kemp roared. He looked around at his fellow spokesmen. "A pitiful effort by Agorwal and his scheming supporters to bring about a favorable settlement for Termalaine in their dispute with Targos!"

Incited by the aura of suspicion that Kemp had infused, Schermont, the new spokesman from Caer-Konig, pointed an accusing finger at Jensin Brent of Caer-Dineval. "What part have you played in this treachery?" he spat at his bitter rival. Schermont had come into his position after the first spokesman from Caer-Konig had been killed on the waters of Lac Dinneshere in a battle with a Dineval boat. Dorim Lugar had been Schermont's friend and leader, and the new spokesman's policies toward hated Caer-Dineval were even more iron-handed than those of his predecessor.

Regis and Bruenor sat back quietly in helpless dismay through all of the initial bickering. Finally Cassius slammed his gavel down, snapping its handle in two and quieting the others long enough to make a point. "A few moments of silence!" he commanded. "Hold your venomous words and listen to the messenger of grim tidings!" The others fell back to their seats and remained silent, but Cassius feared that the damage had already been done.

He turned the floor over to Regis.

Honestly terrified by what he had learned from the captive orc, Regis passionately told of the battle his friends had won over the verbeeg lair and on the grass of Daledrop. "And Bruenor has captured one of the orcs that was escorting the giants," he said emphatically. Some of the spokesmen sucked in their breath at the notion of such creatures banding together, but Kemp and some of the others, ever suspicious of the more immediate threats of their rivals, and already decided on the true purpose of the meeting, remained unconvinced.

"The orc told us," Regis continued grimly, "of the coming of a powerful wizard, Akar Kessell, and his vast host of goblins and giants! They mean to conquer Ten-Towns!" He thought that his dramatics would prove effective.

But Kemp was outraged. "On the word of an orc, Cassius? You summoned us in from the lakes at this critical time on the threat of a stinking orc?"

"The halfling's tale is not an uncommon one," Schermont added. "All of us have heard a captured goblin wag its tongue in any direction it could think of to save its worthless head."

"Or perhaps you had other motives," Kemp hissed, again eyeing Agorwal.

Cassius, though he truly believed the grim tidings, sat back in his chair and said nothing. With tensions on the lakes as high as they were, and the final trading fair of a particularly fruitless fishing season fast approaching, he had suspected that this would occur. He looked resignedly at Bruenor and Regis and shrugged as once again the council degenerated into a shouting match.

Amidst the ensuing commotion, Regis slipped the ruby pendant out from under his waistcoat and nudged Bruenor. They looked at it and each other in disappointment; they had hoped that the magical gem wouldn't be needed.

Regis pounded his gavel in a call for the floor and was granted it by Cassius. Then, as he had done five years previous, he hopped up on the table and walked toward his chief antagonist.

But this time the result wasn't what Regis had expected. Kemp had spent many hours over the last five years reflecting on that council before the barbarian invasion. The spokesman was glad of the final outcome of that whole situation, and in truth, realized that he and all of Ten-Towns were indebted to the halfling for making them heed his warning. Yet it bothered Kemp more than a little that his initial stance had been so easily swayed. He was a brawling type whose first love, even above fishing, was battle, but his mind was keen and always alert to danger. He had observed Regis several times over the last few years and had listened intently to tales of the halfling's prowess in the art of persuasion. As Regis approached, the burly spokesman averted his eyes.

"Be gone, trickster!" he growled, shoving his chair defensively back from the table. "You seem to have a strange way of convincing people of your point of view, but I'll not fall under your spell this time!" He addressed the other spokesmen. "Ware the halfling! He has some magic about him, be sure!"

Kemp understood that he would have no way of proving his claims, but he also realized that he wouldn't have to. Regis looked about, flustered and unable to even answer the spokesman's accusations. Even Agorwal, though the spokesman from Termalaine tactfully tried to hide the fact, would no longer look Regis straight in the eye.

"Sit down, trickster!" Kemp taunted. "Your magic's no good once we're on to you!"

Bruenor, silent up to now, suddenly leaped up, his face contorted with rage. "Is this, too, a trick, dog of Targos?" the dwarf challenged. He pulled a sack from his belt and rolled its contents, a severed verbeeg head, down the table toward Kemp. Several of the spokesmen jumped back in horror, but Kemp remained unshaken.

"We have dealt with rogue giants many times before," the spokesman replied coolly.

"Rogues?" Bruenor echoed incredulously. "Two score o' the beasts we cut down, orcs and ogres besides!"

"A passing band," Kemp explained evenly, stubbornly. "And all dead, so you have said. Why, then, does this become a matter for the council? If it is accolades you desire, mighty dwarf, then you shall have them!" His voice dripped with venom, and he watched Bruenor's reddening face with deep pleasure. "Perhaps Cassius could make a speech in your honor before all of the people of Ten-Towns."

Bruenor slammed his fists onto the table, eyeing all of the men about him in an open threat to anyone who would continue Kemp's insults. "We have come before ye to help ye save yer homes an' yer kin!" he roared. "Might be that ye believe us and ye'll do something to survive. Or might be that ye'll hear the word's o' the dog o' Targos and ye'll do nothin'. Either way, I've had enough o' ye! Do as ye will, and may yer gods show ye favor!" He turned and stalked out of the room.

Bruenor's grim tone brought many of the spokesmen to realize that the threat was simply too grave to be passed off as the deception of a desperate captive, or even as a more insidious plan by Cassius and some conspirators. Yet Kemp, proud and arrogant, and certain that Agorwal and his nonhuman friends, the halfling and the dwarf, were using the facade of an invasion to gain some advantage over the superior city of Targos, would not budge. Second only to Cassius in all of Ten-Towns, Kemp's opinion carried great weight, especially to the people of Caer-Konig and Caer-Dineval, who, in light of Bryn Shander's unshakable neutrality in their struggle, sought the favor of Targos.

Enough spokesmen remained suspicious of their rivals and were willing to accept Kemp's explanation to prevent Cassius from bringing the council to decisive action. The lines were soon clearly drawn.

Regis watched the spectacle as the opposing sides volleyed back and forth, but the halfling's own credibility had been destroyed, and he had no impact on the rest of the meeting. In the end, little was decided. The most that Agorwal, Glensather, and Muldoon could squeeze out of Cassius was a public declaration that, "A general warning should go out to every household in Ten-Towns. Let the people know of our grim tidings, and let them be assured that

I shall make room within the walls of Bryn Shander for every person who so desires our protection."

Regis eyed the divided spokesmen. Without unity, the halfling wondered how much protection even the high walls of Bryn Shander could offer.

20

A SLAVE TO NO MAN

"No arguin'," Bruenor snarled, though none of his four friends standing beside him on the rocky slopes of the climb had any intention of speaking against the decision. In their foolish pettiness and pride, the majority of the spokesmen had doomed their communities to almost certain destruction and neither Drizzt, Wulfgar, Catti-brie, nor Regis expected the dwarves to join in such a hopeless cause.

"When will you block the mines?" Drizzt asked. The drow hadn't yet decided if he would join the dwarves in the self-imposed prison of their caves, but he had planned to act as scout to Bryn Shander at least until Akar Kessell's army moved into the region.

"The preparin'll begin tonight," said Bruenor. "But once they're in place, we've no rush. We'll let the stinkin' orcs come right down our throats afore we drop the tunnels, an' take 'em in the fall. Are ye to stay with us, then?"

Drizzt shrugged his shoulders. Though he was still shunned by most of the people of Ten-Towns, the drow felt a strong sense of loyalty and wasn't sure that he could turn his back on his chosen home, even under suicidal circumstances. And Drizzt had little desire to return to the lightless underworld, even in the hospitable caverns of the dwarven town.

"And what's yer decision?" Bruenor asked Regis.

The halfling, too, was torn between his instincts for survival and his loyalty to Ten-Towns. With the help of the ruby, he had lived well during the last years on Maer Dualdon. But now his cover had been stripped away. After the rumors flowing out of the council, everyone in Bryn Shander whispered about the halfling's magical influence. It wouldn't be long before all of the communities heard about Kemp's accusations and avoided, if not openly shunned, him. Either way, Regis knew that his days of easy living in Lonelywood were nearing an end.

"Thank you for the invitation," he said to Bruenor. "I'll come in before Kessell arrives."

"Good," replied the dwarf. "Ye'll get a room near the boy, so none o' the dwarves has to hear yer bellyachin'!" He flashed Drizzt a good-natured wink.

"Nay," said Wulfgar. Bruenor looked at him curiously, misunderstanding the barbarian's intentions and wondering why he objected to having Regis beside him.

"Watch yerself, boy," the dwarf teased. "If ye're thinkin' ye're to be stayin' beside the girl, then be thinkin' about duckin' yer head from the swing o' me axe!"

Catti-brie chuckled softly, embarrassed yet truly touched.

"Your mines are not the place for me," Wulfgar said suddenly. "My life is on the plain."

"Ye forget that yer life is mine for choosin'!" Bruenor retorted. In truth, his yelling was more the short temper of a father than the outrage of a master.

Wulfgar rose before the dwarf, proud and stern. Drizzt understood and was pleased. Now Bruenor also had an idea of what the barbarian was getting at, and though he hated the thought of separation, he felt more pride in the boy at that moment than ever before.

"My time of indenture is not ended," Wulfgar began, "yet I have repaid my debt to you, my friend, and to your people many times over.

"I am Wulfgar!" he proudly proclaimed, his jaw firm and his muscles tightened with tension. "No more a boy but a man! A free man!"

Bruenor felt the moisture rimming his eyes. For the first time he did nothing to conceal it. He walked out before the huge barbarian and returned Wulfgar's unyielding stare with a look of sincere admiration.

"So ye are," Bruenor observed. "Then might I ask ye, on yer choice, if ye'll stay and fight beside me?"

Wulfgar shook his head. "My debt to you is paid, in truth. And forever I shall name you as my friend . . . dear friend. But I have another debt yet to pay." He looked out to Kelvin's Cairn and beyond. The countless stars shone clearly over the tundra, making the open plain seem even more vast and empty. "Out there, in another world!"

Catti-brie sighed and shuffled uncomfortably. She alone fully understood the vague picture that Wulfgar was painting. And she wasn't pleased with his choice.

Bruenor nodded, respecting the barbarian's decision. "Go then, and live well," he said, straining to hold his breaking voice even as he moved to the rocky trail. He paused for one last moment and looked back at the tall, young barbarian. "Yer a man, there's none to argue that," he said over his shoulder. "But don't ye never forget that ever ye'll be me boy!"

"I shan't," Wulfgar whispered softly as Bruenor disappeared into the tunnel. He felt Drizzt's hand on his shoulder.

"When do you leave?" the drow asked.

"Tonight," Wulfgar replied. "These grim days offer no leisure."

"And where do you go?" Catti-brie asked, already knowing the truth, and also the vague answer that Wulfgar would give.

The barbarian turned his misty gaze back out to the plain. "Home."

He started back down the trail, Regis following. But Catti-brie waited behind and motioned for Drizzt to do likewise.

"Say your farewells to Wulfgar this night," she told the drow. "I do not believe that he shall ever return."

"Home is a place for him to choose," Drizzt replied, guessing that the news about Heafstaag joining Kessell had played a part in Wulfgar's decision. He watched the departing barbarian with respect. "He has some private matters to attend to."

"More than you know," Catti-brie said. Drizzt looked at her curiously. "Wulfgar has an adventure in mind," she explained. She hadn't meant to break her trust with Wulfgar, but figured that Drizzt Do'Urden, above anyone else, might be able to find a way to help. "One that I believe has been put upon him before he is ready."

"Matters of the tribe are his own business," Drizzt said, guessing what the girl was suggesting. "The barbarians have their own ways and do not welcome outsiders."

"Of the tribes, I agree," said Catti-brie. "Yet Wulfgar's path, unless I am mistaken, does not lead directly home. He has something else ahead of him, an adventure that he has often hinted at but never fully explained. I only know that it involves great danger and a vow that even he fears is above his ability to fulfill alone."

Drizzt looked over the starry plain and considered the girl's words. He knew Catti-brie to be shrewd and observant beyond her years. He did not doubt her guesses.

The stars twinkled above the cool night, the celestial dome engulfing the flat rim of the horizon. A horizon as yet unmarked by the fires of an advancing army, Drizzt noted.

Perhaps he had time.

ALTHOUGH CASSIUS'S PROCLAMATION REACHED EVEN THE MOST remote of the towns within two days, few groups of refugees came down the roads to Bryn Shander. Cassius had fully expected this, or he never would have made the bold offer of sheltering all who would come. Bryn Shander was a fair-sized city, and her present population was not as large as it had once been. There were many vacant buildings within the walls, and an entire section of the city, reserved for visiting merchant caravans, lay empty at the present time. However, if even half of the people of the other nine communities sought refuge, Cassius would be hard-pressed to honor his pledge.

The spokesman wasn't worried. The people of Ten-Towns were a hardy folk and lived under the threat of a goblin invasion every day. Cassius knew that it would take more than an abstract warning to make them leave their homes. And with the allegiance between the towns at such a low point, few of the town leaders would take any action at all to convince their people to flee.

As it turned out, Glensather and Agorwal were the only spokesmen to arrive at the gates of Bryn Shander. Nearly all of Easthaven stood behind their leader, but Agorwal had less than half of the people of Termalaine behind him. The rumors from the arrogant city of Targos, itself nearly as well-defended as Bryn Shander, made it clear that none of its people would leave. Many of Termalaine's fishermen, fearing the economic advantage that Targos would gain over them, had refused to give up the most lucrative month of the fishing season.

Such was also the case with Caer-Konig and Caer-Dineval. Neither of the bitter enemies dared give any edge to the other, and not a single person from either city fled to Bryn Shander. To the people of these embattled communities, the orcs were but a distant threat that would have to be dealt with if it ever materialized, but the fighting with their immediate neighbors was brutally real and evident in all their daily routines.

On the western outskirts, the town of Bremen remained fiercely independent of the other communities, viewing Cassius's offer as a feeble attempt by Bryn Shander to reaffirm its position of leadership. Good Mead and Dougan's Hole in the south had no intention of hiding in the walled city or of sending any troops to aid in the fighting. These two towns on Redwaters, smallest of the lakes and poorest in terms of knuckleheads, could not afford any time away from the boats. They had heeded the call for unity five years previous under the threat of a barbarian invasion, and though they had suffered the worst losses of all the towns in the battle, they had gained the least.

Several groups filtered in from Lonelywood, but many of the folk of the northernmost town preferred to stay out of the way. Their hero had lost face, and even Muldoon now viewed the halfling in a different light and passed the warning of invasion off as a misunderstanding, or perhaps even a calculated hoax.

The greater good of the region had fallen beneath the lesser personal gains of stubborn pride, with most of the people of Ten-Towns confusing unity with dependence.

REGIS RETURNED TO BRYN SHANDER TO MAKE SOME PERSONAL arrangements on the morning after Wulfgar departed. He had a friend coming from Lonelywood with his prized belongings, so he remained in the city, watching in dismay as the days drifted by without any real preparations being made to meet the coming army. Even after the council, the halfling had held out some hope that the people would realize the impending doom and band together, but now he came to believe that the dwarves' decision to abandon Ten-Towns and lock themselves into their mines was the only option they had if they wished to survive.

Regis partially blamed himself for the coming tragedy, convinced that he had gotten careless. When he and Drizzt had concocted plans to use political situations and the power of the ruby to force the towns into unity against the barbarians, they had spent many hours predicting the initial responses of the spokesmen and weighing the worth of each town's alliance. This time, though,

Regis had placed more faith in the people of Ten-Towns and in the stone, figuring that he could simply employ its power to sway any of the few remaining doubters of the severity of the situation.

Yet Regis could not sustain his own guilt as he heard the arrogant and mistrusting responses coming in from the towns. Why should he have to trick the people into defending themselves? If they were stupid enough to let their own pride bring about their destruction, then what responsibility, or even what right, did he have to rescue them?

"You get what you deserve!" the halfling said aloud, smiling in spite of himself when he realized that he was beginning to sound as cynical as Bruenor.

But callousness was his only protection against such a helpless situation. He hoped that his friend from Lonelywood would arrive soon.

His sanctuary lay underground.

AKAR KESSELL SAT ON THE CRYSTAL THRONE IN THE HALL OF Scrying, the third level of Cryshal-Tirith, his fingers tapping nervously on the arm of the great chair as he stared intently at the dark mirror before him. Biggrin was long overdue with the report on the reinforcement caravan. The last summons the wizard had received from the lair had been suspicious, with no one on the end to greet his reply. Now the mirror in the lair revealed only blackness, resisting all of the wizard's attempts to scry out the room.

If the mirror had been broken, Kessell would have been able to sense the shift in his visions. But this was more mysterious, for something he could not understand was blocking his distance sight. The dilemma unnerved him, made him think that he had been deceived or discovered. His fingers continued to rap nervously.

"Perhaps it is time to make a decision," Errtu, in its customary place at the side of the wizard's throne, suggested.

"We have not yet reached our fullest strength," Kessell retorted. "Many goblin tribes and a large clan of giants have not come in. And the barbarians are not yet ready."

"The troops thirst for battle," Errtu pointed out. "They fight with each other—you may find that your army will soon fall apart around you!"

Kessell agreed that holding so many goblin tribes together for long was a risky and dangerous proposition. Perhaps it would be better if they marched at once. But still, the wizard wanted to be certain. He wanted his forces at their strongest.

"Where is Biggrin?" Kessell wailed. "Why hasn't he answered my summons?"

"What preparations are the humans now making?" Errtu asked abruptly.

But Kessell was not listening. He rubbed the sweat from his face. Maybe the shard and the demon had been right about sending the less conspicuous barbarians to the lair. What must the fishermen be thinking if they found such an unusual combination of monsters lairing in their area? How much had they guessed?

Errtu noted Kessell's discomfort with grim satisfaction.

The demon and the shard had been pushing Kessell to strike much earlier, as soon as Biggrin's messages had stopped coming in. But the cowardly wizard, needing more assurance that his numbers were overwhelming, had continued to delay.

"Shall I go to the troops?" Errtu asked, confident that Kessell's resistance was gone.

"Send runners to the barbarians and to the tribes that have not yet joined us," Kessell instructed. "Tell them that to fight beside us is to join in the feast of victory! But those who do not fight beside us shall fall before us! Tomorrow we march!"

Errtu rushed from the tower without delay, and soon cheers for the onset of war echoed throughout the huge encampment. Goblins and giants raced excitedly about, breaking down tents and packing supplies. They had anticipated this moment for long tendays, and now they wasted no time in making the final preparations.

That same night, the vast army of Akar Kessell pulled up its camp and began its long march toward Ten-Towns.

Back in the routed verbeeg lair, the scrying mirror sat unmoved and unbroken, securely covered by the heavy blanket that Drizzt Do'Urden had thrown over it.

EPILOGUE

He ran under the bright sun of day, he ran under the dim stars of the night, ever with the east wind in his face. His long legs and great strides carried him tirelessly, a mere speck of movement in the empty plain. For days Wulfgar pushed himself to the absolute limits of his endurance, even hunting and eating on the run, stopping only when exhaustion felled him in his tracks.

Far to the south of him, rolling out of the Spine of the World like a toxic cloud of foul-smelling vapors, came the goblin and giant forces of Akar Kessell. With minds warped by the willpower of the Crystal Shard, they wanted only to kill, only to destroy. Only to please Akar Kessell.

Three days out from the dwarven valley, the barbarian came across the jumbled tracks of many warriors all leading toward a common destination. He was glad that he was able to find his people so easily, but the presence of so many tracks told him that the tribes were gathering, a fact that only emphasized the urgency of his mission. Spurred by necessity, he charged onward.

It wasn't fatigue but solitude that was Wulfgar's greatest enemy. He fought hard to keep his thoughts on the past during the long hours, recalling his vow to his dead father and contemplating the possibilities of his victories. He avoided any thought of his present path, though, understanding well that the sheer desperation of his plan might well destroy his resolve.

Yet this was his only chance. He was not of noble blood, and he had no Rights of Challenge against Heafstaag. Even if he defeated the chosen king, none of his people would recognize him as their leader. The only way that one such as he could legitimatize a claim to tribal kingship was through an act of heroic proportions.

He bounded on, toward the same goal that had lured many would-be kings before him to their deaths. And in the shadows behind him, cruising with the graceful ease that marked his race, came Drizzt Do'Urden.

Ever eastward, toward the Reghed Glacier and a place called Evermelt.

Toward the lair of Ingeloakastimizilian, the white dragon the barbarians simply called "Icingdeath."

PART THREE
CRYSHAL-TIRITH

What does Wulfgar see when he looks out over the tundra—
when his crystal blue eyes stare across the dark plain to the
points of light that mark the fires of his people's encampment?

Does he view the past, perhaps, with a longing to return to
that place and those ways? Does he view the present,
comparing that which he has learned with me and Bruenor with
those harsh lessons of life among his nomadic tribesmen?

Or does Wulfgar see the future, the potential for change, for
bringing new and better ways to his people?

A bit of all three, I would guess. That is the turmoil within
Wulfgar, I suspect, the simmering fire behind those blue eyes. He
fights with such passion! Some of that comes from his
upbringing among the fierce tribesmen, the war games of the
barbarian boys, often bloody, sometimes even fatal. Part of that
passion for battle stems from Wulfgar's inner turmoil, the
frustration he must feel when he contrasts his lessons at my
hands and at Bruenor's hands with those gained in his years
among his own people.

Wulfgar's people invaded Ten-Towns, entered with merciless
rage ready to slaughter anyone who stood in their path without

regard. How does Wulfgar reconcile that truth with the fact
that Bruenor Battlehammer did not let him die on the field,
that the dwarf saved him, though he tried to kill Bruenor in
battle (though the foolish young lad made the mistake of
swatting Bruenor on the head!)? How does Wulfgar reconcile
the love Bruenor has shown him against his previous notions of
dwarves as hateful, merciless enemies? For that is how the
barbarians of Icewind Dale surely view dwarves, a lie that they
perpetuate among themselves so they may justify their
murderous raiding ways. It is not so different than the lies that
the drow tell themselves to justify their hatred of anyone who is
not drow.

But now Wulfgar has been faced with the truth of Bruenor
and the dwarves. Irrevocably. He must weigh that personal
revelation against every "truth" he spent his years of childhood
learning. He must come to accept that what his parents and all
the elders of the tribe told to him were lies. I know from
personal experience that this is no easy thing to reconcile. For to
do so is to admit that a great part of your own life was no more
than a lie, that a great part of that which makes you who you
are is wrong. I recognized the ills of Menzoberranzan early on,
because its teachings went against logic and went against that
which was in my heart. Yet even though those wrongs were
painfully obvious, those first steps that carried me out of my
homeland were not easy ones.

The errors of the barbarians of Icewind Dale pale compared
to those of the drow, and so the steps that Wulfgar must take
emotionally away from his people will be even more difficult, I
fear. There is far more truth in the ways of the barbarians, more
justification for their actions, warlike though they may be, yet it
falls upon Wulfgar's strong, but painfully young, shoulders to
differentiate between the ways of his people and those of his new
friends, to accept compassion and acceptance above the solid
walls of prejudice that have so encapsulated his entire youth.

I do not envy him the task before him, the confusion, the frustration.

It is good that he fights every day — I only pray that in a blind fit while playing out that frustration, my sparring companion does not tear the head from my shoulders.

—Drizzt Do'Urden

21
THE ICY TOMB

At the base of the great glacier, hidden off in a small dell where one of the ice spurs wound through broken rifts and boulders, was a place the barbarians called Evermelt. A hot spring fed a small pool, the warmed waters waging a relentless battle against ice floes and freezing temperatures. Tribesmen stranded inland by early snows, who could not find their way to the sea with the reindeer herd, often sought refuge at Evermelt, for even in the coldest months of winter, unfrozen, sustaining water could be found here. And the warming vapors of the pool made the temperatures of the immediate area bearable, if not comfortable. Yet the warmth and drinking water were only a part of Evermelt's worth.

Beneath the opaque surface of the misty water lay a hoard of gems and jewels, gold and silver, that rivaled the treasure of any king in this entire region of the world. Every barbarian had heard of the legend of the white dragon, but most considered it to be just a fanciful tale recounted by self-important old men for the amusement of children. For the dragon hadn't emerged from its hidden lair in many, many years.

Wulfgar knew better, though. In his youth his father had accidentally stumbled upon the entrance to the secret cave. When

Beornegar later learned the legend of the dragon, he understood the potential value of his discovery and had spent years collecting all of the information he could find concerning dragons, especially white dragons, and Ingeloakastimizilian in particular.

Beornegar had been killed in a battle between tribes before he could make his attempt at the treasure, but living in a land where death was a common visitor, he had foreseen that grim possibility and had imparted his knowledge to his son. The secret did not die with him.

WULFGAR FELLED A DEER WITH A THROW OF AEGIS-FANG AND carried the beast the last few miles to Evermelt. He had been to this place twice before, but when he came upon it now, as always, its strange beauty stole his breath. The air above the pool was veiled in steam, and chunks of floating ice drifted through the misty waters like meandering ghost ships. The huge boulders surrounding the area were especially colorful, with varying hues of red and orange, and they were encapsulated in a thin layer of ice that caught the fire of the sun and reflected brilliant bursts of sparkling colors in startling contrast to the dull gray of the misted glacier ice. This was a silent place, sheltered from the mournful cry of the wind by walls of ice and rock, free of any distractions.

After his father was killed, Wulfgar had vowed, in tribute to the man, to make this journey and fulfill his father's dream. Now he approached the pool reverently, and though other matters pressed in on him, he paused for reflection. Warriors of every tribe on the tundra had come to Evermelt with the same hopes as he. None had ever returned.

The young barbarian resolved to change that. He firmed his proud jaw and set to work skinning the deer. The first barrier that he had to overcome was the pool itself. Beneath its surface the waters were deceptively warm and comfortable, but anyone who emerged from the pool into the air would be frozen dead in minutes.

Wulfgar peeled away the hide of the animal and began scraping away the underlying layer of fat. He melted this over a small fire until it attained the consistency of thick paint, then smeared it over every inch of his body. Taking a deep breath to steady himself and focus his thoughts on the task at hand, he took hold of Aegis-fang and waded into Evermelt.

Under the deadening veil of mist, the waters appeared serene, but as soon as he moved away from the edges of the pool, Wulfgar could feel the strong, swirling currents of the hot stream.

Using a jutting rock overhang as a guidepost, he approximated the exact center of the pool. Once there, he took a final breath and, confident of his father's instructions, opened himself to the currents and let himself sink into the water. He descended for a moment, then was suddenly swept away by the main flow of the stream toward the north end of the pool. Even beneath the mist the water was cloudy, forcing Wulfgar to trust blindly that he would break free of the water before his breath ran out.

He was within a few feet of the ice wall at the pool's edge before he could see the danger. He braced himself for the collision, but the current suddenly swirled, sending him deeper. The dimness darkened to blackness as he entered a hidden opening under the ice, barely wide enough for him to slip through, though the unceasing flow of the stream gave him no choice.

His lungs cried for air. He bit down on his lip to keep his mouth from bursting open and robbing him of the last wisps of precious oxygen.

Then he broke into a wider tunnel where the water flattened out and dropped below the level of his head. He hungrily gasped in air, but he was still sliding along helplessly in the rushing water.

One danger was past.

The slide twisted and turned, and the roar of a waterfall clearly sounded up ahead. Wulfgar tried to slow his ride, but couldn't find a handhold or any kind of a brace, for the floor and walls were of ice smoothed under centuries of the flowing stream. The barbarian tossed wildly, Aegis-fang flying from his hands as he futilely tried to drive them into the solid ice. Then he came into a wide and deep cavern and saw the drop before him.

A few feet beyond the crest of the fall were several huge icicles that stretched from the domed ceiling down below Wulfgar's line of sight. He saw his only chance. When he approached the lip of the drop, he sprang outward, wrapping his arms around an icicle. He dropped quickly as it tapered, but saw that it widened again as it neared the floor, as though a second icicle had grown up from the floor to meet this one.

Safe for a moment, he gazed around the strange cavern in awe. The waterfall captured his imagination. Steam rose from the chasm, adding surrealistic flavor to the spectacle. The stream poured over the drop, most of it continuing on its way through a small chasm, barely a crack in the floor thirty feet below at the base of the fall. The droplets that cleared the chasm, though, solidified as they separated from the main flow of the stream and bounced away in all directions as they hit the cavern's ice floor. Not yet completely hardened, the cubes stuck fast where they landed, and all about the base of the waterfall were strangely sculpted piles of broken ice.

Aegis-fang flew over the drop, easily clearing the small chasm to smash into one such sculpture, scattering shards of ice. Though his arms were numbed from the icicle slide, Wulfgar quickly rushed over to the hammer, already freezing fast where it had landed, and heaved it free of the ice's hardening grip.

Under the glassy floor where the hammer had cracked away the top layers, the barbarian noticed a dark shadow. He examined it more closely, then backed away from the grizzly sight. Perfectly preserved, one of his predecessors had apparently gone over the long drop, dying in the deepening ice where he had landed. How many others, Wulfgar wondered, had met this same fate?

He didn't have time to contemplate it further. One of his other concerns had been dispelled, for much of the cavern's roof was only a few feet below the daylit surface and the sun found its way in through those parts that were purely ice. Even the smallest glow coming from the ceiling was reflected a thousand times on the glassy floors and walls, and the whole cavern virtually exploded in sparkling bursts of light.

Wulfgar felt the cold acutely, but the melted fat had protected him sufficiently. He would survive the first dangers of this adventure.

But the spectre of the dragon loomed somewhere up ahead.

Several twisting tunnels led off of the main chamber, carved by the stream in long-past days when its waters ran high. Only one of these was large enough for a dragon, though. Wulfgar contemplated searching out the others first, to see if he might possibly find a less obvious way into the lair. But the glare and distortions of light and the countless icicles hanging from the ceiling like a predator's teeth dizzied him, and he knew that if he got lost or wasted too much time, the night would fall over him, stealing his light and dropping the temperature below even his considerable tolerance.

So he banged Aegis-fang on the floor to clear away any remaining ice that clung to it and started straight ahead down the tunnel he believed would lead him to the lair of Ingeloakastimizilian.

THE DRAGON SLEPT SOUNDLY BESIDE ITS TREASURE IN THE LARGest chamber of the ice caves, confident after many years of solitude that it would not be disturbed. Ingeloakastimizilian, more commonly known as Icingdeath, had made the same mistake that many of its kin, with their lairs in similar caves of ice, had made. The flowing stream that offered entrance to and escape from the caves had diminished over the years, leaving the dragon trapped in a crystalline tomb.

Icingdeath had enjoyed its years of hunting deer and humans. In the short time the beast had been active, it had earned quite a respectable reputation for havoc and terror. Yet dragons, especially white ones who are rarely active in their cold environments, can live many centuries without meat. Their selfish love of their treasure can sustain them indefinitely, and Icingdeath's hoard, though small compared to the vast mounds of gold collected by the huge reds and blues that lived in more populated areas, was the largest of any of the tundra-dwelling dragons.

If the dragon had truly desired freedom, it could probably have broken through the cavern's ice ceiling. But Icingdeath considered the risk too great, and so it slept, counting its coins and gems in dreams that dragons considered quite pleasant.

The slumbering worm didn't fully realize, though, just how careless it had become. In its unbroken snooze, Icingdeath hadn't moved in decades. A cold blanket of ice had crept over the long form, gradually thickening until the only clear spot was a hole in front of the great nostrils, where the rhythmic blasts of exhaled snores had kept the frost away.

And so Wulfgar, cautiously stalking the source of the resounding snores, came upon the beast.

Viewing Icingdeath's splendor, enhanced by the crystalline ice blanket, Wulfgar looked upon the dragon with profound awe. Piles of gems and gold lay all about the cavern under similar blankets, but Wulfgar could not pull his eyes away. Never had he viewed such magnificence, such strength.

Confident that the beast was helplessly pinned, he dropped the hammer's head down by his side. "Greetings, Ingeloakastimizilian," he called, respectfully using the beast's full name.

The pale blue orbs snapped open, their seething flames immediately apparent even under their icy veil. Wulfgar stopped short at their piercing glare.

After the initial shock, he regained his confidence. "Fear not, mighty worm," he said boldly. "I am a warrior of honor and shall not kill you under these unfair circumstances." He smiled wryly. "My lust shall be appeased by simply taking your treasure!"

But the barbarian had made a critical mistake.

A more experienced fighter, even a knight of honor, would have looked beyond his chivalrous code, accepted his good fortune as a blessing, and slain the worm as it slept. Few adventurers, even whole parties of adventurers, had ever given an evil dragon of any color such a chance and lived to boast of it.

Even Icingdeath, in the initial shock of its predicament, had thought itself helpless when it had first awakened to face the barbarian. The great muscles, atrophied from inactivity, could not resist the weight and grip of the ice prison. But when Wulfgar mentioned the treasure, a new surge of energy blew away the dragon's lethargy.

Icingdeath found strength in anger, and with an explosion of power beyond anything the barbarian had ever imagined, the dragon flexed its cordlike muscles, sending great chunks of ice flying away. The entire cavern complex trembled violently, and Wulfgar, standing on the slippery floor, was thrown down on his back. He rolled aside at the very last moment to dodge the spearlike tip of a falling icicle dislodged by the tremor.

Wulfgar regained his feet quickly, but when he turned, he found himself facing a horned white head, leveled to meet his eyes. The dragon's great wings stretched outward, shaking off the last remnants of its blanket, and the blue eyes bore into Wulfgar.

The barbarian desperately looked around for an escape. He pondered throwing Aegis-fang, but knew that he couldn't possibly kill the monster with a single strike. And inevitably, the killing breath would come.

Icingdeath considered its foe for a moment. If it breathed, it would have to settle for frozen flesh. It was a dragon, after all, a terrible worm, and it believed, probably rightly so, that no single human could ever defeat it. This huge man, however, and particularly the magical hammer, for the dragon could sense its might, disturbed the worm. Caution had kept Icingdeath alive through many centuries. It would not close to melee with this man.

The cold air gathered in its lungs.

Wulfgar heard the intake of air and reflexively dived to the side. He couldn't fully escape the blast that followed, a frosting cone of unspeakable cold, but his agility, combined with the deer fat, kept him alive. He landed behind a block of ice, his legs actually burned by the cold and his lungs aching. He needed a moment to recover, but he saw the white head lifting slowly into the air, taking away the angle of the meager barrier.

The barbarian could not survive a second breath.

Suddenly, a globe of darkness engulfed the dragon's head, and a black-shafted arrow, and then another, whirred by the barbarian and thudded unseen behind the blackness.

"Attack boy! Now!" cried Drizzt Do'Urden from the entrance to the chamber.

The disciplined barbarian instinctively obeyed his teacher. Grimacing through the pain, he moved around the ice block and closed in on the thrashing worm.

Icingdeath swung its great head to and fro, trying to shake free of the dark elf's spell. Hate consumed the beast as yet another stinging arrow found its mark. The dragon's only desire was to kill. Even blinded, its senses were superior; it marked out the drow's direction easily and breathed again.

But Drizzt was well-versed in dragon lore. He had gauged his distance from Icingdeath perfectly, and the strength of the deadly frost fell short. The barbarian charged in on the distracted dragon's side and slammed Aegis-fang with all of his great might against the white scales. The dragon winced in agony. The scales held under the blow, but the dragon had never felt such strength from a human and didn't care to test its hide against a second strike. It turned to release a third blast of breath on the exposed barbarian.

But another arrow cracked home.

Wulfgar saw a great gob of dragon blood splatter on the floor beside him, and he watched the globe of darkness lurch away. The dragon roared in anger. Aegis-fang struck again, and a third time.

One of the scales cracked and flaked away, and the sight of exposed flesh renewed Wulfgar's hopes of victory.

Icingdeath had lived through many battles, though, and was far from finished. The dragon knew how vulnerable it was to the powerful hammer and kept its concentration focused enough to retaliate. The long tail circled over the scaly back and cracked into Wulfgar just as the barbarian had begun another swing. Instead of the satisfaction of feeling Aegis-fang crushing through dragon flesh, Wulfgar found himself slammed against a frozen mound of gold coins twenty feet away.

The cavern spun all about him, his watering eyes heightening the starred reflections of light and his consciousness slipping away. But he saw Drizzt, scimitars drawn, advancing boldly toward Icingdeath. He saw the dragon poised to breathe again.

He saw, with crystalline clarity, the immense icicle hanging from the ceiling above the dragon.

Drizzt walked forward. He had no strategy against such a formidable foe; he hoped that he would spot some weakness before the dragon killed him. He thought that Wulfgar was out of the battle, and probably dead, after the mighty slash of the tail, and was surprised when he saw sudden movement off to the side.

Icingdeath sensed the barbarian's move as well and sent its long tail to squelch any further threat to its flank.

But Wulfgar had already played his hand. With the last burst of strength he could muster, he snapped up from the mound and launched Aegis-fang high into the air.

The dragon's tail struck home and Wulfgar didn't know if his desperate attempt was successful. He thought that he saw a lighter spot appear on the ceiling before he was thrown into blackness.

Drizzt bore witness to their victory. Mesmerized, the drow watched the silent descent of the huge icicle.

Icingdeath, blinded to the danger by the globe of darkness and thinking that the hammer had flown wildly, waved its wings. The clawed forelegs had just begun to lift up when the ice spear smashed into the dragon's back, driving it back to the floor.

With the ball of darkness planted on its head, Drizzt couldn't see the dragon's dying expression.

But he heard the killing "crack" as the whiplike neck, launched by the sudden reversal of momentum, rolled upward and snapped.

22

BY BLOOD OR BY DEED

The heat of a small fire brought Wulfgar back to consciousness. He came to his senses groggily and, at first, could not comprehend his surroundings as he wriggled out of a blanket that he did not remember bringing. Then he recognized Icingdeath, lying dead just a few yards away, the huge icicle rooted firmly in the dragon's back. The globe of darkness had dissipated, and Wulfgar gawked at how accurate the drow's approximated bowshots had been. One arrow protruded from the dragon's left eye, and the black shafts of two others stuck out from the mouth.

Wulfgar reached down to grasp the security of Aegis-fang's familiar handle. But the hammer was nowhere near him. Fighting the pervading numbness in his legs, the barbarian managed to stand up, searching around frantically for his weapon. And where, he wondered, was the drow?

Then he heard the tapping coming from a side chamber. Stifflegged, he moved cautiously around a bend. There was Drizzt, standing atop a hill of coins, breaking away its icy covering with Wulfgar's warhammer.

Drizzt noticed Wulfgar approaching and bowed low in greeting. "Well met, Dragon's Bane!" he called.

"And to you, friend elf," Wulfgar responded, thoroughly pleased to see the drow again. "You have followed me a long way."

"Not too far," Drizzt replied, chopping another chunk of ice off the treasure. "There was little excitement to be found in Ten-Towns, and I could not let you forge ahead in our competition of kills! Ten and one-half to ten and one-half," he declared, smiling broadly, "and a dragon to split between us. I claim half the kill!"

"Yours and well earned," Wulfgar agreed. "And claim to half the booty."

Drizzt revealed a small pouch hanging on a fine silver chain around his neck. "A few baubles," he explained. "I need no riches and doubt that I would be able to carry much out of here, anyway! A few baubles will suffice."

He sifted through the portion of the pile he had just freed from the ice, uncovering a gem-encrusted sword pommel, its black ada-mantite hilt masterfully sculpted into the likeness of the toothed maw of a hunting cat. The lure of the intricate workmanship pulled at Drizzt, and with trembling fingers he slid the rest of the weapon out from under the gold.

A scimitar. Its curving blade was of silver, and diamond-edged. Drizzt raised it before him, marveling at its lightness and perfect balance.

"A few baubles . . . and this," he corrected.

EVEN BEFORE HE HAD ENCOUNTERED THE DRAGON, WULFGAR wondered how he would escape the underground caverns. "The current of the water is too strong and the ledge of the waterdrop too high to go back through Evermelt," he said to Drizzt, though he knew that the drow would have surmised the same thing. "Even if we somehow find our way through those barriers, I have no more deer blubber to protect us from the cold when we leave the water."

"I also have no mind to pass through the waters of Evermelt again," Drizzt assured the barbarian. "Yet I rely on my considerable experience to bring me into such situations prepared! Thus the wood for the fire and the blanket that I put upon you, both wrapped in sealskin. And also this." He produced a three-pronged grapple and some light but strong cord from his belt. He had already discovered an escape route.

Drizzt pointed up to a small hole in the roof above them. The icicle that had been dislodged by Aegis-fang had taken part of the chamber's ceiling with it. "I cannot hope to throw the hook so high, but your mighty arms should find the toss a minor challenge."

"In better times, perhaps," relied Wulfgar. "But I have no strength to make the attempt." The barbarian had come closer to death than he realized when the dragon's breath had descended upon him, and with the adrenaline of the fight now used up, he felt the pervading cold keenly. "I fear that my unfeeling hands could not even close upon the hook!"

"Then run!" yelled the drow. "Let your chilled body warm itself."

Wulfgar was off at once, jogging around the wide chamber, forcing his blood to circulate through his numbed legs and fingers. In a short while, he began to feel the inner warmth of his own body returning.

It took him only two throws to put the grapple through the hole and get it to catch fast on some ice. Drizzt was the first to go, the agile elf veritably running up the cord.

Wulfgar finished his business in the cavern, collecting a bag of riches and some other items he knew he would need. He had much more difficulty than Drizzt in ascending the cord, but with the drow's assistance from above, he managed to scramble onto the ice before the westering sun dipped below the horizon.

They camped beside Evermelt, feasting on venison and enjoying a much-needed and well-deserved rest in the comfort of the warming vapors.

Then they were off again before dawn, running west. They ran side by side for two days, matching the frenzied pace that had brought them so far east. When they came upon the trails of the gathering barbarian tribes, both of them knew that the time had come for them to part.

"Farewell, good friend," said Wulfgar as he bent low to inspect the trails. "I shall never forget what you have done for me."

"And to you, Wulfgar," Drizzt replied somberly. "May your mighty warhammer terrorize your enemies for years to come!" He sped off, not looking back, but wondering if he would ever see his large companion alive again.

WULFGAR PUT ASIDE THE URGENCY OF HIS MISSION TO PAUSE and ponder his emotions when he first viewed the large encampment of the assembled tribes. Five years before, proudly carrying the standard of the Tribe of the Elk, the younger Wulfgar had marched to a similar gathering, singing the Song of Tempus and sharing strong mead with men who would fight, and possibly die, beside him. He had viewed battle differently then, as a glorious test of a warrior. "Innocent savagery," he mumbled, listening to the contradiction of the words as he recalled his ignorance in those days so long ago. But his perceptions had undergone a considerable change. Bruenor and Drizzt, by becoming his friends and teaching him the intricacies of their world, had personalized the people he had previously looked upon merely as enemies, forcing him to face the brutal consequences of his actions.

A bitter bile welled in Wulfgar's throat at the thought of the tribes launching another raid against Ten-Towns. Even more repulsive, his proud people were marching to war alongside goblins and giants.

As he neared the perimeter, he saw that there was no Hengorot, no ceremonial Mead Hall, in all the camp. A series of small tents, each bearing the respective standards of the tribal kings, comprised the center of the assembly, surrounded by the open campfires of common soldiers. By reviewing the banners, Wulfgar could see that nearly all of the tribes were present, but their combined strength was little more than half the size of the assembly five years previous. Drizzt's observations that the barbarians hadn't yet recovered from the massacre on Bryn Shander's slopes rang painfully true.

Two guardsmen came out to meet Wulfgar. He had made no attempt to conceal his approach, and now he placed Aegis-fang at his feet and raised his hands to show that his intentions were honorable.

"Who are you that comes unescorted and uninvited to the council of Heafstaag?" asked one of the guards. He sized up the stranger, greatly impressed by Wulfgar's obvious strength and by the mighty weapon lying at his feet. "Surely you are no beggar, noble warrior, yet you are unknown to us."

"I am known to you, Revjak, son of Jorn the Red," Wulfgar replied, recognizing the man as a fellow tribesman. "I am Wulfgar, son of Beornegar, warrior of the Tribe of the Elk. I was lost to you five years ago, when we marched upon Ten-Towns," he explained, carefully choosing his phrases to avoid the subject of their defeat. Barbarians did not talk of such unpleasant memories.

Revjak studied the young man closely. He had been friends with Beornegar, and he remembered the boy, Wulfgar. He counted the years, comparing the boy's age when he last saw him against the apparent age of this young man. He was soon satisfied that the similarities were more than coincidental. "Welcome home, young warrior!" he said warmly. "You have fared well!"

"I have indeed," replied Wulfgar. "I have seen great and wondrous things and learned much wisdom. Many are the tales that I shall tell, but in truth, I have not the time to idly converse. I have come to see Heafstaag."

Revjak nodded and immediately began leading Wulfgar through the rows of firepits. "Heafstaag will be glad of your return."

Too quietly to be heard Wulfgar replied, "Not so glad."

A CURIOUS CROWD GATHERED AROUND THE IMPRESSIVE YOUNG warrior as he neared the central tent of the encampment. Revjak went inside to announce Wulfgar to Heafstaag and returned immediately with the king's permission for Wulfgar to enter.

Wulfgar hoisted Aegis-fang upon his shoulder, but did not move toward the flap that Revjak held open. "What I have to say shall be spoken openly and before all the people," he said loudly enough for Heafstaag to hear. "Let Heafstaag come to me!"

Confused murmurs sprouted up all about him at these words of challenge, for the rumors that had been running throughout the crowd did not speak of Wulfgar, the son of Beornegar, as a descendant of royal bloodlines.

Heafstaag rushed out of the tent. He moved to within a few feet of the challenger, his chest puffed out and his one good eye glaring at Wulfgar. The crowd hushed, expecting the ruthless king to slay the impertinent youth at once.

But Wulfgar matched Heafstaag's dangerous stare and did not back away an inch. "I am Wulfgar," he proclaimed proudly, "son of Beornegar, son of Beorne before him; warrior of the Tribe of the Elk, who fought at the Battle of Bryn Shander; wielder of Aegis-fang, the Giant Foe"—he held the great hammer high before him—"friend to dwarven craftsmen and student to a ranger of Gwaeron Windstrom, giant-killer and lair-invader, slayer of the frost giant chieftain, Biggrin." He paused for a moment, his eyes squinted by a spreading smile, heightening the anticipation of his next proclamation. When he was satisfied that he held the crowd's fullest attention, he continued, "I am Wulfgar, Dragon's bane!"

Heafstaag flinched. No living man on all the tundra had claim to such a lofty title.

"I claim the Right of Challenge," Wulfgar growled in a low, threatening tone.

"I shall kill you," Heafstaag replied with as much calm as he could muster. He feared no man, but was wary of Wulfgar's huge shoulders and corded muscles. The king had no intention of risking his position at this time, on the brink of an apparent victory over the fishermen of Ten-Towns. If he could discredit the young warrior, then the people would never allow such a fight. They would force Wulfgar to relinquish his claim, or they would kill him at once. "By what birthright do you make such a claim?"

"You would lead our people at the beckon of a wizard," Wulfgar retorted. He listened closely to the sounds of the crowd to measure their approval or disapproval of his accusation. "You would have them raise their swords in a common cause with goblins and orcs!" No one dared protest aloud, but Wulfgar could sense that many of the other warriors were secretly enraged about the coming battle. That would explain the absence of the Mead Hall, as well, for Heafstaag was wise enough to realize that simmering anger often exploded in the high emotions of such a celebration.

Revjak interposed before Heafstaag could reply with words or with weapon. "Son of Beornegar," Revjak said firmly, "you have as yet earned no right to question the orders of the king. You have declared an open challenge; the rules of tradition demand that you justify, by blood or by deed, your right to such a fight."

Excitement revealed itself in Revjak's words, and Wulfgar knew immediately that his father's old friend had intervened to prevent the start of an unrecognized, and therefore unofficial, brawl. The older man obviously had faith that the impressive young warrior could comply with the demands. And Wulfgar further sensed that Revjak, and perhaps many others, hoped the challenge would be successfully carried through.

Wulfgar straightened his shoulders and grinned confidently at his opponent, gaining strength in the continuing proof that his people were following Heafstaag's ignoble course simply because they were bound to the one-eyed king and could produce no suitable challengers to defeat him.

"By deed," he said evenly. Without releasing Heafstaag from his stare, Wulfgar unstrapped the rolled blanket he carried on his back and produced two spearlike objects. He tossed them casually to the ground before the king. Those in the crowd who could clearly see the spectacle gasped in unison, and even unshakable Heafstaag paled and rocked back a step.

"The challenge cannot be denied!" cried Revjak.

The horns of Icingdeath.

THE COLD SWEAT ON HEAFSTAAG'S FACE REVEALED HIS TENSION as he buffed the last burrs from the head of his huge axe. "Dragon's bane!" he huffed unconvincingly to his standard bearer, who had just entered the tent. "More likely that he stumbled upon a sleeping worm!"

"Your pardon, mighty king," the young man said. "Revjak has sent me to tell you that the appointed time is upon us."

"Good!" sneered Heafstaag, running his thumb across the shining edge of the axe. "I shall teach the son of Beornegar to respect his king!"

The warriors from the Tribe of the Elk formed a circle around the combatants. Though this was a private event for Heafstaag's people, the other tribes watched with interest from a respectable distance. The winner would hold no formal authority over them, but he would be the king of the most powerful and dominant tribe on the tundra.

Revjak stepped within the circle and moved between the two opponents. "I proclaim Heafstaag!" he cried, "King of the Tribe of the Elk!" He went on to read the one-eyed king's long list of heroic deeds.

Heafstaag's confidence seemed to return during the reciting, though he was a bit confused and angry that Revjak had chosen to proclaim him first. He placed his hands on his wide hips and glared around threateningly at the closest onlookers, smiling as they backed away from him, one by one. He did the same to his opponent, but again his bullying tactics failed to intimidate Wulfgar.

"And I proclaim Wulfgar," Revjak continued, "son of Beornegar and challenger to the throne of the Tribe of the Elk!" The reciting of Wulfgar's list took much less time than Heafstaag's, of course. But the final deed that Revjak proclaimed brought a degree of parity to the two.

"Dragon's bane!" Revjak cried, and the crowd, respectfully silent up to this point, excitedly began recounting the numerous rumors that had begun concerning Wulfgar's slaying of Icingdeath.

Revjak looked to the two combatants and stepped out of the circle.

The moment of honor was upon them.

They waded around the circle of battle, cautiously stalking and measuring each other for hints of weakness. Wulfgar noted the impatience on Heafstaag's face, a common flaw among barbarian warriors. He would have been much the same were it not for the blunt lessons of Drizzt Do'Urden. A thousand humiliating slaps from the drow's scimitars had taught Wulfgar that the first blow was not nearly as important as the last.

Finally, Heafstaag snorted and roared in. Wulfgar also growled aloud, moving as if he would meet the charge head-on. But then he sidestepped at the last moment and Heafstaag, pulled by the momentum of his heavy weapon, stumbled past his foe and into the first rank of onlookers.

The one-eyed king recovered quickly and charged back out, doubly enraged, or so Wulfgar believed. Heafstaag had been king for many years and had fought in countless battles. If he had never learned to adjust his fighting technique, he would have long ago been slain. He came at Wulfgar again, by all appearances more out of control than the first time. But when Wulfgar moved out of the path, he found Heafstaag's great axe waiting for him. The one-eyed king, anticipating the dodge, swung his weapon sideways, gashing Wulfgar's arm from shoulder to elbow.

Wulfgar reacted quickly, thrusting Aegis-fang out defensively to deter any follow-up attacks. He had little weight behind his swing, but its aim was true and the powerful hammer knocked

Heafstaag back a step. Wulfgar took a moment to examine the blood on his arm.

He could continue the fight.

"You parry well," Heafstaag growled as he squared off just a few steps from his challenger. "You would have served our people well in the ranks. A loss it is that I must kill you!" Again the axe arced in, raining blow after blow in a furious assault meant to end the fight quickly.

But compared to the whirring blades of Drizzt Do'Urden, Heafstaag's axe seemed to move sluggishly. Wulfgar had no trouble deflecting the attacks, even countering now and then with a measured jab that thudded into Heafstaag's broad chest.

Blood of frustration and weariness reddened the one-eyed king's face. "A tiring opponent will often move with all of his strength at once," Drizzt had explained to Wulfgar during the ten-days of training. "But rarely will he move in the apparent direction, the direction that he thinks you think he is moving in."

Wulfgar watched intently for the expected feint.

Resigned that he could not break through the skilled defenses of his younger and faster foe, the sweating king brought the great axe up over his head and lunged forward, yelling wildly to emphasize the attack.

But Wulfgar's reflexes were honed to their finest fighting edge, and the overemphasis that Heafstaag placed upon the attack told him to expect a change in direction. He raised Aegis-fang as if to block the feigned blow, but reversed his grip even as the axe dropped down off of Heafstaag's shoulder and came in deceptively low in a sidelong swipe.

Trusting fully in his dwarven-crafted weapon, Wulfgar shifted his front foot back, turning to meet the oncoming blade with a similarly angled cut from Aegis-fang.

The heads of the two weapons slammed together with incredible force. Heafstaag's axe shattered in his hands, and the violent vibrations knocked him backward to the ground.

Aegis-fang was unharmed. Wulfgar could have easily walked over and finished Heafstaag with a single blow.

Revjak clenched his fist in anticipation of Wulfgar's imminent victory.

"Never confuse honor with stupidity!" Drizzt had scolded Wulfgar after his dangerous inaction with the dragon. But Wulfgar wanted more from this battle than to simply win the leadership of his tribe; he wanted to leave a lasting impression on all of the witnesses. He dropped Aegis-fang to the ground and approached Heafstaag on even terms.

The barbarian king didn't question his good fortune. He sprang at Wulfgar, wrapping his arms about the younger man in an attempt to drive him backward to the ground.

Wulfgar leaned forward to meet the attack, planting his mighty legs firmly, and stopped the heavier man in his tracks.

They grappled viciously, exchanging heavy blows before managing to lock each other close enough to render punches ineffective. Both combatants' eyes were blue and puffy, bruises and cuts welled on face and chest alike.

Heafstaag was the wearier, though, his barrel chest heaving with each labored breath. He wrapped his arms around Wulfgar's waist and tried again to twist his relentless opponent to the ground.

Then Wulfgar's long fingers locked onto the sides of Heafstaag's head. The younger man's knuckles whitened, the huge muscles in his forearms and shoulders tightened. He began to squeeze.

Heafstaag knew at once that he was in trouble, for Wulfgar's grip was mightier than a white bear's. The king struggled wildly, his huge fists slugging into Wulfgar's exposed ribs, hoping only to break Wulfgar's deadly concentration.

This time one of Bruenor's lessons spurred him on: "Think o' the weasel, boy, take the minor hits, but never, never let 'em go once yer on!" His neck and shoulder muscles bulged as he drove the one-eyed king to his knees.

Horrified at the power of the grip, Heafstaag pulled at the

younger man's iron-hard forearms, trying vainly to relieve the growing pressure.

Wulfgar realized that he was about to kill one of his own tribe. "Yield!" he shouted at Heafstaag, seeking some more acceptable alternative.

The proud king answered with a final punch.

Wulfgar turned his eyes to the sky. "I am not like him!" he yelled helplessly, vindicating himself to any who would listen. But there was only one path left open to him.

The young barbarian's huge shoulders reddened as the blood surged through them. He saw the terror in Heafstaag's eye transcend into incomprehension. He heard the crack of bone, he felt the skull squash beneath his mighty hands.

Revjak should have then stepped into the circle and heralded the new King of the Tribe of the Elk.

But like the other witnesses around him, he stood unblinking, his jaw hanging open.

HELPED BY THE GUSTS OF THE COLD WIND AT HIS BACK, DRIZZT sped across the last miles to Ten-Towns. On the same night that he had split from Wulfgar, the snowcapped tip of Kelvin's Cairn came into view. The sight of his home drove the drow onward even faster, yet a nagging hint on the edge of his senses told him that something was out of the ordinary. A human eye could never have caught it, but the keen night vision of the drow finally sorted it out, a growing pillar of blackness blotting out the horizon's lowest stars south of the mountain. And a second, smaller column, south of the first.

Drizzt stopped short. He squinted his eyes to be sure of his guess. Then he started again, slowly, needing the time to sort through an alternate route that he could take.

Caer-Konig and Caer-Dineval were burning.

23

BESIEGED

Caer-Dineval's fleet trolled the southernmost waters of Lac Dinneshere, taking advantage of the areas left open when the people of Easthaven fled to Bryn Shander.

Caer-Konig's ships were fishing their familiar grounds by the lake's northern banks. They were the first to see the coming doom.

Like an angry swarm of bees, Kessell's foul army swept right around the northern bend of Lac Dinneshere and roared down Icewind Pass.

"Up anchor!" cried Schermont and many other ship's captains as soon as they had recovered from the initial shock. But they knew even then that they could not get back in time.

The leading arm of the goblin army tore into Caer-Konig.

The men on the boats saw the flames leap up as buildings were put to the torch. They heard the blood-crazed hoots of the vile invaders.

They heard the dying screams of their kin.

The women, children, and old men who were in Caer-Konig had no thoughts of resistance. They ran. For their lives, they ran. And the goblins chased them and cut them down.

Giants and ogres rushed down to the docks, squashing the pitiful humans who beckoned helplessly to the returning fleet, or forcing them into the cold death of the lake's waters.

The giants carried huge sacks, and as the brave fishermen rushed into port, their vessels were pummeled and crippled by hurled boulders.

Goblins continued to flow into the doomed city, yet the bulk of the vast army's trailing edge flowed past and continued on toward the second town, Caer-Dineval. By this time, the people in Caer-Dineval had seen the smoke and heard the screams and were already in full flight to Bryn Shander, or out on the docks begging their sailors to come home.

But Caer-Dineval's fleet, though they caught the strength of the east wind in their rush back across the lake, had miles of water before them. The fishermen saw the pillars of smoke growing over Caer-Konig, and many suspected what was happening and understood that their flight, even with their sails so full of wind, would be in vain. Still, groans of shock and disbelief could be heard on every deck when the black cloud began its ominous climb from the northernmost sections of Caer-Dineval.

Then Schermont made a gallant decision. Accepting that his own town was doomed, he offered his help to his neighbors. "We cannot get in!" he cried to a captain of a nearby ship. "Pass the word: away south! Dineval's docks are yet clear!"

FROM A PARAPET ON BRYN SHANDER'S WALL, REGIS, CASSIUS, Agorwal, and Glensather watched in horror as the wicked force flowed down the stretch away from the two sacked cities, gaining on the fleeing people of Caer-Dineval.

"Open the gates, Cassius!" Agorwal cried. "We must go out to them! They have no chance of gaining the city unless we slow the pursuit!"

"Nay," replied Cassius somberly, painfully aware of his greater responsibilities. "Every man is needed to defend the city. To go out onto the open plain against such overwhelming numbers would be futile. The towns on Lac Dinneshere are doomed!"

"They are helpless!" Agorwal shot back. "Who are we if we cannot defend our kinfolk? What right do we have to stand watching from behind this wall while our people are slaughtered?"

Cassius shook his head, resolute in his decision to protect Bryn Shander.

But then other refugees came running down the second pass, Bremen's Run, fleeing the open town of Termalaine in their hysteria when they saw the cities across the way put to the torch. More than a thousand refugees were now within sight of Bryn Shander. Judging their speed and the distance remaining, Cassius estimated that they would converge on the wide field just below the principal city's northern gates.

Where the goblins would catch them.

"Go," he told Agorwal. Bryn Shander couldn't spare the men, but the field would soon run red with the blood of women and children.

Agorwal led his valiant men down the northeastern road in search of a defensible position where they could dig in. They chose a small ridge, actually more like a crest where the road dipped slightly. Entrenched and ready to fight and die, they waited as the last of the refugees ran past, terrified, screaming because they believed they had no chance of reaching the safety of the city before the goblins descended upon them.

Smelling human blood, the fastest runners of the invading army were right behind the trailing people, mostly mothers clutching their babies. Intent on their easy victims, the lead monsters never even noticed Agorwal's force until the waiting warriors were upon them.

By then it was too late.

The brave men of Termalaine caught the goblins in a crossfire of arrows and then followed Agorwal into a fierce sword rush. They fought fearlessly, as men who had accepted what fate had dealt them. Dozens of monsters lay dead in their tracks and more fell with each passing minute as the enraged warriors pressed into their ranks.

But the line seemed endless. As one goblin fell, two replaced it. The men of Termalaine were soon engulfed in a sea of goblins.

Agorwal gained a high point and looked back toward the city. The fleeing women were a good distance across the field, but moving slowly. If his men broke their ranks and fled, they would overtake the refugees before the slopes of Bryn Shander. And the monsters would be right behind.

"We must go out and support Agorwal!" Glensather yelled at Cassius. But this time the spokesman from Bryn Shander remained resolute.

"Agorwal has accomplished his mission," Cassius responded. "The refugees will make the wall. I'll not send more men out to die! Even if the combined strength of all of Ten-Towns were on the field, it would not be able to defeat the foe before us!" Already the wise spokesman understood that they could not fight Kessell on even terms.

The kindly Glensather looked crestfallen. "Take some troops down the hill," Cassius conceded. "Help the exhausted refugees up the final climb."

Agorwal's men were hard-pressed now. The spokesman from Termalaine looked back again and was appeased; the women and children were safe. He scanned up to the high wall, aware that Regis, Cassius, and the others could see him, a solitary figure on the small rise, though he could not pick them out among the throng of spectators that lined Bryn Shander's parapets.

More goblins poured into the fray, now joined by ogres and verbeeg. Agorwal saluted his friends in the city. His contented smile was sincere as he spun around and charged back down the grade to join his victorious troops in their finest moment.

Then Regis and Cassius watched the black tide roll over every one of the brave men of Termalaine.

Below them, the heavy gates slammed shut. The last of the refugees were in.

WHILE AGORWAL'S MEN HAD WON A VICTORY OF HONOR, THE only force that actually battled Kessell's army that day and survived were the dwarves. The clan from Mithral Hall had spent days in industrious preparation for this invasion, yet it nearly passed them by altogether. Held by the wizard's compelling will into discipline unheard of among goblins, especially varied and rival tribes, Kessell's army had definite and direct plans for what they had to accomplish in the initial surge. As of this point, the dwarves were not included.

But Bruenor's boys had other plans. They weren't about to bury themselves in their mines without getting to lop off at least a few goblin heads, or without crushing the kneecaps of a giant or two.

Several of the bearded folk climbed to the southern tip of their valley. When the trailing edge of the evil army flowed past, the dwarves began to taunt them, shouting challenges and curses against their mothers. The insults weren't even necessary. Orcs and goblins despise dwarves more than anything else alive, and Kessell's straightforward plan flew from their minds at the mere sight of Bruenor and his kin. Ever hungry for dwarven blood, a substantial force broke away from the main army.

The dwarves let them close in, goading them with taunts until the monsters were nearly upon them. Then Bruenor and his kin slipped back over the rocky ledge and down the steep drop.

"Come an' play, stupid dogs," Bruenor chuckled wickedly as he disappeared from sight. He pulled a rope off of his back. There was one little trick he had thought up that he was anxious to try out.

The goblins charged into the rocky vale, outnumbering the dwarves four to one. And they were backed by a score of raging ogres.

The monsters didn't have a chance.

The dwarves continued to coax them on, down the steepest part of the valley, to the narrow, sloping ledges on the cliff face that crossed in front of the numerous entrances to the dwarven caves. An obvious place for an ambush, but the stupid goblins, frenzied at the sight of their most-hated enemies, came on anyway, heedless of the danger.

When the majority of the monsters were on the ledges and the rest were making the initial descent into the vale, the first trap was sprung. Catti-brie, heavily armed but positioned in the back of the inner tunnels, pulled a lever, dropping a post on the vale's upper crest. Tons of rocks and gravel tumbled down upon the tail of the monster's line, and those who managed to keep their precarious balance and escape the brunt of the avalanche found the trails behind them buried and closed to any escape.

Crossbows twanged from concealed nooks, and a group of dwarves rushed out to meet the lead goblins.

Bruenor wasn't with them. He had hidden himself farther back on the trail and watched as the goblins, intent on the challenge up ahead, passed him by. He could have struck then, but he was after larger prey, waiting for the ogres to come into range. The rope had already been carefully measured and tied off. He slipped one of its looped ends around his waist and the other securely over a rock, then pulled two throwing axes from his belt.

It was a risky ploy, perhaps the most dangerous the dwarf had ever tried, but the sheer thrill of it became obvious in the form of a wide grin across Bruenor's face when he heard the lumbering ogres approaching. He could hardly contain his laughter when two of them crossed before him on the narrow trail.

Leaping from his concealment, Bruenor charged at the surprised ogres and threw the axes at their heads. The ogres twisted and managed to deflect the halfhearted throws, but the hurled weapons were merely a diversion.

Bruenor's body was the true weapon in this attack.

Surprised, and dodging from the axes, the two ogres were put off balance. The plan was falling into place perfectly; the ogres could hardly find their footing. Twitching the powerful muscles in his stubby legs, Bruenor launched himself into the air, crashing into the closest monster. It fell with him onto the other.

And they tumbled, all three, over the edge.

One of the ogres managed to lock its huge hand onto the dwarf's face, but Bruenor promptly bit it, and the monster recoiled. For a moment, they were a falling jumble of flailing legs and arms, but then Bruenor's rope reached its length and sorted them out.

"'ave a nice landing, boys," Bruenor called as he broke free of the fall. "Give the rocks a big kiss for me!"

The backswing on the rope dropped Bruenor into the entrance of a mineshaft on the next-lowest ledge as his helpless victims dropped to their deaths. Several goblins in line behind the ogres had watched the spectacle in blank amazement. Now they recognized the opportunity of using the hanging cord as a shortcut to one of the caves, and one by one they climbed onto the rope and started down.

But Bruenor had anticipated this as well. The descending goblins couldn't understand why the rope felt so slick in their hands.

When Bruenor appeared on the lower ledge, the end of the rope in one hand and a lighted torch in the other, they figured it out.

Flames leaped up the oiled twine. The topmost goblin managed to scramble back on the ledge; the rest took the same route as the unfortunate ogres before them. One nearly escaped the fatal fall, landing heavily on the lower ledge. Before he could even regain his feet, though, Bruenor kicked him over.

The dwarf nodded approvingly as he admired the successful results of his handiwork. That was one trick he intended to remember. He slapped his hands together and darted back down the shaft. It sloped upward farther back to join the higher tunnels.

On the upper ledge, the dwarves were fighting a retreating action. Their plan was not to clash in a death fight outside, but to lure the monsters into the entrances of the tunnels. With the desire to kill blotting out any semblance of reason, the dimwitted invaders readily complied, assuming that their greater numbers were pushing the dwarves back into a corner.

Several tunnels soon rang out with the clash of sword on sword. The dwarves continued to back away, leading the monsters completely into the final trap. Then, from somewhere deeper in the caves, a horn sounded. On cue, the dwarves broke away from the melee and fled down the tunnels.

The goblins and ogres, thinking that they had routed their enemies, paused only to whoop out victory cries, then surged after the dwarves.

But deeper in the tunnels several levers were pulled. The final trap was sprung, and all of the tunnel entrances simply collapsed. The ground shook violently under the weight of the rock drop; the entire face of the cliff came crashing down.

The only monsters that survived were the ones at the very front of the lines. And disoriented, battered by the force of the drop and dizzied by the blast of dust, they were immediately cut down by the waiting dwarves.

Even the people as far away as Bryn Shander were shaken by the tremendous avalanche. They flocked to the north wall to watch the rising cloud of dust, dismayed, for they believed that the dwarves had been destroyed.

Regis knew better. The halfling envied the dwarves, safely entombed in their long tunnels. He had realized the moment he saw the fires rising from Caer-Konig that his delay in the city, waiting for his friend from Lonelywood, had cost him his chance to escape.

Now he watched helplessly and hopelessly as the black mass advanced toward Bryn Shander.

THE FLEETS ON MAER DUALDON AND REDWATERS HAD PUT BACK to their home ports as soon as they realized what was happening. They found their families safe for the present time, except for the fishermen of Termalaine who sailed into a deserted town. All that the men of Termalaine could do as they reluctantly put back out to sea was hope that their kin had made it to Bryn Shander or some other sanctuary, for they saw the northern flank of Kessell's army swarming across the field toward their doomed city.

Targos, the second strongest city and the only one other than Bryn Shander with any hope of holding out for any length of time against the vast army, extended an invitation for Termalaine's ships to tie up at her docks. And the men of Termalaine, soon to be numbered among the homeless themselves, accepted the hospitality of their bitter enemies to the south. Their disputes with Kemp's people seemed petty indeed against the weight of the disaster that had befallen the towns.

BACK IN THE MAIN BATTLE, THE GOBLIN GENERALS THAT LED Kessell's army were confident they could overrun Bryn Shander before nightfall. They obeyed their leader's plan to the letter. The main body of the army veered away from Bryn Shander and moved down the swath of open ground between the principal city and Targos, thus cutting any possibility of the two powerful cities linking their forces.

Several of the goblin tribes had broken away from the main group and were bearing down on Termalaine, intent on sacking their third city of the day. But when they found the place deserted, they abstained from burning the buildings. Part of Kessell's army now had a ready-made camp where they could wait out the coming siege in comfort.

Like two great arms, thousands of monsters raced south from the main force. So vast was Kessell's army that it filled the miles of field between Bryn Shander and Termalaine and still had enough numbers to encircle the hill of the principal city with thick ranks of troops.

Everything had happened so quickly that when the goblins finally stalled their frenzied charge, the change seemed overly dramatic. After a few minutes of breath-catching calm, Regis felt the tension growing once again.

"Why don't they just get it over with?" he asked the two spokesmen standing beside him.

Cassius and Glensather, more knowledgeable in the ways of warfare, understood exactly what was happening.

"They are in no hurry, little friend," Cassius explained. "Time favors them."

Then Regis understood. During his many years in the more populated southlands, he had heard many vivid tales describing the terrible horrors of a siege.

The image of Agorwal's final salute out in the distance came back to him then, the contented look on the spokesman's face and his willingness to die valiantly. Regis had no desire to die in any way, but he could imagine what lay before him and the cornered people of Bryn Shander.

He found himself envying Agorwal.

24

CRYSHAL-TIRITH

Drizzt soon came upon the battered ground where the army had crossed. The tracks came as no surprise to the drow, for the smoke pillars had already told him much of what had transpired. His only remaining question was whether or not any of the towns had held out, and he trotted on toward the mountain wondering if he had a home to return to.

Then he sensed a presence, an otherworldly aura that strangely reminded him of the days of his youth. He bent to check the ground again. Some of the marks were fresh troll tracks, and a scarring on the ground that could not have been caused by any mortal being. Drizzt looked around nervously, but the only sound was the mourn of the wind and the only silhouettes on the horizons were the peaks of Kelvin's Cairn before him and the Spine of the World far to the south. Drizzt paused to consider the presence for a few moments, trying to bring the familiarity he felt into better focus.

He moved on tentatively. He understood the source of his recollections now, though their exact details remained elusive. He knew what he was following.

A demon had come to Icewind Dale.

Kelvin's Cairn loomed much larger before Drizzt caught up to the band. His sensitivity to creatures of the lower planes, brought about by centuries of associating with them in Menzoberranzan, told him that he was nearing the demon before it came into sight.

And then he saw the distant forms, a half-dozen trolls marching in a tight rank, and in their midst, towering over them, was a huge monster of the Abyss. No minor mane or midge, Drizzt knew at once, but a major demon. Kessell must be mighty indeed if he held this formidable monster under his control!

Drizzt followed them at a cautious distance. The band was intent on their destination, though, and his caution was unnecessary. But Drizzt wasn't about to take any chances at all, for he had many times witnessed the wrath of such demons. They were commonplace in the cities of the drow, further proof to Drizzt Do'Urden that the ways of his people were not for him.

He moved in closer, for something else had grabbed his attention. The demon was holding a small object which radiated such powerful magic that the drow, even at this distance, could sense it clearly. It was too masked by the demon's own emanations for Drizzt to get any clear perspectives on it, so he backed off cautiously once again.

The lights of thousands of campfires came into view as the party, and Drizzt, approached the mountain. The goblins had set scouts in this very area, and Drizzt realized that he had gone as far south as he could. He broke off his pursuit and headed for the better vantage points up the mountain.

The time best suited to the drow's underworld vision was the lightening hours just before sunrise, and though he was tired, Drizzt was determined to be in position by then. He quickly climbed up the rocks, gradually working his way around to the southern face of the mountain.

Then he saw the campfires encircling Bryn Shander. Farther to the east, embers glowed in the rubble that had been Caer-Konig and Caer-Dineval. Wild shouts rang out from Termalaine, and

Drizzt knew that the city on Maer Dualdon was in the hands of the enemy.

And then predawn blued the night sky, and much more became apparent. Drizzt first looked to the south end of the dwarven valley and was comforted that the wall opposite him had collapsed. Bruenor's people were safe at least, and Regis with them, the drow supposed.

But the sight of Bryn Shander was less comforting. Drizzt had heard the boasts of the captured orc and had seen the tracks of the army and their campfires, but he could never have imagined the vast assemblage that opened up before him when the light increased.

The sight staggered him.

"How many goblin tribes have you collected, Akar Kessell?" he gasped. "And how many of the giants call you master?"

He knew that the people in Bryn Shander would survive only as long as Kessell let them. They could not hope to hold out against this force.

Dismayed, he turned to seek out a hole where he could get some rest. He could be of no immediate help here, and exhaustion was heightening his hopelessness, preventing him from thinking constructively.

As he started away from the mountain face, sudden activity on the distant field caught his attention. He couldn't make out individuals at this great distance, the army seemed just a black mass, but he knew that the demon had come forth. He saw the blacker spot of its evil presence wade out to a cleared area only a few hundred yards below the gates of Bryn Shander. And he felt the supernatural aura of the powerful magic he had earlier sensed, like the living heart of some unknown life form, pulsating in the demon's clawed hands.

Goblins gathered around to watch the spectacle, keeping a respectable distance between them and Kessell's dangerously unpredictable captain.

"What is that?" asked Regis, crushed in among the watching throng on Bryn Shander's wall.

"A demon," Cassius answered. "A big one."

"It mocks our meager defenses!" Glensather cried. "How can we hope to stand against such a foe?"

The demon bent low, involved in the ritual to call out the dweomer of the crystalline object. It stood the Crystal Shard upright on the grass and stepped back, bellowing forth the obscure words of an ancient spell, rising to a crescendo as the sky began to brighten with the sun's imminent appearance.

"A glass dagger?" Regis asked, puzzled by the pulsating object.

Then the first ray of dawn broke the horizon. The crystal sparkled and summoned the light, bending the sunbeam's path and absorbing its energy.

The shard flared again. The pulsations intensified as more of the sun crept into the eastern sky, only to have its light sucked into the hungry image of Crenshinibon.

The spectators on the wall gaped in horror, wondering if Akar Kessell held power over the sun itself. Only Cassius had the presence of mind to connect the power of the shard with the light of the sun.

Then the crystal began to grow. It swelled as each pulse attained its peak, then shrank back a bit while the next throb grew. Everything around it remained in shadow, for it greedily consumed all the sunlight. Slowly, but inevitably, its girth widened and its tip rose high into the air. The people on the wall and the monsters on the field had to avert their eyes from the brightened power of Cryshal-Tirith. Only the drow from his distant vantage point and the demon who was immune to such sights witnessed another image of Crenshinibon being raised. The third Cryshal-Tirith grew to life. The tower released its hold on the sun as the ritual was completed, and all the region was bathed in morning sunlight.

The demon roared at its successful spellcasting and strode

proudly into the new tower's mirrored doorway, followed by the trolls, the wizard's personal guard.

The besieged inhabitants of Bryn Shander and Targos looked upon the incredible structure with a confused mixture of awe, appreciation, and terror. They could not resist the unearthly beauty of Cryshal-Tirith, but they knew the consequences of the tower's appearance. Akar Kessell, master of goblins and giants, had come.

GOBLINS AND ORCS FELL TO THEIR KNEES, AND ALL THE VAST army took up the chant of "Kessell! Kessell!" paying homage to the wizard with a fanatical devotion that brought shivers to the human witnesses to the spectacle.

Drizzt, too, was unnerved by the extent of the influence and devotion the wizard exerted over the normally independent goblin tribes. The drow determined at that moment that the only chance for survival for the people of Ten-Towns lay in the death of Akar Kessell. He knew even before he had considered any of the possible options that he would try to get to the wizard. For now, though, he needed to rest. He found a shadowed hole just back from the face of Kelvin's Cairn and let his exhaustion overtake him.

Cassius was also tired. The spokesman had stayed on the wall throughout the cold night, examining the campsites to determine how much of the natural enmity between the unruly tribes remained. He had seen some minor discord and name-calling, but nothing extreme enough to give him hope that the army would fall apart early into the siege. He couldn't understand how the wizard had achieved such a dramatic unification of the arch foes. The appearance of the demon and the raising of Cryshal-Tirith had shown him the incredible power that Kessell commanded. He had soon drawn the same conclusions as the drow.

Unlike Drizzt, though, the spokesman from Bryn Shander did not retire when the field calmed again, despite the protests of Regis and Glensather, concerned for his health. On his shoulders,

Cassius carried the responsibility for the several thousand terrified
people that lay huddled within his city's walls, and there would be
no rest for him. He needed information; he needed to find a weak
link in the wizard's seemingly impregnable armor.

And so the spokesman watched diligently and patiently
throughout the first long, uneventful day of the siege, noting the
boundaries that the goblin tribes staked out as their own, and the
order of hierarchy that determined the distance of each group
from the center spot of Cryshal-Tirith.

AWAY TO THE EAST, THE FLEETS OF CAER-KONIG AND CAER-
Dineval moored alongside the docks of the deserted city of Easthaven. Several crews had gone ashore to gather supplies, but most
of the people had remained on the boats, unsure of how far east
Kessell's black arm extended.

Jensin Brent and his counterpart from Caer-Konig had taken
full control of their immediate situation from the decks of the
Mist Seeker, the flagship of Caer-Dineval. All disputes between
the two cities had been called off, temporarily at least—though
promises of continued friendship were heard on the decks of every
ship on Lac Dinneshere. Both spokesmen were agreed that they
would not yet leave the waters of the lake and flee, for they realized
that they had nowhere to go. All of the ten towns were threatened
by Kessell, and Luskan was fully four hundred miles away and
across the path of Kessell's army. The ill-equipped refugees couldn't
hope to reach it before the first of winter's snows caught up with
them.

The sailors that had disembarked soon returned to the docks
with the welcomed news that Easthaven had not yet been touched
by the darkness. More crews were ordered ashore to collect extra
food and blankets, but Jensin Brent played it cautiously, thinking
it wise to keep most of the refugees out on the water beyond Kessell's reach.

More promising news came a short time later.

"Signals from Redwaters, Spokesman Brent!" the watchman atop the *Mist Seeker*'s crow's nest called out. "The people of Good Mead and Dougan's Hole are unharmed!" He held up his news-bearer, a small glasspiece crafted in Termalaine and designed to focus the light of the sun for signaling across the lakes, using intricate though limited signaling codes. "My calls have been answered!"

"Where are they, then?" Brent asked excitedly.

"On the eastern banks," the watchman replied. "They sailed out of their villages, thinking them undefendable. None of the monsters have yet approached, but the spokesmen felt that the far side of the lake would be safer until the invaders have departed."

"Keep the communication open," Brent ordered. "Let me know when you have more news."

"Until the invaders have departed?" Schermont echoed incredulously as he moved to Jensin Brent's side.

"A foolishly hopeful assessment of the situation, I agree," said Brent. "But I am relieved that our cousins to the south yet live!"

"Do we go to them? Join our forces?"

"Not yet," answered Brent. "I fear that we would be too vulnerable on the open ground between the lakes. We need more information before we can take any effective action. Let us keep the communications flowing between the two lakes. Gather volunteers to carry messages to Redwaters."

"They shall be sent off immediately," agreed Schermont as he headed away.

Brent nodded and looked back across the lake at the dying plume of smoke above his home. "More information," he muttered to himself.

Other volunteers headed out later that day into the more treacherous west to scout out the situation in the principal city.

Brent and Schermont had done a masterful job in quelling the panic, but even with the substantial gains in organization, the initial shock of the sudden and deadly invasion had left most of the survivors of Caer-Konig and Caer-Dineval in a state of utter despair. Jensin Brent was the glowing exception. The spokesman from Caer-Dineval was a courageous fighter who steadfastly refused to yield until the last breath had left his body. He sailed his proud flagship around the moorings of the others, rallying the people with his cries of promised revenge against Akar Kessell.

Now he watched and waited on the *Mist Seeker* for the critical news from the west. In mid-afternoon, he heard the call he had prayed for.

"She stands!" the watcher on the crow's nest cried out ecstatically when the newsbearer's signal flashed in. "Bryn Shander stands!"

Suddenly, Brent's optimism took on credibility. The miserable band of homeless victims assumed an angry posture bent on vengeance. More messengers were dispatched at once to carry the news to Redwaters that Kessell hadn't yet achieved complete victory.

On both lakes, the task of separating the warriors from the civilians soon began in earnest, with the women and children moving to the heaviest and least seaworthy boats, and the fighting men boarding the fastest vessels. The designated warships were then moved to the outbound moorings, where they could put out quickly across the lakes. Their sails were checked and tightened in preparation for the wild run that would carry their brave crews to war.

Or, by Jensin Brent's furious decree, "The run that would carry their brave crews to victory!"

REGIS HAD REJOINED CASSIUS ON THE WALL WHEN THE NEWS-bearer's signal had been spotted on the southwestern banks of Lac Dinneshere. The halfling had slept for most of the night and day, figuring that he might as well die doing the thing he loved to do best. He was surprised when he awakened, expecting his slumber to last into eternity.

Cassius was beginning to view things a bit differently, though. He had compiled a long list of potential breakdowns in Akar Kessell's unruly army: orcs bullying goblins and giants in turn bullying both. If he could only find a way for them to hold out long enough for the obvious hatred between the goblin races to take its toll on Kessell's force. . . .

And then, the signal from Lac Dinneshere and subsequent reports of similar flashes on the far side of Redwaters had given the spokesman sincere hope that the siege might well disintegrate and Ten-Towns survive.

But then the wizard made his dramatic appearance and Cassius's hopes were dashed.

It began as a pulse of red light circling within the glassy wall at the base of Cryshal-Tirith. Then a second pulse, this one blue, started up the tower, rotating in the opposite direction. Slowly they circled the diameter of the tower, blending into green as they converged, then separating and continuing on their way. All who could see the tantalizing show stared apprehensively, unsure of what would happen next, but convinced that a display of tremendous power was forthcoming.

The circling lights sped up, their intensity increasing with their velocity. Soon the entire base of the tower was ringed in a green blur, so bright that the onlookers had to avert their eyes. And out of the blur stepped two hideous trolls, each bearing an ornate mirror.

The lights slowed and stopped altogether.

The mere sight of the disgusting trolls filled the people of Bryn Shander with revulsion, but intrigued, none would turn away. The monsters walked right to the base of the city's sloping hill and stood facing each other, aiming their mirrors diagonally toward each other, but still catching the reflection of Cryshal-Tirith.

Twin beams of light shot down from the tower, each striking one of the mirrors and converging with the other halfway between the trolls. A sudden pulse from the tower, like the flash of a lightning stroke, left the area between the monsters veiled in smoke, and when it cleared, instead of the converging beams of light, stood a thin, crooked shell of a man in a red, satiny robe.

Goblins fell to their knees again and hid their faces in the ground. Akar Kessell had come.

He looked up in the direction of Cassius on the wall, a cocky smile stretched across his thin lips. "Greetings, spokesman of Bryn Shander!" he cackled. "Welcome to my fair city!" He laughed wryly.

Cassius had no doubt that the wizard had picked him out, though he had no recollection of ever seeing the man and didn't understand how he had been recognized. He looked to Regis and Glensather for an explanation, but they both shrugged their shoulders.

"Yes, I know you, Cassius," Kessell said. "And to you, good Spokesman Glensather, my greetings. I should have guessed that you would be here; ever were the people of Easthaven willing to join in a cause, no matter how hopeless!"

Now it was Glensather's turn to stare dumbfounded at his companions. But again, there were no explanations forthcoming.

"You know of us," Cassius replied to the apparition, "yet you are unknown to us. It seems that you hold an unfair advantage."

"Unfair?" protested the wizard. "I hold every advantage, foolish man!" Again the laugh. "You know of me—at least Glensather does."

The spokesman from Easthaven shrugged his shoulders again in reply to Cassius's inquiring glance. The gesture seemed to anger Kessell.

"I spent several months living in Easthaven," the wizard snapped. "In the guise of a wizard's apprentice from Luskan! Clever, don't you agree?"

"Do you remember him?" Cassius asked Glensather softly. "It could be of great import."

"It is possible that he stayed in Easthaven," Glensather replied in the same whispered tones, "though no group from the Hosttower has come into my city for several years. Yet we are an open city, and many foreigners arrive with every passing trading caravan. I tell you the truth, Cassius, I have no recollection of the man."

Kessell was outraged. He stamped his foot impatiently, and the smile on his face was replaced by a pouting pucker.

"Perhaps my return to Ten-Towns will prove more memorable, fools!" he snapped. He held his arms outstretched in self-important proclamation. "Behold Akar Kessell, the Tyrant of Icewind Dale!" he cried. "People of Ten-Towns, your master has come!"

"Your words are a bit premature—" Cassius began, but Kessell cut him short with a frenzied scream.

"Never interrupt me!" the wizard shouted, the veins in his neck taut and bulging and his face turning as red as blood.

Then, as Cassius quieted in disbelief, Kessell seemed to regain a measure of his composure. "You shall learn better, proud Cassius," he threatened. "You shall learn!"

He turned back to Cryshal-Tirith and uttered a simple word of command. The tower went black for a moment, as though it refused to release the reflections of the sun's light. Then it began to glow, far within its depths, with a light that seemed more its own than a reflection of the day. With each passing second, the hue shifted and the light began to climb and circle the strange walls.

"Behold Akar Kessell!" the wizard proclaimed, still frowning. "Look upon the splendor of Crenshinibon and surrender all hope!"

More lights began flashing within the tower's walls, climbing and dropping randomly and spinning about the structure in a frenzied dance that cried out for release. Gradually they were working their way up to the pointed pinnacle, and it began to flare as if on fire, shifting through the colors of the spectrum until its white flame rivaled the brightness of the sun itself.

Kessell cried out as a man in ecstasy.

The fire was released.

It shot out in a thin, searing line northward toward the unfortunate city of Targos. Many spectators lined Targos's high wall, though the tower was much farther away from them than it was from Bryn Shander, and it appeared as no more than a flashing speck on the distant plain. They had little idea of what was happening beneath the principal city, though they did see the ray of fire coming toward them.

But by then it was too late.

The wrath of Akar Kessell roared into the proud city, cutting a swath of instant devastation. Fires sprouted all along its killing line. People caught in the direct path never even had a chance to cry out before they were simply vaporized. But those who survived the initial assault, women and children and tundra-toughened men alike, who had faced death a thousand times and more, did scream. And their wails carried out across the still lake to Lonelywood and Bremen, to the cheering goblins in Termalaine, and down the plain to the horrified witnesses in Bryn Shander.

Kessell waved his hand and slightly altered the angle of the release, thus arcing the destruction throughout Targos. Every major structure within the city was soon burning, and hundreds of people lay dead or dying, pitifully rolling about on the ground to extinguish the flames that engulfed their bodies or gasping helplessly in a desperate search for air in the heavy smoke.

Kessell reveled in the moment.

But then he felt an involuntary shudder wrack his spine. And the tower, too, seemed to quiver. The wizard clutched at the relic, still tucked under the folds of his robe. He understood that he had pushed the limits of Crenshinibon's strength too far.

Back in the Spine of the World, the first tower that Kessell had raised crumbled into rubble. And far out on the open tundra, the second did likewise. The shard pulled in its borders, destroying the tower images that sapped away its strength.

Kessell, too, had been wearied by the effort, and the lights of the remaining Cryshal-Tirith began to calm and then to wane. The ray fluttered and died.

But it had finished its business.

When the invasion had first come, Kemp and the other proud leaders of Targos had promised their people that they would hold the city until the last man had fallen, but even the stubborn spokesman realized that they had no choice but to flee. Luckily, the city proper, which had taken the brunt of Kessell's attack, was on high ground overlooking the sheltered bay area. The fleets remained unharmed. And the homeless fishermen of Termalaine were already on the docks, having stayed with their boats after they had docked in Targos. As soon as they had realized the unbelievable extent of the destruction that was occurring in the city proper, they began preparing for the imminent influx of the war's latest refugees. Most of the boats of both cities sailed out within minutes of the attack, desperate to get their vulnerable sails safely away from the windblown sparks and debris. A few vessels remained behind, braving the growing hazards to rescue any later arrivals on the docks.

The people on Bryn Shander's dock wept at the continued screams of the dying. Cassius, though, consumed by his quest to seek out and understand the apparent weakness that Kessell had just revealed, had no time for tears. In truth, the cries affected him as deeply as anyone, but unwilling to let the lunatic Kessell view any hints of weakness from him, he transformed his visage from sorrow to an iron grimace of rage.

Kessell laughed at him. "Do not pout, poor Cassius," the wizard taunted. "It is unbecoming."

"You are a dog," Glensather retorted. "And unruly dogs should be beaten!"

Cassius stayed his fellow spokesman with an outstretched hand. "Be calm, my friend," he whispered. "Kessell will feed off of our panic. Let him talk—he reveals more to us than he believes."

"Poor Cassius," Kessell repeated sarcastically. Then suddenly, the wizard's face twisted in outrage. Cassius noted the abrupt swing keenly, filing it away with the other information he had collected.

"Mark well what you have witnessed here, people of Bryn Shander!" Kessell sneered. "Bow to your master, or the same fate shall befall you! And there is no water behind you! You have nowhere to run!"

He laughed wildly again and looked all about the city's hill, as though he was searching for something. "What are you to do?" he cackled. "You have no lake!

"I have spoken, Cassius. Hear me well. You will deliver an emissary unto me tomorrow, an emissary to bear the news of your unconditional surrender! And if your pride prevents such an act, remember the cries of dying Targos! Look to the city on the banks of Maer Dualdon for guidance, pitiful Cassius. The fires shall not have died when the morrow dawns!"

Just then a courier raced up to the spokesman. "Many ships have been spotted moving out from under the blanket of smoke in Targos. Newsbearer signals have already begun coming in from the refugees."

"And what of Kemp?" Cassius asked anxiously.

"He lives," the courier answered. "And he has vowed revenge."

Cassius breathed a sigh of relief. He wasn't overly fond of his peer from Targos, but he knew that the battle-seasoned spokesman would prove a valuable asset to Ten-Towns' cause before all was through.

Kessell heard the conversation and growled in disdain. "And where shall they run?" he asked Cassius.

The spokesman, intent on studying this unpredictable and unbalanced adversary, did not reply, but Kessell answered the question for him.

"To Bremen? But they cannot!" He snapped his fingers, beginning the chain of a prearranged message to his westernmost forces. At once, a large group of goblins broke rank and started out to the west.

Toward Bremen.

"You see? Bremen falls before the night is through, and yet another fleet will scurry out onto their precious lake. The scene shall be repeated in the town in the wood with predictable results. But what protection will the lakes offer these people when the merciless winter begins to fall?" he shouted. "How fast shall their ships sail away from me when the waters are frozen around them?"

He laughed again, but this time more seriously, more dangerously. "What protection do any of you have against Akar Kessell?"

Cassius and the wizard held each other in unyielding glares. The wizard barely mouthed the words, but Cassius heard him clearly. "What protection?"

OUT ON MAER DUALDON, KEMP BIT BACK HIS FRUSTRATED RAGE as he watched his city tumble in flames. Soot-blackened faces stared back to the burning ruins in horrified disbelief, shouting impossible denials and openly crying for their lost friends and kin.

But like Cassius, Kemp converted his despair into constructive anger. As soon as he learned of the goblin force departing for Bremen, he dispatched his fastest ship to warn the people of that distant city and to inform them of the happenings across the lake. Then he sent a second ship toward Lonelywood to beg for food and bandages, and perhaps an invitation to dock.

Despite their obvious differences, the spokesmen of the ten towns were in many ways alike. Like Agorwal, who had been happy to sacrifice everything for the good of the people, and Jensin Brent, who refused to yield to despair, Kemp of Targos set about rallying his people for a retaliatory strike. He didn't yet know how he would accomplish the feat, but he knew that he had not had his final say in the wizard's war.

And poised upon the wall of Bryn Shander, Cassius knew it, too.

25

ERRTU

Drizzt crawled out of his hidden chamber as the last lights of the setting sun began fading away. He scanned the southern horizon and was again dismayed. He had needed to rest, but he couldn't help feeling pangs of guilt when he saw the city of Targos burning, as though he had neglected his duty to bear witness to the suffering of Kessell's helpless victims.

Yet the drow had not been idle even during the hours of the meditative trance the elves called sleep. He had journeyed back into the underworld of his distant memories in search of a particular sensation, the aura of a powerful presence he had once known. Though he had not gotten close enough for a good look at the demon he had followed the previous night, something about the creature had struck a familiar chord in his oldest recollections.

A pervading, unnatural emanation surrounded creatures from the lower planes when they walked on the material world, an aura that the dark elves, more so than any other race, had come to understand and recognize. Not only this type of demon, but this particular creature itself, was known to Drizzt. It had served his people in Menzoberranzan for many years.

"Errtu," he whispered as he sorted through his dreams.

Drizzt knew the demon's true name. It would come to his call.

THE SEARCH TO FIND AN APPROPRIATE SPOT FROM WHICH HE
could call the demon took Drizzt over an hour, and he spent several more preparing the area. His goal was to take away as many of
Errtu's advantages—size and flight in particular—as he could,
though he sincerely hoped that their meeting would not involve
combat. People who knew the drow considered him daring, sometimes even reckless, but that was against mortal enemies who
would recoil from the stinging pain of his whirring blades. Demons, especially one of Errtu's size and strength, were a different
story altogether. Many times during his youth Drizzt had witnessed the wrath of such a monster. He had seen buildings thrown
down, solid stone torn by the great clawed hands. He had seen
mighty human warriors strike the monster with blows that would
fell an ogre, only to find, in their dying horror, that their weapons were useless against such a powerful being from the lower
planes.

His own people usually fared better against demons, actually
receiving a measure of respect from them. Demons often allied
with drow on even terms, or even served the dark elves outright,
for they were wary of the powerful weapons and magic the drow
possessed. But that was back in the underworld, where the strange
emanations from the unique stone formations blessed the metals
used by the drow craftsmen with mysterious and magical properties. Drizzt had none of the weapons from his homeland, for their
strange magic could not withstand the light of day; though he had
been careful to keep them protected from the sun, they became
useless shortly after he moved to the surface. He doubted that the
weapons he now carried would be able to harm Errtu at all. And
even if they did, demons of Errtu's stature could not be truly destroyed away from their native planes. If it came to blows, the most
that Drizzt could hope to do was banish the creature from the
Material Plane for one hundred years.

He had no intentions of fighting.

Yet he had to try something against the wizard who threatened the towns. His goal now was to gain some knowledge that might reveal a weakness in the wizard, and his method was deception and disguise, hoping that Errtu remembered enough about the dark elves to make his story credible, yet not too much to strip away the flimsy lies that would hold it together.

The place he had chosen for the meeting was a sheltered dell a few yards from the mountain's cliff face. A pinnacled roof formed by converging walls covered half of the area—the other half was open to the sky—but the entire place was set back into the mountainside behind high walls, safely out of view of Cryshal-Tirith. Now Drizzt worked with a dagger, scraping runes of warding on the walls and floor in front of where he would sit. His mental image of these magical symbols had fuzzied over the many years, and he knew that their design was far from perfect. Yet he realized that he would need any possible protection that they might offer if Errtu turned on him.

When he was finished, he sat cross-legged under the roofed section, behind the protected area, and tossed out the small statuette that he carried in his pack. Guenhwyvar would be a good test for his warding inscriptions.

The great cat answered the summons. It appeared in the other side of the cubby, its keen eyes scanning the area for any potential danger that threatened its master. Then, sensing nothing, it turned a curious glance on Drizzt.

"Come to me," Drizzt called, beckoning with his hand. The cat strode toward him, then stopped abruptly, as though it had walked into a wall. Drizzt sighed in relief when he saw that his runes held some measure of strength. His confidence was bolstered considerably, though he realized that Errtu would push the power of the runes to their absolute limits—and probably beyond.

Guenhwyvar lolled its huge head in an effort to understand what had deterred it. The resistance hadn't really been very strong, but the mixed signals from its master, calling for it yet warding it away, had confused the cat. It considered gathering its strength and walking right through the feeble barrier, but its master seemed pleased that it had stopped. So the cat sat where it was and waited.

Drizzt was busy studying the area, searching out the optimum place for Guenhwyvar to spring from and surprise the demon. A deep ledge on one of the high walls just beyond the portion that converged into a roof seemed to offer the best concealment. He motioned the cat into position and instructed it not to attack until his signal. Then he sat back and tried to relax, intent on his final mental preparations before he called the demon.

Across the valley in the magical tower, Errtu crouched in a shadowy corner of Kessell's harem room keeping its ever-vigilant guard over the evil wizard at play with his mindless girls. A seething fire of hatred burned in Errtu's eyes as it looked upon the foolish Kessell. The wizard had nearly ruined everything with his show of power that afternoon and his refusal to tear down the vacated towers behind him, further draining Crenshinibon's strength.

Errtu had been grimly satisfied when Kessell had come back into the Cryshal-Tirith and confirmed, through the use of scrying mirrors, that the other two towers had fallen to pieces. Errtu had warned Kessell against raising a third tower, but the wizard, frail of ego, had grown more stubborn with each passing day of the campaign, envisioning the demon's, or even Crenshinibon's, advice as a ploy to undermine his absolute control.

And so Errtu was quite receptive, even relieved, when it heard Drizzt's call floating down the valley. At first it denied the possibility of such a summons, but the inflections of its true name being spoken aloud sent involuntary shudders running along the demon's spine. More intrigued than angered at the impertinence of some mortal daring to utter its name, Errtu slipped away from the distracted wizard and moved outside Cryshal-Tirith.

Then the call came again, cutting through the harmony of the wind's endless song like a whitecapped wave on a still pond.

Errtu spread its great wings and soared northward over the plain, speeding toward the summoner. Terrified goblins fled from the darkness of the demon's passing shadow, for even in the faint glimmer of a thin moon, the creature of the Abyss left a wake of blackness that made the night seem bright in comparison.

Drizzt sucked in a tense breath. He sensed the unerring approach of the demon as it veered away from Bremen's Run and swept upward over the lower slopes of Kelvin's Cairn. Guenhwyvar lifted its head off its paws and growled, also sensing the approach of the evil monster. The cat ducked to the very back of the deep ledge and lay flat and still, awaiting its master's command, confident that its heightened abilities of stealth could protect it even against the highly tuned senses of a demon.

Errtu's leathery wings folded up tight as it alighted on the ledge. It immediately pinpointed the exact location of the summoner and though it had to tuck its broad shoulders to pass through the narrow entrance to the dell, it charged straight in, intent on appeasing its curiosity and then killing the blasphemous fool that dared utter its name aloud.

Drizzt fought to hold his edge of control when the huge demon pushed in, its bulk filling the small area beyond his tiny sanctuary, blocking out the starlight before him. There could be no turning back from his dangerous course. He had no place to run.

The demon stopped suddenly in amazement. It had been centuries since Errtu had looked upon a drow, and it certainly never expected to find one on the surface, in the frozen wastelands of the farthest north.

Somehow Drizzt found his voice. "Greetings, master of chaos," he said calmly, bowing low. "I am Drizzt Do'Urden, of the house of Daermon N'a'shezbaernon, ninth family to the throne of Menzoberranzan. Welcome to my humble camp."

"You are a long way from home, drow," the demon said with obvious suspicion.

"As are thee, great demon of the Abyss," Drizzt replied coolly. "And lured to this high corner of the world for similar reasons, unless I miss my guess."

"I know why I am here," answered Errtu. "The business of the drow has ever been outside my understanding—or caring."

Drizzt stroked his slender chin and chuckled in feigned confidence. His stomach was tied in knots, and he felt the beginnings of a cold sweat coming on. He chuckled again and fought against the fear. If the demon sensed his unease, his credibility would be greatly diminished. "Ah, but this time, for the first time in many years, it seems that the roads of our business have crossed, mighty purveyor of destruction. My people have a curiosity, perhaps even a vested interest, in the wizard that you apparently serve!"

Errtu squared its shoulders, the first flickers of a dangerous flame evident in its red eyes. "Serve?" it echoed incredulously, the even tone of its voice quivering, as though it bordered on the edge of an uncontrollable rage.

Drizzt was quick to qualify his observation. "By all appearances, guardian of chaotic intentions, the wizard holds some power over you. Surely you work alongside Akar Kessell!"

"I serve no human!" Errtu roared, shaking the cave's very foundation with an emphatic stamp of its foot.

Drizzt wondered if the fight that he could not hope to win was about to begin. He considered calling out Guenhwyvar so that they could at least land the first blows.

But the demon suddenly calmed again. Convinced that it had half-guessed the reason for the unexpected presence of the drow, Errtu turned a scrutinizing eye on Drizzt. "Serve the wizard?" it laughed. "Akar Kessell is puny even by the low standards of humans! But you know this, drow, and do not dare to deny it. You are here, as I am here, for Crenshinibon, and Kessell be damned!"

The confused look on Drizzt's face was genuine enough to throw Errtu off balance. The demon still believed that it had guessed correctly, but it couldn't understand why the drow didn't comprehend the name. "Crenshinibon," it explained, sweeping its clawed hand to the south. "An ancient bastion of unspeakable power."

"The tower?" Drizzt asked.

Errtu's uncertainty bubbled up in the form of explosive fury. "Play no games of ignorance with me!" the demon bellowed. "The drow lords know well the power of Akar Kessell's artifact, or else they would not have come to the surface to seek it out!"

"Very well, you've guessed at the truth," Drizzt conceded. "Yet I had to be certain that the tower on the plain was indeed the ancient artifact that I seek. My masters show little mercy to careless spies."

Errtu smiled wickedly as it remembered the unholy torture chambers of Menzoberranzan. Those years it had spent among the dark elves had been enjoyable indeed!

Drizzt quickly pressed the conversation in a direction that might reveal some weaknesses of Kessell or his tower. "One thing has kept me puzzled, awesome spectre of unbridled evil," he began, careful to continue his string of unduplicated compliments. "By what right does this wizard possess Crenshinibon?"

"None at all," Errtu said. "Wizard, bah! Measured against your own people, he is barely an apprentice. His tongue twitches uneasily when he utters even the simplest of spells. But fate often plays such games. And more to the enjoyment, I say! Let Akar Kessell have his brief moment of triumph. Humans do not live a very long time!"

Drizzt knew that he was pursuing a dangerous line of questions, but he accepted the risk. Even with a major demon standing barely ten feet away, Drizzt figured that his chances for survival at this moment were better than those of his friends in Bryn Shander. "Still, my masters are concerned that the tower may be harmed in the coming battle with the humans," he bluffed.

Errtu took another moment to consider Drizzt. The appearance of the dark elves complicated the demon's simple plan to inherit Crenshinibon from Kessell. If the mighty drow lords of the huge city of Menzoberranzan truly had designs upon the relic, the demon knew that they would get it. Certainly Kessell, even with the power of the shard behind him, could not withstand them. The mere presence of this drow changed the demon's perceptions of its relationship with Crenshinibon. How Errtu wished that it could simply devour Kessell and flee with the relic before the dark elves were too involved!

Yet Errtu had never considered the drow as enemies, and the demon had come to despise the bumbling wizard. Perhaps an alliance with the dark elves could prove beneficial to both sides.

"Tell me, unequaled champion of darkness," Drizzt pressed, "is Crenshinibon in peril?"

"Bah!" snorted Errtu. "Even the tower that is merely a reflection of Crenshinibon is impervious. It absorbs all attacks directed against its mirrored walls and reflects them back on their source! Only the pulsating crystal of strength, the very heart of Cryshal-Tirith, is vulnerable, and that is safely hidden away."

"Inside?"

"Of course."

"But if someone were to get into the tower," Drizzt reasoned, "how well protected would he then find the heart?"

"An impossible task," the demon replied. "Unless the simple fishermen of Ten-Towns have some spirit at their service. Or perhaps a high priest, or an archmage to weave spells of unveiling. Surely your masters know that Cryshal-Tirith's door is invisible and undetectable to any beings inherent to the present plane the tower rests upon. No creature of this material world, your race included, could find its way in!"

"But—" Drizzt pressed anxiously.

Errtu cut him short. "Even if someone stumbled into the structure," he growled, impatient with the relentless stream of impossible suppositions, "he would have to pass by me. And the limit of Kessell's power within the tower is considerable indeed, for the wizard has become an extension of Crenshinibon itself, a living outlet for the Crystal Shard's unfathomable strength! The heart lies beyond the very focal point of Kessell's interaction with the tower, and up to the very tip . . ." The demon stopped, suddenly suspicious of Drizzt's line of questioning. If the lore-wise drow lords were truly intent upon Crenshinibon, why weren't they more aware of its strengths and weaknesses?

Errtu understood its mistake then. It examined Drizzt once again, but with a different focus. When it had first encountered the drow, stunned by the mere presence of a dark elf in this region, it had searched for deception in the physical attributes of Drizzt himself to determine if his drow features were an illusion, a clever yet simple shape-alteration trick within the power of even a minor mage.

When Errtu was convinced that a true drow and no illusion stood before it, it had accepted the credibility of Drizzt's story as consistent with the characteristics of the dark elves' style.

Now, though, the demon scoured the peripheral clues beyond Drizzt's black skin, noting the items he carried and the area he had staked out for their meeting. Nothing that Drizzt had upon his person, not even the weapons sheathed on his hips, emanated the distinct magical properties of the underworld. Perhaps the drow masters had outfitted their spies more appropriately for the surface world, Errtu reasoned. From what it had learned of the dark elves during its many years of service in Menzoberranzan, this drow's presence was certainly not outrageous.

But creatures of chaos survived by trusting no one.

Errtu continued his scan for a clue of Drizzt's authenticity. The only item the demon had spotted that reflected on Drizzt's heritage was a thin silver chain strung around his slender neck, a piece of jewelry common among the dark elves for holding a small pouch of wealth. Concentrating upon this, Errtu discovered a second chain, finer than the first, weaving in and out of the other. The demon followed the almost imperceptible crease in Drizzt's jerkin created by the long chain.

Unusual, it noted, and possibly revealing. Errtu pointed at the chain, spoke a command word, and raised its outstretched finger into the air.

Drizzt tensed when he felt the emblem slipping up from under his leather jerkin. It passed up over the neckline of the garment and dropped to the extent of the chain, hanging openly upon his chest.

Errtu's evil grin widened along with its squinting eyes. "Unusual choice for a drow," it hissed sarcastically. "I would have expected the symbol of Lolth, demon queen of your people. She would not be pleased!" From nowhere, it seemed, a many-thonged whip appeared in one of the demon's hands and a jagged, cruelly notched blade in the other.

At first, Drizzt's mind whirled down a hundred avenues, exploring the most feasible lies he could spin to get him out of this fix. But then he shook his head resolutely and pushed the lies away. He would not dishonor his deity.

At the end of the silver chain hung a gift from Regis, a carving the halfling had done from the bone of one of the few knuckleheads he had ever hooked. Drizzt had been deeply touched when Regis presented it to him, and he considered it the halfling's finest work. It twirled around on the long chain, its gentle grades and shading giving it the depth of a true work of art.

It was a white unicorn head, the symbol of the goddess Mielikki.

"Who are you, drow?" Errtu demanded. The demon had already decided that it would have to kill Drizzt, but it was intrigued by such an unusual meeting. A dark elf that followed the Lady of the Forest? And a surface dweller as well! Errtu had known many drow over the centuries, but had never even heard of one that had abandoned the drow's wicked ways. Cold-hearted killers, one and all, that had taught even the great demon of chaos a trick or two concerning the methods of excruciating torture.

"I am Drizzt Do'Urden, that much is true," Drizzt replied

evenly. "He who forsook the House of Daermon N'a'shezbaernon."
All fear had flown from Drizzt when he accepted beyond any hope
that he would have to battle the demon. Now he assumed the calm
readiness of a seasoned fighter, prepared to seize any advantage
that might fall his way. "A ranger humbly serving Gwaeron Windstrom, hero of the goddess Mielikki." He bowed low in accordance
with a proper introduction.

As he straightened, he drew his scimitars. "I must defeat you,
scar of vileness," he declared, "and send you back to the swirling
clouds of the bottomless Abyss. There is no place in the sunlit
world for one of your kind!"

"You are confused, elf," the demon said. "You have lost the way
of your heritage, and now you dare to presume that you might
defeat me!" Flames sprang to life from the stone all around Errtu.
"I would have killed you mercifully, with one clean stroke, out of
respect for your kin. But your pride distresses me; I shall teach you
to desire death! Come, feel the sting of my fire!"

Drizzt was already nearly overwhelmed by the heat of Errtu's
demon fire, and the brightness of the flames stung his sensitive
eyes so that the bulk of the demon seemed only the dulled blur of
a shadow. He saw the darkness extend to the demon's right and
knew that Errtu had raised its terrible sword. He moved to defend,
but suddenly the demon lurched to the side and roared in surprise
and outrage.

Guenhwyvar had latched firmly onto its upraised arm.

The huge demon held the panther at arm's length, trying to pin
the cat between its forearm and the rock wall to keep the tearing
claws and teeth away from a vital area. Guenhwyvar gnawed and
raked the massive arm, tearing demon flesh and muscle.

Errtu winced away the vicious attack and determined to deal
with the cat later. The demon's main concern remained the drow,
for it respected the potential power of any of the dark elves. Errtu
had seen too many foes fall beneath one of the dark elves' countless
tricks.

The many-thonged whip lashed out at Drizzt's legs, too quickly for the drow, still reeling from the sudden burst of brightness of the flames, to deflect the blow or dodge aside. Errtu jerked the handle as the thongs tangled about the slender legs and ankles, the demon's great strength easily dropping Drizzt to his back.

Drizzt felt the stinging pain all through his legs, and he heard the rush of air pressed out of his lungs when he landed on the hard stone. He knew that he must react without delay, but the glare of the fire and Errtu's sudden strike had left him disoriented. He felt himself being dragged along the stone, felt the intensity of the heat increasing. He managed to lift his head just in time to view his tangled feet entering the demon fire.

"And so I die," he stated flatly.

But his legs did not burn.

Drooling to hear the agonized screams of its helpless victim, Errtu gave a stronger tug on the whip and pulled Drizzt completely into the flames. Though he was totally immolated, the drow barely felt warmed by the fire.

And then, with a final hiss of protest, the hot flames suddenly died away.

Neither of the opponents understood what had happened, both assuming that the other had been responsible.

Errtu struck quickly again. Bringing a heavy foot down upon Drizzt's chest, it began grinding him into the stone. The drow flailed out in desperation with one weapon, but it had no effect on the otherworldly monster.

Then Drizzt swung his other scimitar, the blade he had taken from the dragon's hoard.

Hissing like water on fire, it entered Errtu's knee joint. The hilt of the weapon heated up when the blade tore into the demon's flesh, nearly burning Drizzt's hand. Then it grew icy cold, as though dousing Errtu's hot life force with a cold strength of its own. Drizzt understood then what had extinguished the fires.

The demon gaped in blank horror, then screamed in agony.

Never had it felt such a sting! It leaped back and tossed about wildly, trying to escape the weapon's terrible bite, dragging Drizzt, who could not let go of the hilt. Guenhwyvar was thrown in the violence of the demon's rage, flying from the monster's arm to crash heavily into a wall.

Drizzt eyed the wound incredulously as the demon backed away. Steam poured from the hole in Errtu's knee; and the edges of the cut were iced over!

But Drizzt, too, had been weakened by the strike. In its struggle with the mighty demon, the scimitar had drawn upon its wielder's life force, pulling Drizzt into the battle with the fiery monster.

Now the drow felt as though he hadn't even the strength left to stand. But he found himself lunging forward, blade fully extended before him, as if pulled by the scimitar's hunger.

The cubby entrance was too narrow. Errtu could neither dodge nor spring away.

The scimitar found the demon's belly.

The explosive surge as the blade touched the core of Errtu's life force drained away Drizzt's strength, tossing him backward. He cracked against the stone wall and crumpled, but managed to keep himself alert enough to witness the titanic struggle still raging.

Errtu got out onto the ledge. The demon was staggering now, trying to spread its wings. But they drooped weakly. The scimitar glowed white with power as it continued its assault. The demon could not bear to grasp it and tear it free, though the embedded blade, its magic quelching the fires it had been wrought to destroy, was surely winning the conflict.

Errtu knew that it had been careless, overconfident in its ability to destroy any mortal in single combat. The demon hadn't considered the possibility of such a wicked blade; it had never even heard of a weapon with such a sting.

Steam poured from Errtu's exposed entrails and enveloped the combatants. "And so you have banished me, treacherous drow!" it spat.

Dazed, Drizzt watched in amazement as the white glow intensified and the black shadow diminished.

"A hundred years, drow!" Errtu howled. "Not such a long time for the likes of you or me!" The vapor thickened as the shadow seemed to melt away.

"A century, Drizzt Do'Urden!" came Errtu's fading cry from somewhere far away. "Look over your shoulder then! Errtu shall not be far behind!"

The vapor wafted up into the air and was gone.

The last sound Drizzt heard was the clang of the metal scimitar falling to the stone ledge.

26

RIGHTS OF VICTORY

Wulfgar leaned back in his chair at the head of the main table in the hastily constructed Mead Hall, his foot tapping nervously at the long delays necessitated by the demands of proper tradition. He felt that his people should already be on the move, but it was the restoration of the traditional ceremonies and celebrations that had immediately separated, and placed him above, the tyrant Heafstaag in the eyes of the skeptical and ever-suspicious barbarians.

Wulfgar, after all, had walked into their midst after a five-year absence and challenged their long-standing king. One day later, he had won the crown, and the day after that, he had been coronated King Wulfgar of the Tribe of the Elk.

And he was determined that his reign, short though he intended it to be, would not be marked by the threats and bullying tactics of his predecessor's. He would ask the warriors of the assembled tribes to follow him into battle, not command them, for he knew that a barbarian warrior was a man driven almost exclusively by fierce pride. Stripped of their dignity, as Heafstaag had done by refusing to honor the sovereignty of each individual king, the tribesmen were no better in battle than ordinary men. Wulfgar

knew that they would need to regain their proud edge if they were
to have any chance at all against the wizard's overwhelming numbers.

Thus Hengorot, the Mead Hall, had been raised and the Challenge of the Song initiated for the first time in nearly five years. It
was a short, happy time of good-natured competition between
tribes who had been suffocated under Heafstaag's unrelenting
domination.

The decision to raise the deerskin hall had been difficult for
Wulfgar. Assuming that he still had time before Kessell's army
struck, he had weighed the benefits of regaining tradition against
the pressing need of haste. He only hoped that in the frenzy of
pre-battle preparations, Kessell would overlook the absence of the
barbarian king, Heafstaag. If the wizard was at all sharp, it wasn't
likely.

Now he waited quietly and patiently, watching the fires return
to the eyes of the tribesmen.

"Like old times?" Revjak asked, sitting next to him.

"Good times," Wulfgar responded.

Satisfied, Revjak leaned back against the tent's deerskin wall,
granting the new chief the solitude he obviously desired. And
Wulfgar resumed his wait, seeking the best moment to unveil his
proposition.

At the far end of the hall, an axe-throwing competition was
beginning. Similar to the tactics Heafstaag and Beorg had used to
seal a pact between the tribes at the last Hengorot, the challenge
was to hurl an axe from as great a distance as possible and sink it
deeply enough into a keg of mead to open a hole. The number of
mugs that could be filled from the effort within a specified count
determined the success of the throw.

Wulfgar saw his chance. He leaped from his stool and demanded, by rights of being the host, the first throw. The man who
had been selected to judge the challenge acknowledged Wulfgar's
right and invited him to come down to the first selected distance.

"From here," Wulfgar said, hoisting Aegis-fang to his shoulder. Murmurs of disbelief and excitement arose from all corners of the hall. The use of a warhammer in such a challenge was unprecedented, but none complained or cited rules. Every man who had heard the tales, but not witnessed firsthand the splitting of Heafstaag's great axe, was anxious to see the weapon in action. A keg of mead was placed upon a stool at the back end of the hall.

"Another behind it!" Wulfgar demanded. "And another behind that!" His concentration narrowed on the task at hand and he didn't take the time to sort out the whispers he heard all around him.

The kegs were readied, and the crowd backed out of the young king's line of sight. Wulfgar grasped Aegis-fang tightly in his hands and sucked in a great breath, holding it in to keep himself steady. The unbelieving onlookers watched in amazement as the new king exploded into movement, hurling the mighty hammer with a fluid motion and strength unmatched among their ranks.

Aegis-fang tumbled, head over handle, the length of the long hall, blasting through the first keg, and then the second and beyond, taking out not only the three targets and their stools, but continuing on to tear a hole in the back of the Mead Hall. The closest warriors hurried to the opening to watch the remainder of its flight, but the hammer had disappeared into the night. They started out to retrieve it.

But Wulfgar stopped them. He sprang onto the table, lifting his arms before him. "Hear me, warriors of the northern plains!" he cried. Their mouths already agape at the unprecedented feat, some fell to their knees when Aegis-fang suddenly reappeared in the young king's hands.

"I am Wulfgar, son of Beornegar and King of the Tribe of the Elk! Yet I speak to you now not as your king but as a kindred warrior, horrified at the dishonor Heafstaag tried to place upon us all!" Spurred on by the knowledge that he had gained their attention and respect, and by the confirmation that his assumptions of their true desires had not been in error, Wulfgar seized the moment. These people had cried out for deliverance from the tyrannical reign of the one eyed king, and, beaten almost to extinction in their last campaign and now about to fight beside goblins and giants, they longed for a hero to gain them back their lost pride.

"I am the dragonslayer!" he continued. "And by right of victory I possess the treasures of Icingdeath!"

Again the private conversations interrupted him, for the now unguarded treasure had become a subject for debate. Wulfgar let them continue their gossip for a long moment to heighten their interest in the dragon's gold.

When they finally quieted, he went on. "The tribes of the tundra do not fight in a common cause with goblins and giants!" he decreed to rousing shouts of approval. "We fight against them!"

The crowd suddenly hushed. A guard rushed into the tent, but did not dare interrupt the new king.

"I leave with the dawn for Ten-Towns," Wulfgar stated. "I shall battle against the wizard Kessell and the foul horde he has pulled from the holes of The Spine of the World!"

The crowd did not respond. They accepted the notion of battle against Kessell eagerly, but the thought of returning to Ten-Towns to help the people who had nearly destroyed them five years before had never occurred to them.

But the guard now intervened. "I fear that your quest shall be in vain, young king," he said. Wulfgar turned a distressed eye upon the man, guessing the news he bore. "The smoke clouds from great fires are even now rising above the southern plain."

Wulfgar considered the distressing news. He had thought that he would have more time. "Then I shall leave tonight!" he roared at the stunned assembly. "Come with me, my friends, my fellow warriors of the north! I shall show you the path to the lost glories of our past!"

The crowd seemed torn and uncertain. Wulfgar played his final card.

"To any man who will go with me, or to his surviving kin if he should fall, I offer an equal share of the dragon's treasure!"

He had swept in like a mighty squall off the Sea of Moving Ice. He had captured the imagination and heart of every barbarian warrior and had promised them a return to the wealth and glory of their brightest days.

That very night, Wulfgar's mercenary army charged out of their encampment and thundered across the open plain.

Not a single man remained behind.

27

THE CLOCK OF DOOM

Bremen was torched at dawn.

The people of the small, unwalled village had known better than to stand and fight when the wave of monsters rolled across the Shaengarne River. They put up token resistance at the ford, firing a few bursts of arrows at the lead goblins just to slow the ranks long enough for the heaviest and slowest ships to clear the harbor and reach the safety of Maer Dualdon. The archers then fled back to the docks and followed their fellow townsmen.

When the goblins finally entered the city, they found it completely deserted. They watched angrily as the sailing ships moved back toward the east to join the flotilla of Targos and Termalaine. Bremen was too far out of the way to be of any use to Akar Kessell, so, unlike the city of Termalaine which had been converted into a camp, this city was burned to the ground.

The people on the lake, the newest in the long line of homeless victims of Kessell's wanton destruction, watched helplessly as their homes fell in smoldering splinters.

From the wall of Bryn Shander, Cassius and Regis watched, too.

"He has made yet another mistake," Cassius told the halfling.

"How so?"

"Kessell has backed the people of Targos and Termalaine, Caer-Konig and Caer Dineval, and now Bremen into a corner," Cassius explained. "They have nowhere to go now; their only hope lies in victory."

"Not much of a hope," Regis remarked. "You have seen what the tower can do. And even without it, Kessell's army could destroy us all! As he said, he holds every advantage."

"Perhaps," Cassius conceded. "The wizard believes that he is invincible, that much is certain. And that is his mistake, my friend. The meekest of animals will fight bravely when it is backed against a wall, for it has nothing left to lose. A poor man is more deadly than a rich man because he puts less value on his own life. And a man stranded homeless on the frozen steppes with the first winds of winter already beginning to blow is a formidable enemy indeed!

"Fear not, little friend," Cassius continued. "At our council this morning, we shall find a way to exploit the wizard's weaknesses."

Regis nodded, unable to dispute the spokesman's simple logic and unwilling to refute his optimism. Still, as he scanned the deep ranks of goblins and orcs that surrounded the city, the halfling held out little hope.

He looked northward, where the dust had finally settled on the dwarven valley. Bruenor's Climb was no more, having toppled with the rest of the cliff face when the dwarves closed up their caverns.

"Open a door for me, Bruenor," Regis whispered absently. "Please let me in."

COINCIDENTALLY, BRUENOR AND HIS CLAN WERE, AT THAT VERY moment, discussing the feasibility of opening a door in their tunnels. But not to let anyone in. Soon after their smashing success against the ogres and goblins on the ledges outside their mines, the fighting longbeards had realized that they could not sit idly by while orcs and goblins and even worse monsters destroyed the world around them. They were eager to take a second shot at Kessell. In their underground womb, they had no idea if Bryn Shander was still standing, or if Kessell's army had already rolled over all of Ten-Towns, but they could hear the sounds of an encampment above the southernmost sections of their huge complex.

Bruenor was the one who had proposed the idea of a second battle, mainly because of his own anger at the imminent loss of his closest non-dwarven friends. Shortly after the goblins that had escaped the tunnel collapse had been cut down, the leader of the clan from Mithral Hall gathered the whole of his people around him.

"Send someone to the farthest ends o' the tunnels," he instructed. "Find out where the dogs'll do their sleepin'."

That night, the sounds of the marching monsters became obvious far in the south, under the field surrounding Bryn Shander. The industrious dwarves immediately set about reconditioning the little-used tunnels that ran in that direction. And when they had gotten under the army, they dug ten separate upward shafts, stopping just shy of the surface.

A special gleam had returned to their eyes: the sparkle of a dwarf who knows that he's about to chop off a few goblin heads. Bruenor's devious plan had endless potential for revenge with minimal risk. With five minutes' notice, they could complete their new exits. Less than a minute beyond that, their entire force would be up in the middle of Kessell's sleeping army.

THE MEETING THAT CASSIUS HAD LABELED A COUNCIL WAS TRULY more of a forum where the spokesman from Bryn Shander could unveil his first retaliatory strategies. Yet none of the gathered leaders, even Glensather, the only other spokesman in attendance, protested in the least. Cassius had studied every aspect of the entrenched goblin army and the wizard with meticulous attention to detail. The spokesman had outlined a layout of the entire force, detailing the most potentially explosive rivalries among the goblin and orc ranks and his best estimates about the length of time it would take for the inner fighting to sufficiently weaken the army.

Everyone in attendance was agreed, though, that the cornerstone holding the siege together was Cryshal-Tirith. The awesome power of the crystalline structure would cow even the most disruptive orcs into unquestioning obedience. Yet the limits of that power, as Cassius saw it, were the real issue.

"Why was Kessell so insistent on an immediate surrender?" the spokesman reasoned. "He could let us sit under the stress of a siege for a few days to soften our resistance!"

The others agreed with the logic of Cassius's line of thinking but had no answers for him.

"Perhaps Kessell does not command as strong a hold over his charges as we believe," Cassius himself proposed. "Might it be that the wizard fears his army will disintegrate around him if stalled for any length of time?"

"It might," replied Glensather of Easthaven. "Or maybe Akar Kessell simply perceives the strength of his advantage and knows that we have no choice but to comply. Do you, perhaps, confuse confidence with concern?"

Cassius paused for a moment to reflect on the question. "A point well taken," he said at length. "Yet immaterial to our plans." Glensather and several others cocked a curious eye at the spokesman.

"We must assume the latter," Cassius explained. "If the wizard is truly in absolute control of the gathered army, then anything we might attempt shall prove futile in any case. Therefore, we must act on the assumption that Kessell's impatience reveals well-founded concern.

"I do not perceive the wizard as an exceptional strategist. He has embarked on a path of destruction that he assumed would cow us into submission, yet which, in reality, has actually strengthened the resolve of many of our people to fight to the last. Long-standing rivalries between several of the towns, bitterness that a wise leader of an invading force would surely have twisted into an excellent advantage, have been mended by Kessell's blatant disregard of finesse and his displays of outrageous brutality."

Cassius knew by the attentive looks he was receiving that he was gaining support from every corner. He was trying to accomplish two things in this meeting: to convince the others to go along with the gamble he was about to unveil, and to lift their outlook and give them back some shred of hope.

"Our people are out there," he said, sweeping his arm in a wide arc. "On Maer Dualdon and Lac Dinneshere, the fleets have gathered, awaiting some sign from Bryn Shander that we shall support them. The people of Good Mead and Dougan's Hole do likewise on the southern lake, fully armed and knowing full well that in this struggle there is nothing left at all for any survivors if we are not victorious!" He leaned forward over the table, alternately catching and holding the gaze of each man seated before him, and concluded grimly, "No homes. No hope for our wives. No hope for our children. Nowhere left to run."

Cassius continued to rally the others around him and was soon backed by Glensather, who had guessed at the spokesman's goal of increasing morale and recognized the value of it. Cassius searched for the most opportune moment. When the majority of the assembled leaders had replaced their frowns of despair with the determined grimace of survival, he put forth his daring plan.

"Kessell has demanded an emissary," he said, "and so we must deliver one."

"You or I would seem the most obvious choice," Glensather intervened. "Which shall it be?"

A wry smile spread across Cassius's face. "Neither," he replied. "One of us would be the obvious choice if we intended to go along with Kessell's demands. But we have one other option." He turned his gaze squarely upon Regis. The halfling squirmed uncomfortably, half-guessing what the spokesman had in mind. "There is one among us who has attained an almost legendary reputation for his considerable abilities of persuasion. Perhaps his charismatic appeal shall win us some valuable time in our dealings with the wizard."

Regis felt ill. He had often wondered when the ruby pendant was going to get him into trouble too deep to climb out of.

Several other people eyed Regis now, apparently intrigued by the potential of Cassius's suggestion. The stories of the halfling's charm and persuasive ability, and the accusation that Kemp had made at the council a few tendays earlier, had been told and retold a thousand times in every one of the towns, each storyteller typically enhancing and exaggerating the tales to increase his own importance. Though Regis hadn't been thrilled with losing the power of his secret—people seldom looked him straight in the eye anymore—he had come to enjoy a certain degree of fame. He hadn't considered the possible negative side effects of having so many people looking up to him.

"Let the halfling, the former spokesman from Lonelywood, represent us in Akar Kessell's court," Cassius declared to the nearly unanimous approval of the assembly. "Perhaps our small friend will be able to convince the wizard of the error of his evil ways!"

"You are mistaken!" Regis protested. "They are only rumors . . ."

"Humility," Cassius interrupted, "is a fine trait, good halfling. And all gathered here appreciate the sincerity of your self-doubts and appreciate even more so your willingness to pit your talents against Kessell in the face of those self-doubts!"

Regis closed his eyes and did not reply, knowing that the motion would surely pass whether he approved or not.

It did, without a single dissenting vote. The cornered people were quite willing to grab at any sliver of hope they could find.

Cassius moved quickly to wrap up the council, for he believed that all other matters—problems of overcrowding and food hoarding—were of little importance at a time like this. If Regis failed, every other inconvenience would become immaterial.

Regis remained silent. He had only attended the council to lend support to his spokesmen friends. When he took his seat at the table, he had no intentions of even actively participating in the discussions, let alone becoming the focal point of the defense plan.

And so the meeting adjourned. Cassius and Glensather exchanged knowing winks of success, for everyone left the room feeling a bit more optimistic.

Cassius held Regis back when he moved to leave with the others. The spokesman from Bryn Shander shut the door behind the last of them, desiring a private briefing with the principal character of the first stages of his plan.

"You could have spoken to me about all of this first!" Regis grumbled at the spokesman's back as soon as the door was closed. "It seems only right that I should have been given the opportunity to make a decision in this matter!"

Cassius wore a grim visage as he turned to face the halfling. "What choice do any of us have?" he asked. "At least this way we have given them all some hope."

"You overestimate me," Regis protested.

"Perhaps you underestimate yourself," Cassius said. Though the halfling realized that Cassius would not back away from the plan that he had set in motion, the spokesman's confidence relayed an altruistic spirit to Regis that was genuinely comforting.

"Let us pray, for both our sakes, that the latter is the truth," Cassius continued, moving to his seat at the table. "But I truly believe this to be the case. I have faith in you, even if you do not. I remember well what you did to Spokesman Kemp at the council five years ago, though it took his own declaration that he had been tricked to make me realize the truth of the situation. A masterful job of persuasion, Regis of Lonelywood, and more so because it held its secret for so long!"

Regis blushed and conceded the point.

"And if you can deal with the stubborn likes of Kemp of Targos, you should find Akar Kessell easy prey!"

"I agree with your perceptions of Kessell as something less than a man of inner strength," said Regis, "but wizards have a way of uncovering wizardlike tricks. And you forget the demon. I would not even attempt to deceive one of its kind!"

"Let us hope that you shall not have to deal with that one," Cassius agreed with a visible shudder. "Yet I feel that you must go to the tower and try to dissuade the wizard. If we cannot somehow hold the gathered army at bay until its own inner turmoil becomes our ally, then we are surely doomed. Believe me, as I am your friend, that I would not ask you to journey into such peril if I saw any other possible path." A pained look of helpless empathy had clearly worn through the spokesman's earlier facade of rousing optimism. His concern touched Regis, as would a starving man crying out for food.

Even beyond his feelings for the overly pressured spokesman, Regis was forced to admit the logic of the plan and the absence of other avenues to explore. Kessell hadn't given them much time to regroup after the initial attack. In the razing of Targos, the wizard had demonstrated his ability to likewise destroy Bryn Shander, and the halfling had little doubt that Kessell would carry out his vile threat.

So Regis came to accept his role as their only option. The halfling wasn't easily spurred to action, but when he made up his mind to do something, he usually tried to do it properly.

"First of all," he began, "I must tell you in the strictest of confidence that I do indeed have magical aid." A glimmer of hope returned to Cassius's eyes. He leaned forward, anxious to hear more, but Regis calmed him with an outstretched palm.

"You must understand, however," the halfling explained, "that I do not, as some tales claim, have the power to pervert what is in a person's heart. I could not convince Kessell to abandon his evil path any more than I could convince Spokesman Kemp to make peace with Termalaine." He rose from his cushioned chair and paced around the table, his hands clasped behind his back. Cassius watched him in uncertain anticipation, unable to figure out exactly what he was leading up to with his admission and then disclaimer of power.

"Sometimes, though, I do have a way of making someone view his surroundings from a different perspective," Regis admitted. "Like the incident you have referred to, when I convinced Kemp that embarking upon a certain preferable course of action would actually help him to achieve his own aspirations.

"So tell me again, Cassius, all that you have learned about the wizard and his army. Let us see if we might discover a way to make Kessell doubt the very things that he has come to rely upon!"

The halfling's eloquence stunned the spokesman. Even though he hadn't looked Regis in the eye, he could see the promise of truth in the tales he had always presumed to be exaggerated.

"We know from the newsbearer that Kemp has taken command of the remaining forces of the four towns on Maer Dualdon," Cassius explained. "Likewise, Jensin Brent and Schermont are poised upon Lac Dinneshere, and combined with the fleets on Redwaters, they should prove a powerful force indeed!

"Kemp has already vowed revenge, and I doubt if any of the other refugees entertain thoughts of surrender or fleeing."

"Where could they go?" Regis muttered. He looked pitifully at Cassius, who had no words of comfort. Cassius had put on a show of confidence and hope for the others at the council and for the people in the town, but he could not look at Regis now and make hollow promises.

Glensather suddenly burst back into the room. "The wizard is back on the field!" he cried. "He has demanded our emissary—the lights on the tower have started again!"

The three rushed from the building, Cassius reiterating as much of the pertinent information as he could.

Regis silenced him. "I am prepared," he assured Cassius. "I don't know if this outrageous scheme of yours has any chance of working, but you have my vow that I'll work hard to carry out the deception."

Then they were at the gate. "It must work," Cassius said, clapping Regis on the shoulder. "We have no other hope." He started to turn away, but Regis had one final question that he needed answered.

"If I find that Kessell is beyond my power?" he asked grimly. "What am I to do if the deception fails?"

Cassius looked around at the thousands of women and children huddled against the chill wind in the city's common grounds. "If it fails," he began slowly, "if Kessell cannot be dissuaded from using the power of the tower against Bryn Shander," he paused again, if only to delay having to hear himself utter the words, "you are then under my personal orders to surrender the city."

Cassius turned away and headed for the parapets to witness the critical confrontation. Regis didn't hesitate any longer, for he knew that any pause at this frightening juncture would probably cause him to change his mind and run to find a hiding place in some dark hole in the city. Before he even had the chance to reconsider, he was through the gate and boldly marching down the hill toward the waiting specter of Akar Kessell.

Kessell had again appeared between two mirrors borne by trolls, standing with arms crossed and one foot tapping impatiently. The evil scowl on his face gave Regis the distinct impression that the wizard, in a fit of uncontrollable rage, would strike him dead before he even reached the bottom of the hill. Yet the halfling had to keep his eyes focused on Kessell to even continue his approach. The wretched trolls disgusted and revulsed him beyond anything he had ever encountered, and it took all of his willpower to move anywhere near them. Even from the gate, he could smell the foul odor of their rotting stench.

But somehow he made it to the mirrors and stood facing the evil wizard.

Kessell studied the emissary for quite a while. He certainly hadn't expected a halfling to represent the city and wondered why Cassius hadn't come personally to such an important meeting. "Do you come before me as the official representative of Bryn Shander and all who now reside within her walls?"

Regis nodded. "I am Regis of Lonelywood," he answered, "a friend to Cassius and former member of the Council of Ten. I have been appointed to speak for the people within the city."

Kessell's eyes narrowed in anticipation of his victory. "And do you bear their message of unconditional surrender?"

Regis shuffled uneasily, purposely shifting so that the ruby pendant would start into motion on his chest. "I desire private council with thee, mighty wizard, that we might discuss the terms of the agreement."

Kessell's eyes widened. He looked at Cassius upon the wall. "I said unconditional!" he shrieked. Behind him, the lights of Cryshal-Tirith began to swirl and grow. "Now you shall witness the folly of your insolence!"

"Wait!" pleaded Regis, jumping around to regain the wizard's attention. "There are some things that you should be aware of before all is decided!"

Kessell paid little attention to the halfling's rambling, but the ruby pendant suddenly caught his attention. Even through the protection offered by the distance between his physical body and the window of his image projection, he found the gem fascinating.

Regis couldn't resist the urge to smile, though only slightly, when he realized that the eyes of the wizard no longer blinked. "I have some information that I am sure you will find valuable," the halfling said quietly.

Kessell signaled for him to continue.

"Not here," Regis whispered. "There are too many curious ears about. Not all of the gathered goblins would be pleased to hear what I have to say!"

Kessell considered the halfling's words for a moment. He felt curiously subdued for some reason that he couldn't yet understand. "Very well, halfling," he agreed. "I shall hear your words." With a flash and a puff of smoke, the wizard was gone.

Regis looked back over his shoulder at the people on the wall and nodded.

Under telepathic command from within the tower, the trolls shifted the mirrors to catch Regis's reflection. A second flash and puff of smoke, and Regis, too, was gone.

On the wall, Cassius returned the halfling's nod, though Regis had already disappeared. The spokesman breathed a bit easier, comforted by the last look Regis had thrown him and by the fact that the sun was setting and Bryn Shander still stood. If his guess, based on the timing of the wizard's actions, was correct, Cryshal-Tirith drew most of its energy from the light of the sun.

It appeared that his plan had bought them at least one more night.

EVEN THROUGH HIS BLEARY EYES, DRIZZT RECOGNIZED THE DARK shape that hovered over him. The drow had banged his head when he had been thrown from the scimitar's hilt and Guenhwyvar, his loyal companion, had kept a silent vigil throughout the long hours the drow had remained unconscious, even though the cat had also been battered in the fight with Errtu.

Drizzt rolled into a sitting position and tried to reorient himself to his surroundings. At first he thought that dawn had come, but then he realized that the dim sunlight was coming from the west. He had been out for the better part of a day, drained completely, for the scimitar had sapped his vital energy in its battle with the demon.

Guenhwyvar looked even more haggard. The cat's shoulder hung limp from its collision with the stone wall, and Errtu had torn a deep cut into one of its forelegs.

More than injuries, though, fatigue was wearing on the magical beast. It had overstayed the normal limits of its visit to the Material Plane by many hours. The cord between its home plane and the drow's was only kept intact by the cat's own magical energy, and each passing minute that it remained in this world drew away a bit of its strength.

Drizzt stroked the muscled neck tenderly. He understood the sacrifice Guenhwyvar had made for his sake, and he wished that he could comply with the cat's needs and send it back to its own world.

But he could not. If the cat returned to its own plane, it would be hours before it would regain the strength required to reestablish a link back to this world. And he needed the cat now.

"A bit longer," he begged. The faithful beast lay down beside him without any hint of protest. Drizzt looked upon it with pity and petted the neck once again. How he longed to release the cat from his service! Yet he could not.

From what Errtu had told him, the door to Cryshal-Tirith was invisible only to beings of the Material Plane.

Drizzt needed the cat's eyes.

28

A LIE WITHIN A LIE

Regis rubbed the after-image of the blinding flash out of his eyes and found himself again facing the wizard. Kessell lounged on a crystal throne, leaning back against one of its arms with his legs casually thrown over the other. They were in a squared room of crystal, giving a slick visual impression, but feeling as solid as stone. Regis knew immediately that he was inside the tower. The room was filled with dozens of ornate and strangely shaped mirrors. One of these in particular, the largest and most decorative, caught the halfling's eye, for a fire was ablaze within its depths. At first Regis looked opposite the mirror, expecting to see the source of the image, but then he realized that the flames were not a reflection but an actual event occurring within the dimensions of the mirror itself.

"Welcome to my home," the wizard laughed. "You should consider yourself fortunate to witness its splendor!" But Regis fixed his gaze upon Kessell, studying the wizard closely, for the tone of his voice did not resemble the characteristic slur of others he had entranced with the ruby.

"You'll forgive my surprise when first we met," Kessell continued. "I did not expect the sturdy men of Ten-Towns to send a halfling to do their work!" He laughed again, and Regis knew that something had disrupted the charm he had cast upon the wizard when they were outside.

The halfling could guess what had happened. He could feel the throbbing power of this room; it was evident that Kessell fed off of it. With his psyche outside, the wizard had been vulnerable to the magic of the gemstone, but in here his strength was quite beyond the ruby's influence.

"You said that you had information to tell me," Kessell demanded suddenly. "Speak now, the whole of it, or I shall make your death an unpleasant one!"

Regis stuttered, trying to improvise an alternative tale. The insidious lies he had planned to weave would have little value on the unaffected wizard. In fact, in their obvious weaknesses they might reveal much of the truth about Cassius's strategies.

Kessell straightened on his throne and leaned over the halfling, imposing his gaze upon his counterpart. "Speak!" he commanded evenly.

Regis felt an iron will insinuating itself into all of his thoughts, compelling him to obey Kessell's every command. He sensed that the dominating force wasn't emanating from the wizard, though. Rather it seemed to be coming from some external source, perhaps the unseen object that the wizard occasionally clutched in a pocket of his robes.

Those of halfling stock possessed a strong natural resistance to such magic, however, and a countering force—the gemstone— helped Regis fight back against the insinuating will and gradually push it away. A sudden idea came over Regis. He had certainly seen enough individuals fall under his own charms to be able to imitate their revealing posture. He slouched a bit, as though he had suddenly been put completely at ease, and focused his blank stare on an image in the corner of the room beyond Kessell's shoulder. He felt his eyes drying out, but he resisted the temptation to blink.

"What information do you desire?" he responded mechanically.

Kessell slumped back again confidently. "Address me as Master Kessell," he ordered.

"What information do you desire, Master Kessell?"

"Good," the wizard smirked to himself. "Admit the truth, half-ling, the story you were sent to tell me was a deception."

Why not? Regis thought. A lie flavored with the sprinklings of truth becomes that much stronger. "Yes," he answered. "To make you think that your truest allies plotted against you."

"And what was the purpose?" Kessell pressed, quite pleased with himself. "Surely the people of Bryn Shander know that I could easily crush them even without any allies at all. It seems a feeble plan to me."

"Cassius had no intentions of trying to defeat you, Master Kessell," Regis said.

"Then why are you here? And why didn't Cassius simply surrender the city as I demanded?"

"I was sent to plant some doubts," replied Regis, blindly improvising to keep Kessell intrigued and occupied. Behind the facade of his words, he was trying to put together some kind of an alternate plan. "To give Cassius more time to lay out his true course of action."

Kessell leaned forward. "And what might that course of action be?"

Regis paused, searching for an answer.

"You cannot resist me!" Kessell roared. "My will is too great! Answer or I shall tear the truth from your mind!"

"To escape," Regis blurted, and after he had said it, several possibilities opened up before him.

Kessell reclined again. "Impossible," he replied casually. "My army is too strong at every point for the humans to break through."

"Perhaps not as strong as you believe, Master Kessell," Regis baited. His path now lay clear before him. A lie within another lie. He liked the formula.

"Explain," Kessell demanded, a shadow of worry clouding his cocky visage.

"Cassius has allies within your ranks."

The wizard leaped from his chair, trembling in rage. Regis marveled at how effectively his simple imitation was working. He wondered for an instant if any of his own victims had likewise reversed the dupe on him. He put the disturbing thought away for future contemplation.

"Orcs have lived among the people of Ten-Towns for many months now," Regis went on. "One tribe actually opened up a trading relationship with the fishermen. They, too, answered your summons to arms, but they still hold loyalties, if any of their kind ever truly hold loyalties, to Cassius. Even as your army was entrenching in the field around Bryn Shander, the first communications were exchanged between the orc chieftain and orc messengers that slipped out of Bryn Shander."

Kessell smoothed his hair back and rubbed his hand nervously across his face. Was it possible that his seemingly invincible army had a secret weakness?

No, none would dare oppose Akar Kessell!

But still, if some of them were plotting against him—if all of them were plotting against him—would he know? And where was Errtu? Could the demon be behind this?

"Which tribe?" he asked Regis softly, his tone revealing that the halfling's news had humbled him.

Regis drew the wizard fully into the deception. "The group that you sent to sack the city of Bremen, the Orcs of the Severed Tongue," he said, watching the wizard's widening eyes with complete satisfaction. "My job was merely to prevent you from taking any action against Bryn Shander before the fall of night, for the orcs shall return before dawn, presumably to regroup in their assigned position on the field, but in actuality, to open a gap in your western flank. Cassius will lead the people down the western slope to the open tundra. They only hope to keep you disorganized long enough to give them a solid lead. Then you shall be forced to pursue them all the way to Luskan!"

Many weak points were apparent in the plan, but it seemed a reasonable gamble for people in such a desperate situation to attempt. Kessell slammed his fist down on the arm of the throne. "The fools!" he growled.

Regis breathed a bit easier. Kessell was convinced.

"Errtu!" he screamed suddenly, unaware that the demon had been banished from the world.

There was no reply. "Oh, damn you, demon!" Kessell cursed. "You are never about when I most need you!" He spun on Regis. "You wait here. I shall have many more questions for you later!" The roaring fires of his anger simmered wickedly. "But first I must speak with some of my generals. I shall teach the Orcs of the Severed Tongue to oppose me!"

In truth, the observations Cassius had made had labeled the Orcs of the Severed Tongue as Kessell's strongest and most fanatical supporters.

A lie within a lie.

OUT ON THE WATERS OF MAER DUALDON LATER THAT EVENING, the assembled fleet of the four towns watched suspiciously as a second group of monsters flowed out from the main force and headed in the direction of Bremen.

"Curious," Kemp remarked to Muldoon of Lonelywood and the spokesman from the burned city of Bremen, who were standing on the deck of Targos' flagship beside him. All of Bremen's populace was out on the lake. Certainly the first group of orcs, after the initial bowshots, had met no further resistance in the city. And Bryn Shander stood intact. Why, then, was the wizard further extending his line of power?

"Akar Kessell confuses me," said Muldoon. "Either his genius is simply beyond me or he truly makes glaring tactical errors!"

"Assume the second possibility," Kemp instructed hopefully, "for anything that we might try shall be in vain if the first is the truth!"

So they continued repositioning their warriors for an opportune strike, moving their children and womenfolk in the remaining boats to the as yet unassailed moorings of Lonelywood, similar to the strategies of the refugee forces on the other two lakes.

On the wall of Bryn Shander, Cassius and Glensather watched the division of Kessell's forces with deeper understanding.

"Masterfully done, halfling," Cassius whispered into the night wind.

Smiling, Glensather put a steadying hand on his fellow spokesman's shoulder. "I shall go and inform our field commanders," he said. "If the time for us to attack comes, we shall be ready!"

Cassius clasped Glensather's hand and nodded his approval. As the spokesman from Easthaven sped away, Cassius leaned upon the ridge of the wall, glaring determinedly at the now darkened walls of Cryshal-Tirith. Through gritted teeth, he declared openly, "The time shall come!"

FROM THE HIGH VANTAGE POINT OF KELVIN'S CAIRN, DRIZZT Do'Urden had also witnessed the abrupt shift of the monster army. He had just completed the final preparations for his courageous assault on Cryshal-Tirith when the distant flickers of a large mass of torches suddenly flowed away to the west. He and Guenhwyvar sat quietly and studied the situation for a short while, trying to find some clue as to what had prompted such action.

Nothing became apparent, but the night was growing long and he had to make haste. He wasn't sure if the activity would prove helpful, by thinning out the camp's ranks, or disruptive, by heightening the remaining monsters' state of readiness. Yet he knew that the people of Bryn Shander could not afford any delays. He started down the mountain trail, the great panther trailing along silently behind him.

He made the open ground in good time and started his hasty trot down the length of Bremen's Run. If he had paused to study his surroundings or put one of his sensitive ears to the ground, he might have heard the distant rumble from the open tundra to the north of yet another approaching army.

But the drow's focus was on the south, his vision narrowed upon the waiting darkness of Cryshal-Tirith as he made haste. He was traveling light, carrying only items he believed essential to the task. He had his five weapons: the two scimitars sheathed in their leather scabbards on his hips, a dagger tucked in his belt at the middle of his back, and the two knives hidden in his boots. His holy symbol and pouch of wealth was around his neck and a small sack of flour, left over from the raid on the giant's lair, still hung on his belt—a sentimental choice, a comforting reminder of the daring adventures he had shared with Wulfgar. All of his other supplies, backpack, rope, waterskins, and other basic items of everyday survival on the harsh tundra, he had left in the small cubby.

He heard the shouts of goblin merrymaking when he crossed by the eastern outskirts of Termalaine. "Strike now, sailors of Maer Dualdon," the drow said quietly. But when he thought about it, he was glad that the boats remained out on the lake. Even if they could slip in and strike quickly at the monsters in the city, they could not afford the losses they would suffer. Termalaine could wait; there was a more important battle yet to be fought.

Drizzt and Guenhwyvar approached the outer perimeter of Kessell's main encampment. The drow was comforted by signs that the commotion within the camp had quieted. A solitary orc guard leaned wearily on its spear, halfheartedly watching the empty blackness of the northern horizon. Even had it been wary, it would not have noticed the stealthy approach of the two shapes, blacker than the darkness of night.

"Call in!" came a command from somewhere in the distance.

"Clear!" replied the guard.

Drizzt listened as the check was called in from various distant spots. He signaled for Guenhwyvar to hold back, then crept up within throwing range of the guard.

The tired orc never even heard the whistle of the approaching dagger.

And then Drizzt was beside it, silently breaking its fall into the darkness. The drow pulled his dagger from the orc's throat and laid his victim softly on the ground. He and Guenhwyvar, unnoticed shadows of death, moved on.

They had broken through the only line of guards that had been set on the northern perimeter and now easily picked their way among the sleeping camp. Drizzt could have killed dozens of orcs and goblins, even a verbeeg, though the cessation of its thundering snores might have drawn attention, but he couldn't afford to slow his pace. Each passing minute continued to drain Guenhwyvar, and now the first hints of a second enemy, the revealing dawn, were becoming apparent in the eastern sky.

The drow's hopes had risen considerably with the progress he had made, but he was dismayed when he came upon Cryshal-Tirith. A group of battle-ready ogre guards ringed the tower, blocking his way.

He crouched beside the cat, undecided on what they should do. To escape the breadth of the huge camp before the dawn exposed them, they would have to flee back the way they came. Drizzt doubted that Guenhwyvar, in its pitiful state, could even attempt that route. Yet to go on meant a hopeless fight with a group of ogres. There seemed no answer to the dilemma.

Then something happened back in the northeast section of the encampment, opening a path for the stealthy companions. Sudden shouts of alarm sprang up, drawing the ogres a few long strides away from their posts. Drizzt thought at first that the murdered orc guard had been discovered, but the cries were too far to the east.

Soon the clang of steel on steel rang out in the predawn air. A battle had been joined. Rival tribes, Drizzt supposed, though he could not spot the combatants from this distance.

His curiosity wasn't overwhelming, however. The undisciplined ogres had moved even farther away from their appointed positions. And Guenhwyvar had spotted the tower door. The two didn't hesitate for a second.

The ogres never even noticed the two shadows enter the tower behind them.

A STRANGE SENSATION, A BUZZING VIBRATION, CAME OVER Drizzt as he passed through Cryshal-Tirith's entryway, as though he had moved into the bowels of a living entity. He continued on, though, through the darkened hallway that led to the tower's first level, marveling at the strange crystalline material that comprised the walls and floors of the structure.

He found himself in a squared hall, the bottom chamber of the four-roomed structure. This was the hall where Kessell often met with his field generals, the wizard's primary audience hall for all but his top-ranking commanders.

Drizzt peered around at the dark forms in the room and the deeper shadows that they created. Though he sighted no movement, he sensed that he was not alone. He knew that Guenhwyvar had the same uneasy feelings, for the fur on the scruff of the black-coated neck was ruffled and the cat let out a low growl.

Kessell considered this room a buffer zone between himself and the rabble of the outside world. It was the one chamber in the tower that he rarely visited. This was the place where Akar Kessell housed his trolls.

29
OTHER OPTIONS

The dwarves of Mithral Hall completed the first of their secret exits shortly after sunset. Bruenor was the first to climb to the top of the ladder and peek out from under the cut sod at the settling monster army. So expert were the dwarven miners that they had been able to dig a shaft right up into the middle of a large group of goblins and ogres without even alerting the monsters in the least.

Bruenor was smiling when he came back down to rejoin his clansmen. "Finish th' other nine," he instructed as he moved down the tunnel, Catti-brie beside him. "Tonight's sleep'll be a sound one for some o' Kessell's boys!" he declared, patting the head of his belted axe.

"What role am I to play in the coming battle?" Catti-brie asked when they moved away from the other dwarves.

"Ye'll get to pull one o' the levers an' collapse the tunnels if any o' the swine come down," Bruenor replied.

"And if you are all killed on the field?" Catti-brie reasoned. "Being buried alone in these tunnels does not hold much promise for me."

Bruenor stroked his red beard. He hadn't considered that consequence, figuring only that if he and his clan were cut down on the field, Catti-brie would be safe enough behind the collapsed tunnels. But how could she live down here alone? What price would she pay for survival?

"Do ye want to come up an' fight then? Ye're fair enough with a sword, an' I'll be right beside ye!"

Catti-brie considered the proposition for a moment. "I'll stay with the lever," she decided. "You'll have enough to look after your own head up there. And someone has to be here to drop the tunnels; we cannot let goblins claim our halls as their home!

"Besides," she added with a smile, "it was stupid of me to worry. I know that you will come back to me, Bruenor. Never have you, nor any of your clan, failed me!" She kissed the dwarf on the forehead and skipped away.

Bruenor smiled after her. "Suren yer a brave girl, my Catti-brie," he muttered.

The work on the tunnels was finished a few hours later. The shafts had been dug and the entire tunnel complex around them had been rigged to collapse to cover any retreating action or squash any goblin advance. The entire clan, their faces purposely blackened with soot and their heavy armor and weapons muffled under layers of dark cloth, lined up at the base of the ten shafts. Bruenor went up first to investigate. He peeked out and smiled grimly. All around him ogres and goblins had bedded down for the night.

He was about to give the signal for his kinsmen to move when a commotion suddenly started up in the camp. Bruenor remained at the top of the shaft, though he kept his head beneath the sod layer (which got him stepped on by a passing goblin), and tried to figure out what had alerted the monsters. He heard shouts of command and a clatter like a large force assembling.

More shouts followed, calls for the death of the Severed Tongue. Though he had never heard that name before, the dwarf easily guessed that it described an orc tribe. "So, they're fightin' amongst themselves, are they?" he muttered softly, chuckling. Realizing that the dwarves' assault would have to wait, he climbed back down the ladder.

But the clan, disappointed in the delay, did not disperse. They were determined that this night's work would indeed be done. So they waited.

The night passed its midpoint and still the sounds of movement came from the camp above. Yet the wait wasn't dulling the edge of the dwarves' determination. Conversely, the delay was sharpening their intensity, heightening their hunger for goblin blood. These fighters were also blacksmiths, craftsmen who spent long hours adding a single scale to a dragon statue. They knew patience.

Finally, when all was again quiet, Bruenor went back up the ladder. Before he had even poked his head through the turf, he heard the comforting sounds of rhythmic breathing and loud snores.

Without further delay, the clan slipped out of the holes and methodically set about their murderous work. They did not revel in their roles as assassins, preferring to fight sword against sword, but they understood the necessity of this type of raid, and they placed no value whatsoever on the lives of goblin scum.

The area gradually quieted as more and more of the monsters entered the silent sleep of death. The dwarves concentrated on the ogres first, in case their attack was discovered before they were able to do much damage. But their strategy was unnecessary. Many minutes passed without retaliation.

By the time one of the guards noticed what was happening and managed to shout out a cry of alarm, the blood of more than a thousand of Kessell's charges wetted the field.

Cries went up all about them, but Bruenor did not call for a retreat. "Form up!" he commanded. "Tight around the tunnels!" He knew that the mad rush of the first wave of counterattackers would be disorganized and unprepared.

The dwarves formed into a tight defensive posture and had little trouble cutting the goblins down. Bruenor's axe was marked with many more notches before any goblin had even taken a swing at him.

Gradually, though, Kessell's charges became more organized. They came at the dwarves in formations of their own, and their growing numbers, as more and more of the camp was roused and alerted, began to press heavily on the raiders. And then a group of ogres, Kessell's elite tower guard, came charging across the field.

The first of the dwarves to retreat, the tunnel experts who were to make the final check on the preparations for the collapse, put their booted feet on the top rungs of the shaft ladders. The escape into the tunnels would be a delicate operation, and efficient haste would be the deciding factor in its success or failure.

But Bruenor unexpectedly ordered the tunnel experts to come back out of the shafts and the dwarves to hold their line.

He had heard the first notes of an ancient song, a song that, just a few years before, would have filled him with dread. Now, though, it lifted his heart with hope.

He recognized the voice that led the stirring words.

A SEVERED ARM OF ROTTED FLESH SPLATTED ON THE FLOOR, YET another victim of the whirring scimitars of Drizzt Do'Urden.

But the fearless trolls crowded in. Normally, Drizzt would have known of their presence as soon as he entered the square chamber. Their terrible stench made it hard for them to hide. These ones, though, hadn't actually been in the chamber when the drow entered. As Drizzt had moved deeper into the room, he tripped a magical alarm that bathed the area in wizard's light and cued the guardians. They stepped in through the magical mirrors that Kessell had planted as watchposts throughout the room.

Drizzt had already dropped one of the wretched beasts, but now he was more concerned with running than fighting. Five others replaced the first and were more than a match for any fighter.

Drizzt shook his head in disbelief when the body of the troll he had beheaded suddenly rose again and began flailing blindly.

And then, a clawed hand caught hold of his ankle. He knew without looking that it was the limb he had just cut free.

Horrified, he kicked the grotesque arm away from him and turned and sprinted to the spiraling stairway that ran up to the tower's second level from the back of the chamber. At his earlier command Guenhwyvar had already limped weakly up the stairs and now waited on the platform at the top.

Drizzt distinctly heard the sucking footsteps of his sickening pursuers and the scratching of the severed hand's filthy nails as it also took up the chase. The drow bounded up the stairway without looking back, hoping that his speed and agility would give him enough of a lead to find some way of escaping.

For there was no door on the platform.

The landing at the top of the stairs was rectangular and about ten feet across at its widest length. Two sides were open to the room, a third caught the lip of the cresting stairwell, and the fourth was a flat sheet of mirror, extending the exact length of the platform and secured between it and the chamber's ceiling. Drizzt hoped that he would be able to understand the nuances of this unusual door, if that was what the mirror actually was, when he examined it from the platform's level.

It wouldn't be that easy.

Though the mirror was filled with the reflection of an ornate tapestry hanging on the wall of the chamber directly opposite it, its surface appeared perfectly smooth and unbroken by any cracks or handles that might indicate a concealed opening. Drizzt sheathed his weapons and ran his hands across the surface to see if there was a handle hidden from his sharp eyes, but the even glide of the glass only confirmed his observation.

The trolls were on the stairway.

Drizzt tried to push his way through the glass, speaking all of the command words of opening he had ever learned, searching for an extra-dimensional portal similar to the ones that had held Kessell's hideous guards. The wall remained a tangible barrier.

The lead troll reached the halfway point on the stairs.

"There must be a clue somewhere!" the drow groaned. "Wizards love a challenge, and there is no sport to this!" The only possible answer lay in the intricate designs and images of the tapestry. Drizzt stared at it, trying to sort through the thousands of interwoven images for some special hint that would show him the way to safety.

The stench flowed up to him. He could hear the slobbering of the ever-hungry monsters.

But he had to control his revulsion and concentrate on the myriad images.

One thing in the tapestry caught his eye: the lines of a poem that wove through all of the other images along the top border. In contrast to the dulling colors of the rest of the ancient artwork, the calligraphed letters of the poem held the contrasting brightness of a newer addition. Something Kessell had added?

Come if ye will
To the orgy within,
But first ye must find the latch!
Seen and not seen,
Been yet not been
And a handle that flesh cannot catch.

One line in particular stood out in the drow's mind. He had heard the phrase "Been yet not been" in his childhood days in Menzoberranzan. They referred to Urgutha Forka, a vicious demon that had ravaged the planet with a particularly virulent plague in the ancient times when Drizzt's ancestors had walked on the surface. The surface elves had always denied the existence of Urgutha Forka, blaming the plague on the drow, but the dark elves knew better. Something in their physical make-up had kept them immune to the demon, and after they realized how deadly it was to their enemies, they had worked to fulfill the suspicions of the light elves by enlisting Urgutha as an ally.

Thus the reference "Been yet not been" was a derogatory line in a longer drow tale, a secret joke on their hated cousins who had lost thousands to a creature they denied even existed.

The riddle would have been impossible to anyone unaware of the tale of Urgutha Forka. The drow had found a valuable advantage. He scanned the reflection of the tapestry for some image that had a connection to the demon. And he found it on the far edge of the mirror at belt height: a portrayal of Urgutha itself, revealed in all of its horrible splendor. The demon was depicted smashing the skull of an elf with a black rod, its symbol. Drizzt had seen this same portrayal before. Nothing seemed out of place or hinted at anything unusual.

The trolls had turned the final corner of their ascent. Drizzt was nearly out of time.

He turned and searched the source of the image for some discrepancy. It struck him at once. In the original tapestry Urgutha was striking the elf with its fist; there was no rod!

"Seen and not seen."

Drizzt spun back on the mirror, grasping at the demon's illusory weapon. But all he felt was smooth glass. He nearly cried out in frustration.

His experience had taught him discipline, and he quickly regained his composure. He moved his hand back away from the mirror, attempting to position his own reflection at the same depth he judged the rod to be at. He slowly closed his fingers, watching his hand's image close around the rod with the excitement of anticipated success.

He shifted his hand slightly.

A thin crack appeared in the mirror.

The leading troll reached the top of the stairs, but Drizzt and Guenhwyvar were gone.

The drow slid the strange door back into its closed position, leaned back, and sighed with relief. A dimly lit stairway led up before him, ending with a platform that opened into the tower's second level. No door blocked the way, just hanging strands of beads, sparkling orange in the torchlight of the room beyond. Drizzt heard giggling,

Silently, he and the cat crept up the stairs and peeked over the rim of the landing. They had come to Kessell's harem room.

It was softly lit with torches glowing under screening shades. Most of the floor was covered with overstuffed pillows, and sections of the room were curtained off. The harem girls, Kessell's mindless playthings, sat in a circle in the center of the floor, giggling with the uninhibited enthusiasm of children at play. Drizzt doubted that they would notice him, but even if they did, he wasn't overly concerned. He understood right away that these pitiful, broken creatures were incapable of initiating any action against him.

He kept alert, though, especially of the curtained boudoirs. He doubted that Kessell would have put guards here, certainly none as unpredictably vicious as trolls, but he couldn't afford to make any mistakes.

With Guenhwyvar close at his side, he slipped silently from shadow to shadow, and when the two companions had ascended the stairs and were on the landing before the door to the third level, Drizzt was more relaxed.

But then the buzzing sound that Drizzt had heard when he first entered the tower returned. It gathered strength as it continued, as though its song came from the vibrations of the very walls of the tower. Drizzt looked all around for a possible source.

Chimes hanging from the room's ceiling began to tinkle eerily. The fires of the torches on the walls danced wildly.

Then Drizzt understood.

The structure was awakening with a life of its own. The field outside remained under the shadow of night, but the first fingers of dawn brightened the tower's high pinnacle.

The door suddenly swung open into the third level, Kessell's throne room.

"Well done!" cried the wizard. He was standing beyond the crystal throne across the room from Drizzt, holding an unlit candle and facing the open door. Regis stood obediently at his side, wearing a blank expression on his face.

"Please enter," Kessell said with false courtesy. "Fear not for my trolls that you injured, they will surely heal!" He threw his head back and laughed.

Drizzt felt a fool; to think that all of his caution and stealth had served no better purpose than to amuse the wizard! He rested his hands on the hilts of his sheathed scimitars and stepped through the doorway.

Guenhwyvar remained crouched in the shadows of the stairway, partly because the wizard had said nothing to indicate that he knew of the cat, and partly because the weakened cat didn't want to expend the energy of walking.

Drizzt halted before the throne and bowed low. The sight of Regis standing beside the wizard disturbed him more than a little, but he managed to hide that he recognized the halfling. Regis likewise had shown no familiarity when he had first seen the drow, though Drizzt couldn't be sure if that was a conscious effort or if the halfling was under the influence of some type of enchantment.

"Greetings, Akar Kessell," Drizzt stammered in the broken accent of denizens of the underworld, as though the common tongue of the surface was foreign to him. He figured that he might as well try the same tactics he had used against the demon. "I am sent from my people in good faith to parley with you on matters concerning our common interests."

Kessell laughed aloud. "Are you indeed!" A wide smile spread across his face, replaced abruptly with a scowl. His eyes narrowed evilly. "I know you, dark elf. Any man who has ever lived in Ten-Towns has heard the name of Drizzt Do'Urden in tale or in jest! So keep your lies unspoken!"

"Your pardon, mighty wizard," Drizzt said calmly, changing tactics. "In many ways, it seems, you are wiser than your demon."

The self-assured look disappeared from Kessell's face. He had been wondering what had prevented Errtu from answering his summons. He looked at the drow with more respect. Had this solitary warrior slain a major demon?

"Allow me to begin again," Drizzt said. "Greetings, Akar Kessell." He bowed low. "I am Drizzt Do'Urden, ranger of Gwaeron Windstrom, guardian of Icewind Dale. I have come to kill you."

The scimitars leaped out of their sheaths.

But Kessell moved, too. The candle he held suddenly flickered to life. Its flame was caught in the maze of prisms and mirrors that cluttered the entire chamber, focused and sharpened at each reflecting spot. Instantaneously with the lighting of the candle, three concentrated beams of light enclosed the drow in a triangular prison. None of the beams had touched him, but he sensed their power and dared not cross their path.

Drizzt clearly heard the tower humming as daylight filtered down its length. The room brightened considerably as several of the wall panels which had appeared mirrorlike in the torchlight showed themselves to be windows.

"Did you believe that you could walk right in here and simply dispose of me?" Kessell asked incredulously. "I am Akar Kessell, you fool! The Tyrant of Icewind Dale! I command the greatest army that has ever marched on the frozen steppes of this forsaken land!

"Behold my army!" He waved his hand and one of the scrying mirrors came to life, revealing part of the vast encampment that surrounded the tower, complete with the shouts of the awakening camp.

Then a death cry sounded from somewhere in the unseen reaches of the field. Instinctively, both the drow and the wizard tuned their ears on the distant clamor and heard the continuing ring of battle. Drizzt looked curiously at Kessell, wondering if the wizard knew what was happening in the northern section of his camp.

Kessell answered the drow's unspoken question with a wave of his hand. The image in the mirror clouded over with an inner fog for a moment, then shifted to the other side of the field. The shouts and clanging of the battle rang out loudly from within the depths of the scrying instrument. Then, as the mist cleared, the image of Bruenor's clansmen, fighting back to back in the midst of a sea of goblins, came clear. The field all around the dwarves was littered with the corpses of goblins and ogres.

"You see how foolish it is to oppose me?" Kessell squealed.

"It appears to me that the dwarves have done well."

"Nonsense!" Kessell screamed. He waved his hand again, and the fog returned to the mirror. Abruptly, the Song of Tempus resounded from within its depths. Drizzt leaned forward and strained to catch a glimpse of an image through the veil, anxious to see the leader of the song.

"Even as the stupid dwarves cut down a few of my lesser fighters, more warriors swarm to join the ranks of my army! Doom is upon you all, Drizzt Do'Urden! Akar Kessell is come!"

The fog cleared.

With a thousand fervent warriors behind him, Wulfgar approached the unsuspecting monsters. The goblins and orcs who were closest to the charging barbarians, holding unbending faith in the words of their master, cheered at the coming of their promised allies.

Then they died.

The barbarian horde drove through their ranks, singing and killing with wild abandonment. Even through the clatter of weapons, the sound of the dwarves joining in the Song of Tempus could be heard.

Wide-eyed, jaw hanging open, trembling with rage, Kessell waved the shocking image away and swung back on Drizzt. "It does not matter!" he said, fighting to keep his tone steady. "I shall deal with them mercilessly! And then Bryn Shander shall topple in flames!

"But first, you, traitorous drow," the wizard hissed. "Killer of your own kin, what gods have you left to pray to?" He puffed on the candle, causing its flame to dance on its side.

The angle of reflection shifted and one of the beams landed on Drizzt, boring a hole completely through the hilt of his old scimitar, and then drove deeper, cutting through the black skin of his hand. Drizzt grimaced in agony and clutched at his wound as the scimitar fell to the floor and the beam returned to its original path.

"You see how easy it is?" Kessell taunted. "Your feeble mind cannot begin to imagine the power of Crenshinibon! Feel blessed that I allowed you to feel a sample of that power before you died!"

Drizzt held his jaw firm, and there was no sign of pleading in his eyes as he glared at the wizard. He had long ago accepted the possibility of death as an acceptable risk of his trade, and he was determined to die with dignity.

Kessell tried to goad the sweat out of him. The wizard swayed the deadly candle tantalizingly about, causing the rays to shift back and forth. When he finally realized that he would not hear any whimpering or begging out of the proud ranger, Kessell grew tired of the game. "Farewell, fool," he growled and puckered his lips to puff on the flame.

Regis blew out the candle.

Everything seemed to come to a complete halt for several seconds. The wizard looked down at the halfling, whom he thought to be his slave, in horrified amazement. Regis merely shrugged his shoulders, as if he was as surprised by his uncharacteristically brave act as Kessell.

Relying on instinct, the wizard threw the silver plate that held the candle through the glass of the mirror and ran screaming toward the back corner of the room to a small ladder hidden in the shadows. Drizzt had just taken his first steps when the fires within the mirror roared. Four evil red eyes stared out, catching the drow's attention, and two hellhounds bounded through the broken glass.

Guenhwyvar intercepted one, leaping past its master and crashing headlong into the demon hound. The two beasts tumbled back toward the rear of the room, a black and tawny-red blur of fangs and claws, knocking Regis aside.

The second dog unleashed its fire breath at Drizzt, but again, as with the demon, the fire didn't bother the drow. Then it was his turn to strike. The fire-hating scimitar rang in ecstasy, cleaving the charging beast in half as Drizzt brought it down. Amazed at the power of the blade but not having time even to gawk at his mutilated victim, Drizzt resumed his chase.

He reached the bottom of the ladder. Up above, through the open trap door to the tower's highest floor, came the rhythmic flashing of a throbbing light. Drizzt felt the intensity of the vibrations increasing with each pulse. The heart of Cryshal-Tirith was beating stronger with the rising sun. Drizzt understood the danger that he was heading into, but he didn't have the time to stop and ponder the odds.

And then he was once again facing Kessell, this time in the smallest room of the structure. Between them, hanging eerily in midair, was the pulsating hunk of crystal—Cryshal-Tirith's heart. It was four-sided and tapered like an icicle. Drizzt recognized it as a miniature replica of the tower he stood in, though it was barely a foot long.

An exact image of Crenshinibon.

A wall of light emanated from it, cutting the chamber in half, with the drow on one side and the wizard on the other. Drizzt knew from the wizard's snicker that it was a barrier as tangible as one of stone. Unlike the cluttered scrying room below, only one mirror, appearing more like a window in the tower's wall, adorned this room, just to the side of the wizard.

"Strike the heart, drow," Kessell laughed. "Fool! The heart of Cryshal-Tirith is mightier than any weapon in the world! Nothing that you could ever do, magical or otherwise, could even put the slightest scratch upon its pure surface! Strike it; let your foolish impertinence be revealed!"

Drizzt had other plans, though. He was flexible and cunning enough to realize that some foes could not be defeated with force alone. There were always other options.

He sheathed his remaining weapon, the magical scimitar, and began untying the rope that secured the sack to his belt. Kessell looked on curiously, disturbed by the drow's calm, even when his death seemed inevitable. "What are you doing?" the wizard demanded.

Drizzt didn't reply. His actions were methodical and unshaken. He loosened the drawstring on the sack and pulled it open.

"I asked you what you were doing!" Kessell scowled as Drizzt began walking toward the heart. Suddenly the replica seemed vulnerable to the wizard. He had the uncomfortable feeling that perhaps this dark elf was more dangerous than he had originally estimated.

Crenshinibon sensed it, too. The Crystal Shard telepathically instructed Kessell to unleash a killing bolt and be done with the drow.

But Kessell was afraid.

Drizzt neared the crystal. He tried to put his hand over it, but the light wall repulsed him. He nodded, expecting as much, and pulled back the sack's opening as wide as it would go. His concentration was solely on the tower itself; he never looked at the wizard or acknowledged his ranting.

Then he emptied the bag of flour over the gemstone.

The tower seemed to groan in protest. It darkened.

The wall of light that separated the drow from the wizard disappeared.

But still Drizzt concentrated on the tower. He knew that the layer of suffocating flour could only block the gemstone's powerful radiations for a short time.

Long enough, though, for him to slip the now empty bag over it and pull the drawstring tight. Kessell wailed and lurched forward, but halted before the drawn scimitar.

"No!" the wizard cried in helpless protest. "Do you realize the consequences of what you have done?" As if in answer, the tower trembled. It calmed quickly, but both the drow and the wizard sensed the approaching danger. Somewhere in the bowels of Cryshal-Tirith, the decay had already begun.

"I understand completely," replied Drizzt. "I have defeated you, Akar Kessell. Your short reign as self-proclaimed ruler of Ten-Towns is ended."

"You have killed yourself, drow!" Kessell retorted as Cryshal-Tirith shuddered again, this time even more violently. "You cannot hope to escape before the tower crumbles upon you!"

The quake came again. And again.

Drizzt shrugged, unconcerned. "So be it," he said. "My purpose is fulfilled, for you, too, shall perish."

A sudden, crazy cackle exploded from the wizard's lips. He spun away from Drizzt and dived at the mirror embedded in the tower wall. Instead of crashing through the glass and falling to the field below, as Drizzt expected, Kessell slipped into the mirror and was gone.

The tower shook again, and this time the trembling did not relent. Drizzt started for the trap door but could barely keep his footing. Cracks appeared along the walls.

"Regis!" he yelled, but there was no answer. Part of the wall in the room below had already collapsed; Drizzt could see the rubble at the base of the ladder. Praying that his friends had already escaped, he took the only route left open to him.

He dived through the magic mirror after Kessell.

30
THE BATTLE OF ICEWIND DALE

The people of Bryn Shander heard the fighting out on the field, but it wasn't until the lightening of full dawn that they could see what was happening. They cheered the dwarves wildly and were amazed when the barbarians crashed into Kessell's ranks, hacking down goblins with gleeful abandon.

Cassius and Glensather, in their customary positions upon the wall, pondered the unexpected turn of events, undecided as to whether or not they should release their forces into the fray.

"Barbarians?" gawked Glensather. "Are they our friends or foes?"

"They kill orcs," Cassius answered. "They are friends!"

Out on Maer Dualdon, Kemp and the others also heard the clang of battle, though they couldn't see who was involved. Even more confusing, a second fight had begun, this one to the southwest, in the town of Bremen. Had the men of Bryn Shander come out and attacked? Or was Akar Kessell's force destroying itself around him?

Then Cryshal-Tirith suddenly fell dark, its once glassy and vibrant sides taking on an opaque, deathly stillness.

"Regis," muttered Cassius, sensing the tower's loss of power. "If ever a hero we had!"

The tower shuddered and shook. Great cracks appeared over the length of its walls. Then it broke apart.

The monster army looked on in horrified disbelief as the bastion of the wizard they had come to worship as a god came crashing down.

The horns in Bryn Shander began to blow. Kemp's people cheered wildly and rushed for the oars. Jensin Brent's forward scouts signaled back the startling news to the fleet on Lac Dinneshere, who in turn relayed the message to Redwaters. Throughout the temporary sanctuaries that hid the routed people of Ten-Towns came the same command.

"Charge!"

The army assembled inside the great gates of Bryn Shander's wall poured out of the courtyard and onto the field. The fleets of Caer-Konig and Caer-Dineval on Lac Dinneshere and Good Mead and Dougan's Hole in the south lifted their sails to catch the east wind and raced across the lakes. The four fleets assembled on Maer Dualdon rowed hard, bucking that same wind in their haste to get revenge.

In a whirlwind rush of chaos and surprise, the final Battle of Icewind Dale had begun.

REGIS ROLLED OUT OF THE WAY AS THE EMBATTLED CREATURES tumbled past again, claws and fangs tearing and ripping in a desperate struggle. Normally, Guenhwyvar would have had little trouble dispatching the helldog, but in its weakened state the cat found itself fighting for its life. The hound's hot breath seared black fur; its great fangs bit into muscled neck.

Regis wanted to help the cat, but he couldn't even get close enough to kick at its foe. Why had Drizzt run off so abruptly?

Guenhwyvar felt its neck being crushed by the powerful maw. The cat rolled, its greater weight taking the dog over with it, but the hold of the canine jaws was not broken. Dizziness swept over the cat from lack of air. It began to send its mind back across the planes, to its true home, though it lamented having failed its master in his time of need.

Then the tower went dark. The startled hellhound relaxed its grip slightly, and Guenhwyvar was quick to seize the opportunity. The cat planted its paws against the dog's ribs and shoved free of the grasp, rolling away into the blackness.

The helldog scanned for its foe, but the panther's powers of stealth were beyond even the considerable awareness of its keen senses. Then the dog saw a second quarry. A single bound took it to Regis.

Guenhwyvar was playing a game that it knew better now. The panther was a creature of the night, a predator that struck from the blackness and killed before its prey even sensed its presence. The helldog crouched for a strike at Regis, then dropped as the panther landed heavily upon its back, claws raking deeply into the rust-colored hide.

The dog yelped only once before the killing fangs found its neck.

Mirrors cracked and shattered. A sudden hole in the floor swallowed Kessell's throne. Blocks of crystalline rubble began falling all about as the tower shuddered in its death throes. Screams from the harem chamber below told Regis that a similar scene of destruction was common throughout the structure. He was gladdened when he saw Guenhwyvar dispatch the helldog, but he understood the futility of the cat's heroics. They had nowhere to run, no escape from the death of Cryshal-Tirith.

Regis called Guenhwyvar to his side. He couldn't see the cat's body in the blackness, but he saw the eyes, intent upon him and circling around, as though the cat was stalking him. "What?" the halfling balked in astonishment, wondering if the stress and the wounds the dog had inflicted upon Guenhwyvar had driven the cat into madness.

A chunk of wall crashed right beside him, sending him sprawling to the floor. He saw the cat's eyes rise high into the air; Guen-hwyvar had sprung.

Dust choked him, and he felt the final collapse of the crystal tower begin. Then came a deeper darkness as the black cat engulfed him.

DRIZZT FELT HIMSELF FALLING.

The light was too bright; he couldn't see. He heard nothing, not even the sound of air rushing by. Yet he knew for certain that he was falling.

And then the light dimmed in a gray mist, as though he were passing through a cloud. It all seemed so dreamlike, so completely unreal. He couldn't recall how he had gotten into this position. He couldn't recall his own name.

Then he dropped into a deep pile of snow and knew that he was not dreaming. He heard the howl of the wind and felt its freezing bite. He tried to stand and get a better idea of his surroundings.

And then he heard, far away and below, the screams of the raging battle. He remembered Cryshal-Tirith, remembered where he had been. There could only be one answer.

He was on top of Kelvin's Cairn.

THE SOLDIERS OF BRYN SHANDER AND EASTHAVEN, FIGHTING arm in arm with Cassius and Glensather at their head, charged down the sloping hill and drove hard into the confused ranks of goblins. The two spokesmen had a particular goal in mind: They wanted to cut through the ranks of monsters and link up with Bruenor's charges. On the wall a few moments before, they had seen the barbarians attempting the same strategy, and they figured that if all three armies could be brought together in flanking support, their slim chances would be greatly improved.

The goblins gave way to the assault. In their absolute dismay and surprise at the sudden turn of events, the monsters were unable to organize any semblance of a defensive line.

When the four fleets on Maer Dualdon landed just north of the ruins of Targos, they encountered the same disorganized and disoriented resistance. Kemp and the other leaders had figured that they could easily gain a foothold on the land but their main concern was that the large goblin forces occupying Termalaine would sweep down behind them if they pushed in from the beach and cut off their only escape route.

They needn't have worried, though. In the first stages of the battle, the goblins in Termalaine had indeed rushed out with every intention of supporting their wizard. But then Cryshal-Tirith had tumbled down. The goblins were already skeptical, having heard rumors throughout the night that Kessell had dispatched a large force to wipe out the Orcs of the Severed Tongue in the conquered city of Bremen. And when they saw the tower, the pinnacle of Kessell's strength, crash down in ruins, they had reconsidered their alternatives, weighing the consequences of the choices before them. They fled back to the north and the safety of the open plain.

BLOWING SNOW ADDED TO THE HEAVY VEIL ATOP THE MOUNTAIN. Drizzt kept his eyes down, but he could hardly see his own feet as he determinedly placed one in front of the other. He still held the magical scimitar, and it glowed a pale light, as though it approved of the frigid temperatures.

The drow's numbing body begged him to start down the mountain, and yet he was moving farther along the high face, to one of the adjacent peaks. The wind carried a disturbing sound to his ears—the cackle of insane laughter.

And then he saw the blurred form of the wizard, leaning out over the southern precipice, trying to catch a glimpse of what was happening on the battlefield below.

"Kessell!" Drizzt shouted. He saw the form shift abruptly and knew that the wizard had heard him, even through the howl of the wind. "In the name of the people of Ten-Towns, I demand that you surrender to me! Quickly, now, lest this unrelenting breath of winter freeze us where we stand!"

Kessell sneered. "You still do not understand what it is you face, do you?" he asked in amazement. "Do you truly believe that you have won this battle?"

"How the people below fare I do not yet know," Drizzt answered. "But you are defeated! Your tower is destroyed, Kessell, and without it you are but a minor trickster!" He continued moving while they talked and was now only a few feet from the wizard, though his opponent was still a mere black blur in a gray field.

"Do you wish to know how they fare, drow?" Kessell asked. "Then look! Witness the fall of Ten-Towns!" He reached under his cloak and pulled out a shining object—a crystal shard. The clouds seemed to recoil from it. The wind halted within the wide radius of its influence. Drizzt could see its incredible power. The drow felt the blood returning to his numbed hands in the light of the crystal. Then the gray veil was burned away, and the sky before them was clear.

"The tower destroyed?" Kessell mocked. "You have broken just one of Crenshinibon's countless images! A sack of flour? To defeat the most powerful relic in the world? Look down upon the foolish men who dare to oppose me!"

The battlefield was spread wide before the drow. He could see the white, wind-filled sails of the boats of Caer-Dineval and Caer-Konig as they neared the western banks of Lac Dinneshere.

In the south, the fleets of Good Mead and Dougan's Hole had already docked. The sailors met no initial resistance, and even now were forming up for an inland strike. The goblins and orcs that had formed the southern half of Kessell's ring had not witnessed the fall of Cryshal-Tirith. Though they sensed the loss of power and guidance, and as many of them remained where they were or deserted their comrades and fled as rushed around Bryn Shander's hill to join in the battle.

Kemp's troops were also ashore, shoving off cautiously from the beaches with a wary eye to the north. This group had landed into the thickest concentration of Kessell's forces, but also into the area that was under the shadow of the tower, where the fall of Cryshal-Tirith had been the most disheartening. The fishermen found more goblins interested in running away than ones intent on a fight.

In the center of the field, where the heaviest fighting was taking place, the men of Ten-Towns and their allies also seemed to be faring well. The barbarians had nearly joined with the dwarves. Spurred by the might of Wulfgar's hammer and the unrivaled courage of Bruenor, the two forces were tearing apart all that stood between them. And they would soon become even more formidable, for Cassius and Glensather were close by and moving in at a steady pace.

"By the tale my eyes tell me, your army does not fare well," Drizzt retorted. "The 'foolish' men of Ten-Towns are not defeated yet!"

Kessell raised the Crystal Shard high above him, its light flaring to an even greater level of power. Down on the battlefield, even at the great distance, the combatants understood at once the resurgence of the powerful presence they had known as Cryshal-Tirith. Human, dwarf, and goblin alike, even those locked in mortal combat, paused for a second to look at the beacon on the mountain. The monsters, sensing the return of their god, cheered wildly and abandoned their heretofore defensive posture. Encouraged by the glorious reappearance of Kessell, they pressed the attack with savage fury.

"You see how my mere presence incites them!" Kessell boasted proudly.

But Drizzt wasn't paying attention to the wizard or the battle below. He was standing in puddles of water now from snow melting under the warmth of the shining relic. He was intent on a noise that his keen ears had caught among the clatter of the distant fighting. A rumble of protest from the frozen peaks of Kelvin's Cairn.

"Behold the glory of Akar Kessell!" the wizard cried, his voice magnified to deafening proportions by the power of the relic he held. "How easy it shall be for me to destroy the boats on the lake below!"

Drizzt realized that Kessell, in his arrogant disregard for the dangers growing around him, was making a flagrant mistake. All that he had to do was delay the wizard from taking any decisive actions for the next few moments. Reflexively, he grabbed the dagger at the back of his belt and flung it at Kessell, though he knew that Kessell was joined in some perverted symbiosis with Crenshinibon and that the small weapon had no chance of hitting its mark. The drow was hoping to distract and anger the wizard to divert his fury away from the battlefield.

The dagger sped through the air. Drizzt turned and ran.

A thin beam shot out from Crenshinibon and melted the weapon before it found its mark, but Kessell was outraged. "You should bow down before me!" he screamed at Drizzt. "Blasphemous dog, you have earned the distinction of being my first victim of the day!" He swung the shard away from the ledge to point it at the fleeing drow. But as he spun he sank, suddenly up to his knees in the melting snow.

Then he, too, heard the angry rumbles of the mountain.

Drizzt broke free of the relic's sphere of influence, and, without hesitating to look back, he ran, putting as much distance between himself and the southern face of Kelvin's Cairn as he could.

Immersed up to his chest now, Kessell struggled to get free of the watery snow. He called upon the power of Crenshinibon again, but his concentration wavered under the intense stress of impending doom.

Akar Kessell felt weak again for the first time in years. Not the

Tyrant of Icewind Dale, but the bumbling apprentice who had murdered his teacher.

As if the Crystal Shard had rejected him.

Then the entire side of the mountain's snowcap fell. The rumble shook the land for many miles around. Men and orcs, goblins and even ogres, were thrown to the ground.

Kessell clutched the shard close to him when he began to fall. But Crenshinibon burned his hands, pushed him away. Kessell had failed too many times. The relic would no longer accept him as its wielder.

Kessell screamed when he felt the shard slipping through his fingers. His shriek, though, was drowned out by the thunder of the avalanche. The cold darkness of snow closed around him, falling, tumbling with him on the descent. Kessell desperately believed that if he still held the Crystal Shard, he could survive even this. Small comfort when he settled onto a lower peak of Kelvin's Cairn.

And half of the mountain's cap landed on top of him.

THE MONSTER ARMY HAD SEEN THEIR GOD FALL AGAIN. THE thread that had incited their momentum quickly began to unravel. But in the time that Kessell had reappeared, some measure of coordinating activity had taken place. Two frost giants, the only remaining true giants in the wizard's entire army, had taken command. They called the elite ogre guard to their side and then called for the orc and goblin tribes to gather around them and follow their lead.

Still, the dismay of the army was obvious. Tribal rivalries that had been buried under the iron-fisted domination of Akar Kessell resurfaced in the form of blatant mistrust. Only fear of their enemies kept them fighting, and only fear of the giants held them in line beside the other tribes.

"Well met, Bruenor!" Wulfgar sang out, splattering another

goblin head, as the barbarian horde finally broke through to the dwarves.

"An' to yerself, boy!" the dwarf replied, burying his axe into the chest of his own opponent. "Time's almost passed that ye got back! I thought that I'd have to kill yer share o' the scum, too!"

Wulfgar's attention was elsewhere, though. He had discovered the two giants commanding the force. "Frost giants," he told Bruenor, directing the dwarf's gaze to the ring of ogres. "They are all that hold the tribes together!"

"Better sport!" Bruenor laughed. "Lead on!"

And so, with his principal attendants and Bruenor beside him, the young king started smashing a path through the goblin ranks.

The ogres crowded in front of their newfound commanders to block the barbarian's path.

Wulfgar was close enough by then.

Aegis-fang whistled past the ogre ranks and took one of the giants in the head, dropping it lifeless to the ground. The other, gawking in disbelief that a human had been able to deliver such a deadly blow against one of its kind from such a distance, hesitated for only a brief moment before it fled the battle.

Undaunted, the vicious ogres charged in on Wulfgar's group, pushing them back. But Wulfgar was satisfied, and he willingly gave ground before the press, anxious to rejoin the bulk of the human and dwarven army.

Bruenor wasn't so willing, though. This was the type of chaotic fighting that he most enjoyed. He disappeared under the long legs of the leading line of ogres and moved, unseen in the dust and confusion, among their ranks.

From the corner of his eye, Wulfgar saw the dwarf's odd departure. "Where are you off to?" he shouted after him, but battle-hungry Bruenor couldn't hear the call and wouldn't have heeded it anyway.

Wulfgar couldn't view the flight of the wild dwarf, but he could approximate Bruenor's position, or at least where the dwarf had just been, as ogre after ogre doubled over in surprised agony, clutching a knee, hamstring, or groin.

Above all of the commotion, those orcs and goblins who weren't engaged in direct combat kept a watchful eye on Kelvin's Cairn, awaiting the second resurgence.

But settled now on the lower slopes of the mountain, there was only snow.

LUSTING FOR REVENGE, THE FIGHTING MEN OF CAER-KONIG AND Caer-Dineval brought their ships in under full sail, sliding them up recklessly onto the sands of the shallows to avoid the delays of mooring in deeper waters. They leaped from the boats and splashed ashore, rushing into the battle with a fearless frenzy that drove their opponents away.

Once they had established themselves on the land, Jensin Brent brought them together in a tight formation and turned them south. The spokesman heard the fighting far off in that direction and knew that the men of Good Mead and Dougan's Hole were cutting a swath north to join up with his men. His plan was to meet them on the Eastway and then drive westward toward Bryn Shander with his reinforced numbers.

Many of the goblins on this side of the city had long since fled, and many more had gone northwest to the ruins of Cryshal-Tirith and the main fighting. The army of Lac Dinneshere made good speed toward their goal. They reached the road with few losses and dug in to wait for the southerners.

KEMP WATCHED ANXIOUSLY FOR THE SIGNAL FROM THE LONE ship sailing on the waters of Maer Dualdon. The spokesman from Targos, appointed commander of the forces of the four cities of the lake, had moved cautiously thus far for fear of a heavy assault from the north. He held his men in check, allowing them to fight only the monsters that came to them, though this conservative stance, with the sounds of raging battle howling across the field, was tearing at his adventurous heart.

As the minutes had dragged along with no sign of goblin reinforcements, the spokesman had sent a small schooner to run up the coastline and find out what was delaying the occupying force in Termalaine.

Then he spied the white sails gliding into view. Riding high upon the small ship's bow was the signal flag that Kemp had most desired but least expected: the red banner of the catch, though in this instance, it signaled that Termalaine was clear and the goblins were fleeing northward.

Kemp ran to the highest spot he could find, his face flushed with a vengeful desire. "Break the line, boys!" he shouted to his men. "Cut me a swath to the city on the hill! Let Cassius come back and find us sitting on the doorstep of his town!"

They shouted wildly with every step, men who had lost homes and kin and seen their cities burned out from under them. Many of them had nothing left to lose. All that they could hope to gain was a small taste of bitter satisfaction.

THE BATTLE RAGED FOR THE REMAINDER OF THE MORNING, MAN and monster alike lifting swords and spears that seemed to have doubled their weight. Yet exhaustion, though it slowed their reflexes, did nothing to temper the anger that burned in the blood of every combatant.

The battle lines grew indistinguishable as the fighting wore on, with troops getting hopelessly separated from their commanders. In many places, goblins and orcs fought against each other, unable, even with a common foe so readily available, to sublimate their long-standing hatred for the rival tribes. A thick cloud of dust enveloped the heaviest concentrations of fighting; the dizzying clamor of steel grating on steel, swords banging against shields, and the expanding screams of death, agony, and victory degenerated the structured clash into an all-out brawl.

The sole exception was the group of battle-seasoned dwarves. Their ranks did not waver or disintegrate in the least, though Bruenor had not yet returned to them after his strange exit.

The dwarves provided a solid platform for the barbarians to strike from and for Wulfgar and his small group to mark for their return. The young king was back among the ranks of his men just as Cassius and his force linked up. The spokesman and Wulfgar exchanged intent stares, neither certain of where he stood with the other. Both were wise enough to trust fully in their alliance for the present, though. Both understood that intelligent foes put aside their differences in the face of a greater enemy.

Supporting each other would be the only advantage that the newly banded allies enjoyed. Together, they outnumbered and could overwhelm any individual orc or goblin tribe they faced. And since the goblin tribes would not work in unison, each group had no external support on its flanks. Wulfgar and Cassius, following and supporting each other's movements, sent out defensive spurs of warriors to hold off perimeter groups, while the main force of the combined army blasted through one tribe at a time.

Though his troops had cut down better than ten goblins for every man they had lost, Cassius was truly concerned. Thousands of the monsters had not even come in contact with the humans or raised a weapon yet, and his men were nearly dropping with fatigue. He had to get them back to the city. He let the dwarves lead the way.

Wulfgar, also apprehensive about his warriors' ability to maintain their pace, and knowing that there was no other escape route, instructed his men to follow Cassius and the dwarves. This was a gamble, for the barbarian king wasn't even certain that the people of Bryn Shander would let his warriors into the city.

Kemp's force had made impressive initial headway in their charge to the slopes of the principal city, but as they neared their goal, they ran up against heavier and more desperate concentrations of humanoids. Barely a hundred yards from the hill, they were bogged down and fighting on all sides.

The armies rolling in from the east had done better. Their rush down the Eastway had met with little resistance, and they were the first to reach the hill. They had sailed madly across the breadth of the lakes and ran and fought all the way across the plain, yet Jensin Brent, the lone surviving spokesman of the original four, for Schermont and the two from the southern cities had fallen on the Eastway, would not let them rest. He clearly heard the heated battle and knew that the brave men in the northern fields, facing the mass of Kessell's army, needed any support they could get.

Yet when the spokesman led his troops around the final bend to the city's north gate, they froze in their tracks and looked upon the spectacle of the most brutal battle they had ever seen or even heard of in exaggerated tales. Combatants battled atop the hacked bodies of the fallen; fighters who had somehow lost their weapons bit and scratched at their opponents.

Brent surmised at once that Cassius and his large force would be able to make it back to the city on their own. The armies of Maer Dualdon, though, were in a tight spot.

"To the west!" he cried to his men as he charged toward the trapped force. A new surge of adrenaline sent the weary army in full flight to the rescue of their comrades. On orders from Brent, they came down off of the slopes in a long, side-by-side line, but when they reached the battlefield, only the middle group continued forward. The groups at the ends of the formation collapsed into the middle, and the whole force had soon formed a wedge, its tip breaking all the way through the monsters to reach Kemp's embattled armies.

Kemp's men eagerly accepted the lifeline, and the united force was soon able to retreat to the northern face of the hill. The last stragglers stumbled in at the same time as the army of Cassius, Wulfgar's barbarians, and the dwarves broke free of the closest ranks of goblins and climbed the open ground of the hill. Now, with the humans and dwarves joined as one force, the goblins moved in tentatively. Their losses had been staggering. No giants or ogres remained, and several entire tribes of goblins and orcs lay dead. Cryshal-Tirith was a pile of blackened rubble, and Akar Kessell was buried in a frozen grave.

The men on Bryn Shander's hill were battered and wobbly with exhaustion, yet the grim set of their jaws told the remaining monsters unequivocally that they would fight on to their last breath. They had backed into the final corner; there would be no further retreat.

Doubts crept into the mind of every goblin and orc that remained to carry on the war. Though their numbers were still probably sufficient to complete the task, many more of them would yet fall before the fierce men of Ten-Towns and their deadly allies would be put down. Even then, which of the surviving tribes would claim victory? Without the guidance of the wizard, the survivors of the battle would certainly be hard-pressed to fairly divide the spoils without further fighting.

The Battle of Icewind Dale had not followed the course that Akar Kessell had promised.

31
VICTORY?

The men of Ten-Towns, along with their dwarven and barbarian allies, had fought their way from all sides of the wide field and now stood unified before the northern gate of Bryn Shander. And while their army had achieved a singular fighting stance, with all of the once-separate groups banded together toward the common goal of survival, Kessell's army had gone down the opposite road. When the goblins had first charged into Icewind Pass, their common purpose was victory for the glory of Akar Kessell. But Kessell was gone and Cryshal-Tirith destroyed, and the cord that had held together the long-standing, bitter enemies, the rival orc and goblin tribes, had begun to unravel.

The humans and dwarves looked upon the mass of invaders with returning hope, for on all the outer fringes of the vast force dark shapes continued to break away and flee from the battlefield and back to the tundra.

Still, the defenders of Ten-Towns were surrounded on three sides with their backs to Bryn Shander's wall. At this point the monsters made no move to press the attack, but thousands of goblins held their positions all around the northern fields of the city.

Earlier in the battle, when the initial attacks had caught the invaders by surprise, the leaders of the engaged defending forces would have considered such a lull in the fighting disastrous, stealing their momentum and allowing their stunned enemies to regroup into more favorable formations.

Now, though, the break came as a two-fold blessing: It gave the soldiers a desperately needed rest and let the goblins and orcs fully absorb the beating they had taken. The field on this side of the city was littered with corpses, many more goblin than human, and the crumbled pile that was Cryshal-Tirith only heightened the monsters' perceptions of their staggering losses. No giants or ogres remained to bolster their thinning lines, and each passing second saw more of their allies desert the cause.

Cassius had time to call all the surviving spokesmen to his side for a brief council.

A short distance away, Wulfgar and Revjak were meeting with Fender Mallot, the appointed leader of the dwarven forces in light of Bruenor's disturbing absence.

"Glad we are o' yer return, mighty Wulfgar," Fender said. "Bruenor knew ye'd be back."

Wulfgar looked out over the field, searching for some sign that Bruenor was still out there swinging. "Have you any news of Bruenor at all?"

"Ye, yerself, were the last to see 'im," Fender replied grimly.

And then they were silent, scanning the field.

"Let me hear again the ring of your axe," Wulfgar whispered.

But Bruenor could not hear him.

"JENSIN," CASSIUS ASKED THE SPOKESMAN FROM CAER-DINEVAL, "where are your womenfolk and children? Are they safe?"

"Safe in Easthaven," Jensin Brent replied. "Joined, by now, by the people of Good Mead and Dougan's Hole. They are well provisioned and watched. If Kessell's wretches make for the town, the people shall know of the danger with ample time left for them to put back out onto Lac Dinneshere."

"But how long could they survive on the water?" Cassius asked. Jensin Brent shrugged noncommittally. "Until the winter falls, I should guess. They shall always have a place to land though, for the remaining goblins and orcs could not possibly encompass even half of the lake's shoreline."

Cassius seemed satisfied. He turned to Kemp.

"Lonelywood," Kemp answered to his unspoken question. "And I'll wager that they're better off than we are! They've enough boats in dock there to found a city in the middle of Maer Dualdon."

"That is good," Cassius told them. "It leaves yet another option open to us. We could, perhaps, hold our ground here for a while, then retreat back within the walls of the city. The goblins and orcs, even with their greater numbers, couldn't hope to conquer us there!"

The idea seemed to appeal to Jensin Brent, but Kemp scowled. "So our folk may be safe enough," he said, "but what of the barbarians?"

"Their women are sturdy and capable of surviving without them," Cassius replied.

"I care not the least for their foul-smelling women," Kemp blustered, purposely raising his voice so that Wulfgar and Revjak, holding their own council not far away, could hear him. "I speak of these wild dogs, themselves! Surely you're not going to open your door wide in invitation to them!"

Proud Wulfgar started toward the spokesmen.

Cassius turned angrily on Kemp. "Stubborn ass!" he whispered harshly. "Our only hope lies in unity!"

"Our only hope lies in attacking!" Kemp retorted. "We have them terrified, and you ask us to run and hide!"

The huge barbarian king stepped up before the two spokesmen, towering above them. "Greetings, Cassius of Bryn Shander," he said politely. "I am Wulfgar, son of Beornegar, and leader of the tribes who have come to join in your noble cause."

"What could your kind possibly know of nobility?" Kemp interrupted. Wulfgar ignored him.

"I have overheard much of your discussion," he continued, un-shaken. "It is my judgment that your ill-mannered and ungrateful advisor," he paused for control, "has proposed the only solution."

Cassius, still expecting Wulfgar to be enraged at Kemp's insults, was at first confused.

"Attack," Wulfgar explained. "The goblins are uncertain now of what gains they can hope to make. They wonder why they ever followed the evil wizard to this place of doom. If they are allowed to find their battle lust again, they will prove a more formidable foe."

"I thank you for your words, barbarian king," Cassius replied. "Yet it is my guess that this rabble will not be able to support a siege. They will leave the fields before a tenday has passed!"

"Perhaps," said Wulfgar. "Yet even then your people shall pay dearly. The goblins leaving of their own choice will not return to their caves empty-handed. There are still several unprotected cities that they could strike at on their way out of Icewind Dale.

"And worse yet, they shall not leave with fear in their eyes. Your retreat shall save the lives of some of your men, Cassius, but it will not prevent the future return of your enemies!"

"Then you agree that we should attack?" Cassius asked.

"Our enemies have come to fear us. They look about and see the ruin we have brought down upon them. Fear is a powerful tool, es-pecially against cowardly goblins. Let us complete the rout, as your people did to mine five years ago . . ."—Cassius recognized the pain in Wulfgar's eyes as he recalled the incident—". . . and send these foul beasts scurrying back to their mountain homes! Many years shall pass before they venture out to strike at your towns again."

Cassius looked upon the young barbarian with profound re-spect, and also deep curiosity. He could hardly believe that these proud tundra warriors, who vividly remembered the slaughter they had suffered at the hands of Ten-Townsmen, had come to the aid of the fishing communities. "My people did indeed rout yours, noble king. Brutally. Why, then, have you come?"

"That is a matter we shall discuss after we have completed our task," Wulfgar answered. "Now, let us sing! Let us strike terror into the hearts of our enemies and break them!"

He turned to Revjak and some of his other leaders. "Sing, proud warriors!" he commanded. "Let the Song of Tempus foretell the death of the goblins!" A rousing cheer went up throughout the barbarian ranks, and they lifted their voices proudly to their god of war.

Cassius noted the immediate effect the song had on the closest monsters. They backed away a step and clutched their weapons tightly.

A smile crossed the spokesman's face. He still couldn't understand the barbarians' presence, but explanations would have to wait. "Join our barbarian allies!" he shouted to his soldiers. "Today is a day of victory!"

The dwarves had taken up the grim war chant of their ancient homeland. The fishermen of Ten-Towns followed the words of the Song of Tempus, tentatively at first, until the foreign inflections and phrases easily rolled from their lips. And then they joined in fully, proclaiming the glory of their individual towns as the barbarians did of their tribes. The tempo increased; the volume moved toward a powerful crescendo. The goblins trembled at the growing frenzy of their deadly enemies. The stream of deserters flowing away from the edges of the main gathering grew thicker and thicker.

And then, as one killing wave, the human and dwarven allies charged down the hill.

DRIZZT HAD BEEN ABLE TO SCRAMBLE FAR ENOUGH AWAY FROM the southern face to escape the fury of the avalanche, but he still found himself in a dangerous predicament. Kelvin's Cairn wasn't a high mountain, but the top third was perpetually covered with deep snow and brutally exposed to the icy wind that gave this land its name.

Even worse for the drow, his feet had gotten wet in the melt caused by Crenshinibon, and now, as the moisture hardened around his skin to ice, movement through the snow was painful.

He resolved to plod on, making for the western face, which offered the best protection against the wind. His motions were violent and exaggerated, expending all of the energy that he could to keep the circulation flowing through his veins. When he reached the lip of the mountain's peak and started down, he had to move more tentatively, fearing that any sudden jolts would deliver him into the same grim fate that had befallen Akar Kessell.

His legs were completely numb now, but he kept them moving, almost having to force his automatic reflexes.

But then he slipped.

WULFGAR'S FIERCE WARRIORS WERE THE FIRST TO CRASH INTO the goblin line, hacking and pushing back the first rank of monsters. Neither goblin nor orc dared stand before the mighty king, but in the crowded confusion of the fighting few could find their way out of his path. One after another they fell to the ground.

Fear had all but paralyzed the goblins, and their slight hesitation had spelled doom for the first groups to encounter the savage barbarians.

Yet the downfall of the army ultimately came from farther back in the ranks. The tribes who had not even been involved in the fighting began to ponder the wisdom of continuing this campaign, for they recognized that they had gained enough of an advantage over their homeland rivals, weakened by heavy losses, to expand their territories back in the Spine of the World. Shortly after the second outburst of fighting had begun, the dust cloud of stamping feet once again rose above Icewind Pass as dozens of orc and goblin tribes headed home.

And the effect of the mass desertions on those goblins who could not easily flee was devastating. Even the most dim-witted goblin understood its people's chance for victory against the stubborn defenders of Ten-Towns lay in the overwhelming weight of their numbers.

Aegis-fang thudded repeatedly as Wulfgar, charging in alone, swept a path of devastation before him. Even the men of Ten-Towns shied away from him, unnerved by his savage strength. But his own people looked upon him with awe and tried their best to follow his glorious lead.

Wulfgar waded in on a group of orcs. Aegis-fang slammed home on one, killing it and knocking those behind it to the ground. Wulfgar's backswing with the hammer produced the same results on his other flank. In one burst, more than half of the group of orcs were killed or lying stunned.

Those remaining had no desire to move in on the mighty human.

Glensather of Easthaven also waded in on a group of goblins, hoping to incite his people with the same fury as his barbarian counterpart. But Glensather wasn't an imposing giant like Wulfgar, and he didn't wield a weapon as mighty as Aegis-fang. His sword cut down the first goblin he encountered, then spun back deftly and felled a second. The spokesman had done well, but one element was missing from his attack—the critical factor that elevated Wulfgar above other men. Glensather had killed two goblins, but he had not caused the chaos in their ranks that he needed to continue. Instead of fleeing, as they did before Wulfgar, the remaining goblins pressed in behind him.

Glensather had just come up beside the barbarian king when the cruel tip of a spear dived into his back and tore through, driving out the front of his chest.

Witnessing the gruesome spectacle, Wulfgar brought Aegis-fang over the spokesman, driving the head of the spear-wielding goblin down into its chest. Glensather heard the hammer connect behind him and even managed to smile his thanks before he fell dead to the grass.

The dwarves worked differently than their allies. Once again formed into their tight, supportive formation, they mowed down rows of goblins simultaneously. And the fishermen, fighting for the lives of their women and children, fought, and died, without fear.

In less than an hour, every group of goblins had been smashed, and half an hour after that, the last of the monsters fell dead to the bloodstained field.

DRIZZT RODE THE WHITE WAVE OF FALLING SNOW DOWN THE side of the mountain. He tumbled helplessly, trying to brace himself whenever he saw the jutting tip of a boulder in his path. As he neared the base of the snowcap, he was thrown clear of the slide and sent bouncing through the gray rocks and boulders, as though the mountain's proud, unconquerable peaks had spit him out like an uninvited guest.

His agility—and a strong dose of pure luck—saved him. When he at last was able to stop his momentum and find a perch, he discovered that his numerous injuries were superficial, a scrape on his knee, a bloodied nose, and a sprained wrist being the worst of them. In retrospect, Drizzt had to consider the small avalanche a blessing, for he had made swift progress down the mountain, and he wasn't even certain that he could have otherwise escaped Kessell's frosty fate without it.

The battle in the south had begun again by this time. Hearing the sounds of the fighting, Drizzt watched curiously as thousands of goblins passed by on the other side of the dwarven valley, running up Icewind Pass on the first legs of their long journey home. The drow couldn't be sure of what was happening, though he was familiar with the cowardly reputation of goblins.

He didn't give it too much thought, though, for the battle was no longer his first concern. His vision followed a narrow path, to the mound of broken black stonework that had been Cryshal-

Tirith. He finished his descent from Kelvin's Cairn and headed down Bremen's Run toward the rubble.

He had to find out if Regis or Guenhwyvar had escaped.

VICTORY.

It seemed a small comfort to Cassius, Kemp, and Jensin Brent as they looked around at the carnage on the scarred field. They were the only three spokesmen to have survived the struggle; seven others had been cut down. "We have won," Cassius declared grimly. He watched helplessly as more soldiers fell dead, men who had suffered mortal wounds earlier in the battle but had refused to fall down and die until they had seen it through. More than half of all the men of Ten-Towns lay dead, and many more would later die, for nearly half of those still alive had been grievously wounded. Four towns had been burned to the ground and another one looted and torn apart by occupying goblins.

They had paid a terrible price for their victory.

The barbarians, too, had been decimated. Mostly young and inexperienced, they had fought with the tenacity of their breeding and died accepting their fate as a glorious ending to their life's tale.

Only the dwarves, disciplined by many battles, had come through relatively unscathed. Several had been slain, a few others wounded, but most were all too ready to take up the fight again if only they could have found more goblins to bash! Their one great lament, though, was that Bruenor was missing.

"Go to your people," Cassius told his fellow spokesmen. "Then return this evening to council. Kemp shall speak for all the people of the four towns of Maer Dualdon, Jensin Brent for the people of the other lakes."

"We have much to decide and little time to do it," Jensin Brent said. "Winter is fast approaching."

"We shall survive!" Kemp declared with his characteristic defiance. But then he was aware of the sullen looks his peers had cast upon him, and he conceded a bit to their realism. "Though it will be a bitter struggle."

"So it shall be for my people," said another voice. The three spokesmen turned to see the giant Wulfgar striding out from the dusty, surrealistic scene of carnage. The barbarian was caked in dirt and spattered with the blood of his enemies, but he looked every bit the noble king. "I request an invitation to your council, Cassius. There is much that our people can offer to each other in this harsh time."

Kemp growled. "If we need beasts of burden, we'll buy oxen."

Cassius shot Kemp a dangerous look and addressed his unexpected ally. "You may indeed join the council, Wulfgar, son of Beornegar. For your aid this day, my people owe yours much. Again I ask you, why did you come?"

For the second time that day, Wulfgar ignored Kemp's insults. "To repay a debt," he replied to Cassius. "And perhaps to better the lives of both our peoples."

"By killing goblins?" Jensin Brent asked, suspecting that the barbarian had more in mind.

"A beginning," Wulfgar answered. "Yet there is much more that we may accomplish. My people know the tundra better than even the yetis. We understand its ways and know how to survive. Your people would benefit from our friendship, especially in the hard times that lay ahead for you."

"Bah!" Kemp snorted, but Cassius silenced him. The spokesman from Bryn Shander was intrigued by the possibilities.

"And what would your people gain from such a union?"

"A connection," Wulfgar answered. "A link to a world of luxuries that we have never known. The tribes hold a dragon's treasure in their hands, but gold and jewels do not provide warmth on a winter night, nor food when game is scarce.

"Your people have much rebuilding to do. My people have the wealth to assist in that task. In return, Ten-Towns will deliver my people into a better life!" Cassius and Jensin Brent nodded approvingly as Wulfgar laid out his plan.

"Finally, and perhaps most important," the barbarian concluded, "is the fact that we need each other, for the present at least. Both of our peoples have been weakened and are vulnerable to the dangers of this land. Together, our remaining strength would see us through the winter."

"You intrigue and surprise me," Cassius said. "Attend the council, then, with my personal welcome, and let us put in motion a plan that will benefit all who have survived the struggle against Akar Kessell!"

As Cassius turned, Wulfgar grabbed Kemp's shirt with one of his huge hands and easily hoisted the spokesman from Targos off the ground. Kemp swatted at the muscled forearm, but realized that he had no chance of breaking the barbarian's iron grip.

Wulfgar glared at him dangerously. "For now," he said, "I am responsible for all my people. Thus have I disregarded your insults. But when the day comes that I am no longer king, you would do well to cross my path no more!" With a flick of his wrist, he tossed the spokesman to the ground.

Kemp, too intimidated for the present to be angry or embarrassed, sat where he landed and did not respond. Cassius and Brent nudged each other and shared a low chuckle.

It lasted only until they saw the girl approaching, her arm in a bloody sling and her face and auburn hair caked with layers of dust. Wulfgar saw her, too, and the sight of her wounds pained him more than his own ever could.

"Catti-brie!" he cried, rushing to her. She calmed him with an outstretched palm.

"I am not badly injured," she assured Wulfgar stoically, though it was obvious to the barbarian that she had been sorely injured. "Though I dare not think of what would have befallen me if Bruenor had not arrived!"

"You have seen Bruenor?"

"In the tunnels," Catti-brie explained. "Some orcs found their way in—perhaps I should have collapsed the tunnel. Yet there weren't many, and I could hear that the dwarves were doing well on the field above.

"Bruenor came down then, but there were more orcs at his back. A support beam collapsed; I think Bruenor cut it out, and there was too much dust and confusion."

"And Bruenor?" Wulfgar asked anxiously.

Catti-brie looked back across the field. "Out there. He has asked for you."

BY THE TIME DRIZZT REACHED THE RUBBLE THAT HAD BEEN Cryshal-Tirith, the battle was over. The sights and sounds of the horrible aftermath pressed in all about him, but his goal remained unchanged. He started up the side of the broken stones.

In truth, the drow thought himself a fool for following such a hopeless cause. Even if Regis and Guenhwyvar hadn't gotten out of the tower, how could he possibly hope to find them?

He pressed on stubbornly, refusing to give in to the inescapable logic that scolded him. This was where he differed from his people, this was what had driven him, finally, from the unbroken darkness of their vast cities. Drizzt Do'Urden allowed himself to feel compassion.

He moved up the side of the rubble and began digging around the debris with his bare hands. Larger blocks prevented him from going very deep into the pile, yet he did not yield, even squeezing into precariously tight and unstable crevices. He used his burned left hand little, and soon his right was bleeding from scraping. But he continued on, moving first around the pile, then scaling higher.

He was rewarded for his persistence, for his emotions. When he reached the top of the ruins, he felt a familiar aura of magical power. It guided him to a small crevice between two stones. He reached in tentatively, hoping to find the object intact, and pulled out the small feline figurine. His fingers trembled as he examined it for damage. But he found none—the magic within the object had resisted the weight of the rubble.

The drow's feelings at the find were mixed, however. Though he was relieved that Guenhwyvar had apparently survived, the presence of the figurine told him that Regis had probably not escaped to the field. His heart sank. And sank even further when a sparkle within the same crevice caught his eye. He reached in and pulled out the golden chain with the ruby pendant, and his fears were confirmed.

"A fitting tomb for you, brave little friend," he said somberly, and he decided at that moment to name the pile Regis's Cairn. He could not understand, though, what had happened to separate the halfling from his necklace, for there was no blood or anything else on the chain to indicate that Regis had been wearing it when he died.

"Guenhwyvar," he called. "Come to me, my shadow." He felt the familiar sensations in the figurine as he placed it on the ground before him. Then the black mist appeared and formed into the great cat, unharmed and somewhat restored by the few hours it had spent back on its own plane.

Drizzt moved quickly toward his feline companion, but then he stopped as a second mist appeared a short distance away and began to solidify.

Regis.

The halfling sat with eyes closed and his mouth opened wide, as though he was about to take an enjoyable and enormous bite out of some unseen delicacy. One of his hands was clenched to the side of his eager jowls, and the other open before him.

As his mouth snapped shut on empty air, his eyes snapped open in surprise. "Drizzt!" he groaned. "Really, you should ask before you steal me away! This perfectly marvelous cat had caught me the juiciest meal!"

Drizzt shook his head and smiled with a mixture of relief and disbelief.

"Oh, splendid," Regis cried. "You have found my gemstone. I thought that I had lost it; for some reason it didn't make the journey with the cat and me."

Drizzt handed the ruby back to him. The cat could take someone along on its travels through the planes? Drizzt resolved to explore this facet of Guenhwyvar's power later.

He stroked the cat's neck, then released it back to its own world where it could further recuperate. "Come, Regis," he said grimly. "Let us see where we might be of assistance!"

Regis shrugged resignedly and stood to follow the drow. When they crested the top of the ruins and saw the carnage spread out below them, the halfling realized the enormity of the destruction. His legs nearly faltered under him, but he managed, with some help from his agile friend, to make the descent.

"We won?" he asked Drizzt when they neared the level of the field, unsure if the people of Ten-Towns had labeled what he saw before him victory or defeat.

"We survived," Drizzt corrected.

A shout went up suddenly as a group of fishermen, seeing the two companions, rushed toward them, yelling with abandon. "Wizard-slayer and tower-breaker!" they cried.

Drizzt, ever humble, lowered his eyes.

"Hail Regis," the men continued, "the hero of Ten-Towns!"

Drizzt turned a surprised but amused eye on his friend. Regis merely shrugged helplessly, acting as much the victim of the error as Drizzt.

The men caught hold of the halfling and hoisted him to their shoulders. "We shall carry you in glory to the council taking place within the city!" one proclaimed. "You, above all others, should have a say in the decisions that will be made!" Almost as an afterthought, the man said to Drizzt, "You can come too, drow."

Drizzt declined. "All hail Regis," he said, a smile splayed across his face. "Ah, little friend, ever you have the fortune to find gold in the mud where others wallow!" He clapped the halfling on the back and stood aside as the procession began.

Regis looked back over his shoulder and rolled his eyes as though he were merely going along for the ride.

But Drizzt knew better.

THE DROW'S AMUSEMENT WAS SHORT-LIVED.

Before he had even moved away from the spot, two dwarves hailed him.

"It is good that we have found ye, friend elf," said one. The drow knew at once that they bore grim news.

"Bruenor?" he asked.

The dwarves nodded. "He lies near death, even now he might be gone. He has asked for ye."

Without another word, the dwarves led Drizzt across the field to a small tent they had set up near their tunnel exits and escorted him in.

Inside, candles flickered softly. Beyond the single cot, against the wall opposite the entrance, stood Wulfgar and Catti-brie, their heads bent reverently.

Bruenor lay on the cot, his head and chest wrapped in blood-stained bandages. His breathing was raspy and shallow, as though each breath would be his last. Drizzt moved solemnly to his side, stoically determined to hold back the uncharacteristic tears that welled in his lavender eyes. Bruenor would prefer strength.

"Is it . . . the elf?" Bruenor gasped when he saw the dark form over him.

"I have come, dearest of friends," Drizzt replied.

"To see . . . me on me way?"

Drizzt couldn't honestly answer so blunt a question. "On your way?" He forced a laugh from his constricting throat. "You have suffered worse! I'll hear no talk of dying—who then would find Mithral Hall?"

"Ah, my home. . . ." Bruenor settled back at the name and

seemed to relax, almost as if he felt that his dreams would carry him through the dark journey before him. "Ye're to come with me, then?"

"Of course," Drizzt agreed. He looked to Wulfgar and Catti-brie for support, but lost in their own grief, they kept their eyes averted.

"But not now, no, no," Bruenor explained. "Wouldn't do with the winter so close!" He coughed. "In the spring. Yes, in the spring!" His voice trailed away and his eyes closed.

"Yes, my friend," Drizzt agreed. "In the spring. I shall see you to your home in the spring!"

Bruenor's eyes cracked open again, their deathly glaze washed away by a hint of the old sparkle. A contented smile widened across the dwarf's face, and Drizzt was happy that he had been able to comfort his dying friend.

The drow looked back to Wulfgar and Catti-brie and they, too, were smiling.

At each other, Drizzt noted curiously.

Suddenly, to Drizzt's surprise and horror, Bruenor sat up and tore away the bandages.

"There!" he roared to the amusement of the others in the tent. "Ye've said it, and I have witnesses to the fact!"

Drizzt, after nearly falling over with the initial shock, scowled at Wulfgar. The barbarian and Catti-brie fought hard to subdue their laughter.

Wulfgar shrugged, and a chuckle escaped. "Bruenor said that he would cut me down to the height of a dwarf if I said a word!"

"And so he would have!" Catti-brie added. The two of them made a hasty exit. "A council in Bryn Shander," Wulfgar explained hastily. Outside the tent, their laughter erupted unheeded.

"Damn you, Bruenor Battlehammer!" the drow scowled. Then, unable to stop himself, he threw his arms around the barrel-shaped dwarf and hugged him.

"Get it over with," Bruenor groaned, accepting the embrace.

"But be quick. We've a lot o' work to do through the winter! Spring'll be here sooner than ye think, and on the first warm day we leave for Mithral Hall!"

"Wherever that might be," Drizzt laughed, too relieved to be angered by the trick.

"We'll make it, drow!" Bruenor cried. "We always do!"

EPILOGUE

The people of Ten-Towns and their barbarian allies found the winter following the battle a difficult one, but by pooling their talents and resources, they managed to survive. Many councils were held throughout those long months with Cassius, Jensin Brent, and Kemp representing the people of Ten-Towns, and Wulfgar and Revjak speaking for the barbarian tribes. The first order of business was to officially recognize and condone the alliance of the two peoples, though many on both sides were strongly opposed.

Those cities left untouched by Akar Kessell's army were packed full of refugees during the brutal winter. Reconstruction began with the first signs of spring. When the region was well on its way to recovery, and after the barbarian expedition following Wulfgar's directions returned with the dragon's treasure, councils were held to divide the towns among the surviving people. Relations between the two peoples almost broke down several times and were held together only by the commanding presence of Wulfgar and the continued calm of Cassius.

When all was finally settled, the barbarians were given the cities of Bremen and Caer-Konig to rebuild, the homeless of Caer-

Konig were moved into the reconstructed city of Caer-Dineval, and the refugees of Bremen who did not wish to live among the tribesmen were offered homes in the newly built city of Targos.

It was a difficult situation, where traditional enemies were forced to put aside their differences and live in close quarters. Though victorious in the battle, the people of the towns could not call themselves winners. Everyone had suffered tragic losses; no one had come out better for the fight.

Except Regis.

The opportunistic halfling was awarded the title of First Citizen and the finest house in all of Ten-Towns for his part in the battle. Cassius readily surrendered his palace to the "tower-breaker." Regis accepted the spokesman's offer and all of the other numerous gifts that rolled in from every city, for though he hadn't truly earned the accolades awarded him, he justified his good fortune by considering himself a partner of the unassuming drow. And since Drizzt Do'Urden wasn't about to come to Bryn Shander and collect the rewards, Regis figured that it was his duty to do so.

This was the pampered lifestyle that the halfling had always desired. He truly enjoyed the excessive wealth and luxuries, though he would later learn that there was indeed a hefty price to be paid for fame.

DRIZZT AND BRUENOR HAD SPENT THE WINTER IN PREPARATION for their search for Mithral Hall. The drow intended to honor his word, though he had been tricked, because life hadn't changed much for him after the battle. Although he was in truth the hero of the fight, he still found himself barely tolerated among the people of Ten-Towns. And the barbarians, other than Wulfgar and Revjak, openly avoided him, mumbling warding prayers to their gods whenever they inadvertently crossed his path.

But the drow accepted the shunning with his characteristic stoicism.

"THE WHISPERS IN TOWN SAY THAT YOU HAVE GIVEN YOUR VOICE at council to Revjak," Catti-brie said to Wulfgar on one of her many visits to Bryn Shander.

Wulfgar nodded. "He is older and wiser in many ways."

Catti-brie drew Wulfgar under the uncomfortable scrutiny of her dark eyes. She knew that there were other reasons for Wulfgar stepping down as king. "You mean to go with them," she stated flatly.

"I owe it to the drow," was Wulfgar's only explanation as he turned away, in no mood to argue with the fiery girl.

"Again you parry the question," Catti-brie laughed. "You go to pay no debt! You go because you choose the road!"

"What could you know of the road?" Wulfgar growled, pulled in by the girl's painfully accurate observation. "What could you know of adventure?"

Catti-brie's eyes sparkled disarmingly. "I know," she stated flatly. "Every day in every place is an adventure. This you have not yet learned. And so you chase down the distant roads, hoping to satisfy the hunger for excitement that burns in your heart. So go, Wulfgar of Icewind Dale. Follow your heart's trail and be happy!

"Perhaps when you return you will understand the excitement of simply being alive." She kissed him on the cheek and skipped to the door.

Wulfgar called after her, pleasantly surprised by her kiss. "Perhaps then our discussions will be more agreeable!"

"But not as interesting!" was her parting response.

ONE FINE MORNING IN EARLY SPRING, THE TIME FINALLY CAME for Drizzt and Bruenor to leave. Catti-brie helped them pack their overstuffed sacks.

"When we've cleared the place, I'll take ye there!" Bruenor told the girl one more time. "Sure yer eyes'll shine when ye see the rivers runnin' silver in Mithral Hall!"

Catti-bric smiled indulgently.

"Ye're sure ye'll be all right, then?" Bruenor asked more seriously. He knew that she would, but his heart flooded with fatherly concern.

Catti-brie's smile widened. They had been through this discussion a hundred times over the winter. Catti-brie was glad that the dwarf was going, though she knew that she would miss him dearly, for it was clear that Bruenor would never truly be contented until he had at least tried to find his ancestral home.

And she knew, better than anyone, that the dwarf would be in fine company.

Bruenor was satisfied. The time had come to go.

The companions said their goodbyes to the dwarves and started off for Bryn Shander to bid farewell to their two closest friends.

They arrived at Regis's house later in the morning, and found Wulfgar sitting on the steps waiting for them, Aegis-fang and his pack by his side.

Drizzt eyed the barbarian's belongings suspiciously as they approached, half-guessing Wulfgar's intentions. "Well met, King Wulfgar," he said. "Are you off to Bremen, or perhaps Caer-Konig, to oversee the work of your people?"

Wulfgar shook his head. "I am no king," he replied. "Councils and speeches are better left to older men; I have had more of them than I can tolerate. Revjak speaks for the men of the tundra now."

"Then what o' yerself?" asked Bruenor.

"I go with you," Wulfgar replied. "To repay my last debt."

"Ye owe me nothin'!" Bruenor declared.

"To you I am paid," Wulfgar agreed. "And I have paid all that I owe to Ten-Towns, and to my own people as well. But there is one debt I am not yet free of." He turned to face Drizzt squarely. "To you, friend elf."

Drizzt didn't know how to reply. He clapped the huge man on the shoulder and smiled warmly.

"COME WITH US, RUMBLEBELLY," BRUENOR SAID AFTER THEY had finished an excellent lunch in the palace. "Four adventurers, out on the open plain. It'll do ye some good an' take a bit o' that belly o' yers away!"

Regis grasped his ample stomach in both hands and jiggled it. "I like my belly and intend to keep it, thank you. I may even add some more to it!

"I cannot begin to understand why you all insist on going on this quest, anyway," he said more seriously. He had spent many hours during the winter trying to talk Bruenor and Drizzt out of their chosen path. "We have an easy life here; why would you want to leave?"

"There is more to living than fine food and soft pillows, little friend," said Wulfgar. "The lust of adventure burns our blood. With peace in the region, Ten-Towns cannot offer the thrill of danger or the satisfaction of victory." Drizzt and Bruenor nodded their assent, though Regis shook his head.

"An' ye call this pitiful place wealth?" Bruenor chuckled, snapping his stubby fingers. "When I return from Mithral Hall, I'll build ye a home twice this size an' edged in gems like ye never seen afore!"

But Regis was determined that he had witnessed his last adventure. After the meal was finished, he accompanied his friends to the door. "If you make it back . . ."

"Your house shall be our first stop," Drizzt assured him.

They met Kemp of Targos when they walked outside. He was standing across the road from Regis's front step, apparently looking for them.

"He is waiting for me," Wulfgar explained, smiling at the notion that Kemp would go out of his way to be rid of him.

"Farewell, good spokesman," Wulfgar called, bowing low. "Prayne de crabug ahm keike rinedere be-yogt iglo kes gron"

Kemp flashed an obscene gesture at the barbarian and stalked away. Regis nearly doubled over with laughter.

Drizzt recognized the words, but was puzzled as to why Wulfgar had spoken them to Kemp. "You once told me that those words were an old tundra battle cry," he remarked to the barbarian. "Why would you offer them to the man you most despise?"

Wulfgar stammered over an explanation that would get him out of this jam, but Regis answered for him.

"Battle cry?" the halfling exclaimed. "That is an old barbarian housemother's curse, usually reserved for adulterous old barbarian housefathers." The drow's lavender eyes narrowed on the barbarian as Regis continued. "It means: May the fleas of a thousand reindeer nest in your genitals."

Bruenor broke down into laughter, Wulfgar soon joining him. Drizzt couldn't help but go along.

"Come, the day is long," the drow said. "Let us begin this adventure—it should prove interesting!"

"Where will you go?" Regis asked somberly. A small part of the halfling actually envied his friends; he had to admit that he would miss them.

"To Bremen, first," replied Drizzt. "We shall complete our provisions there and strike out to the southwest."

"Luskan?"

"Perhaps, if the fates deem it."

"Good speed," Regis offered as the three companions started out without further delay.

Regis watched them disappear, wondering how he had ever picked such foolish friends. He shrugged it away and turned back to his palace—there was plenty of food left over from lunch.

He was stopped before he got through the door.

"First Citizen!" came a call from the street. The voice belonged to a warehouseman from the southern section of the city, where the merchant caravans loaded and unloaded. Regis waited for his approach.

"A man, First Citizen," the warehouseman said, bowing apologetically for disturbing so important a person. "Asking about you. He claims to be a representative from the Heroes Society in Luskan, sent to request your presence at their next meeting. He said that he would pay you well."

"His name?"

"He gave none, just this!" The warehouseman opened a small pouch of gold.

It was all that Regis needed to see. He left at once for the rendezvous with the man from Luskan.

Once again, sheer luck saved the halfling's life, for he saw the stranger before the stranger saw him. He recognized the man at once, though he hadn't seen him in years, by the emerald-encrusted dagger hilt protruding from the sheath on his hip. Regis had often contemplated stealing that beautiful weapon, but even he had a limit to his foolhardiness. The dagger belonged to Artemis Entreri.

Pasha Pook's prime assassin.

THE THREE COMPANIONS LEFT BREMEN BEFORE DAWN THE NEXT day. Anxious to begin the adventure, they made good time and were far out into the tundra when the first rays of the sun peeked over the eastern horizon behind them.

Still, Bruenor was not surprised when he noticed Regis scrambling across the empty plain to catch up with them.

"Got 'imself into trouble again, or I'm a bearded gnome," the dwarf snickered to Wulfgar and Drizzt.

"Well met," said Drizzt. "But haven't we already said our farewells?"

"I decided that I could not let Bruenor run off into trouble without me being there to pull him out," Regis puffed, trying to catch his breath.

"Yer comin?" groaned Bruenor. "Ye've brought no supplies, fool halfling!"

"I don't eat much," Regis pleaded, an edge of desperation creeping into his voice.

"Bah! Ye eat more'n the three of us together! But no mind, we'll let ye tag along anyway."

The halfling's face brightened visibly, and Drizzt suspected that the dwarf's guess about trouble wasn't far off the mark.

"The four of us, then!" proclaimed Wulfgar. "One to represent each of the four common races: Bruenor for the dwarves, Regis for the halflings, Drizzt Do'Urden for the elves, and myself for the humans. A fitting troupe!"

"I hardly think the elves would choose a drow to represent them," Drizzt remarked.

Bruenor snorted. "Ye think the halflings'd choose Rumblebelly for their champion?"

"You're crazy, dwarf," retorted Regis.

Bruenor dropped his shield to the ground, leaped around Wulfgar, and squared off before Regis. His face contorted in mock rage as he grasped Regis by the shoulders and hoisted him into the air.

"That's right, Rumblebelly!" Bruenor cried wildly. "Crazy I am! An' never cross one what's crazier than yerself!"

Drizzt and Wulfgar looked at each other with knowing smiles.

It was indeed going to be an interesting adventure.

And with the rising sun at their back, their shadows standing long before them, they started off on their way.

To find Mithral Hall.

ACKNOWLEDGMENTS

Whenever an author takes on a project like this, especially if it is his first novel, there are invariably a number of people who help him accomplish the task. The writing of *The Crystal Shard* was no exception.

Publishing a novel involves three elements: a degree of talent; a lot of hard work; and a good measure of luck. The first two elements can be controlled by the author, but the third involves being in the right place at the right time and finding an editor who believes in your ability and dedication to the task at hand.

Therefore, my greatest thanks go to TSR, and especially to Mary Kirchoff, for taking a chance on a first time author and guiding me throughout the process.

Writing in the 1980s has become a high-tech chore as well as an exercise in creativity. In the case of *The Crystal Shard*, luck once again worked on my side. I consider myself lucky to have a friend like Brian P. Savoy, who loaned me his software expertise in smoothing out the rough edges.

My thanks also to my personal opinion-givers, Dave Duquette and Michael LaVigueur, for pointing out strengths and weaknesses in the rough draft, to my brother, Gary Salvatore, for his work on the maps of Icewind Dale, and to the rest of my AD&D™ game group, Tom Parker, Daniel Mallard, and Roland Lortie, for their continued inspiration through the development of eccentric characters fit to wear the mantle of a hero in a fantasy novel.

And finally; to the man who truly brought me into the world of the AD&D™ game, Bob Brown. Since you moved away (and took the pipe smoke with you) the atmosphere around the gaming table just hasn't been the same.

—R.A. Salvatore, 1988

ABOUT THE AUTHOR

R.A. SALVATORE's books have sold more than thirty-five million copies, have landed on many bestseller lists, and have been translated into numerous foreign languages. When he isn't writing, Salvatore and his wife, Diane, along with their Japanese spaniels, Dexter and Pikel, bounce coast-to-coast to see their grandchildren. Salvatore hits the gym and coaches and plays on Clan Battlehammer, a softball team that includes most of his family. His gaming group still meets on Sundays to play D&D or DemonWars or whatever the Sadist . . . err, Game Master, decides.

ABOUT THE TYPE

This book was set in Caslon, a typeface first designed in 1722 by William Caslon (1692–1766). Its widespread use by most English printers in the early eighteenth century soon supplanted the Dutch typefaces that had formerly prevailed. The roman is considered a "workhorse" typeface due to its pleasant, open appearance, while the italic is exceedingly decorative.